Under the
Sitka Tree

A Novel

TL Alton

My life has been
enriched Erna,
by our many years of
friendship!
I gift you this book, I
wrote, for who so ever
reads it, may my
storytelling shine thru!
Kindly, (Tonya)
TL Alton

PSALM 147:3

Introduction

I have written this in my mind, a thousand times, with varied
turbulence, peace, hurt and grace. Everything that has taken place since
the original draft, twenty years ago, has altered my life in a multitude of
ways. Times which have tested my faith and my sanity. During the low
times of dealing with my Bipolar, I felt as if the commotion of the waves
swirling in my mind would consume me. However, it was when my
thoughts collided within, that I found my writer's voice. A town carved
out of a mountainside, where a bustling community once resided. For me,
it was a place where the skyline touched the heavens and the mountains
peaked, along the sprawling, British Columbia coastline.

The urge to write about a 1950's Canadian, coastal town, saw me
immerse myself in several years of research. This was due to several
timelines connected to the slave trade, Japanese internment in Canada,
and the Residential schools. I was deeply humbled by those who
entrusted me with their own stories of hardship and survival. For it was
through their courage, I found character.

I made contact with a woman, who grew up in Ocean Falls, BC.
Through Sharen Kish's insight, I gained a better understanding
of the townspeople and the characters I was creating. Due to her
communication with me, I was also invited over the years and
attended two reunions of the "Rain People of Ocean Falls."

In the beginning of working on my novel, I was also in the midst of writing for a small newspaper. As time passed by, I could not stop the characters in my novel from wanting their stories to be told.

I would scribble notes onto pieces of papers, later to be collected and laid out on my desk.

All the while I worked on the storyline, my young daughter Shayla, would watch, with curiosity.

Shayla was also creative. She had grown up with me, writing on a desk in the same area, as our living space. Many times over the years, she would come and share her poetry with me. As a tribute to the spark of creativity we shared, two of our poems are hidden in plain sight, amongst the pages and interwoven into the storyline.

Over the years, my health issues became a problem, I no longer could ignore. The flow of my story writing was interrupted, as I faced battles with mental health. After the wrong diagnosis and treatment, I came close to losing my life.

As a mother, I was failing, while trying desperately to survive. The one thing I had not counted on, was the monsters I battled privately, were now spilling forward into real life.

Later, I was diagnosed with Bipolar. Years of depression and mania, were wreaking havoc on my system and I struggled to stay alive in a world that was bent on my destruction.

It was then I began to give my life over to the Lord and trust in him for all things to strengthen me.

After nearly dying, my prayers were answered by a precise diagnosis, given to me by Doctor Gregory Hudson, who saved my life. He offered me assurances, the life-long medications I would be placed on, would change my world for the better. Due to his genuine care and supportive nature, I returned to writing with a clarity I did not have before.

Whenever I felt restless, I would reach for "Sitka" and get lost amongst the pages. While waiting for the regiment of medications to help balance me out, my illness would see me stay awake until 4am; as I learned to come to grips, with my mental disorder.

When I found myself a single mother, it was my daughter who encouraged me to continue writing and more importantly, to keep working on my book. One day, as I sat around our kitchen table, Shayla came to me and made a simple request: Could she read what I had written so far? I felt a wave of anxiety overcome me, as I wanted the book to be perfect – before I presented it to her. I wanted to be in print and published; all the things I had dreamt of. Therefore, I only handed over a few pages. She soon retreated to her bedroom, and I carried on. A while passed before Shayla emerged.

Sitting down beside me, I could see tears in her eyes. Placing the pages onto the table, she leaned across and offered me her pinky finger. I was unsure of what to expect. Yet when my daughter spoke again, her words have carried me through, the rest of writing this book.

Taking a deep breath, Shayla exhaled, then said: "Momma, you need to promise me that you will get your book published – no matter whatever happens – as this is the proof of God's love."

I sat there in awe of how she had understood so much, in the very little I gave her to read. Leaning into her, I took my pinky and as we hooked ours together, I said to her:

"Babygirl, a promise is a promise."

A time after, when I finally had a proper diagnosis of Bipolar and the medications were making a difference, I still had honest concerns. I worried the filaments of my creativity would eventually disappear, that I would be robbed of that spark within and would be left only with the ashes of my words. For me, it was like climbing aboard a rocket to space, yet there would be no lift-off.

It took weeks to realize that I had more insight, clarity and less chaos. My eyes had been opened and I saw how things were coming together – instead of being divided apart.

Through a second lease on life, I was able to attend writing conferences, courses and festivals. The dark cloud that I had been cloaked in, was now removed and the light that was always there, was allowed to shine in me.

For my readers, this is what my novel is about…the balance of darkness and light; forged in forgiveness.

Acknowledgments

This journey also saw a massive group of collective souls encourage, support and stand by me throughout times of upheaval.

From my early days of writing a weekly column, I met TJ Wallis. Her no-nonsense approach instilled in me the need to remain focussed and committed to my writing. I am most grateful for the opportunities she gave me, the second chances I needed to believe in myself and most of all, to begin again.

In Sarah Kube, I found a true alliance to the forests and all things shining, my love is rooted in our endearing friendship. I thank you for the care packages that sustained me, the gifting from your heart to mine and the passion for the written word; including all things Sitka.

I am grateful to Sherry Brown, who has been the keeper of our friendship during times of loss. For her fiery spirit of resilience and anchor within the community of wellness, I thank Amanda Swoboda.

To Judy Dowd, who saw me rise and fall. Thank you for loving me for who I am and seeing me through the struggles, I have overcome. I am grateful for your generous heart and helping me endure many difficult times.

Most of all, I have been honoured to know of your daughter Lindsay, through over the times of your heartfelt sharing. In her passing, I believe many years ago on Christmas Day, when you and I first met, Lindsay and Shayla brought us together; as we shared a connection in our sorrow.

To Leeann, I am grateful for our childhood friendship as it was an inspiration for the bond between two characters in my book. Your courage and resilience, taught me the importance of never giving up. I was blessed by your forgiveness and compassion. As well, Shayla was blessed by the love of her Aunty and someone to confide in.

To Terry Stofer, Thank you for your serving heart that lifted me up. Your patience, guidance and compassion saw you tend to my adversities, as you carried me through the trials of life. I am grateful for the love you extended to me.

To Michelle Wells, I thank you for your interest in my story that was a reminder of my abilities and for your generous heart, friendship and loving support.

Even though some individuals have moved on or let go; there are blessings for the memories we shared, and are part of the chapters of my life.

To those who are my brothers and sisters in Christ, I am humbled by those who came along side me, and I thank you for all you gave from your nurturing hearts; meals, shelter and the provisions to survive another day. To Bev and Cam, whose gifting allowed me to get out of sleeping in my car and into a clean, warm bed for several nights, I am grateful for all you shared with me!

For I was hungry, and you gave me something to eat, I was thirsty, and you gave me something to drink, I was a stranger and you invited me in.
– Matthew 25:35

For Leanna, whose serving heart saw me gain monthly housing for a longer period of time, there has never been a time, when you did not rise to the call of assisting me! Your kind words of scripture shared, encouragement given and countless blessings, throughout the years, have helped uplift me out of times of darkness. Your caring ways of sharing the blessings from God, putting unity into church community and sharing in fellowship, has brought such light into my life.

My heartfelt thanks to Cindy and Gary Bruton, who took in a struggling soul and truly extended compassion and God's mercy to me. The above scripture is the way you genuinely live your lives in serving and helping others. Thank you for the amazing, kind-hearted gesture of welcoming me into your home and to get to know your family. For the countless gift cards that bought myself and those in need, many meals. For the times, I was in despair, and you lead me more to God, the one who is in control and makes All things Possible.

I want to thank Ruth Sanderson and family for the chance to live amongst the stars as a Provincial Parks Operator, while I dreamt of completing my book.

I give my deepest thanks to my mother Dee and brother Brad, for I have been able to see blessings, buried in the pieces of brokenness. To my cousin Lisa, who helped me to carry on and to Mara Plican and Tristan Murphy – our hearts are forever changed by the sorrow in the passing of Margaret, Shayla and Matthew. To my cousin Michael, who was the first to devote his valued time to reading and editing my novel, I would like to extend my genuine thanks.

I want to thank George, who was the one person in the printing business that created my silver foil, tree business cards. He also had the brilliant idea, to scan my Faith/Piper key, and to have it be a part of my book. From the onset, I was inspired to creatively include the skeleton key in my storyline. To weave into the chapters, the placement of something that was small, yet would lead to opening the door – to something bigger. I also believe that one of my characters inspired him to have a connection – to all things golden. I want to express my sincerest gratitude for George's help, which sent ripples into my novel. He was there from the beginning and long after, I was blessed by the components of what the key represents.

I need to say a heartfelt thank you to my editor Liam Ford, who stepped into the world of Ospero Falls and welcomed the moments of endless connections.

To Karen L. Smith, Thank you for taking me back to the beginning.

To Dr. Jazlin Ebenezer, who took in a wounded soul and through her gentle teaching, prayer and belief in me, encouraged me to embrace the light that shines within. To Dr. Sudesh Ebenezer, I thank you for the years of friendship.

I give thanks to the one man who shared the passion of the written word, along with me – Christopher Sherman and his wife Ayako.

I want to thank the former citizens of Ocean Falls, BC. My sincerest gratitude to Sharen, Maureen and Joyce, along with Greg. They were kind enough, to share some of their stories of growing up, in this central coast community.

A heartfelt thank you to Sharen, who offered her personal reflections of life found in Ocean Falls. I am grateful for the compassion she has always shown me and for the inspiration, to a place that will always be special in my heart.

Through my research, I gained insight to hearing of what life was like in their wonderful Canadian community. This gave me a chance, to weave some of the beauty and enchantment into Ospero Falls, BC (a place of hope), that I created in my own novel.

To Dela Wilkins, I thank you for your insight and friendship; you have always offered encouragement and purpose in my life.

To Erna, whom I have shared three decades of friendship with, I cherish our conversations and always being a beautiful light, even in the darkness.

To Monique of Trace of Grey Designs and also Claudia – years ago, your beautiful hearts wrapped around me and shone love into a mother's bereaved soul. Thank you immensely, for the generous gifting of the leather heart that says mine and graces the cover of my book. Your encouraging words have been such a blessing!

I want to thank Benjamin Lee, whose help on several chapters, provided further insight. I am grateful that he asked valid questions, which allowed me to connect with him, as a reader.

To Alicia, whose home with Ryan, I was welcomed in. You took up my cause and created a Go Fund Me page that saw me find stability and shelter. Thank you for the times of laughter, love and gratitude.

My deepest gratitude to Dini Steyn, my former TESL Professor, guidance mentor and friend. Thank you for believing in me, beyond the classroom and encouraging me to find my place in this world, as a writer. The years of friendship you gave me, your insight and confidence in my abilities and your many pebble releases for my daughter, showed me the compassionate heart you have, in all things you accomplish.

To Karen Alexander Hoshal, We met during Black History Month in a library, where you gave a presentation. Thank you for your kindness and insight in looking over an important part of a timeline in my book, connected to slavery. Your positive feedback-contributed to the way I better understood- what it meant for my characters to be free.

There is deepest appreciation to Shania, whose faith, creativity and inspiring words saw me find solace, in the places where darkness wanted to settle – within the cracks. Thank you for the light shining within.

To Christine, I am full of gratitude, for when I needed to find freedom in nature, your guidance went beyond the mountains and forest. I Thank you for taking a stand.

To Jenn and Tim van Akker, Thank you for providing safe shelter, when I was displaced. I am grateful for you sharing your home and the hearts that dwelled in it.

To Robert and Lillian Anderson, I am grateful for you opening up your home and for you Lillian, your beautiful, caring heart to me, when I had nowhere else to go. Thank you Lillian for the nourishing meals and fellowship we took part in. From you, my faith deepened and grew. I am thankful for the many times you included me in your family and the forgiveness that was found within your soul.

I want to express my sincere thank you to Saanich Baptist Church. God knows all of the mercy and grace I was given, along with help in sustaining myself.

I am grateful to the Lord, for the opportunity to see me lead individuals, in the bereavement support group, Griefshare. Throughout my own grief journey, I was able to understand the true meaning of Psalm 147:3.

Thank you also to the worship team, as many times I came into church weary, with heavy burdens upon me. Through your voices praising God and raising the church roof, I left with my heart and soul uplifted.

To Lorraine Broughton, In our time spent together and through your kindness, I was offered shelter, food and your generosity. I remember our conversations about the loss of your daughter Ellen and my daughter Shayla. I am thankful for your compassion and how you welcomed me into your home.

To the late Karen Hill, your novel, *Cafe Babanussa,* was like a comforting friend, in my writing process. Your journey held me steadfast, throughout my own bouts of Bipolar.

In your own struggles, I found an anchor of hope. In your candidness, there was a connection and with every chapter I finished of mine, your book was by my side. Thank you, for through you, I was able to embrace the two decade journey of writing my own novel- with a sense of accomplishment – instead of discord.

I want to express my deepest Thanks to Jane for the many years of friendship and support she gifted me. Always a believer in my dreams of writing; Jane encouraged me, when at times I needed it the most.

To Lori Halls and family, It was when in my moments of shame, loss and despair that you shined in the greatest examples of Matthew 25:35-40. Thank you from my heart to yours, for the miles driven, laughter and tears shared over the years.

I am deeply grateful for the blessings of your generosity that has no bounds!

In knowing everyone has a beautiful story to share, ours is infused with love, heartache and sorrow, for that I wish our friendship had a different ending. However, the countless memories we shared- are ones where Shayla would want us to cherish. In a world filled with regret, we are not defined by the moments that take our breath away – rather we are defined by the ones where forgiveness can be found… amongst the pages of this book.

To all of those bereaved and whose loved ones have passed away: We can take comfort in knowing, we are surrounded daily, by the love they left us in our hearts.

To the God whose ink is in my pen all of these years and continues to be, your name is above the depression I have experienced and the displacement I encountered. It was during the tragic loss I and countless others experienced – when Shayla was welcomed into the heavens on December 12th, 2011, that my faith grew stronger.

I have felt the love of so many mentioned above, those who helped nourished me in many amazing ways and saw me overcome adversity.

I would like to sincerely thank Marty Aitken for his recommendations, for they led me to Leon Oldale's professional services. Leon helped me, in so many wonderful ways; including the direction I needed to take with my book.

I would like to offer my gratitude to Island Blue Press for helping me keep a mother's promise.

— *TL Alton*

PROLOGUE

Under the Sitka Tree
BY TL ALTON

THE SITKA SPRUCE ROSE FROM THE FERTILE GROUND, IN prominence. The natural curve of its broad trunk silhouetted the tree, encircled by light. For over 200 years, a river of roots connected to its heartwood. Having a solid foundation; this tree's existence was to provide. To grant protection by offering shade and rest. To halt erosion, while releasing oxygen. A succession of rings rippled outward. Within it – the tree held an ancient connection to the land. Stretched out in nature's sloping canopy were a multitude of limbs. Poking from the upturned, stiff branches, were clusters of bluish-green needles. Each cross section, permeated with brackish vapour in the air; arising from exposed seaweed at low tide. Soft, ginger cones with pliable scales, dotted the branches and peppered the ground. Enriched by the shoreline, clay earth, and infusion of the sun – these elements provided the substances of life.

A doe and her fawn, grazed on the lichen near the trunk. Under the emergent layer of the spruce, a spotted owl hooted, neighbouring an abandoned nest – of a bald eagle. The deer scattered as a woman approached. She knelt and touched the trunk of the tree where it met the forest floor. Letting her fingers climb upwards, she thought about the flow of nature's energy, in the stately spruce. Abruptly, her shoulders drooped. Throughout her life, she had the viewed the tree as an adversary. Picking up a dispersed cone and holding it in her palm, the woman recalled words shared with her about the Creator. She marvelled at mother nature's design of the thin, uneven edges. Something so harmless, yet as a whole tree, it had such deep impact within her family.

This prompted the woman to draw a deep sigh in, then exhale. Looking up at the grandeur before her, she struggled to form the words of appreciation.

As a young girl, Katrina was told about the importance of giving thanks, for what you take from nature.

Closing her hand around the cone, she thought back to stories being told to her. The ones about the First Nations union with the majestic coniferous tree, steeped in tradition. The First Nations participation in winter ceremonies, honoured the trees' lives, for the protection they gave. For many believed the needles, had the capacity to ward off evil thoughts. It was customary to gather under the boughs collected from Sitka trees. They used the boughs to shield the dancers from the cold, winter ash draping the slumbering forest, in a flow of endless white.

Katrina's thoughts drifted back to her upbringing.

Over the years, she felt her perception of the tree, had been misshapen by distorted lies.

Or had it been tales infused with truth? Katrina had come to face the one obstacle in her life, which held the answers. In acknowledging the wildness that was part of who she was, she also understood her need for answers, came from a place of abandonment. Determined to unleash what held her back all these years, she stepped away, to analyze her opponent. Abruptly her attention was drawn beyond the tree. Scanning the jagged lines of the mountainside, she could see the custom of logging, had made the area vulnerable. This caused the spruce to stand out, in the former ancient forest, of old growth. Further up, an area of exposed stumps revealed the law of supply and demand. A section of cut and felled trees, with their trunks still tethered to the earth, gathered in a mournful display of age defining rings. There was a separation of nature – where over the years and left behind – were hundreds of root systems, remaining intact.

In conflict to the other trees nearby, whose lifecycles had been severed, this tree embodied survival. For within the massive tower was the heartwood; whose purpose was to support the life of the Sitka. The correlation to Katrina's resilience and the spruce, triggered her empathy. Impulsively, she opened her arms and wrapped them around the purplish, grey bark of the trunk. A succession of her tears, abruptly released, onto the scales of the Sitka. Suddenly, a flicker of light in the distance caught Katrina's attention. Slowly, a lone figure approached out of the mist, dangling the source of illumination; in their hand.

Chapter I

Commemoration

EARLIER THAT SPRING, AN ELDERLY MAN NAMED CHRISTIAN, STOOD beneath the tree. With the pounding of rain upon him, his pigmented skin felt the stinging of every droplet, causing his tenuous arthritic bones to ache. Laying beside him on the ground was a lantern, its flame snuffed out from the storm. In the creases of his hand, he held a skeleton key. Wrapping his fingers around the cold metal, he cursed at the object. He was torn, knowing the key would reveal the answers to a loved one's questions, yet would cause ramifications. His gnarled, trembling fingers reached for the craggy bark, powerless to fully reclaim what was once lost. As he collapsed against the tree, his eyes fell upon the overgrown, granite stone, buried at its base.

An hour later, Christian James O'Connelly, returned to the cabin that was his secluded haven. Sitting on the porch, he watched as the rain let up. Rocking back and forth on the weathered swing, he remembered to place a cushion before sitting on the wood, which was splintered beyond repair. There he sat staring at the chipped green paint, as the bench creaked rhythmically, lulling him into a daydream. Adjusting his glasses, Christian peered out at the sea a few miles away from his cabin. The view reminded him of the expressive artwork of the Canadian painter, Robert Bateman, whom he held in high regard. A squirrel scampered past, searching for its harvest. Christian's brow furrowed over another silent reminder of the impending, bitter, winter.

Squinting, he glanced off in the distance, at the mountain crests sculpted from earth and wind. The overshadowing inclines taunted him. He frowned, recalling as a young lad when his father Jack had said, "Nature shows mercy to no one."

Many years later, Christian now fully understood the consequence of those words.

Peering out at the dignified Sitka trees, his lips curved into a smile, remembering his boyhood conquests, in the forest.

Almost immediately, the smile was replaced with a scowl. The regrets triggered by a Sitka spruce, replayed over in his mind, and felt within his heart, the grief he carried.

Catching a glimpse of himself, in the window, he pulled his right hand up and through his hair. The divided Picasso reflection, highlighted his unruly salt-and-pepper mane, in a disorderly way. Nevertheless, since he lived alone, he had no reason to groom himself. Christian's pale face, was etched with lines, connecting his past with the present. The result, was a rugged appearance, which gave him a hardened edgy appearance. Breathing deeply in, he sighed, imagining the face of the dapper, young, lad looking back at him. It was then out of the corner of his eye, he spotted on the rusting bar stool, a large weathered medical bag. Christian sucked in a deep breath, as he tried to avoid the painful memories attached to it.

* * *

Turning back to his viewpoint from the porch swing, he refocussed his attention on the beauty of the landscape before him. The central coast air was crisp and pierced his nostrils. He breathed in the scent of balsam fir, Sitka spruce, and Ponderosa pine. It reminded him of the musk perfume his soulmate once wore. Combined with the aroma of the ocean breeze, it was as if she were standing right before him.

Her name, was Skylar Reigh Falls. Memories of her reddish-blonde locks, fragrant with wintergreen shampoo, made him yearn. He pictured her grin, outlined in angular cheekbones. Her face highlighted by a wave of freckles, across her delicate features. It was as if a paintbrush, dipped in golden sand, had kissed her face.

He remembered how her olive eyes captured angles of the sunlight. A radiance, almost ethereal, surrounded her wherever she went.

His skin tingled recalling how she spoke of her connection to the natural world.

Autumn had been her favourite season. It was when the world came alive with splashes of beautiful, multi-coloured foliage. She treasured the time stretched out on the woodlands surface, enveloped in the delicate foliage of red alder trees. Inhaling the bouquet of the forest, she would exclaim, "My heart beats with Mother Nature!"

From the moment Skylar and her family moved into Ospero Falls, seven-year-old Christian knew his life had changed forever.

She was younger than Christian and painfully shy at five years old. Like a pair of mismatched bookends, they were drawn together, yet were set apart due to their families. Both shared in loneliness, as neither of them had any siblings. However, Skylar seemed to hold things inside, never letting on what was truly happening behind closed doors. In her shyness, she drew on a vivid imagination. Even at a young age, he would come to discover, Skylar was a beautiful storyteller. Christian remembered in their later years; it was her words that had drawn him to her. He had often revelled in their isolation, growing up within a small Canadian coastal town; had only brought them closer together. Throughout the years they knew one other, Skylar was always a significant part of his life. Even now she consumed his everyday thoughts. Like a landscape scorched by wildfire, his memories were seared by her image.

Drifting off to sleep, Christian imagined her warm breath upon his skin.

The next morning upon waking up, the sunshine filtered into Christian's window. The particles of light were an unwelcome display, as he fought the same nostalgia to which he clung. Memories of her filled his thoughts, stirring the torment felt within.

Secluded by the overgrown thickets of Salmonberries, Christian would be satisfied each day to sit on the porch swing. However, he had a purpose. It was the love of his granddaughter, Lily, who he tenderly liked to call "Lilybug," as she brought him much joy.

In recent years, as Lily grew into a teenager, she still enjoyed him referring to her by the nickname and even more now when in his company. Once a week, she took the half-hour ferry ride from Averston to Ospero Falls, British Columbia and biked several kilometres to his cabin. Lily had found a shortcut, on the outskirt of town, which saw her frequently drop in to see her grandfather. Although her family worried about her going alone into the woods, she felt it was important to visit. She resented that no one else seemed to care about him, as she found comfort in listening to his tales. Clinging to his every word, Lily sought stability, away from the turmoil of her home life. Sometimes, she would bravely ask him about the bitterness within her household. Despite his devotion to his granddaughter, Christian never answered her directly. Instead, he told her that the secrets dividing their family, was forged in betrayal.

All the while unbeknown to Lily, remnants of the unrevealed past were confined inside one room of the cabin, waiting to be revealed.

Christian knew one day; she would not settle for his excuses.

Therefore, he mulled over the advice once given to him, by the woman he loved:

Search within yourself, for where our roots run deep in darkness, our fears can be overcome by the light.

Chapter 2

Recollections

ONE LATE AUGUST MORNING, WITH THE LUSTRE OF THE SEA teeming with life below, Lily left her home in Averston and boarded the ferry to Ospero Falls. It was a secluded town along the Canadian coastline. Anticipating another great day with Grandpa C.C., as she fondly called her grandfather, it would be one filled with stories.

Leaning her bicycle against the railing, she caught a glimpse of herself in the ferry window. Pulling out her Village Lip Lickers balm, Lily glided it across her mouth, the taste of juicy watermelon was her favourite. With a twisted mane of caramel hair and eyes of tourmaline, Lily, 15, resembled a young starlet of the '40s.

Ever since she was a little girl, Lily adored her grandfather. She treasured the love for literature he had passed on in quotations from the works of William Wordsworth, Robert Louis Stevenson, and Elizabeth Barrett Browning. He shared how his father Jack, had taught him to appreciate the splendour of words.

Her grandfather always spoke fondly of his childhood and politely of Lily's grandmother Jacqueline. This was one of the reasons, why Lily never understood the resentment toward him, by her family. She had heard the rumours, claiming Jacqueline was to blame for all of the hostility. This drew her to occupy herself in things that required an imagination, as an escape. Lily loved to daydream, almost as much as she adored reading. Walking through the woods surrounding her grandfather's cabin, the young girl would often let her imagination run wild.

One day as she perched herself upon a rock, her focus was on a mound of burnished leaves. Letting her creativity take hold, she would envision fairies with their gossamer wings flittering around the decaying life.

When noises from the forest interrupted her fantasies, her eyes would turn to the shaded canopy of trees.

In her mind, she could see a woman emerge wielding a sword, her entwined copper tresses matching a firestone gem embedded in its handle. All of these things came to life when she painted, as Lily was an enthusiast of the outdoors and all its magnificent creatures. She had a wonderful teacher in her grandfather, who Lily had learned a lot from about the wilderness. He taught her the names of the animals inhabiting the woodlands, along with the many rocks that permeated the forest ground with their meanings. Over the years, he had shared the importance of respecting all the elements and artistry of nature. It was a filament of ingenuity, connecting granddaughter to grandfather.

As the ferry docked half an hour later, Lily mounted the bike, and pushed off. The summer breeze brought relief, as she moved along swiftly, towards her destination of her grandfather's house. She arrived around 10 o'clock to the smell of Red Rose tea wafting through the entrance of the cabin. Grandpa C.C. always had a fresh pot steeping upon her arrival. On the weekends when his granddaughter came to visit him, he picked fresh wildflowers, before Lily arrived. The fragrance of pine intermingled with the scent of the bouquet.

"Grandpa C.C., are you in the kitchen?"

Christian emerged from the breakfast nook with the teapot and two Wedgwood teacups.

"Greetings my Lilybug," he responded.

They were white and decorated with a wisp of vine that enclosed a scarlet corn poppy. When he saw them in a catalogue, he knew Lily would love them. It was his gift to her last Christmas, and she adored them. After using them, she always washed them and returned them to the shelf, knowing they gave her another reason to return.

Receiving a peck on the cheek, she followed him to the cushioned bench seat. There they sat for hours, chatting idly and sipping tea.

He tired easily and was finding it hard to keep awake; by two o'clock in the afternoon his eyes drooped, and his head bobbed forward.

Reaching for the patchwork quilt C.C.'s mother Sophia had made, Lily covered him. Later on, she would wake him up before supper. She did not mind when her grandfather occasionally nodded off, as it gave her time to explore. Quietly, she wandered back inside.

* * *

Long before Lily was born, Christian had renovated the cabin.

One of the additions to the cabin was a loft. The wooden stairs leading up to it creaked with each step, a reminder that her presence there was strictly forbidden.

"You don't want to go up there Lilybug," Christian always said. "It's musty-full of cobwebs and old junk. I wouldn't want to see you get hurt."

To her delight, her grandfather had redone the guestroom, for Lily's overnight visits on the weekends. She recalled the pleasant surprise of opening the guestroom door for the first time. A splendid array of delicate pastel colours filled the space. In the middle, a quilt adorned with hand-stitched songbirds and red poppies, covered an oak bed frame. The bed complimented the interlocking pine logs, which was the structure of the home. Her favourite accent was a string of lights, encased in a tinted green bottle. When plugged in, the lights cast sparks that danced off the walls, reminding her of lightning bugs. Although she treasured the charming room, the mystery surrounding the loft, drew her upstairs. Over the years, she had tried several times to gain entry. However, she was dismayed each time, to find the door locked. Today, though, Lily was determined.

She had to know what hidden treasure lay within the secret room – and, more importantly, why her grandfather had kept it from her.

She remembered once seeing him place a key into a lace-trimmed handkerchief but could not find it anywhere.

Determined not to give up, Lily looked back downstairs, when something caught her eye. On the lower shelf of a cabinet, tucked inside an old watering can, was a piece of lace sticking out.

She knelt to gently pick up the tarnished antique and reached inside.

Pulling out the frilled cloth, the young girl placed it on her knees and delicately undid the weathered string that entwined it. With sweaty palms and a heartbeat pounding as fast as a hummingbird's wings, she felt she was about to faint. Inside was a unique, silver, skeleton key, with a heart at the top enclosing a cross. The key, heavy in her palm, had the word FAITH inscribed on one side. Turning it over, she read the word PIPER. Caressing the key, she knew it was for the lock on the door. Puzzled why no one entered the loft, and eager to find out what lay within, Lily grabbed the cabinet for balance and pulled herself up. Stepping towards the door, her hands began to shake. Even though she was disobeying her grandfather, Lily convinced herself she had to know, what existed behind the door. The young girl placed the key into the hole below the doorknob. Turning it left then right, she heard the lock click open. Pausing, she listened for any signs of life from downstairs. Satisfied it was safe to continue, Lily pushed open the massive pine door. Upon entering the room, she gasped. The sight before her was filled with more grandeur than she had imagined. Yards of Victorian lacework cascaded from every corner of the room and draped the furniture elegantly. A wrought-iron bedframe adorned with red hearts on its porcelain posts lay in the centre of the room. The quilt spread across the bed was stitched with an intricate pattern of ruby songbirds. Everything appeared to be untouched.

The loft reminded her of the turrets on a castle, the ones her grandfather read to her about, from his collection of stories.

Intrigued by the dainty ornaments, Lily's eyes fell upon the nightstand, where a delicate woodcarving of a bird lay on its side. Even the curtains, sewn from creamy satin, draped the windows with patterns of sparrows. The shapes cut away to the inside trim of Calais lace.

Her attention turned to a mannequin in the corner, wearing a vintage dress. Around the collar, was a necklace, with a gold heart-shaped locket that was engraved with a cross.

The jewellery offset the scoop neckline, trimmed with red lace poppies.

The sleeves were sheer, while each cuff was a solid pattern of hand-stitched sweetbriar. Lily stepped around in the back of the dress. Complementing the ivory outfit, around the waist, in the back was a red bow, with a flower button. Looking down, Lily smiled as she saw an embroidered Sitka spruce on the trailing edge of the dress. She wondered who once owned the vintage dress? Continuing her search, the young girl saw a white sheet, draped over something meant to be kept hidden. Taking a few steps toward it, her attention was diverted to an arrangement of pictures, on the top of an oak vanity. They intrigued her more as she hoped they held more answers. She immediately recognized the picture of her grandfather as a young man. Beside it, in a silver frame, was a colour snapshot of C.C. leaning against a massive Sitka spruce tree. Standing beside him was a girl Lily didn't know. The tight, small curls complemented her oval face. Though curious who the girl was, Lily was more fascinated by the magnificent tree in the background. The lofty branches overwhelmed C.C. and the mystery girl. Lily examined the photograph more closely. She noticed what appeared to be a tree house, hidden among the towering limbs, which only increased her wonder. Next to the photo was a black-and-white picture of a baby wrapped in a blanket with a single sparrow stitched into the fabric.

Turning over the photograph there was no name to identify the child. Another black-and-white snapshot caught her interest. It was of a young woman smiling. She was petite, with long cascading curls. Her full lips drew upwards to rounded cheekbones; the arc of her curvy frame extended her sharp features. She turned over the picture and saw writing on the back.

In a whisper, she read the words:
Always remember the songbirds flying above our Sitka tree.
With never-ending love... On the other side. Xo

As Lily reread the words, they struck her as being familiar. She was intrigued by the mysterious woman's identity, yet more troubled by her grandfather's secret room. This made her feel justified, in snooping among his personal belongings. Moving around the room, she spotted a cross-stitch of a tree leaned against a woven basket. Next to it was a small, wooden box. Lily could see there was a songbird painted on the lid. She wondered what it contained. Like a child in a candy store, her focus darted from one item to another. The next thing to grab her attention was a polished heart-shaped stone. Picking it up, she peered at the glints of crimson and fuchsia. Unexpectedly, she heard the creaking of stairs outside the room. Panic overcame her, but it was too late. Standing in the doorway, with his teeth clenched, was her grandfather. The expression on his face frightened her, as she had never seen her grandfather so angry! Her hands began to tremble. Fear overcame her, and the stone she was holding, slipped from her fingers. She watched, stunned, as it sliced through the air. When it struck the floor, it shattered, splitting the remnants of nostalgia into two, fragmented pieces.

"What have you done?" Christian bellowed, "You promised me you'd never enter the loft; how could you do this?"

Lily felt like a speck on the floor, among the remains of the stone.

She broke into a sprint and rushed past her grandfather.

Running down the stairs two at a time, she did not stop until she arrived at her bicycle, leaning against the wooden gate outside. She was soon too far away to hear her grandfather calling her name.

Christian slumped against the loft door. Replacing the outburst, was his remorse over what he had done. Tears pooled in his eyes as his mind replayed the unhappy scene. Overwhelmed, he began to sob.

Lily sat quietly on the pier, her body shaking. She had managed to pedal her bicycle so fast, her legs felt like those of her rag doll, Pugsley. Looking at her foot, she noticed a tiny piece of lace, caught in her woven sandal. How could she have been so thoughtless? Lily wondered. She had no right to invade his privacy! Still puzzled by it all, there remained many unanswered questions. Who was the young woman in the photograph? Why did her grandfather have a secret room and who was the baby in the photograph? Reaching down, she picked the lace from her sandal. Gradually, she realized she might never get the answers she needed. Within moments, her rosy cheeks felt the stinging of her tears. As a gust of wind picked up, the ferry came into view. Despite all that had transpired, Lily was still determined to find out, what was behind the mystery of the loft.

Later that evening Christian, who had reluctantly gone downstairs, sat in his rocker. Years of teetering back and forth had left its mark. The wooden floor underneath was worn by two distinct grooves. The rocking of the chair kept time with the ticking of a grandfather clock. Christian glanced upon the mantelpiece to the photograph of Lily. Full of remorse, he turned to concentrate instead on the blaze of the fire. However, the flames with the warped images reflecting on the cabin walls, brought no comfort.

The ringing of the telephone startled him. He feared the call would be an unpleasant one. Shuffling his arthritic body towards the kitchen, Christian picked up the receiver. Clearing his throat, he answered, "Hello?"

"Who the hell do you think you are?" He recognized the voice of his daughter, Katrina.

"Damn you, Christian, what right do you have to send Lily home in tears?"

She was demanding an answer but wouldn't let him speak. "Lily's been crying in her room and won't not tell me what's wrong. I know you have something to do with this!"

"I am really sorry. I didn't mean to hurt Lily."

"You always have some pathetic excuse!"

"I know," he whispered, "you're right. As usual, I wasn't thinking."

"How many times have I had to plead with you to not involve Lily in your misery?

Do you know how much shit I'll catch from Marty if he finds out about this?"

"I know. Please don't tell Marty how I've upset Lily. I beg of you, Katrina – I couldn't live with myself if you cut me out of her life."

A dull quiet filled the air. For a moment, he thought she had hung up on him.

"I'm sorry, Christian, but you've brought this on yourself. It's out of my hands now and not my decision to make."

"I know, but what about how Lily feels?"

"I don't think you understand what I'm trying to tell you. I'm phoning on her behalf.

"Lily says she never wants to see you again!"

The words tugged like an anchor on his heart. He felt the room start to spin. Seizing a kitchen chair, he buckled into it, a tightness in his chest.

Struggling to speak, he tried to say the words, yet the moment was lost, as he heard the click of the connection being severed.

As the moonlight filtered through the cabin windows, Christian's head pounded from the hangover of the adrenaline rush. Beads of sweat stuck to his forehead, and his breathing remained laboured. The day's events had taken their toll on him, and it took all his strength to reach for the patchwork quilt he loved so dearly.

Tonight, he would sleep in the chair by the telephone, just in case his Lilybug changed her mind and decided to call.

This time, he would not give up so easily.

* * *

For the next several days, Christian centred his life around the telephone. He nibbled on smoked cheese and peppered jerky in the kitchen. He took only breaks to make tea and go to the bathroom. He even moved the rocking chair beside the phone, so he would not miss a call.

Gradually he went back to his regular routine. As the days turned into weeks, he still he had not heard from Lily. Over time, he realized that his past tormenting him had torn him away from his granddaughter. The many letters and cards he had sent went unanswered, and he wondered if she had bothered to read them.

It was nearing Thanksgiving when the telephone rang. Christian quickly picked up the handset.

"Hello, Lilybug?"

"Hey Christian! It's Frank. Jeez, I haven't heard from you in weeks, buddy. How the heck have you been?"

"I've been okay," he mumbled, sinking into the chair.

"You were expecting to hear from Lily today?"

"Yeah, Frank, I was hoping she would call."

"I wondered if she was okay. As I haven't run into her on the ferry as I often do.

Is everything all right between you two?"

"Yes, Frank, things are fine." He was in no mood to tell Frank how he had treated Lily. "In fact, I'm expecting Lily to drop by any day now." He was glad Frank could not see his face flush with embarrassment.

"Well, what would you say if I swung by tonight for a game of crib?"

Frank lived a half-hour away across the sea, in Averston, not far from Lily.

It was a place where women wrapped their Stormy pink lips around dry martinis, as rings of Diamond Solitaire clinked on their glasses.

"You know," Christian feigned a yawn, "maybe another time."

"Well, I say you don't need the beauty rest, as you're a hell of a lot better looking than the catfish we use to snag!" Frank chuckled.

"Thanks, Frank," Christian laughed half-heartedly. "Give me a call another day."

After Christian hung up the telephone, he was angry with himself, for spending so long talking to Frank. What if his granddaughter had called?

Chapter 3

Camouflage

A FRIGID, SEPTEMBER MORNING CREPT INTO THE CORNERS OF THE studio, where Lily liked to paint.

She lived with her parents Marty and Katrina Cadwaladers, in Averston. The coastal community was an excellent place to raise a family. The antique lampposts that decorated every street were draped with hanging baskets of fuchsias, black-eyed Susans, and begonias.

The Cadwaladers occupied a stately home with four bedrooms and as many bathrooms.

Although once considered prestigious, the dwelling was less stately, compared to the new upscale neighbours. Lily's father worked for a marketing company. He was often away for weeks to secure new contracts, which meant he could not spend a lot of time with his daughter.

Staring out at the storm gathering over the sea, Lily's breath matched in unison, with the surf pounding the coastline. The unrestrained weather, reminded her of the storms brewing, within her own family. In addition to having an absent father, Lily had to deal with an overbearing mother. It was the discipline she received, which suffocated her at times. Her mother's domineering ways reminded the young girl of her grandmother Jacqueline, who had never shared Grandpa's C.C.'s love of the written word. Lily's grandmother chastised her daughter unremittingly, with their spats mostly to do with Christian. The matriarch of the family, Jaqueline was cold and distant. She was outspoken in her request to never refer to her as grandmother; rather by her name, which seemed off putting to Lily.

Yet, after hearing Jacqueline constantly put down Christian for sharing his love of poetry with his granddaughter, Lily was content with keeping a distance from her grandmother.

After Jacqueline moved in with Lily and her parents, she took charge.

Next, she proceeded to infiltrate her bitterness towards Christian, by poisoning Katrina's relationship with him.

This resulted in placing a further wedge between father and daughter.

In the years to follow, Jacqueline saw Christian as a painful splinter, an unremovable reminder that they had never belonged together. Therefore, she refused to acknowledge his existence.

When Jacqueline finally died, Christian thought he would be relieved of the burden of her hatred. But he was disappointed when Katrina carried on her legacy. Still, he tried to be a part of her life. When Lily was born, he offered his love and financial support. Yet he knew it could never make up for the years he had missed with Katrina – or his acts of unfaithfulness to her mother.

Turning from the window, she walked over and sat on a stool to take a break. As she rested on the seat, Lily saw that one of the compartments of the storage cabinet was sticking out farther than the others. She pulled it out. Crammed in behind were half a dozen letters and cards bundled together. Grabbing them, she gasped on recognizing the writing to be her grandfather's. Each was addressed to her – and unopened. Putting them on the drawing board, she undid the string and sifted through the pile. Lily wondered why her mother hid the letters and soon became angry at the notion of what she had done. Sorting through the pile, the shape of one envelope struck her as unusual. Picking it up, Lily opened it. Gently, she pulled the card out and, fascinated by its construction, examined it closer. On the front was a photograph of a Sitka spruce, the same one she had seen in her grandfather's loft. Attached to the card, scalloped in lace, was a sparrow brooch made from green aventurine. The eye of the bird was a small pearl. Removing the brooch, the young girl opened the card.

To her amazement, she found the key to the loft inside. Bound to it, was a strand of lace and in it, was a handwritten message:

My dearest Lilybug,

Please, always remember the beauty of life is rooted in simpler things.

If you want the answers you are searching for, come back.

With sincerest apologies and regrets,

Love Grandpa C.C.

Overcome with emotion, Lily brushed tears from her cheeks. Soon, her fury at her mother for hiding the letters, overpowered her sadness. Her life had been shrouded by veils of deceit, and she was tired of it. She recognized the lace from the handkerchief. It was the same one tucked into the watering can in her grandfather's cabin. She removed it and peeled the tape off the key.

Placing the key in her back pocket, she set the card upon the cabinet. Lily then attached the brooch to her blouse.

Standing up, she gathered a fistful of cards and headed downstairs, to find her mother.

Lily saw her mom stretched out in a lounging chair by the indoor swimming pool. Holding tightly onto her precious mail, Katrina's daughter smacked the mail with such force at her mother's leg, prompting Katrina to scream.

"What the hell did you do that for?"

"Look at the mail, mother."

Katrina looked down. Realizing she was cornered, she stood up.

"I was only trying to protect you," she stammered. "At first, I was going to burn the letters, but I decided to hide them instead. I was just waiting to see if you still wanted to talk to your grandfather."

"You're lying! Don't try to cover this up…"

"Lily! Don't you talk to me that way!"

"You're nothing but a bold-faced liar!"

The slap across Lily's face swung her head to the side and back, and the sound echoed over the pool water.

Katrina's hands were trembling, as she saw her daughter's cheek turn red, from the handprint remaining upon it.

Tears ran from her bulging eyes.

"Get out!" Katrina screamed. "Go back to your room now!"

Lily's instincts told her to listen. However, as she passed into the foyer of their home, she quickly pulled on her boots and bolted out the door. Without much thought given to it, Lily had left behind in her room, her warm, down jacket. As she hurried away, she regretted not bundling up or taking her bike. She was anxious when she realized her wallet was still on the dresser at home. All that mattered was getting away from her mother – and to the ferry.

A heaviness settled in as she walked, knowing how much distance lay ahead.

As she walked, she heard the crunch of the frosted, autumn leaves underneath her boots. In her mind, she replayed all that transpired. Abruptly, her cold fingers reached for the pin still attached to her blouse. Suddenly, her thoughts were interrupted by the rumble of a vehicle in the distance.

From behind her, appeared a Chevy Silverado. The truck's windshield was fogged up. As the vehicle neared Lily, it slowed to a stop. The window rolled down to reveal her grandfather's friend Frank. She breathed a sigh of relief.

"Jeez, Lily, what are you doing out in the cold?"

"It's a long story, and I feel like a block of ice! Can you give me a lift to the ferry?"

"I can do better than that," Frank winked. "I'll take you right to your grandfather's doorstep."

He leaned over and as Frank opened the passenger door, the sparrow brooch Lily was wearing, caught his attention. It was something he had not seen in years. Before he had a chance to ask about it, Lily eager to get warm, jumped inside.

As Frank drove to the ferry, he offered Lily a warm cup of coffee out of his thermos and an extra parka he had stashed behind the seat. Grabbing the jacket, Frank paused for a moment, when he saw the pin but said nothing.

It was not until they arrived at the dock, several kilometres away, that she felt the blood returning to her fingertips.

"You know, Lily, it's none of my business what's troubling you these days. However, I do know your grandfather has been missing you dearly. He is a complex man. Your parents raised you differently; you have your family's privileged circumstances, to shield you from the outside world."

It was true, she had been born into wealth and was spoiled with whatever her heart desired.

"I think I know what you're trying to say," Lily replied.

She remarked, "Thank you. I'm so glad you came along."

As the ferry sped through the frigid waters, wind clipped the peaks of the whitecaps nipping at the hull. None of the passengers ventured outside.

When the ferry docked, Frank started the truck and drove off. He knew it would be quicker to take the shortcut, to bypass Ospero Falls and go straight to Christian's home.

Approaching Grandpa C.C.'s log cabin, Lily remembered the key and thought of the world she had left behind. Yet she always felt at home, with the surrounding wilderness, that comforted her among the townspeople of Ospero Falls.

Driving up to the cabin, the colours of autumn burst with intensity, as if nature's vacuum seal had popped opened. When the truck came to a stop, she was happy to see smoke billowing out of the chimney.

"Looks like he's home," Frank said.

They looked at each other and laughed, as they both knew how silly Frank's statement was. Christian was a recluse. Delivery boys brought him all the supplies he needed; visitors knew to phone first before dropping by. Lily was the only one who never needed an invitation. She was welcome any time.

"Are you coming in?" she asked.

"No, afraid not. I just remembered that I offered to help Samuel Benson with his woodpile today. Take it easy on your grandfather, dear and remember, he was expecting me today" said Frank, leaning across to open the passenger door. "He loves you very much."

She thanked him and offered his jacket back.

"No, you can keep it. A young outdoorsy lady like yourself, needs to have a good parka to keep her warm."

"You're a nice man, Frank. My grandfather's lucky to have a friend like you."

"And I'm lucky to have a friend like him. He and I have been through a lot together."

She trudged through the uncut grass towards the cabin. The porch swing creaked in the breeze. Standing on the doorstep, she was about to knock, when the door opened.

"Lilybug!" cried Christian. "Oh, my goodness, I'm so delighted to see you! I knew it was only a matter of time before you came. Come in, my dear. I'll brew us some tea."

He hurried off to the kitchen, before she had a chance to reply.

He appeared back in the room, holding a vintage Brown Betty teapot and a rippled amber saucer. On the side, was a selection of vanilla and chocolate Girl Guide cookies.

Since she was a little girl, Lily had enjoyed being served Red Rose from a unique teapot, which had a dragon wrapped around it. Her grandfather called it Moriage and said it was a term used to describe the delicate layering on pieces of pottery.

He once told her it was from Japan and held a special connection to his father, Jack.

"Looks wonderful, Grandpa C.C.," Lily said.

"I'm glad," Christian said, sitting in his rocker and rubbing his chin. "I would rather wait on you than stuffy old Frank any day."

The words seemed to ease their tension as they both began to laugh. Soon followed a brief period of quietness, until Christian finally spoke.

"My dearest Lily, what happened between us was entirely my fault. Throughout your life, there have been too many secrets. The truth needs to be revealed. I sent you the key, as it no longer belongs to me. When I tell you my story/ our story, I promise to share everything. I believe you deserve to find what you have been searching for."

His crescent lids dropped as his brown eyes glistened with tears. She reached out and tenderly touched his hand.

Lily replied, "Oh, Grandpa C.C., I'm sorry, too… I had no right to invade your privacy.

You need to understand that right now in my life, I feel no real sense of connection to my family, except with you. It's as if a part of me is missing, and within this home are the answers I am seeking. Besides," she said, lowering her voice, "I need to know what happened to make my family despise you."

Christian rocked back and forth.

With a sigh he said, "I've a feeling you left home on unpleasant terms, Lilybug, and I must be honest with you, I do not like it one bit.

There is already too much bad blood between your mother and me. If I allow you to stay here without calling her first, then she will loathe me even more."

A lump formed in Lily's throat.

"I thought if anyone would understand it would be you! Why are you making me phone her?

She paused, then stammered out the words… when she's such a wretched person?"

Christian stared at her. "Do not talk that way again, young lady! I will not have any more nonsense. You are forgetting that she still is my daughter, no matter what has happened between us. Your mother has given you the best of everything."

Lily turned her head the other way. "Fine. I'll call, but I'm not going home."

Christian knew better than to push the issue and was in no position to preach.

As she picked up the telephone and dialed, Lily noticed the sofa chair and pillow pushed nearby. Her heart sank, as she realized C.C. had been waiting for her to call.

The phone rang once.

"Hello?"

"It's me… Lily."

"Oh my God, where are you?" Katrina gasped, then added, "I looked all over the house for you!"

Lily hesitated, glancing back at Christian, who gave her a concerned look.

"I'm at Grandpa's and plan on staying here for a while."

Lily tried to say more but was cut off…

"Of course, you would run back to him. What was I thinking?"

"Mom! How can you be so spiteful?"

"You have no idea what has occurred throughout the years between us, so you have no right to talk! I am so tired of how you idolize your grandfather. If only you knew the half of it!"

"Well, mom, you've never allowed me to make my own decisions and now is my chance." Pausing for a moment, she gathered her thoughts and said, "Growing up, you sheltered me from the secrets that are still ruining our lives."

Katrina took a deep breath in, trying hard to hold back her tears.

Lily continued on, "When Grandmother had her stroke; she was trapped inside a mind that all I ever saw her hatred towards Grandpa. Then she died, and I feel you've taken on her unhappiness! I need to know the truth, Mom, to break this cycle we are entangled in. The only person who can give me closure is Grandpa."

"Oh, Lily," Katrina gave into her sobs, "I am so afraid the truth will hurt you more."

"More than the slap you gave me?"

The words sunk into Christian, who upon hearing them, was surprised.

"I am so sorry, Lily, for hitting you. My temper got the best of me. There is simply no excuse for what I did to you. I hope you can forgive me."

Lily had never been struck by her mother before. Whatever secrets her grandfather was keeping, she knew, seriously threatened mom's relationship with her.

Lily added, "I don't understand why everything is being hidden from me?"

Katrina replied, "Please know I have tried to do my best in raising you. I do love you. Despite my actions, I am scared for you to find out the truth of our family. And even if you think I have mistreated your grandfather, I hope that you understand, I let him be a part of your life."

Lily softened as she whispered,

"I will call you back when I am ready. Just give me some time."

"I do hope of one thing, replied Katrina. "That is – your grandfather tells both sides of the story."

Lily glanced towards the kitchen, to see her Grandpa C.C., was tidying the already-clean room.

"Okay, well maybe someday you can speak to your father again yourself. Goodbye, Mom." Lily sighed, as she hung up.

The words brought Christian's movements to a halt. His shoulders sagged as he disappeared from view.

When he appeared again, her grandfather had a slight smile. Motioning for his granddaughter to join him, he said,

"Come with me, Lilybug."

Nearing the stairs, he paused. Turning around, he remarked,

Oh wait, I should probably stoke the fire and refill the teapot first."

She knew he was stalling but waited while he meandered around the cabin.

Lily sat and waited patiently for him to be ready to return to the loft.

Christian returned with hot water and topped up the teapot.

"We'll need this," Christian said, grabbing the tray, then added, "As it will take some time for me to share a story that's been decades in the making."

Looking upwards at the stairs, he added, "Let's continue."

Slowly, they climbed the stairs to the loft. When he reached the door, Christian paled.

"Grandpa C.C., are you alright?"

"I don't know if I'm ready for this," he whispered, leaning against the door frame.

"So many years, too much tragedy."

"Listen," she said, touching his arm, "if you are not prepared to deal with this, I totally understand."

Christian took a deep breath in before exhaling, then replied, "No, Lilybug, I have to rid myself of the enemies lies, which I've tried to keep hidden, far too long."

Christian waited then asked, "Please, will you unlock the door?"

Reaching into her pocket, she pulled out the skeleton key and placed it into the keyhole.

She turned it until the lock clicked.

As the door opened, they saw the room as they had left it on that fateful day – except for the stone that now sat on the bureau, split in two.

Christian put down the tray and moved slowly through the loft, touching each item in the room, with fondness. Reaching the bed, he placed two fingers to his lips, then upon the pillow.

Lily stood in wonder, as she watched her grandfather. Waiting quietly, not wanting to interrupt his thoughts, she saw a rocking chair with the carving of a sandpiper on it. Pulling it near her grandfather, she settled comfortably into it and began to slowly rock.

"Her name was Skylar Reigh Falls," Christian said. "She was a warrior of the forest and a sea-loving beachcomber. She had the gift of discernment and the power to forgive."

He paused, then smiled adding, "You would have liked her, Lilybug."

He grabbed his cup of tea. Sitting opposite his granddaughter in a rocking chair, he smiled. He reached over to the night table, opened the drawer, and felt inside. He pulled out what appeared to be a long strip of bark. Puzzled, Lily glanced at the out-of-place item.

He handed her the strip of bark that bent around its crumbling edges. Glued on one side was a weathered piece of paper.

The ink had faded from the paper, yet she could still make out the handwritten words.

"Please dear, read it out loud for me."

She cleared her throat, then recited the words,

I, Christian James O' Connelly, lay claim to this tree uniting two lovers and declare that our roots here – will never be severed!

Lily looked over to her grandfather.

His eyes were closed.

"Grandpa C.C., are you okay?"

"Yes, dear, I'm fine. I was simply thinking of that day."

"Can I ask you something?" Lily hesitated.

Christian nodded his head, "Yes, of course you can, for today is about providing the answers I should have given you long ago."

Lily cleared her throat and inquired, "You claimed ownership over something produced by our Creator?"

Christian sighed deeply, then replied, "For everything there is a reason. That memento is a piece of your past. It also connects me to Skylar, who was my reason to live. One of her remarkable qualities, was the ability to remain strong and faithful. Even through the darkest moments, she taught me the true meaning of compassion."

"What happened to her?" asked Lily.

Before answering, Christian rubbed his chin, then remarked:

"There are some things you need to know first, to understand what happened so many years ago. I only hope that by delving into the darkness of the past, I can bring more purpose and light to your life. Know that I will always be here for you Lilybug, despite what is revealed."

Although confused, Lily knew she had to be patient as she wanted to hear his story. Knowing he had kept it guarded, Lily had a feeling, it was worth the wait.

* * *

The tale her grandfather was about to tell had become part of the history of a small lumber and fishing town in British Columbia. Throughout the years, many people had retold it, offering various details.

But one fact never changed: near a tiny, coastal community, stood a towering Sitka spruce tree.

The tree's presence in Christian's life, was connected to the hearts of those he loved. Over time, it had withstood many storms. Those who came to know the trees existence, would hear of the numerous tales, affixed to it. Like bonded, wilful branches – fighting against the wind – they never wanted to let go. Therefore, the tendrils of deceptions connected to a treehouse, had remained.

Chapter 4

Innocence

In the spring of 1950, when Christian was four-years-old, he and his family moved to a small town called Ospero Falls. The community was located along the western coastline of Canada, within a complex of straits, fjords, islands, and inlets. Since much of the seaside was unoccupied and road access was unheard of, the only way to the area was by ferry. Hank Stevenson, was the private operator of The Carnelian. It ferried 10 vehicles between Ospero Falls and Averston. The large dock also saw another bigger ferry, transport people and vehicles to Norelton and Oakerson. The surrounding nature abounded with a variety of wildlife, including mountain goats, which impressed the locals with their ability to hang on to the precipitous cliffs. Above the towering peaks of raw, layered basalt that overlooked the town, soared flocks of bald eagles. Their sharp eyes searched for their next fresh meal of salmon, an abundance of oily protein, within the vast ocean. Rushing from the mountains, were numerous thundering waterfalls. Townspeople often gathered at the foot of the discharging freshwater rapids to fly-fish for trout.

The immigration boom, beginning 1867 in the Prairies continued, until the onset of the First World War in 1914. The war stimulated the forest industry, providing Canada with its first export market. Recent immigrants flocked to the towns where work was plentiful. There were jobs within the lumber and pulp-mill industry, for any able-bodied man, who was not afraid of a hard day's labour. With the outbreak of the Second World War, small towns whose men left to serve their country were stricken with labour shortages. An influx of Eastern and Mediterranean Europeans came to work. In nearby Averston, citizens were afraid that foreigners would take over and did not welcome them. Even though they shared a common purpose, the lives of the outsiders were made difficult.

With no labour unions, and a lack of education, many feared losing their jobs.

Jack O'Connelly was not one of them.

After his time of service in the war, he moved to Ospero Falls, so as to provide for his new family. Jack's quiet demeanour was welcome in the small, knit community. The town itself, was created out of possibilities, through the investment of a North American company. Each supporter, saw opportunities from all of the elements within; a waterfall, surrounding mountains and the ocean, could all provide subsistence for those who chose to call Ospero Falls home.

Unlike Averston, a 1/2 hour ferry ride away, which was a town overflowing with indifference.

Jack liked to keep to himself in Ospero Falls, working day after day for the lumber company. He worked along the water's edge, forming logs into booms to be towed to the local mill. Jack was proficient in handling a variety of equipment. His experience saw him toiling laborious hours, in order to afford for his family, the best of what Ospero Falls offered. Jack adored his wife Sophia and his son Christian. Every day he looked forward to walking down the dirt road home, knowing his boy was waiting for him. He delighted in telling Christian elaborate stories about fighting for England back in World War II. To Christian, his father was the embodiment of adventure. When the O'Connelly family first arrived in Ospero Falls, townspeople considered them one of the wealthier families. Sophia's Aunt Gloria, had left her a substantial inheritance when she passed away. However, Jack had his pride and refused to live off the money. Therefore, it sat in the local bank. The house they bought, was a modest structure and needed a bit of sprucing up. Therefore, Sophia recruited her son, Christian's help with painting the front porch and planting flowers.

Sophia dedicated herself to the community. Unlike Jack, she was outgoing. She liked to drop off a fresh-baked fruit pie, for new neighbours, to welcome them to town.

Locals referred to her affectionately as Lady Crocker.

* * *

In the summer of 1953, Sophia busily readied her preserves for the long winter. Pouring gooseberry jelly into canning jars, she would gaze through the kitchen window and smile upon the changing of the seasons. It was a glorious thing to see nature, casting its spell onto Ospero Falls. One day, peering through the window, Sophia's attention was drawn across the street.

An old, Ford truck, rambled into the driveway of a house needing repair.

"Oh, Christian!" Sophia said. "Please go fetch one of my berry pies from the windowsill.

"I see we have some new neighbours to greet."

Christian was curious to see who had moved into the deserted house. He wondered if they had a boy who could be his playmate. Being an only child was lonely, and with his father hard at work, he yearned for a friend. At seven-years-old, he thought it would be nice to have someone with whom he could skip rocks, fish, and build a tree house. As he stared through the window, his mind drifted back to a summer's day he longed to return to. He and Sophia had taken the half-hour ferry ride to Averston, where she had shopping to do. Much to his delight, she gave Christian permission to go exploring for an hour. The dense forest invited him to play underneath its massive, sheltering branches. Christian seized the opportunity to look for the tree of his dreams. It had to have an outstretched canopy for shading and supportive limbs for protection. Once in a National Geographic, he had discovered an awe-inspiring photograph of the majestic Sitka spruce. He was then determined to find a tree just like it. Christian spent the first 20 minutes, walking around and was about to give up, when he spotted an impressive spruce. It stood in a clearing, full of unyielding beauty – the tree he had spent so many starry nights envisioning. The bark was thin, scaly, and purple-grey.

The limbs stretched out from the trunk leaving a clearing perfect for a tree house. As Christian gazed in wonder, the tree seemed to beckon to him: Come and climb! He approached the thick trunk and charted out the steps he would take. Cautiously, he began to ascend, grasping smaller limbs that were soft and flexible to steady himself. His small fingers dug into the trunk, and he felt confident, until some of the bark came off in his hand. Quickly, he slipped down to the base of the tree. Christian looked at the handful of bark and decided to keep it as a reminder of his efforts.

He tucked it into his back pocket. Again, the young boy began the tedious climb upwards. It took him a while to reach the clearing.

But once he sat among the boughs covered in wavy, papery seed cones and stiff, bluish needles, he knew it was worth the effort. Perched comfortably, Christian looked out. He observed the vast, churning waters stretch for miles and listened to the jarring lullaby of surf collide with stone. On the western side tucked within the mountains, he saw an alpine lake, trailing rock flour from a distant glacier. A pinch in his backside reminded him of the bark in his pocket. Making sure he had a stable limb to hold him, he carefully pulled it out to look. The bark was smooth on one side and rough and wrinkly on the other. As he held it out, over the tree limbs, it looked like an old woman's hand with one, gnarled, finger pointing to something. It was then that his gaze following the line of the bark, saw the mansion. He had heard people talk about a house in Averston so enormous, it had to be seen to be believed. Boasting dozens of bedrooms, and extravagantly decorated in silks, brass, and silver, it stood poised on top of a mountain ridge. High gates blocked the outside world from peering in. Despite the owner's desire for privacy, it could not hide the mansion from the probing eyes of a curious child, sitting in a towering tree. Christian's heart began to race.

"One day, that house will be mine!" he declared.

The young boy's thoughts of that day drifted back to his mother in the kitchen. The aroma of the pie wafting throughout the house. Sophia bundling her warm pastry into a checkered tea towel, announced she was off to meet the neighbours. Curious, Christian peered through the yellow polka-dotted curtains. As his mother approached the house, a woman greeted her outside and led her away from the front door, to speak with her. She wore a long sleeve blouse and a sweater. Her dark slacks were thick. The outfit as a whole, was heavy for that time of year.

Christian could not hear what they were talking about, but he saw they were smiling. The lady had accepted the pie and after a few minutes, he grew bored.

Christian was about to give up hope of making a friend, when the front door of the house swung open. There stood a scrawny girl with matted strawberry-blonde curls. Her two front teeth protruded outward from dirt-smudged cheeks. She clutched a doll that caught Christian's attention with its dark skin; a stark contrast to her pale complexion.

His mother asked about the unique, toy doll. The woman, who introduced herself as Victoria, shared how her daughter Skylar had found it in a bin at a local thrift store and would not part with it. Bending down towards the girl, Sophia smiled. The girl withdrew from her, cowering in fright. Suddenly, the front door open to reveal a man in a tattered white T-shirt, staggering toward the woman. His belly spilled out over a reddish-brown snakeskin belt, which held up a pair of ragged jeans. Victoria revealed he was her boyfriend, Trey. Sophia took several steps back when the man began cursing. Startled, she began running towards their house. As Sophia fled, the man angrily shook his fist in the air, swearing loudly for the entire neighbourhood to hear. Sophia darted inside her home, still clutching her warm pie.

Sophia saw her son standing at the window, still with fright. Walking over to him, she hugged Christian tightly and remarked, "Oh, my goodness, I have never encountered such a brute man in my entire life! What rudeness!"

He looked up at her and asked, "Are you alright, Mom?"

"I will be just fine, dear." Sophia patted his head. "You make sure to stay away from them, you hear me? That poor child!"

Christian nodded. Although he knew it was better to listen to his mother, something drew him to the mysterious girl.

The summer months were lonely for Christian. He was disappointed when his parents agreed he would start school the following year. Still, he understood, as studies were considered an addition to helping with the daily chores.

In many families, youngsters piled wood, picked berries, or learned skills on the fishing boats. Jack showed him about the importance of a good work ethic, in the chores he set out for his son.

Christian mowed the lawn with The Clipper, washed all of the baking dishes for his mom and took the neighbours dog, Boots, out for walks. After Christian helped his mother with chores, he also went with her to do errands.

Ospero Falls was home to 2,900 people. Within the town was a post office, customs building, dock warehouse, fire hall, and a bank, in addition to an array of businesses. This included Canetti's Diner, Miss Jean's Boutique, and Dufrayn's General Store. For those needing lodging, the Billows Inn offered comfortable accommodations at a reasonable price. The increase in population and remoteness of Ospero Falls required the building of the Bay hospital, which was equipped with all of the best necessities a hospital could want. This included being staffed with skilled doctors, qualified specialists, and many nurses, who worked on the two floors.

In between the local bakeshop and a jewelry store, Christian and his mother liked to visit Reggie's Place, a one-room bookstore brimming with every kind of fantastic tale. Reggie ensured the unique stockpile covered an array of genres. Though gruff looking, he would twist his silver moustache and with a huff, blame his English ancestry. To the enjoyment of Christian, Reggie would recite poetry on a whim. He shared with many who would listen, his favourite author was D.H. Lawrence, as Reggie was delighted to have accumulated an impressive collection of his books. For a young boy, the bookstore was one of Christian's favourite places to visit. Reggie had befriended him, upon discovering the youngsters enthusiasm for words.

Soon after, he set a bright orange cushion in the corner, where Christian could sit and read. Above the bookstore, was Miss Jeans Boutique, Beside the general store was Canetti's Diner, which housed a soda fountain and the best place to gather for a hotdog, hamburger and golden fries. It also sold penny candy and the thickest hand dipped shakes. Another door down, was Dufrayn's General Store. It was the main place for supplies, brought in from Averston, where fresh meat – especially poultry and fish could be found. Canned goods were the best for they lasted the longest. The fresh fruits and vegetables were bought up quickly. Everyone flocked over to Jakob's Bakery, which was right beside the Post Office. Their best customers were those who worked in the small post office. As they had to endure the sweet and savory smells all day long, which tended to waft over to those sorting the mail, in the early morning hours.

Further down, was The Cedrus Pub, where a crowd of fishermen and loggers gathered to swig beer, while upstairs was Fred's Barbershop. They swapped exaggerated stories of ferocious sea creatures and tales of a beast named Bigfoot. Overindulgence, spurred the need for law enforcement. Within the small police station was a single jail cell.

Over the years, drunks paid visits to the clink to clear their heads, though never for more than a night. There was no need for those to be transferred for further incarceration in Averston, or to be transferred to the courthouse in Norelton, the nearest, larger city.

Ospero Falls saw mostly everyone get along with each other, for when you grew up together, it was like you were family. The folks here lived life in unison, aside from those who liked to reside on the outskirts.

Scattered about the town were bunkhouses and modest homes. Further into the woods, nestled within, were rustic cabins. This is where people from other cultures, such as Japanese, found comfort in being with immigrants from further away places in the world.

While everyone worked together, at the end of their shifts, most returned to their areas of livening that suited them well.

Ospero Falls' only place of learning, The Beech Lacus School, housed students from Grades 1-12. However, the school had trouble retaining teachers, who left to take positions at the private school in Averston. Although Sophia's inheritance could afford such a luxury, Jack refused to place Christian higher above the workers, who he laboured side by side, daily. For entertainment, the Blackfine Theatre provided hours of fun. Christian could still recall the greeting on the marquee, boasting "Wholesome, affordable family entertainment for everyone!"

At the end of the gravel road was Walt's Seascapes pet store. The owner, was a former sailor who entertained the children of Ospero Falls, with whimsical tales of adventures alongside the creatures of the deep. They were never disappointed. Eyes wide, Walt's eager audience envisioned the hammerhead sharks, eels, and stingrays that filled his stories. The children looked up to him, like a Super-hero. Many returned to the store with broken piggy banks.

Captured by Walt's tales, they eagerly brought their purchases home of fishes, hamsters and the occasional parakeet. There was always the supplies needed of goldfish bowls, cages and birdseed, which Walt receiving supplies from Averston.

On Sunday mornings, the people of Ospero Falls assembled for service, in the small church located in the town centre.

* * *

Over the next few weeks, Christian obeyed his mother and stayed away from the house across the street. Rumours had spread through the small town about the strangers who had moved there. Fred Wilson, the barber, claimed the man was the leader of a violent biker gang. Though Tom Severson, the barkeep, swore he had overheard the man had ties to a mobster.

While people gossiped, they could not imagine what was to unfold. One day, Sophia offered to take Christian into Averston. He leapt at the opportunity to see his tree again and make plans to build the best tree house anyone had ever seen. As the 3 o'clock ferry pulled away, Christian sat on the top platform with Sophia, who was preoccupied with a novel. He heard sobbing cries coming from underneath the stairwell. Descending the eroded steps, he felt the tiny hairs on his neck rise. Reaching the bottom, he crouched down and squinted into the musty space underneath. Two wide, green eyes stared back.

"Jeez! What are you doing here?" Christian asked.

The girl sniffled and wiped her nose on her unclean shirt.

"Mommy… Mommy… Mommy!" she wailed.

"It's okay, I'm not gonna hurt you." He reached out his hand and offered it to her.

She flinched, biting her bottom lip. Then she bolted into his arms and squeezed his waist.

"Hey, it's alright! What's your name?"

"S-S-Skylar."

"Where's your mommy?"

"Mommy's hurt," she said, shaking.

Christian felt uneasy, and he knew he needed help. "Come with me upstairs, so I can get my mommy to help your mommy, okay?"

"Bad man!"

"No, it's alright, Skylar! I'm not gonna hurt you!"

Skylar shook her head. "Bad man hurt mommy!"

"Is your daddy the bad man?

"No," she whimpered, "Daddy's dead."

Panic overcame him. Christian ran up the stairs two at a time until he reached his mother.

He grabbed Sophia's arm, startling her.

"Christian James O'Connelly!" she scolded. "What is the meaning of this outburst?"

"Mom, you have to come quick!" Christian panted.

"The little girl that lives across from us is hiding down under the stairs. Her name is Skylar. She says her mom's hurt and her father's dead!"

"Good Lord, Christian! What are you talking about?"

"Mom, you have to believe me and get some help!"

"Okay, sweetie! Let me go talk to Mr. Stevenson. You stay with the little girl."

"Hurry up, Mom!"

Sophia hurried towards the ferry operator's quarters.

The next several hours were a blur to Christian. The coastal police got involved, and the whole town turned out to watch.

Once the story was straightened out and the truth revealed, Christian discovered the bad man turned out to be Trey Wickett, the boyfriend of Skylar's mom Victoria.

The night before, in a drunken rage, Wickett pounded Victoria with his fists. As he walked away, he said, "If you ever mention your dead husband again, I will beat you even harder."

Her husband, Eli Falls, had died in a fire at the mill where he worked when Skylar was only a baby. At the tender age of three, the terrorized little girl found out her daddy, was never coming back to save her.

According to the report, Victoria tried to escape on the ferry with Skylar. Her daughter was already safely tucked aboard when Trey caught up with her. Not realizing Skylar was watching from the ferry window, he wrenched her mother's arm back so hard, Victoria thought it would break.

This was not the first injury Victoria had received at the hands of Trey Wickett. He was not the same man either, when they had met two years earlier, it was when she was leaving her grief support group. Trey seemed to linger, until he finally approached to walk her home. She was hesitate as she was not interested in meeting anyone.

Besides, Trey was in his late forties and not an attractive man. Victoria tried to brush him off gently, yet he pursued her. Finally, after running into him after her group on another two occasions, Victoria finally gave in.

It was the way he initially doted on her that she was fooled. Trey would bring her flowers, which unknown to her, he cut from a neighbours yard. Another time he brought her a picnic basket full of cheese, crackers, olives, and deli meats. Yet Trey failed to mention his sister had prepared it for their grandmother and he had swiped it off the porch, blaming some rotten kids in the area for stealing it.

Trey having been in and out of jail, had a cellmate named Antonio, who was a con artist. Antonio taught him everything he now was putting into practice. The one place Trey learned to target vulnerable women, was the local grief group. Victoria had been attending because of the loss of her husband, Eli.

It did not take long before his yelling turned into slaps and then full punches onto Victoria's small frame. She never went out into public without a long-sleeved blouse, a sweater, and dark slacks, to hide away the endless bruises. There was a part of her that hated who she had become. She was supposed to protect her little girl and felt she had failed Skylar. Victoria struggled to cope with the reality, the monster in their house did not hide underneath a bed, rather he sat with them at every meal.

She tried to escape with her daughter to Ospero Falls, however Trey would never let her go.

When they showed up in the close community, it was not new beginnings they found, rather the same horrific pattern of abuse.

Now as she looked back with tears in her blackened eyes at Skylar, the ferry pulled away for Averston. Mr. Stevenson radioed ahead to the police, who were waiting when the ferry docked. The Coastal police arrived in Averston to speak with Skylar.

Once the truth was revealed, Trey was arrested in Ospero Falls for battering his girlfriend. Immediately, the police sent him to a more secure jail, in Averston.

Years later, the next several hours of what transpired, were clear as day to Christian.

Everyone hoped Wickett would vanish, especially Victoria and Skylar. However, no one could anticipate the misery he would unleash; staining the wholesomeness of Ospero Falls.

Chapter 5

Faith Collision

THE FOLLOWING WEEKS, SAW SKYLAR TAKE HER FIRST STEPS OUT OF the vicious cycle of abuse, mother and daughter had been confined in. Slowly, she began to show interest in going outside her home with Victoria. The two of them would walk along the beach, as both found solace in the waters surrounding Ospero Falls. One autumn day, Christian saw them together, by the pier. He was curious when Skylar brought a hand to her pursed lips and tossed something invisible into the sea. It took a minute before he realized she was blowing kisses to the ocean.

On another occasion, Christian watched as Victoria helped her daughter carry a few pots of paint, along with stacks of old paper, down to the shoreline. Taking her time, Skylar thoughtfully selected and assembled pebbles of various shapes and sizes. Next, she rolled out the paper onto a large, sanded log Jack had given her. Picking up a pebble, she would dip it into a vibrant hue and use it as a paintbrush, to create swirls of colour onto her canvas.

Christian's parents were fond of the girl whose laughter brought joy to everyone. Jack wanted to contribute to her happiness. He built her a pair of wooden stilts out of discarded lumber from the mill. Jack walked behind her, patiently guiding the little girl along as she fumbled with them. Jack smiled and with a chuckle said, "This is what's called getting your sea legs."

Meanwhile, back at the O'Connelly home, Sophia taught Victoria to sew and make preserves. Christian often spent his small allowance taking the young girl to see a picture at the Blackfine Theatre.

As winter was now upon them, Skylar was excited about Christmas. Even her mother was looking forward to a new year full of promise.

Jack announced it was time to go into the mountains to pick out a tree.

As Christian towed Skylar on a toboggan, Jack shouldered a large axe and slung a sled across his back. A few hours later, the three were returning with their Christmas tree.

A tall pine bursting with small bunches of evergreen needles, would soon hold the ornaments, passed through the generations. Jack towed the sled holding the tree. Christian trudged along, pulling the toboggan with Skylar on it, over knolls of layered snow.

They stopped at a viewpoint overlooking the town. Jack reached into his parka and pulled out a flare. As Skylar looked on curiously, he cracked it – a signal, Christian knew, to the people waiting below. In the centre of town, Victoria stood beside an enormous Christmas tree. Each branch held charming, little trinkets. Suddenly the whole town and the tree lit up with tinted filaments, as applause filled the air, with those sharing in the holiday joy.

Christian leaned down to Skylar, who was all bundled up in her new winter coat.

"This is all for you," he whispered. "Merry Christmas!"

The evening was celebrated with an assortment of treats including crescent-shaped mincemeat pies, thumbprint cookies, and whipped shortbread. Mulled apple cider and hot cocoa with peppermint sticks warmed the community. Carollers sang a succession of Christmas songs, along the town's dirt roads, which bustled with crowds of people.

* * *

After the presents were opened and the excitement of Christmas had passed, everyone began planning for Ospero Falls' next celebration: New Year's Eve. Skylar looked forward to celebrating her fifth birthday at the O'Connelly home. She liked being born on New Year's Eve, as people were always celebrating with the whole world. Victoria wanted to make Skylar a special dress yet did not have the funds. Sophia generously bought her the material she needed.

Not wanting to bother Jack for the money, Sophia withdrew some funds from her inheritance.

It was the first time in her life she had gone behind his back. However, she believed the end justified the means and did not tell him. Hours were spent, cutting out the dress pattern and sewing it together. Victoria wanted an emerald velvet dress to match her daughter's eyes. Scallops of elegant lace adorned the edges and an ivory bow gathered in the back. The dress was completed in time to present it to Skylar on the day of her party.

No one could have predicted the evil that was lurking in the shadows of Ospero Falls. Unbeknown to the people, including Victoria and Skylar, was the early release of Trey Wickett from Averston's jail. He had changed his appearance dramatically by cutting off his long black hair and shaving his beard and moustache. These changes allowed him to blend in easily with the bustling people shopping along the streets. Trey had come to town for one thing only, and he could almost taste the sweet revenge on the tip of his caustic tongue. He moved swiftly towards Victoria's house. It was almost dusk when he arrived. Heavy clouds blocked out the setting sun. Wickett bit off the end of a cigarette and spat it onto the frosty earth. Striking a match, he lit the tip and breathed in the smoke. Mulling over the plans he had for his former girlfriend and her daughter, Trey Wickett smiled.

Inside the O'Connelly home, the smell of ham and cloves blended with the scent of crackling pine, emitted from the wood stove. Christian sat content on the hardwood floors, munching on a jar of pickled herring. It was a gift from the Ukrainian mailman, Yakiv, who knew it was one of the young boys' favourites. Sophia suggested he ask Skylar to come over and help decorate for her birthday party. He nodded and said he would go over in a few minutes. However, his interest was quickly consumed by the set of toy cars he had received from his father.

Over at Victoria's house, Skylar was in her room twirling in her fancy dress in the mirror, when she saw him.

Standing in the doorway, was the bad man – his finger touching his pursed lips, mimicking a whisper. He did not have to worry about the little girl screaming, as she stiffened with fear. A warm stream of urine cascaded down her thin legs. Seeing it puddle at her feet triggered the rage inside Wickett.

He took two swift strides towards Skylar and, grabbing her arms, he shook her like a dirty rug.

"See what you made me do, you wretched thing!" he growled. "I'm going to teach you a lesson you won't forget."

He pushed her against the wall, and her head hit with such force that her eyes rolled back. The sound vibrated through the divider separating her room from her mother's.

Victoria, who was in the shower, heard the thump. A sick feeling overcame her. Fighting back the queasiness, she grabbed her robe, raced into the room, and screamed. Lying near the bed was Skylar, with her bottom lip split wide open. The dress Victoria had made her daughter was spattered with blood. The little girl stared blankly, unaware of what was happening. Victoria ran to tend to her when she smelled the stench of whisky. Wickett appeared from behind the bedroom door.

"Surprised to see me, baby doll?" he hissed.

Victoria sought out a route of escape, but there was none. Trey slammed the bedroom door, making them his prisoners. She screamed again, knowing it was the last effort, at saving her precious girl.

Christian was busily playing, oblivious to the passing of time, when he heard the dreadful cry. His heart skipped a beat, and his mother came running from the kitchen, visibly shaken.

"Dear God!" she exclaimed. "That terrifying noise came from Victoria's house!"

The hair on his neck stood on end and Christian jumped to his feet.

Jack, who had walked into the house moments earlier, strode into the living room.

"Christian, you stay with your mother," he said. "I'll be right back!"

Christian peered through the curtains. His eyes widened when he looked outside to see his father bend down and pick up a long piece of two-by-four. He made a split decision to disobey his father, not knowing it would haunt him forever. Sophia ran upstairs for a better view of what was happening. She did not hear Christian leave the house to follow Jack.

Crossing the street, Jack heard the awful wails of Victoria begging for her child's life. The front door was ajar, and he rushed up the stairs two at a time. In the chaos, he did not notice Christian behind him.

As Jack flung open the bedroom door, what he saw took him by surprise. Curled up in the corner of the room was Victoria, her head bloodied, and eyes swollen. He looked down at her cradled arm and was appalled by the long gash. She had scratches on her upper legs and thick blood streaming from her inner thighs. Victoria was shouting at Wickett, who had turned his attention to Skylar. Lifting the piece of lumber, Christians' father struck Trey from behind with such force; there was a cracking noise. His body fell to the side with a thud. Christian looked over to see Skylar's dress torn and stained crimson. Jack spun around to see his son standing there, paralyzed with fright.

"What the hell are you doing here, boy? Jack shouted, Get out! And tell your mother to call the police!"

Christian turned and ran down the stairs. His mind replayed over the horrifying scene, of Skylar lying helpless and injured. Reaching the steps of his house, he was overcome with nausea and doubling over, instantly threw-up all of his pickled herring. After Sophia called the police, only a few minutes passed before the house across the street overflowed with officers. They had received Trey Wickett's rap sheet and were not about to take any chances.

Paramedics ushered Victoria and Skylar into an ambulance, which sped away.

Officers brought the dazed Wickett out of the house. A paramedic looked over his injury, shaking his head.

"This guy should not be alive!" he said.

Wickett did not struggle as he was handcuffed and was tossed into the back of a police car. The policeman in charge, Police sergeant Calhoun, spoke to the paramedic. A decision was made for two other Officers to take Trey to the hospital in Averston. Once treated, he would be transported to the jail there. Jack was escorted to another car for questioning. Sophia was in a panic. She drove her and Christian in their Chevy pickup truck to Bay View Hospital.

Upon arriving, she ran to the emergency room. They passed nurses shaking their heads, distraught over what they had seen. One of them, a stocky older woman, blocked their way.

"Not a step further Mrs. O'Connelly," she said. "Only family allowed inside."

"Goodness' sake, Ethel," Sophia said. "You know we are the closest thing they have to family."

"Please, Sophia, come sit down. Once Dr. Gregson is finished his examination, I promise you will be able to see them."

Christian clutched his mother's arm, looking up at her. He could see tears flushing out her sorrow.

"Good Lord, Ethel!" Sophia cried. "What kind of an animal does this to a little girl and her mother?"

Nurse Ethel guided them back to the waiting room and sat down beside Sophia. She glanced around and cleared her throat.

"Word from the other nurses, has it your husband saved Skylar and Victoria's lives," she whispered, "thank the Lord the poor, young girl is alive!"

"I overheard a Police Officer say that monster had grave intentions for her."

"Ethel, watch your tongue! Can't you see my boy's present?"

"Sorry dear, I just figured that after the policeman told his partner that Christian must have witnessed some terrible stuff, he now wants to question your son."

Sophia looked over at Christian. He was trembling. Putting an arm around her son, she held on.

"Oh, honey, I had no idea you saw anything!" she cried.

Suddenly, Dr. Gregson appeared. He came and sat beside Sophia.

"I have had to sedate Miss Falls in consideration of the trauma she has experienced. The gash on her arm required over a dozen stitches. As for Skylar, she suffered a sprained arm, is missing her front teeth and received a concussion. Although Skylar is aware Wickett attacked them, the good news is she says she does not remember what took place. Also, we have found no signs of any serious internal injuries."

Sophia and Christian breathed a sigh of relief.

The waiting room doors swung open. Jack entered, along with the Sergeant. As they neared Sophia and Christian, the boy was nervous, as he had never spoken to the police. As the Sergeant bent down, he extended his hand toward Christian, and smiled.

"Hello Christian. My name is Sergeant Calhoun." They shook hands. "Goodness young man, that is quite a grip you have there." This put the young boy at ease. The Sergeant continued,

"I hear you did a great job in helping your friend Skylar, by running back home and telling your mom to call us."

Christian smiled.

"Listen, I need you to answer a few simple questions in private. Your mom will be right at the door, waiting for you afterwards. Then I will let you be with your family. Is that okay with you?"

Christian nodded. They stood up and went into a quiet area of the room to talk, with Sophia following behind. She sat quietly in another chair as Jack looked on.

Christian nodded yes or shook his head no, answering all of the questions, best he could.

Sergeant Calhoun walked Christian back to his parents.

Dr. Gregson and Nurse Ethel had left to attend to other patients.

"Listen, folks," Calhoun said. "I have spoken with Sheriff Palmer, and the official word is there will be no charges laid against you, Jack."

"I certainly hope not," Sophia said. "My husband saved two lives!"

Jack put his arm around his wife, giving her a gentle squeeze.

"Yes ma'am, we do understand that, yet we still have to go through procedures to find out all the facts. As for Trey Wickett, he is being detained at the Averston jail until we can transfer him to a higher-security facility." He tipped his hat. "I thank you nice folks for your time. I will need Jack to bring Christian down to the police station, as soon as possible, to make an official statement."

"Alright," Jack said. "I will swing by sometime tomorrow."

As Sergeant Calhoun turned to leave, he said, "Every so often, the right thing to do comes about, when the people you care for, their lives at serious risk."

The town clock struck midnight. The sound of people cheering marked the beginning of a new year. The O'Connelly family huddled together as Jack said a special prayer for Victoria and Skylar.

"We praise you God, for watching over these two, innocent souls. We take comfort in casting our fears upon you Jesus. In your name, Amen."

* * *

Meanwhile in Averston, after being looked over and receiving ten stiches, Trey Wickett was now allowed to shower. He knew the drill. Before leaving his cell, Trey's dark brown eyes, stared at the words carved into the concrete by a former prisoner: "As you sow, so shall you reap." He contemplated his future with all of his priors, he was now facing a maximum sentence. Taking his clothes off, Trey entered the shower. The razor he was given for shaving proved easy to remove the blade. He took it and placed it in between his lips, concealing the weapon. Every cell mate he had ever met, had confided what they would use to commit suicide, if ever a time warranted it. Trey thought to himself, this was exactly 'one of those times.' He had been shown by a former cellmate how to make sure to slice your wrists properly. Returning to his cell, Trey ripped his prison shirt and taking a part of it, he tied it around his arm. Smiling he thought, *dead men don't talk.*

Chapter 6

Decree

THE NEXT DAY, JACK BROUGHT CHRISTIAN TO GIVE HIS STATEMENT. Sergeant Calhoun, told them the case would be investigated in Averston, since Trey Wickett had taken his own life there.

While Victoria and Skylar recovered side by side in their hospital beds, the news about the suicide spread quickly.

Arriving at the hospital with flowers and balloons, Nurse Ethel greeted the O'Connelly family with a smile. She escorted them to the Falls' room and slowly opened the door. The scent wafting from numerous flower arrangements filled the room, and balloons bobbed everywhere.

"Good luck finding a spot!" smiled Ethel, as she left.

Skylar had moved from her bed to snuggle with her mother. They were sitting up beside each other when they saw Jack, Sophia, and Christian walked in. Skylar's eyes widened.

"Christian," she grinned, "look at all the balloons!"

Everyone in the room broke out into laughter. Victoria reached out for Jack's hand and tenderly squeezed it.

"How can I ever thank you?" she asked.

Jack looked the two of them over. He was thankful for intervening before anything worse happened.

"Listen," he sighed, "We need to step out as Sergeant Calhoun has some news to tell you."

"Oh, please God, no!" Victoria cried, turning ashen.

"No dear, it's okay!" Sophia said. "We will bring Skylar with us and just be outside, then come back in right after.

Victoria felt overwhelmed by all that had transpired. While Skylar clung onto her mother, everyone could see their scars would take some time to heal.

As Sergeant Calhoun walked in, he waited for the room to clear, in order to speak privately with Victoria.

"Last night, Trey Wickett took his life into his hands."

Victoria's expression turned to shock.

"You mean he's dead?" Victoria asked.

"Yes, however there will be an independent investigation in Averston."

A sense of relief came upon her, and she could not muster a single tear.

"If it's okay with you Sergeant, I do not care to know anymore.

He nodded and replied,

"I understand Ma'am. I will leave it up to you to explain it to your little girl."

As the O'Connelly's came back in, Skylar was lifted by Jack onto her mother's hospital bed.

Abruptly, Victoria began to cry.

"What the matter momma? Skylar asked.

Holding onto her daughter, she said in a gentle tone,

"Sweetie, you don't have to worry about Trey hurting me anymore." She paused then added, "He is never coming back to ever touch us again!"

"So, the bad man is gone?" Skylar asked.

"Yes, my little Songbird," Victoria said, "he will never harm us again."

Suddenly, Skylar began kissing the tears falling on her mother's cheeks.

"It's okay momma, don't be sad."

Jack and Sophia had to turn away, for worry they would begin to cry.

"Ms. Falls," Christian asked, "Why do you call Skylar Songbird?"

"Sweetie," Victoria said to Skylar, "Why don't you tell your friend why I call you that?"

"Mommy loves the skylark bird," Skylar grinned.

"She told me it's a blessing from God showing me how special I am to him."

Christian liked how that sounded. "What's your favourite bird?"

"Sparrows and sandpipers are pretty," she said, her face lighting up.

"You know, Skylar," Jack said, "when you come back home, I am sure I can arrange a trip to Averston. Besides, Christian has been wanting to show me a Sitka spruce, he says would be perfect to build a tree house."

Another week passed before Dr. Gregson authorized Victoria and Skylar's release. Sophia and Christian picked them up in Jack's truck. Pulling into the driveway, they saw residents of Ospero Falls milling about. To their surprise, the house had a new porch and new shingles on the roof. Frilly curtains hung in the windows, and a hand-painted sign with yellow letters declaring,

"The Falls Family."

The townspeople greeted Victoria and Skylar, as they stepped out of the truck.

Ms. Sharen stood with Nanaimo bars from Jacob's Bakery and two bags full of candy, from Krowling's Sweet Shoppe.

Mr. Geri and his boys had cut and stockpiled three cords of wood against the house. Miss Donna held an apple box packed with her favourite childhood toys.

"Oh my…" Victoria said, astounded by the display of generosity.

As she and Skylar entered the house, they smelled fresh paint. The halls wore a coat of soft cream. Several pieces of handmade furniture, including a pine bed belonging to Sophia's late Aunt, were added to the décor. Walking upstairs, Victoria and Skylar paused before they entered the rooms.

Sophia turned to them and gently said, "Our community is a loving one and we support each other. If you chose to not want any of the furnishings or decide to paint it your choice of colours, no one will have any hurt feelings. What was done here, was to welcome you back into new beginnings."

Victoria held back her tears, as Skylar watched on.

"Sophia, what everyone has managed in a week to do is incredible! No one has ever treated us this way and we are thrilled to accept the generosity of Ospero Falls people."

Sophia nodded and opened the doors to each room.

As Skylar entered her mother's old room, she saw a pine bed covered in a mound of pillows. Perched on top was a teddy bear with black button eyes dressed in a rose, satin, ballerina outfit. Underneath, a quilt was draped across the bed. Skylar's fingers caressed the comforter that was made by Sophia, during the winter months. Along its border was an array of crimson poppies. Skylar could not contain her excitement. She jumped onto the bed and fell back into the softness.

The kindness of everyone in the community, touched Victoria.

"All of these things are so magnificent, Sophia," Victoria said, holding back tears.

"But I can't repay you. I can't even pay my bills without a job or money."

"Take what's in my hand," Sophia said. "Do not ever mention it or worry about paying it back. I want to help give you and Skylar a fresh start."

Victoria looked down to the rolls of bills and shook her head.

"No, I could never take money from you."

Sophia pushed the money into her hands.

"As for a job, Ms. Johanna Tamsin at Miss Jean's Boutique is willing to give you a chance, if you want.

The pay is not much, but maybe you would have a response if you placed a sign for a room for rent?

Sophia smiled. "There is a large bed in your room, so if you and Skylar decided to share the one space and main bathroom, that allows for the other room to be made available. It could help bring in a little extra money if you wanted to consider it?"

Victoria was leery of sharing her home with boarders, yet she needed to think of her daughter. She liked the idea of the two of them having their bedroom together.

Sophia spoke softly, "After what you and your daughter have been through, not just anyone can be trusted. This is solely up to you to decide.

"How can I possibly furnish a boarding room properly?" asked Victoria.

Sophia left Christian and Skylar to play, while she opened the bedroom that used to belong to her Skylar.

"The Lord helps those in need," Sophia said, opening the door.

Victoria entered the room to see two single beds, each fitted with beautiful quilts crafted by Sophia from the previous year. On the night tables, were fresh towels.

Along the edge of the wall was a bureau with a floral-pattern washbowl perched on top. In the corner of the room stood a pine wardrobe, which Victoria liked the most.

"My aunt left me these pieces when she passed on," Sophia said. "Jack did not want to clutter our home with them, so they have been sitting under a blanket in the shed since we moved here. You can use them for as long as you wish."

"Thank you for your thoughtfulness," Victoria said, shedding tears.

The laughter of children echoed throughout the hallway as Christian and Skylar danced about, playing a game of tag.

Sophia was about to scold Christian for running inside the house when Victoria stopped her with a touch on the arm.

"Do you know how wonderful a sound like that is to my ears?"

Sophia smiled, knowing the healing had begun.

* * *

As the weeks passed, Trey Wickett's memory slowly began to fade in the small town.

Things had changed, and fortunately they were for the better. The townspeople welcomed Victoria and Skylar, into the community. Jack deepened his connection with Christian, with the two of them taking the ferry to see the spruce tree, discovered by his son. As father and son made their way to the tree together, they needed their snowshoes to travel over the frozen ground.

Years later, Christian still remembered the moment, his father laid eyes on the sprawling Sitka spruce. Jack rubbed his chin, deep in thought. Then, shaking his head in amazement, he said, "Good gracious! You sure know how to pick them. Must be the forest blood we share, rushing throughout your veins, boy!"

* * *

As life returned to normal, the O'Connelly's finally celebrated Skylar's fifth birthday.

Though it was several weeks late, Skylar was surrounded by so much love. The young boy was grateful, the memories of that night had not returned. Christian made the decision to never tell her what he had witnessed. There was a lot that still troubled him and so he made a solemn promise never to bring up the horror of that night.

As the weeks turned into months, Victoria worked hard at Miss Jean's Boutique. She made enough money for food and to pay some bills.

However, the money Sophia had given her was dwindling, and no one had inquired about boarding at her house.

As opportunity would have it, two individuals were following a lead that they hoped would bring new beginnings in the next town over, Ospero Falls.

* * *

On the first day of spring in 1954, the glacier waters rippled with the undercurrents of life. Along the ocean's edge, the solitary sandpiper warned other birds, with a recognizable *plik plik plik*.

The soft ground erupted in yellow shocks of balsamroot, offering a dazzling display of sweeping colour. Dotting the forest, were clusters of castilleja, thrusting forth their ruby paintbrushes.

In town, children jumped in the reflective puddles formed by the downpour, earlier in the morning. During the past weeks Christian, Skylar, and Jack spent many hours, working on plans for the tree house. It would be 10x10 in size, with Jack wanting to keep it simple yet useful. He also knew that more help was needed by another adult. They could hold up the posts and do things Christian was unable to, being only seven years old. On paper, it was rudimentary. Yet in the imagination of a young boy, it was a fortress.

Jack wanted this tree house to be special, yet he also was mindful of not damaging the tree.

"Listen here, I figure under the grand old canopy of branches and limbs of the Sitka, that tree will provide a great deal of shelter, for many years to come. If we can build the treehouse beside the spruce and under the Sitka, instead of actually fastening to it – then that would be the best solution. This way, the tree can continue to grow, and the rain won't get inside because we aren't fastening to the actual tree.

Jack's knowledge of timber, saw him select cedar wood, which was perfectly suited for the build. Christian took notes on paper when his father talked about using 8ft long treated posts for support. On the ferry to Averston, they brought along more supplies. Jack spoke of the plans for the treehouse. The roof would be angled, to protect the treehouse and divert the rain away, from the walls and flooring. Asphalt shingles would keep the roof shielded from the many elements.

Disembarking his truck off the ferry, on the outskirts of Averston, Jack pulled his son closer beside him. As Jack manipulated the pedals,

Christian steered them down the overgrown road, towards their destination. Skylar clapped her hands, excited to see the tree. When they arrived on the back road to leading to the woodlands, they exited the truck. Christian dashed ahead of them, to where the majestic Sitka stood.

Skylar took longer to make her way and Jack slowly walked with her.

Upon seeing the tree's massive trunk, she was in awe.

"We're gonna build a house under there?" she asked, looking at Jack and Christian with wonder.

"Yep," Christian said, "we sure are!" He and Jack chuckled.

They unloaded the truck. Before they started to work, Jack gathered Christian and Skylar near.

"Every single tree in the forest," he said, "is a living part of the woods. These towering giants came long before us. It is important, you never take more than what you need from it. It's also important to offer a prayer before we build. We do this to honour the tree's life."

Looking up at the magnificent tree that graced the blue skyline, Jack raised his hands.

"Hear my words!" Jack boomed. "We give thanks to our Creator for the strength and grace of this beautiful Sitka, and for the refuge each person who climbs into the heart of it will find.

I ask that we are always reminded of the spruce's value in the forest.

In return, we will give this Sitka tree an abundance of laughter and stories but – most importantly – the precious time we spend here, in fellowship."

Skylar gazed at Jack, listening intently. The silence was then broken by Jack patting his son on his shoulder and carrying on with his plans. Gazing up at the tree, he assigned his son a mission. His goal was to scale the Sitka with the materials they had brought.

Christian was determined to show his father how strong he was.

Without hesitation, the young boy swung the yellow rope over a high, sturdy branch. As he climbed the trunk, pulling himself up the tree with a firm grip on to the rope, beads of sweat formed on his forehead. The young boy's hands ached from the thick, twisted cord grating into his palms, while his breathing deepened and grew laboured.

Reaching the top, Christian braced himself in the opening of the spruce. Looking down at his father and Skylar, they appeared to be miniscule.

Triumphantly he claimed, "I, Christian James O'Connelly have mastered this tree. Therefore, I declare, she now belongs to me!"

Skylar shrugged her shoulders. Looking over at Jack, a tear slid down his cheek.

"Are you okay?" she asked.

"Yes dear," he said, swallowing. "I'm fine."

Skylar did not know what all the fuss was about and kicked at the dirt around the tree.

"Why didn't Christian use the ladder, Mr. O'Connelly?"

Jack squatted down and sat Skylar upon his knee.

"In life, it's not always best to take the easy way," he said. "Perseverance prevails where everything else fails."

"What's persa…" she asked, stumbling on the word.

"It means always try your hardest."

Skylar nodded.

"Hey, you two," Christian hollered. "Give me a hand!"

"Well, look who's in charge now!" Jack said, laughing.

Skylar stuck out her tongue at her friend.

Near lunchtime, clouds began to gather. They had work to do, before it started to rain. Jack shared the importance of keeping the materials dry, but away from the heat of the sun. He also shared the value of cleaning all tools and respecting everything used in building. He ended his talk with the significance of mapping and measuring.

For the little girl, all she heard was sun, cleaning and maps.

The next day, was an early morning start in Ospero Falls, as Skylar wanted to help stock Jack's truck with materials. This included a measuring tape, rope, and a level. For Skylar, this meant she could only carry one item at a time. Meanwhile, Jack placed in the back of his truck four western cedarwood posts and a ladder. He also needed to load 8 bags of concrete. Jack knew they would need another adult to help, therefore he asked Walt from the pet store. Being an adventurer, Walt quickly agreed, as his brother offered to run the store for the day. Showing up, he shook hands with Jack. Whistling while helping load the rest of supplies into the truck, he too was excited for the project.

Soon after, the four of them took the ferry over to Averston. As Walt was led to the Sitka spruce, his eyes lit up as he remarked, "Wow – wee! I bet you can look at lots of sea creatures from way up there!" This made Christian smile as he replied, "I've been up this tree and you can see for miles!"

Jack thanked Walt for his help and said, "Best be getting to work, while there's daylight!"

Soon, they set out to measure the distance between the four posts. They would need to sink the supports into the ground, a few feet away from the tree. Afterwards using two 50 lb bags of concrete, each post would be secured in cement. Christian and Walt came to help keep each post level, while Skylar played in the dirt with a stick. Her tiny size only allowed her to watch, for the time being. After, Jack used his level to ensure the correct angles. Walt and Christian filled 1/3 full of water into every hole. Christian liked the next part, as the bags of cement were poured around the posts. A shovel was used to stir up any bubbles and mix the concrete together.

Afterwards, Jack explained the concrete needed to cure for a full 12 hours. After completing their task for the day, Walt and Jack sat up front, while Christian and Skylar sat in the back of the truck. This was only the beginning of their project and when Skylar looked over at Christian beaming with a smile, she knew he was eager for the next part.

Later upon tucking his son into bed, his father tousled his hair.

"It's important to me this gets done, one way or another boy," said Jack.

Christian hung onto every word his father shared with him.

Jack continued, You know, a man's word is as good as his foundation. If he cannot keep a promise, then he ain't no value to others."

Standing up, Jack bent over and kissed his son on his forehead.

"Hope your dreams are all good ones about the Sitka."

On the following day Jack, Christian, and Skylar were back out at the tree. Walt decided to close up his shop Saturday, as his brother was unavailable to come lend a hand. He put a note on his store that said:

"Gone Adventuring!"

There was a lot of work that saw Walt labouring, with Christian by his father's side.

The secured hardened concrete around each post were backfilled in, using the dirt they had dug out. Next, four more posts were fastened all around the tops, using screws to secure the posts, creating the beginning of a platform.

Before long, all posts has been securely fastened to the four pieces of wood, creating a frame for the cross section. Jack then took the pre-measured and cut cross beams. Attaching two posts all around, in a criss-cross pattern, Stewart nailed them securely. Jack made sure to add extra ones, to ensure it would withstand the heavy rains and wind.

Next the truss hangers were measured and placed across from one another. Four nails were used to keep them in place, until they were screwed in. Another four cross beams were securely fitted into, which allowed for the flooring to be installed. Jack and Walt worked side by side, in order to hand screw in the added beams. Christian enjoyed every minute of the building process, while Skylar was bored. She had gathered a group of small smooth pebbles and carefully balanced one on top of the other. There was not much for a little girl her size to do.

The flooring used was several pieces of pre-cut thick, sturdy plywood. Once this was done, everyone took a break. Sophia had packed a wonderful picnic basket filled with mustard, cheese, and ham sandwiches, on her baked bread. A tin of butter tarts, were washed down with homemade lemonade. Afterwards, Jack looked over at Skylar and giving her a wink, he said reassuringly, "Little one, I will need your help later on."

It was during this time Walt mentioned to Jack the project was going to take quite a long time to complete. "Imagine if we were able to get some more help back in Ospero?"

Nodding, Jack agreed. He mulled over the wall supports still needed to be framed for the exterior. He thought of the cedar planks for siding, a small side deck and the asphalt roofing.

Turning to Skylar, Jack asked.

"How many windows do you want?"

Skylar smiled and held up two fingers.

"Do you want a regular door or a trap door, where you come in from the bottom?

Skylar's eyes widened, as she replied,

"I want a secret door on the bottom and a rope ladder!"

Christian chuckled and interjected, "Wow, yeah Skylar that will make it look so cool!"

Skylar beamed.

Jack looked over at Walt.

"I may have bit off just a lot more than I bargained for."

Walt smiled, then remarked, "I know a lot of fisherman, who would love to lend a hand."

This made Jack happy, and he replied,

"Well, thank you Walt! We can work a few more hours on this, then see what you can do to help get this treehouse done!"

It was supper when everyone came back tired, yet happy about what had been accomplished.

Sophia and Victoria, took one look at their loved ones and knew it had been a long day.

On Sunday, everyone was in church. Walt nodded over at Jack. It was a day of rest that he was thankful for. Later, as everyone gathered for treats, along with tea and coffee, Walt approached.

"Good afternoon Jack," said Walt.

Sophia and Victoria smiled, as they went to gather Christian and Skylar.

Walt leaned over and said, "I reckon I have a few guys assembled to help out. They respect you Jack and what your doing for your boy."

Picking up an oatmeal raisin cookie, Jack grinned, then replied,

"I appreciate that being said Walt, but this has always been more than just about Christian."

He winked, then added, "So you propose we can get this project finished?"

Walt excitedly replied, "Next weekend, the boys are willing to meet us out in Averston.

They want a list of things you still need and will come out Friday afternoon and stay through until its done. For each of them, it's a childhood dream!"

Jack smacked Walt on the back in a playful way.

"This means a lot to me and my son, along with Skylar too. That poor little girl's suffered enough."

Walt nodded in agreement. As the two men ate their Sunday goodies, both looked forward to their plans ahead.

Later on, Christian was thrilled to hear more people had come forward to help. The sooner it was built, the more fun Skylar and he could have.

Jack had no idea what to expect when he loaded up his truck on Friday. Upon driving away from the ferry and out to the Sitka, work had already begun on the actual walls of the treehouse. The noise of men milling about, nails being hammered and forms going up, astounded Jack.

He counted ten men, who had come to reconnect with their childhoods and more importantly, to give a little girl a dwelling where she could play and feel safe.

By early evening, everyone gathered to give thanks for all that had been accomplished.

Back in Ospero Falls, Victoria was tidying the house when there was a knock on the door. She was surprised to find an elderly, black woman standing on her porch. Her frayed, plain grey dress matched the wiry, silver strands of hair pulled back into a large bun.

"Hello," Victoria said through the screen door. "May I help you?"

"We've come to see you, ma'am, about the place for rent," she said.

Victoria noticed a small, black girl. Her raven hair was twisted into two tight braids. Chewing her nails, she clutched the ragged edges of the woman's dress.

"Where are you from?" she asked.

"We're from Averston, ma'am. I was cleaning a gentleman's home, but he has passed on. Anyhow, we don't belong in a town like that anymore."

Victoria noticed her worn shoes and the cracks in her skin.

"And who is the young miss?"

"Why, this here is my granddaughter, Gwendolyn-Sue. She's my pride and joy!"

"My name is Victoria Falls," she said, opening the screen door. Extending her hand, she welcomed them inside.

"Nice to meet you, Ms. Falls. My name is Evamya Rosie Grace Walker, but you can call me Evamya."

Victoria led them up the stairs to the bedroom. As Evamya glanced around, she breathed in deeply.

"I like the yellow paint," she said. "it's like sunshine bouncing off your walls."

"Why, you are quite right," Victoria nodded in agreement.

"How much you asking?" Evamya inquired.

Victoria noticed they were not much better off than she was.

"I will tell you what. You can move in right away, as long as I can depend on you to help out making meals, keeping house, and child-rearing."

She was offering free room and board, when she desperately needed money, but she knew it was the right thing to do.

"I appreciate your kindness, ma'am. I reckon you'll be happy with your decision."

Evamya spoke so reassuringly.

"By the way," Victoria said, "my daughter Skylar will be home soon. She is in Averston with the neighbours from across the street."

The girl held firm onto the dress of her grandmother's, reminding Victoria of how timid Skylar use to be.

* * *

It was almost dinnertime when Jack, Christian, and Skylar came home.

As they drove into the Falls' driveway, Christian glanced up and saw a light on in the spare room, shining through the closed curtains.

"Looks like someone has finally moved in," he said, pointing up.

The curtain opened and somebody peered out.

"By golly!" Christian blurted. "You've got a black girl in your house!"

Jack shot his son a look. "Watch your tongue!"

"Jeez Dad, I'm sorry. I didn't mean to say anything bad. But I've only seen a black person in a book!"

Jack replied, "They're no different underneath, from the Japanese people who live around here, whose skins are golden. Heck, even our ivory skin is just that, son – flesh that covers the bone. Have you ever noticed all the colours of a rainbow trout? They complement each other, side by side. Every colour is equal in beauty. That is how God created us. We are just the same as everyone else." He opened the truck door to let Skylar out.

"Looks like you'll have a new friend to play with."

Christian bristled at the thought. Skylar already had a best friend – him!

Standing on her front porch, Skylar turned to wave goodbye.

Chapter 7

Unity

As Skylar entered the house, the smell of cooking oil filled the air. She slipped off her boots and tossed them aside.

"Sweetie," her mother called out, "would you please set your boots on the mat properly and then come into the kitchen?"

Skylar peeked around the corner.

"Well now, who do we have here?" Evamya asked, wiping her hands on the gingham apron she wore.

"Come on, my little Songbird, do not be shy," said Victoria. "Come introduce yourself."

Reluctantly, she came out of the shadows and into the light of the kitchen. As Evamya leaned forward, Skylar breathed in the scent of sweet lavender.

"Your name is Songbird?" Evamya asked. "Why, such a pretty name for such a sweet thing."

"My real name's Skylar Reigh," she whispered, "but most people call me by my nickname, Songbird."

"You don't say, child! My oh my, you must truly be special to have been blessed with two lovely names. My name is Evamya Rosie Grace Walker, but you can call me either Evamya or Gramsy."

Skylar grinned. Victoria gestured for her to sit down.

"Evamya made the most delicious fried chicken I have ever eaten. Are you hungry?"

"No thank you, Momma. Mr. O'Connelly fed us some cornmeal cakes and canned fish. It was yummy!"

"Thank you for the generous compliment about my chicken," Evamya said. "It was one of my momma's favourite recipes.

"However, it sounds like it might have some competition against Mr. O'Connelly's cooking!"

"Jack can only scramble eggs," Victoria said. "The cakes would be my friend Sophia's food. Though he does make the best buttered popcorn!"

Laughter filled the room.

Victoria looked over at her daughter.

"Evamya and her granddaughter Gwendolyn-Sue will be staying with us, in the spare room."

Skylar's eye grew wide.

"Where is she?"

Evamya smiled,

"She's upstairs, using the bathroom, but Gwendolyn-Sue is gonna be down shortly. I hear you two girls are both going on six-years-old," Evamya winked.

Skylar nodded and snuggled into her mother's lap.

"How was the visit to the tree house?"

Skylar's face lit up. "Oh Momma! You should see it's all finished now!

Victoria was surprised.

"My goodness, how is that possible?"

Skylar grinned, "A whole bunch of fishy men came out to help! It looks so pretty in the woods. And guess what?

Victoria and Evamya were holding back their laughter.

"What's that songbird?"

"The tree's taller than our house and the branches stick out all over. Christian said it's a magical place where your wishes come true!"

"Good gracious," Victoria chuckled, "did he really say that?"

Skylar nodded.

"Well then, it must be a very extraordinary tree!"

Standing at the kitchen entryway was the girl Skylar had seen in the window.

Her eyes were large and beautiful, with dark eyelashes that reminded Skylar of the fine hairs on a black feather she had once found in the woods. In an instant, she was reminded of her dark-skinned doll.

"Go on in, Gwendolyn-Sue," coaxed Evamya. "Don't be shy, girl. Introduce yourself!"

"Pleased to meet you, miss," she said, curtsying in front of Skylar.

Skylar looked up at her mother, puzzled by the greeting.

"Why's she calling me miss?"

"Everyone has a particular way of saying hello to people, sweetie," Victoria said.

"Gwendolyn-Sue is just polite, that's all."

Skylar leapt off her mother's lap.

"Hello! My name is Skylar, but you can call me Songbird if you would like."

She tried to curtsy but lost her balance and tumbled forward.

Gwendolyn-Sue caught Skylar and snickered. "Okay, Bird Girl, but I think you need some new legs!"

"Mind your manners!" Evamya chided Gwendolyn.

"Oh Evamya, it is okay," Victoria said, holding back laughter. "You cannot blame the girl for speaking the truth!"

Skylar and Evamya laughed. When they finally settled down, Skylar looked at Gwendolyn.

"Can I call you Gwennie too?" she asked.

"Sure thing, she said with a shrug, as long as I can call you Bird Girl?"

Both girls started to giggle again, while Victoria and Evamya smiled.

* * *

Christian awoke early in the morning. Eager to go over to Skylar's house, he gobbled down his breakfast. It was Sunday and everyone would be attending church in a few hours. He was anxious to learn about the new people who had moved in. He rushed out the door and ran across the street, not stopping, until he stood on the front porch. Evamya answered the door. The aroma of fresh biscuits filled his nostrils.

"Well good morning, boy! My name's Evamya Rosie Grace Walker, but you can call me Evamya or Gramsy. You must be Christian," she winked. "Skylar told me all about you over breakfast."

Christian tried his best not to interrupt, yet blurted out, "Please, may I speak with her?"

"Oh, I am sorry, sweetie. Skylar and my granddaughter Gwendolyn-Sue left over an hour ago to go fishing with Ms. Falls. Both girls begged her to take them before church started."

Christian's heart sank. Fishing was one of the special things he and Skylar shared with his father. Evamya could see the disappointment on his face.

"Honey, why don't you come in and I will fix you up one of Evamya's famous biscuits with black currant jelly."

"No thank you, ma'am," he mumbled.

Shoulders slumped, he turned and walked back towards his house, overwhelmed by jealousy. He suddenly wished the tree house were finished.

Victoria and the girls arrived home an hour before church. Their laughter and the odour of fish wafted in from the door.

"Look what I caught, Gramsy!" Gwendolyn held out two small freshwater trout. "Supper!"

Skylar reached into a fishing pail and pulled out the two trout she had hooked. "There's one for each of us! Wait till I tell Christian at church."

"I hope you mean after the service," Victoria said.

"Yes, Momma. I know. You always say no chit-chatting while Preacher Crane's a-prattling."

At 11 o'clock, the church bell chimed. It was when the townspeople gathered to worship, pray, and listen to the weekly sermon.

Afterwards, Evamya and Gwendolyn-Sue joined the Falls when they went over to the O'Connelly's' for tea and pie. It was the one day of the week the children could eat dessert before a meal.

As Victoria introduced everyone, Evamya winked at Christian, as if to reassure him she had not said anything about his visit earlier that morning. He grinned.

Victoria introduced Evamya to Sophia.

"Wisdom," Evamya said.

"Pardon me?" Sophia asked.

"Your name, it means wisdom."

"I've always known that" Jack said.

Sophia blushed. "Oh, stop teasing now!"

"I'd like you to meet my best friend in the whole wide world," Skylar said to Evamya and Gwendolyn-Sue. "His name is Christian, just like one of God's people!"

He felt his cheeks redden. "Pleased to meet you, ma'am," he said, extending his hand to Evamya.

"Oh sweetie," she smiled and winked, "you call me Evamya or Gramsy, whichever suits you best."

Everyone sat down to relax. Soon, laughter and conversation filled the room. Christian and Skylar told Gwendolyn-Sue about the treehouse. Christian never grew tired of saying how he was meant to find the Sitka spruce. Skylar meanwhile was excited to have two playmates. Her bond with Christian had been made stronger by the things they shared as friends.

When Gwendolyn-Sue went to see the Sitka spruce for the first time in the spring, she gave a whistle and said, "Jesus sure blessed this treehouse!"

* * *

After they were playing, Jack told stories of the forest. Their favourite was the tale of the silver fairy.

The legend, passed from generation to generation, told of a fairy that would leave pieces of silver in exchange for children's teeth.

None of the townspeople knew how a half-pint milk bottle, hanging from a tree branch with twine, came to be. Nor did they know who painted on the bottle, shiny wings, and the words *Silver Fairy*. The real mystery was a single, human tooth dangling from a string wrapped around the neck of the bottle. No one dared to ask who it belonged to, for fear of the answer.

The legend was if you lost a tooth, you placed it in the bottle and walked home through the forest. Upon returning to the forest, you would find a nickel shimmering by the water's edge.

One year, something strange occurred. In a single week, several dozen children of Ospero Falls lost a tooth.

The Silver Fairy bottle was filled with an assortment of baby teeth. The next day, with parents in tow, the children trekked through the woods to see if the Silver Fairy had come.

Upon reaching the bottle, they discovered it was empty. However, in the distance, a shimmering glint came from the lake.

Immersed in the turquoise glacier waters, shone an abundance of nickels; one for every child.

* * *

On June 7th, two days before Christian turned eight, his parents planned a special birthday celebration at the treehouse. They invited Walt, Skylar, and Victoria, along with Gwendolyn-Sue and Evamya, who had made a carrot cake, which was Christian's favourite. Sophia wanted to celebrate the Sitka by doing something unique. She told Jack her idea. He smiled and nodded in agreement. Everyone was eager to go see the Sitka and the treehouse. The morning of the 9th, Sophia made a trip to the bank, to withdraw from the trust account. Arriving at Miss Jean's Boutique, she bought three pairs of children's Saddle shoes, in various sizes. The white shoe had a black saddle in the middle, with white laces. Arriving at Victoria's, the O'Connelly's brought with them the three boxes. Departing onto the ferry for Averston, there was a lot of eagerness.

Aboard the commuter boat, a dozen fishermen had come to join in the festivities.

Making their way to the spruce, the three children hopped along with excitement.

Finally arriving, everyone could finally see the complete treehouse. The slanted asphalt shingled roof, complimented the cedar siding. Two windows were closed with shutters. Off to the side, was a small overhang deck, which looked out to the ocean. The only way in, was through a trap door. Hanging below it, was a rope ladder.

As everyone stood admiring it, Jack motioned over Christian, Skylar and Walt.

As each of them stood side by side, Jack made an announcement.

"This here treehouse deserves our joy for everyone's hard work.

We all gave this build our best efforts, yet we knew it could not have been completed, without the help of the Ospero Falls fishermen."

Jack began to clap, and everyone joined in. The Sitka had brought members of the community together in a special way. As the children gathered with Evamya, Jack gave a nod for Sophia to share.

Standing before all of them, she offered an explanation.

"Our tree is very special, and you children will have lots of fun in it. So, I have for each of you, a pair of Saddle shoes. I want each of you to take a pair and throw them into the tree branches. That way, you will always be a part of the Sitka tree."

Christian thought it was a wonderful idea, however Gwendolyn piped up: "You just wanna toss away a good pair of new shoes?"

Evamya interrupted by saying, "Now hush up Gwendolyn-Sue, you've forgotten your own roots and all your family traditions before you, honouring their journey."

Gwendolyn looked down, as Jack said, "We may have invested our best efforts in building the treehouse, but that spruce – it has given us its protection and each of you a place to climb."

"You know," Victoria chimed in, "it might not make much sense just yet, but give it time. When you see those shoes swinging in the ocean breeze, from the branches of your Sitka, blessed memories will be there."

Removing the shoes from the boxes, each tied their own shoelaces together, to make a pair. Jack helped the girls, while Christian made a double loop. Standing around the tree, Skylar was asked to go first. Her small frame and tiny arms could not reach even the lowest limb. Therefore, Jack came closer for the little girl and lifted her high up onto his shoulders. Holding onto her tightly, Skylar's offering sat upon the lowest branch.

Placing her down, Jack realized he would have to do the same for Gwendolyn, yet Jack asked her permission first. She nodded and he lifted her up. Tossing her shoes, were only a branch higher, yet she was proud of her release. Next, Christian felt he had something to prove and threw his pair of Saddle shoes, as hard as he could. The end result, saw his pair land on the roof of the treehouse.

Both girls burst into giggles, while the rest of them held back their laughter.

Jack rubbed his chin and shook his head, then spoke,

"Well there boy is one heck of a throw. I reckon those Saddles will never be seen again!"

Christian was embarrassed and upset, all at the same time. He figured the shoes would be high up in the canopy, for everyone to look at. Kicking the dirt, he mumbled,

"Dad, why don't you just let me climb up and grab them?"

Jack shook his head and looking over at Sophia he replied, "Your dear mother would pitch a fit if she knew I let you climb this tree! No way son, this is where your shoes will have to stay."

He winked at Christian and ruffled the young boy's hair.

As they returned home, all Christian could think about was his beloved Sitka spruce and the new tree house – with his shoes upon it.

The next afternoon, Skylar hurried over to Christian's porch. When he answered the knock on his door, there she stood.

"C'mon over to my house," Skylar said, grabbing his hand, "I have something to show you!"

They ran across the street and up the stairs to the room Victoria and Skylar shared. Standing in front of the door, Skylar asked Christian to cover his eyes. He heard the creaking door being opened.

"Okay," she whispered, "you can look."

As Christian opened his eyes, there stood his father, sharply dressed in his finest clothes. Beside him was Sophia, in an ivory cream dress with yellow buttercups on the hemline.

They were smiling and holding hands. Evamya and Victoria stood behind them against the bedroom wall.

Skylar grew impatient. "You want to see my surprise from Gwennie and I?"

"Uh huh!" Christian said eagerly.

Evamya and Victoria moved away to reveal a painting right on the wall. To Christian's amazement, there was a replica of his beloved Sitka tree in bright watercolours. It was around the size of a 11 x 14 portrait. Although rudimentary, it was the likeness of the original.

The girls had added spiky, blue-green needles and reddish seed cones, to make it look genuine.

Around the base of the trunk, three stick people held hands. Their names – Christian, Skylar, and Gwendolyn-Sue – were painted in bright orange. The girls had even tried to duplicate the tree house, though the result, looked more like a brown box. White dots were added to resemble shoes hanging from the branches. On top of the treehouse, were two blobs of paint, to signify Christian's pair of Saddles.

Skylar had added a simple v, to represent a bird soaring high, above the tree.

"Oh, wow!" Christian said. "Thank you so much."

"We thought it would be nice for us to have our own tree here," Skylar said, "because we can't always go to the real one."

Victoria bent down in front of Christian. "Within this home," she said, "you are always welcome."

Christian would come to cherish the day's events. Surrounded by the love of family and friends, he felt everything was just as it should be.

* * *

Several weeks passed… The cool wind carried a hint of autumn. Whenever Sophia, Victoria and Evamya made a trip to Averston, Christian, Skylar, and Gwendolyn-Sue came along on the ferry.
They would spend an hour at the tree house, sharing secrets and having

adventures. Christian didn't want the treehouse filled with too much girly things. His Dad brought a rug, a flashlight and two tv trays. On another trip, he added three metal stacking stools. Jack had bought them in the same General Store, that Christian had seen a rustic lantern. It didn't work anymore, he was told, but the boy was drawn to it. He asked his father if he could purchase it with his allowance, which Jack agreed. Christian also brought along some games such as Snakes and Ladders, checkers, and Candyland – Skylar's favourite. They would put two of the stools together and play a game or two. The girls added to the décor, a Laura Secord tin, with a handle. Inside was silly putty, Play-Doh, and a Slinky. For playing outside, they had a Frisbee and two Hula Hoops.

While Christian was looking forward to finally beginning Grade 1, he would miss spending time out at the Sitka tree.

For Skylar, his mention of September only brought unhappiness, as she dreaded the thought of him starting school and leaving her behind. However, he had already been held back a year and was ready. Christian knew he would miss hanging out with the girls, especially Skylar. However, he had never forgotten the day he was up in the Sitka tree and saw the mansion.

On the last day of summer vacation, they ferried over to Averston with Evamya. She knew all the spots to gather berries and left the children to themselves at their beloved Sitka tree.

Christian and Gwendolyn-Sue climbed the rope ladder, feeling the breeze on their faces.

Looking outward through the sprawling branches, nature's carved slate surrounded them.

Skylar stayed below, gathering seed cones in her rose-hemmed skirt.

When they reached the top, Gwendolyn-Sue noticed Christian staring at something across the riverbed.

"What are you looking at?" she asked.

He didn't reply. She climbed out on the branch to look for herself. She peered over the flowing glacier waters to see the mansion and giggled.

"What's so funny?" Christian asked.

"Here you sit staring at some big old house when all this time, I've been in it!"

"There's no way you've been in there!" he sneered.

"Have so! I can prove it, just ask Gramsy!"

"What are you talking about?"

Gwendolyn-Sue knew she had him where she wanted him.

Down below, Skylar started climbing the ladder. "What are you two fighting about now?" she yelled.

"Nothing, Bird Girl! We're just talking, that's all."

Christian could not take it any longer. "Okay, I give. What's the deal?"

"I'll tell you," Gwendolyn-Sue said, "but first I want you to kiss me on the cheek!"

"What the heck you want me to kiss you for?" he winced.

Gwendolyn-Sue looked down for Skylar, who was unaware of her intentions. She bit onto her lower lip.

"Well," she said, avoiding Christian's gaze, "I overheard Ms. Austen tell Mrs. Lola she pitied me because there's no way anyone's ever gonna kiss me, being that I'm a coloured girl! So, I figured since we're friends and all, you'd kiss me on the cheek. Then I can tell her she's a fibber who doesn't know anything about me."

Christian's heart sank at the thought of his friend referred to by the colour of her skin.

He knew the townspeople had welcomed Evamya and Gwendolyn into Ospero Falls, but there were some in Averston, who treated them as outcasts.

He did not think there was any harm in giving Gwendolyn-Sue one quick peck to make her feel better.

As he bent forward, Gwendolyn-Sue leaned in. When Christian was about to kiss her on the left cheek, she turned her head, so his mouth touched hers.

His eyes opened in panic, just as their lips puckered together, and Skylar looked up to see them.

At first, she thought the sun was playing tricks on her eyes. However, she soon realized the awful sight was real. Her eyes filled up with tears.

"I thought you were my friends?" Skylar yelled, letting the cones spill from her dress.

Bursting into tears, she hurried down the ladder to find Evamya, who was picking salmonberries nearby. Christian pushed Gwendolyn-Sue away and tried to regain his composure.

"What did you do that for? Now we've upset Skylar!"

"You're always worried about her instead of how I'm feeling! Skylar's a pretty white girl. No one wants a coloured girl like me?" Tears fell as she looked down at her tattered shoes. "Ms. Austen was right."

Christian was torn between his two friends.

He had to find Skylar, to tell her it was just a mistake.

Skylar found Evamya and collapsed into her arms, sobbing.

"Good gracious child, what's the matter with you? Where's my Gwendolyn-Sue, and Christian?"

She stroked Skylar's locks, which were tangled in a heap of dishevelled curls.

"I hate them!" Skylar said. "And I don't want to talk to them ever again!"

"Hush now, girl, watch your tongue. What could they possibly have done to upset you so?" Skylar's sobs waned. She sniffled and wiped her nose on Evamya's white apron, which was stained with salmonberry juice.

"I saw them Gramsy with my own two eyes… I watched them kiss right in front of me."

"Dear Lord, girl! Do you mean my granddaughter and Christian?"

Skylar nodded. "Just now in the tree house, they were sitting up in the branches, talking, and when I looked up again, they were having a big old kiss… on the lips too!"

She scrunched up her face.

Christian bounded through the bushes. He was panting heavily, and his thick, dark hair lay matted in sweat on his forehead.

"Good heavens, boy! Just who do you think you are pulling a ruse like that?" Evamya demanded. Christian was trying to catch his breath when he looked at Skylar, her eyes puffy and red from crying. He tried to explain. However, she hopped to her feet and backed away from him.

"Get away from me! I don't want to see you!"

"I was just going to try and tell you…"

Evamya stormed forward and grabbed Christian's ear. He shrieked in pain. She dragged him to a large fir stump. Skylar followed, unsure of what was going to happen.

"You've got some talking to do, boy," Evamya hollered, "you hear me?"

Gwendolyn-Sue appeared from behind the bushes with tears in her eyes.

"Gramsy," it's my fault."

"You tell me right now what happened, child, or so help me God."

Christian added, "It's those ladies in town, who taunted Gwennie-Sue."

"Well, go on then, boy!" Evamya said, confused.

"You see, Gwennie-Sue overheard Ms. Austen tell Mrs. Lola that no one's ever gonna kiss such a poor little – "

"Coloured girl like me!" Gwennie-Sue said. She hung her head in shame. Evamya and Skylar's mouths dropped open.

"I just wanted someone to kiss me, because then I could tell them it isn't true."

"Come here, child," Evamya said, eyes filling with tears as she reached out. Gwendolyn ran towards her grandmother and clutched her apron. Meanwhile, Skylar walked up to Christian.

Looking at the dirt, she kicked it with her right shoe.

Christian felt bad but all he could muster up was "I'm sorry!"

Skylar nodded.

Releasing Gwendolyn from her embrace, Evamya sat upon the stump.

"Please," she said, waving over Christian and Skylar, "come and settle in, while I tell you a story."

Chapter 8

Revelations

SKYLAR AND CHRISTIAN SAT ON THE MOIST GRASS BESIDE Gwendolyn-Sue.

"I reckon with all that's happened today, the truth needs telling. The time has come for both of you to hear the facts about Gwendolyn-Sue and I." Evamya looked hesitantly at her. "Besides, I can see that my precious girl needs a reminder of her faith, which has sustained our family through many difficult times."

"I'm sorry, Gramsy," Gwendolyn-Sue said, squirming.

"I do believe you have something to say to your friends?"

"Sorry!" she sputtered.

Skylar threw her arms around Gwendolyn, accepting her apology with a reassuring hug.

"Now then," Evamya said, nodding, "shall we get on with the story?"

* * *

"I've told Gwendolyn this story many times since she was born. It is to remind her of the ordeal her family endured, and so she'll never be ashamed of her colour.

My family came from a place in the south, far away from here, where your blistered bare feet walked on the dirt.

Back in harder times, my grandparents who were known by their Swahili names – Bibi for grandmother and Babu for grandfather, lived far from here in a place called the South. To make it easier for you to understand, in my story, I will call them Grandma and Grandpa. They existed by the grace of God, as they were bound in poverty and kept by a white man, Master Phillips, as slaves.

Now, slaves were people who had no freedom and whose only purpose was to serve their owners. They had to do whatever their masters told them to. Slaves were bought and sold like cattle, treated awfully like animals.

Some people in the South figured Blacks didn't have any right to say or do what they pleased.

My grandparents could not talk with any white person, except to their master, who was a cruel man. They could only speak to people of colour, like their own.

They had no schooling, no proper food. Their shelter was a wooden shack with dirt floors and rags mixed with straw for a bed. No one dared speak against it for fear of being whipped, tied to a tree, or taken into the woods, never to be seen again. They worked long, hard hours in the cotton fields struggling in the sweltering sun, from dawn till dusk.

Master kept them very poor, so there was little chance of ever escaping. If they uttered a word that didn't please the master, they got whipped!

You see, the White folk figured if the Blacks were beaten, kept hungry, and forced to live in filth, then they would become weak. Well, let me tell you, their faith in the good Lord only made them stronger! Try as they might, there was no way anyone was stripping the joy my grandparents felt being Black. My Gramma Keziah, was so proud to carry the name after one of Job's daughters in the Bible. My grandpa's name was Isaac. One day, another black man by the name of Henry, who had been working beside Grandpa, asked if they wanted to escape and find freedom. That meant for them to go into Canada, to a place where they would no longer be slaves.

Now, poor Grandpa was scared at first and wanted nothing to do with it. Then, one night Gramma spoke to him. She begged Grandpa to rethink what Henry had suggested, as she didn't want their future children to be born into slavery.

After much fuss, Grandpa finally gave in, and plans were made.

A few days later, they left at dusk with Henry and followed the North Star. They were told to keep their eyes towards the heavens – on the Big Dipper – and it would lead them to the Promised Land.

"My grandparents escaped in 1850 through a route known now referred to as the Underground Railway. Along the passage, they sang an African American song known as Wade in the Water. The means of their travels, saw them walk through the woods on foot, hip deep in muddy swamp, they navigated and trudged on. After being welcomed onboard a boat operated by people called conductors, my grandparents were taken to Philadelphia. They then were greeted by other helpers, who placed them on a train to New York. After a week of staying with other friends who had escaped, they took their last train waiting to taste freedom, here in Canada. It was a long, exhausting journey that lasted a span of over seven weeks. Upon arriving in Upper Canada, they were welcomed into a 'safe house', where they were given proper food along with clothing and shelter. Poor Gramma was weakened by the harsh travels and Grandpa could only pray she'd live through it all, to one day have a child. The people who cared for her weren't like the mean white folk back South.

"My grandparents eventually settled in a place called Amherstburg, that was smaller than Ospero Falls. It is so far away from here; it would take you 5-6 days by ferry and train. Grandpa worked as a labourer, but this time, they paid him. He also helped build the main church in town. Grandpa had given up hope of becoming a father. He thought the long journey had taken its toll on Grandma, and as a result she couldn't have children. This is why he blamed himself for not leaving the South earlier. Yet all that was pushed aside when in 1855 Grandma gave birth to a healthy, baby boy. They named him Isaiah.

The years passed. In 1875, Isaiah was 20, when he married Rasheda, two years younger. They were my parents. Momma worked odd jobs, cooking, sewing, and selling fresh vegetables. Momma was a wise, sweet woman who wanted lots of children. She ended up with two girls, me in 1877 and then, ten years later, she gave birth to my younger sister Clara.

I have my momma to thank for teaching me everything I know. She used to tell me, 'Evamya Rosie Grace Walker, I gave you several strong names of women, to bring together that fierce spirit you have.'

She was a vivacious African storyteller, who knew the value of keeping her ancestor's stories alive.

Sometimes she would share simple words that had powerful meaning, two of my favourites were the South African word Ubuntu which means we are defined by our kindness towards others. Another word was passed onto her by an elderly woman from India. In an old, different language called Sanskrit, there is a word known as Vilomah, which means a parent whose child has died.

She learned traditional things passed down and had her own way of sharing them.

Momma used to say: 'You only need three things to sustain you in life.'

Evamya picked up a twig and in the dirt drew a large circle. Slowly, she wrote three words inside in the shape of a cross: faith, courage, kindness.

Evamya pointed to each word, drawing a line between and connecting them together in the middle.

"If you have faith, then there is purpose. If you have courage, then you have a heart like a lion, and if you show kindness, well, that says you know the Golden rule of how to treat others."

As Evamya spoke, all three children sat mesmerized by her story. Suddenly, bending forward, the elderly woman blew the dirt around – making the diagram disappear.

Clara and I always dreamed of what it would be like, when we found husbands to marry and have children with.

Unfortunately, we were to be afflicted with lots of bad juju – like bad luck.

Also in my family we had a way of knowing things to come. Like in the Bible, the Holy Spirit guides you."

Evamya looked at her listening audience, before carrying on.

The man I had married, Sirius, died of scarlet fever before we were able to have any children. Clara was just as unsuccessful in motherhood, though she tried for many years, she was without child.

"Finally, long after she had given up hope, Clara became pregnant. Her husband, Jacob, was excited for they'd waited so long. However, several months later, in the darkest hours of the night, a neighbour came banging at their door. He was screaming that the local church, which Grandpa had helped build years earlier, was on fire! Even though my sister didn't want him to leave, Jacob felt he should at least try to lend a hand. Clara told me she knew it would be the last time she would see him alive."

Evamya choked on the words. As the tears pooled in her eyes, she let out a deep sigh. Christian, Skylar and Gwendolyn sat silently, an overwhelming feeling of sorrow hovering over them. Evamya smoothed the threads of her silver hair, before continuing on.

"Sadly, she was right. It was a time of mourning, for my family thought they'd be safe moving to a new country! Word around town was some White folk weren't pleased with Blacks living among them. We never did find out who or what caused the blaze, but Jacob gave his life for it. He ran in when he heard the caretaker was inside. He didn't hesitate for a moment, to sacrifice his life, for someone else's.

Without her beloved Jacob at her side, my sister gave birth one bitter night in a tiny shack to a lovely baby girl."

Evamya pause and then shook her head. "Poor Clara! When that child came out into my arms, there was a lot of blood – too much and my sister drew her last breath."

Evamya's voice trailed off, as she cleared her throat.

"I raised my sister's baby girl Cecilia as my own, but she always knew who her real momma was. I told her about her roots and taught her to be proud of her colour. The years seemed to pass too quickly and one day she came to me with her head hung down in shame. I asked her what are you so sad about? Some man, who already had a family, had fed her a bunch of hogwash about being in love and all. But when Cecilia found herself pregnant, I'd reckon it took him only a few seconds to run as fast as his scrawny chicken legs could carry him. So, there I was, preparing to help my niece raise a baby though she was still so young herself. Regardless of the tragedies that have befallen my relations, my faith had me believing the good Lord was going to bless us this time. Well he did, for a while. But in those days, there were all types of dreadful diseases. God must have needed another angel up in heaven because a year after she gave birth, Cecilia caught a thing called cholera. It was a horrible disease, and she fought long and hard, but the spirit is a powerful thing. You see, when your time is up, you must go. I tried to comfort Cecilia, asking the Lord to end her suffering. I took the baby girl and there I was at my old age, raising another child!"

Evamya glanced over at Gwendolyn-Sue, whose large, dark eyes were downcast.

"You see, I'm not Gwendolyn's grandmother – I'm her great-aunt. I've been raising her since she was a young babe, so that now I'm more like a mother to her. That's why I call her my Opal, she is like a precious gem that reminds me of my faithfulness."

Christian and Skylar could not help but gasp in disbelief.

Gwendolyn-Sue said, "Don't tell anyone."

Skylar replied, "Friends don't tattle!"

"I suppose we still call you Gramsy?" Christian asked.

"Of course!" she smiled.

"I was also wondering", Christian paused then asked, "How do you know so much about your grandparents?"

"Always asking questions!" Evamya winked. "Well, I'll tell you it's a darn good thing us black folk know the importance of family history. My Gramma Keziah always cherished the family tradition of sharing in your own words, where you came from.

As she grew older, she told Isaiah their story of freedom. Oh, how Poppa loved to retell his parent's tale of following the North Star into Canada. I could tell it a thousand times over. It made us so proud.

"Before my Momma and Poppa finally passed on, they told the tales to their kin of how they survived. Their words gave life to the oral history passed onto my sister Clara.

"The night she died; I found a small torn rag in her dress pocket.

"It had drawings of a star, a cross, and the Canadian red leaf – symbols that represented our freedom, faith, and new roots. It was all I had now, to connect our stories with our past.

"Although the sad accounts are of the sufferings my family went through, we have never forgotten where we came from. I reckon Momma wanted everyone to know, just how deep their trust was in the Lord."

Christian had grown restless as he wanted to know more.

"Gwennie mentioned something about her being inside the large house across the river," said Christian, then pausing, he asked "How did you end up there?"

Evamya shook her head. "After Cecilia passed on, there was just the two of us. I had to find work and some white folk took me in for a while, as a housekeeper.

"As time went on, the woman of the house, Laura-Belle, came to me and told me about her wealthy Uncle Wilkes in Averston. She said he had never married and was a miserable old coot that hoarded his money. He needed someone to come and tend to the duties of the house.

After being told of our dire situation, Uncle Wilkes offered me the job. It wasn't much pay, but we could stay there if I minded my business and did my work. Well, of course I jumped at the chance! Now I tell you, nothing I've ever seen before or since comes close to the loveliness of that mansion. If you think it's grand on the outside… my goodness, you should have seen the inside!"

Christian's eyes widened in delight.

"Two years passed, and you know something, I never did get to know the man whose fine clothes I pressed, whose lavish food I prepared, and whose bed I made a thousand times over. For even though he was rich in wealth, he was unsuccessful in finding joy. The objects he once desired, which filled his home, never could take away the loneliness he felt inside. He passed on – a miserable, old man who never knew what it felt like, to be truly loved. On the day of his funeral, the only people who came to pay their respects were Gwendolyn and myself. Not even his niece travelled the short distance to bid him farewell. Afterwards, I put my old clothes back on and boarded the ferry to Ospero Falls. From there on, you know my story."

Christian had lost the smirk on his face, but not his interest.

"Is the house for sale?" he asked.

Evamya glanced over – with a look of disdain.

Taking a deep breath in, she sighed, "Yes child, that wretched mass is for sale at a price only the devil knows!"

Evamya stood. Gathering the basket of salmonberries, she started walking the trail, to the ferry dock.

"Reckon it's best we be on our way, children," she said wearily. "The days are long, and there's still work to be done."

As they approached the riverbed, Christian trailed behind the others. He glanced towards the estate perched upon Rogue's Bluffs.

The captivating charm was replaced with an ominous presence. He felt a breeze on the back of his neck and reached for the collar of his shirt.

"When the hairs on your neck stand up," Evamya yelled back, "you pay attention to them, boy."

Chapter 9

Departure

SEPTEMBER ARRIVED WITH THE LAUGHTER OF CHILDREN RINGING out from the schoolyard. Christian was beginning the first grade, much to the dismay of Skylar and Gwendolyn-Sue. They walked all the way to the tiny schoolhouse with him in silence.

"Ah, come on you two," he said. "There isn't anything to be sulking about. I am just going to school."

He nudged Skylar, trying to make her grin, but to no avail. As he turned and walked down the path to the entrance. Opening the door, a blast of air wafted a cluster of fallen leaves past his feet. Christian smiled, for today was the beginning of a new adventure.

* * *

One autumn morning, Skylar was walking near the upper lake while her mother gathered berries. Hopping alongside the fresh water, something brought her to a standstill. There, lying in front of her, was an injured bird. It was a sandpiper, with a broken wing. Skylar knew it had to be taken to Gramsy to see if she could save it. Bending down, she gently lifted the wounded bird into her palms. Its beady black eyes looked up at her.

She saw her mother up near the bushes picking berries.

"We need to go back to the house!" she hollered.

"I will be right behind you, sweetie."

When Skylar got home, she burst into the kitchen, startling Evamya.

"My Lord! What in heaven's name are you up to?"

Skylar's glum face told Evamya it was serious. She glanced at Skylar's hands clutching something.

"What do you have there?"

Skylar thrust her open hands forward, to reveal the injured bird.

"I found the birdie near the lake's edge while Mommy was collecting her fruit. It's hurt, Gramsy. Is there some way you can help?"

"Of course, child! I'll fix your bird for you." Skylar felt better already. "You know, young miss, what it means when a sparrow pays you a visit?"

"No, Gramsy, I don't."

"A sparrow showing up, means someone's soul is free to fly up to paradise, to be with the Heavenly Father."

Skylar's nose scrunched up. "You mean I have birdies living inside me, when I go to see Jesus?"

Evamya broke into a deep belly laugh.

"You just leave him to me, Songbird. I'll see to it the poor little one gets what he needs. You go on now and wash up, you hear? It's almost suppertime."

Walking away, Skylar turned to see the bird stare directly at her. Nearing the stairs, she was more curious to know how Gramsy was going to make the bird's wing better. Turning around, Skylar crept back towards the kitchen and peeked around the corner.

Evamya hunched over the bird, lying in a cloth on the kitchen table. She held a funny shaped bottle in her one hand. Popping the cork off the small decanter, she poured what appeared to be dirt onto her gnarled fingers, twisted with arthritis. As the soil covered her weathered hands, she slowly began to rub it between her palms.

Next, she gently clutched the delicate wing with her fingertips, massaging the dirt into the feathers, humming all the while. The bird stopped chirping.

For a moment, Skylar feared the worst. Then, miraculously, the bird fluttered both its wings, stood, and hopped towards Evamya. Skylar's eyes widened, mesmerized by the sight before her.

The back door slammed. Skylar quickly scrambled up the stairs so she would not draw any attention to herself. No sooner had she sat on her bed than Gwendolyn-Sue skipped into the room.

"What'cha doing?" she asked.

Skylar whispered. "Have you been in the kitchen?"

Gwendolyn-Sue shook her head, "No, why?" she asked.

Skylar whispered, "I found something and brought it to Gramsy. She's acting strange, I dunno."

Gwen was more than curious.

"Let's go to the kitchen," said Skylar.

As both girls sauntered downstairs, they heard the twittering of a bird coming from the kitchen. Victoria was setting the table.

"What's all the chirping about?" Gwendolyn-Sue asked.

"Your friend here found what she reckoned to be an injured bird," Evamya said with a wink. "However, when I fed it some water and gruel, well, it just perked right up!"

Skylar was confused and thought she might have imagined the whole incident.

Dismissing it from her thoughts, she grinned at her silliness.

Sitting down at the table to eat they bowed their heads to say grace.

Afterwards, they began to eat.

Skylar looked over at the bird. Its tiny, dark eyes seemed to stare at her, and it began to chirp.

"Looks like Bird Girl's made a new friend," Gwendolyn-Sue said.

Later, Christian came by to tell everyone about another exciting day at school.

Walking into the foyer, laughter, and the chirps of a bird, greeted him from the den.

"Good evening, Christian!" Evamya said. "Have you come to enlighten us with your knowledge?"

The girls giggled.

"Want to see my new pet?" Skylar asked.

"The bird is not staying, honey!" Victoria frowned.

"Yes, Momma," Skylar said, rolling her eyes. "I know."

Christian saw a brownish-grey bird on Skylar's lap.

"What kind of bird is it?" he asked.

"It's a solitary sandpiper." she replied

"Well, looks like it knows it's safe with you," smiled Christian.

"He likes being in my arms where it's nice and warm." Skylar cooed.

"Yeah, Bird Girl," Gwen retorted, "Now you'll have to feed him worms from your mouth… just like his momma would!"

Everyone groaned.

"Hey! Skylar, I now know what my special nickname for you is," Christian said. "I'm gonna call you Piper!"

Skylar blushed.

"She's already got a nickname, silly!" Gwendolyn-Sue said.

"Yeah, she does, but that's what everyone else calls her. Besides, Piper sounds better than Bird Girl!"

Gwendolyn-Sue stuck out her tongue, trying to act as if it did not bother her. As for Skylar, her face lit up. Her best friend Christian, had announced in front of everybody, her nickname.

The next day, before supper, the time arrived for the sandpiper to be released. Along the inlet, Evamya joined Skylar to free the bird. She lay her palms flat, which allowed the bird a secure place to take off. Before lifting off, it turned and looked at Skylar one last time and began chirping, grateful for its freedom.

"It's okay," Skylar whispered, "you can go home now."

The bird spread its wings and headed off towards the upper lake.

"See you around, birdie!"

The weeks passed quickly, and the days grew darker. Flurries once again covered the town.

Regardless of the cold, the town's children always relished the first snowfall. Christian played with everyone in the schoolyard – except for one boy named Franklin. His ears looked too big, he wore thick, round glasses, and he had a wide space between his two front teeth.

One day during Christmas break, Christian was walking out of Walt's Seascape. Suddenly, Franklin rounded the corner of the store.

"What'cha doing?" Franklin asked.

Everyone in town knew his father, Oliver, had been sick for some time, and his mother was working two jobs to take care of the family. Christian realized Franklin was lonely.

"I was just heading home to do chores," he said.

"Can I come? I mean… I will give you some help if you need it."

"Sure, Franklin, you can tag along," Christian said, feeling sorry for him.

As they approached Christian's house, they saw Skylar waiting on the porch. She was buttoned up in a pink snowsuit and wore a purple toque, hand knitted by Evamya. Her face was partially covered by a bright yellow scarf.

"You sure could spot her a mile away!" Franklin chuckled.

"Have you looked at yourself?" Christian glared over his shoulder.

"Yeah, I know what you mean… sorry."

Guilt overcame Christian. "I didn't mean it."

Franklin shrugged.

"Hello!" Skylar said, walking down the steps to greet them. "Who's your friend?"

"This is Franklin. He just wanted to hang out with me today."

Skylar stuck out her hand, covered by a mitten with tiny balls of snow clinging to it.

"Nice to meet you," she said.

Franklin grabbed the icy mitt and shook it carefully; afraid his bare hand would stick to it. Christian grinned. "What are you doing here?"

Skylar pointed towards her home and replied, "Everyone's over at my place. Gramsy fixed up some spiced bread pudding and hot chocolate. I came to bring you over."

They headed over to the Falls' house. The sweet smell of ginger and cocoa greeted them.

After Christian's schoolmate was introduced to Evamya and her baking, Jack looked at Franklin with a sombre expression.

"How's your pa doing?" he asked. Sophia frowned.

"He's not doing so well, Mr. O'Connelly. Fever's set in bad and Ma's working hard to keep things together. But thanks for asking."

"Well, when you go home," Jack nodded, "tell your mother if she needs anything to call upon us. You hear me, son?"

"Yes, sir," replied Franklin.

Evamya slid a pair of mittens in front of the boy, whose bare hands were still red from the cold.

"I have here an extra pair for you," she winked. "Just be sure not to lose them."

He smiled sheepishly, showing the gap between his teeth.

"I will be sure to take care of them, ma'am."

"My goodness," Evamya said, letting out a deep laugh. "Please don't call me ma'am! Just like everyone else, you can call me Gramsy."

"Trust me," whispered Christian, "there's some strange names around here!"

The next day, Christian could not help but notice that Franklin's seat was empty. At lunch, he found out his classmate's father, might not make it through the night.

The Whitman's prayed for Oliver to hold on throughout the holidays. Franklin clung to the hope that by some miracle, his father would make it.

However, when school retuned in the new year, Mrs. Ebby addressed the class. Try as she might to remain professional, she could not hide the tears behind her horn-rimmed spectacles.

"Class," she said, "I have some sad news to tell you today. Franklin Whitman's father, Oliver, passed away last night in his sleep. The disease that afflicted that poor man's body overcame him, and now his spirit is with the Lord. God rest his soul. Class will be dismissed early today, as preparations are made for the funeral and potluck at Mrs. Whitman's residence. Please tell your parents to come and pay their respects."

Christian trudged through the snow, numb inside. He did not know what he would say the next time he saw Franklin. A few days later, the young boy did not attend the funeral, choosing instead to play sick in order to stay home.

In the evening, Christian who was lying under a mound of blankets, heard his parents return from Mr. Whitman's wake. His mother was whispering. He could not make out a word she was saying, until his father's thundering voice reverberated through the thin walls.

"That's complete hogwash, woman! Our boy is not sick in bed, he's faking it.

He did not want to pay his respects to a dead man and his family. He figures it's okay to invite the boy into Victoria's home, but when Franklin needed someone to talk to this evening, our cowardly son hid in his bedroom. Right now, Sophia, I swear to God, I am ashamed of him," shouted Jack.

The words stung Christian. His father's approval meant the world to him, and he had let him down. His first reaction was to cry, but anger overwhelmed him. Christian rose from bed, furious. Goaded by his father's scorn, he dressed and slipped out into the frigid night.

Christian ran all the way to Franklin's house.

Breathing heavily, he paused outside the door, then knocked and waited. To his relief, he heard footsteps. Mrs. Whitman answered.

Christian was startled to see the black circles under her eyes.

She looked as if the grief had found its way upon her and was now etched upon her face.

"Please come out of the cold, dear," she said, motioning him inside. "You're bound to take ill, the way you are dressed. What can I do for you?"

Christian cleared his throat. "I'm here to pay respects to you and your son, ma'am, as I'm very sorry to hear about Mr. Whitman."

"Well, that's very kind of you. Aren't you Jack and Sophia's boy?"

"Yes, ma'am."

He looked up to see Franklin walking down the stairs towards them. His eyes were swollen, and red. Christian lowered his head, ashamed of how he had avoided Franklin, when he needed him the most. Mrs. Whitman winced, seeing her boy suffer in silence.

"Honey, look who's come by to see you. It's Christian." She forced a weak smile.

"Franklin told me all about his nice time over at Ms. Fall's house. It was kind of you to invite him along."

Franklin's eyes met Christian's, and they both knew the truth. Christian had only befriended the loner because he felt sorry for him. Nonetheless, Christian's absence at the wake gave Franklin the idea that he simply didn't care. Christian knew it was up to him to set things right.

"Hey Franklin, I'm sorry for not showing up earlier. I've not been to a funeral before and was scared. I didn't know what to expect." His voice trailed off… "I don't have a good excuse."

"You didn't know what to expect?" Franklin blurted. "What about me? It's not like I have been to a lot of funerals.

His mother glanced towards him with a sorrowful look.

Franklin struggled to say how much he was hurt and mumbled,

"I really needed a friend today."

Christian felt terrible and wasn't sure how to reply.

Franklin sighed, his shoulders softening. "I guess it's better late than never."

Christian was relieved. He turned to Mrs. Whitman.

"Can you call my parents and tell them where I am at?"

Mrs. Whitman smiled and nodded.

"Why don't you two head on up to Franklin's room. I will make sure to call and let them know where you are," she said.

The boys sat talking over the next hour about everything from cars to their favourite science-fiction flicks.

When it was time to retrieve his son, Jack drove over in his old pickup. Christian slid into the cold seat ready to hear his father's preaching.

Despite Jack's disappointment over how Christian had first handled the situation, his father was now satisfied with the outcome. Reaching over, he patted his son's shoulder and they returned home.

* * *

Come spring, there was something the young boy needed to do. He had been collecting his allowance for months, intent on buying a toy medical kit he wanted. Taking it out of his piggy bank, Christian went to Miss Jean's Boutique and bought a pair of Saddle shoes. She was thrilled to have sold the last box and would happily re-order some more, if needed.

It was a clear, April day, when Christian invited Franklin over. He shared about the tradition of throwing a pair of shoes up to the branches hanging over their treehouse. Franklin was keen on the idea. The boys went to Jack, who had to keep his emotions in check. As a father, he was overjoyed to see his son do the right thing. Christian asked his father to take them out to Averston, so Franklin could see the Sitka. Since the girls were out fishing, Jack decided to make it a special trip on the ferry, for the three of them. Once at the treehouse, Franklin peered through his glasses, at the majestic beauty. Whistling, he patted Christian on the back and said,

"Of all the trees in this forest, you picked the one that is nature's best."

Christian smiled and replied, "Thank's buddy."

Franklin tied the two shoes together and wound up, as if a pitcher on the mound.

Giving his best efforts, the young boy let go.

A little above the roof of the treehouse, the Saddle shoes found their permanent home. It was an impressive land. While there was a tinge of jealously, Christian remembered his friend had lost his father.

Looking over at Franklin, who was beaming with joy, Christian said, "Your dad would be proud of you!"

Jack walked over and tousling Christian's hair, he said, "You have done right by me, son."

* * *

The summer of 1955, saw four children explore the woods around Ospero Falls. They fished at the upper lake and hung out together at Reggie's bookstore. Often the four friends would spend time out at the Sitka tree. Hank Stevenson, knew the children well and how much the treehouse meant to them. Many trips were taken and the half hour ferry ride, never seemed to go quick enough for the foursome. Sitting up in the treehouse, their legs dangled over the side, as many books were read there. While Christian and Franklin liked anything science fiction,

Gwendolyn enjoyed stories about far off places, like Africa. Skylar would sit upon a stool, where the sunlight trickled through the window. She looked at nature magazine's that had songbirds in them.

In between swimming, beachcombing, and time at their treehouse, the two girls were excited about autumn. They were about to start school. Since Kindergarten was not a requirement, they would be beginning Grade One.

* * *

In September, when Christian and Franklin started 2nd Grade, they walked a nervous Skylar and shy Gwendolyn-Sue, to their classroom. At first, the girls missed Victoria and Evamya. But as time passed, they adapted well to their new surroundings.

There was a great deal to learn for all of them and soon their days were filled with lessons about reading and arithmetic. Christian enjoyed science the most, as he enjoyed learning about the human body. Franklin liked math, as he discovered angles, volume, and mass. Gwendolyn-Sue's favourite subject was social studies as they learned about history. Skylar found it hard to concentrate, as she gazed out the window wanting to play and explore more.

As autumn led into winter, the seasons changes saw Christmas being celebrated.

Soon after another holiday season was filled with traditions, favourite foods, and gifts to keep everyone happy. The O'Connelly family held the meal at their house and invited Olivia and Franklin. It weighed on everyone's hearts; this would be the Whitman's first Christmas without Oliver. As they gathered to eat, a chair and plate had been placed in his memory, next to another empty chair. Before sitting down Skylar had taken a napkin and written Daddy Eli on it, then placed it on the plate. As everyone settled in, Skylar blew a tender kiss to the vacant seat.

* * *

Months later, in early March, life carried on in Ospero Falls. The townspeople's everyday routines saw the community thrive in activities that brought them joy.

Without knowing what was to come in the following years, those in Ospero Falls and connected with the Sitka tree; would encounter unwelcome seasons of abrupt change.

Chapter 10

Sacrifice

As the years passed by, ushering in changes, time saw the four form their own independence. Meanwhile, each individual was searching for an identity to assert themselves. Victoria decided to grant Skylar the space she yearned for and gave the room upstairs to her. Setting up an area to sleep in the sewing room, Victoria thought about the evolving transformations taking place before her. Gone were the days of children's games once played, in exchange for high school studies.

As they grew though, the friends never lost the close bond they shared. Along with the awkwardness of puberty in being young teenagers, came days occupied by thoughts of the future. Both Franklin and Gwendolyn-Sue decided to leave behind their childhood names, opting for shortened versions: Frank and Gwen. Christian retained his full name, as he liked how Skylar called him as such. He shared with her, his dislike for someone referring to him as Chris.

Throughout their school years, Christian and Skylar were a steady couple. They took many rides on the ferry to Averston, which lead them to their special place. In the tree house they helped build amongst the Sitka, they shared secrets – and their first kiss. Christian still recalled the sweetness of her painted cerise mouth. He grinned, thinking of when he lingered on her sensual lips, it sent shivers throughout him.

Over time, the four pairs of Saddle shoes had weathered, but remained a part of the spruce's existence. Skylar had added to the mural, two white spots of paint, high up in the lofty branches. These were Frank's shoes, tossed long ago, after his father had passed. Throughout the years, Christian made several attempts to climb out onto the roof, to retrieve his shoes. Yet his efforts failed, due to the location of them on the steep, angled top. On his last attempt, he had been able to see closer that a bird had built a nest, in the left shoe.

Afterwards, he was resigned to simply let things be.

One morning in May, Evamya came to the Sitka, to both see the tree and ask something from it. Before removing a small piece of bark from the tree, she thanked the Creator. Poking a small hole in it, she looped through a leather cord and threaded a cross made of Howlite. Presenting the necklace to Skylar, Evamya said she believed the tree had brought Christian and Skylar together. She explained how her ancestors use the bark of a tree to represent the bond between two people. The bark represented shelter and strength. Evamya then prayed for continual blessings in their lives.

* * *

In 1961, a new minister arrived in Ospero Falls, to replace the ailing Preacher Crane. His ideas were fresh and his sermons full of inspiration. His name was Reverend Francis, and he was the town's new beacon of light. He was a man of the cloth who kept up with current events and enjoyed celebrating with the community, world events. The Reverend shared at his pulpit, his enthusiasm for space travel. He spoke of Alan Shepard Jr., the first American astronaut to be launched into space in May 1961. Shepard's galactic expedition, captivated millions of people; intrigued by the images of a man, floating collectively amongst the stars.

Although an enthusiastic preacher, one sermon caught the attention of Skylar and Gwen.

Rev. Francis spoke of his dismay over a recent U.S. Supreme Court decision. In 1962, a ban on teaching religion in the classrooms arose from a lawsuit. Public schools did not have the power to encourage school prayer, deeming it unconstitutional. Rev. Francis preached that the only being who has power over prayer is God, and that no government would ever convince him any differently. Whispers filtered through the crowded church, until a resounding voice echoed "Amen!"

Everyone turned to see where it came from.

Abruptly, Evamya began to sing a hymn and clapped her hands in harmony.

A few weeks later, Rev. Francis sermon focussed on the value of serving the Lord with a purpose.

He shared with his congregation, the idea of building a sanctuary, near the upper lake. It would be a place near the mountains, where people could come to worship and seek refuge if needed.

With the townspeople eager to help those in their community, work soon began.

Skylar was the first person to volunteer her time and assisted the project in every way she could. Victoria, Sophia, and Mrs. Whitman held bake sales to raise funds. Miss Lynn's English sweets always sold out first. Everyone enjoyed the British treat of sponge cake, layered with raspberry jam and vanilla buttercream.

Other fresh-baked goods were loaded up in several Radio Flyer wagons. Boys towed the wagons down to the docks to sell the goods to the commercial fishermen, who couldn't resist the aroma of brownies, squares, and warm fruit pies.

The only problem arose, when little Georgie Allman stuck his finger into a pie and Ms. Erna, who was two steps behind, whacked him with a rolled-up newspaper.

The structure for the sanctuary was donated by the local lumber company and Jack cut it. All the town's men gathered to place the pine logs and raise the roof.

During all the excitement, one person was noticeably absent. Evamya had taken ill in the autumn, with a bout of pneumonia.

As the months passed, Evamya slowly recovered, yet she was not the same. She no longer waited by the window for her precious Gwendolyn-Sue to come home from school. Gwen was busy devoting her time to the yearbook committee and photography class. She always carried with her a Kodak Brownie Junior camera, a gift from Evamya.

It was delivered from back east by the Canadian Kodak Company, for her 13th birthday.

Gwen had entered her photographs into several contests and took first place at the autumn fair. Ribbons and the trophy she had won decorated her side of the bedroom.

Every time Evamya entered the room, she sighed deeply, proud of Gwendolyn-Sue's achievements.

Throughout the winter months, Evamya struggled to maintain her health. Although her mind was clear, her body was slowing down.

* * *

The sixties saw continual growth and expansion within the community of Ospero Falls. Meanwhile, the entire world was experiencing a revolution of shocking events. The early sixties saw continual growth.

It was November 22, 1963, when the evening televisions and radios shared the shocking announcement U.S. President John F. Kennedy had been assassinated. Though prayer was stricken in the classroom, people in their communities, got on their knees to seek answers.

Gwen and Skylar held each other in tears, while Frank and Christian went to the house, to console them in their grief.

Ospero Falls was full of citizens from several ethnic backgrounds, who had family members in the States. The local paper, Ocean Side News, delivered the next day headlines that said:

"Contribution to the Human Spirit is Gone!"

The story shared what many felt all over North America: "It did not matter JFK was a president of the USA. The loss felt throughout homes, schools and businesses was the abrupt death of a man whose support of civil rights, resonated globally. The American dream had been forever marred by violence. Indeed, the reporter wrote:

JFK's death exposed people's vulnerability; in a world pulsating, with revolution.

Many months passed, before anyone could concentrate on other matters. Even the holidays had been subdued and a quieter atmosphere rung in the new years, while people across the world sought a reason to celebrate.

In times of unrest, many sought answers through praying and there was a continual increase in attendance at church. Once spring arrived and the wildflowers were on display, there was a sense of positive change to come.

On the eve of July 2, 1964, The news anchor reported:
An announcement was made by President Johnson declaring it official – signing into law, the Civil Rights Act. The law prohibits employment discrimination based on race, colour, religion, sex, and national origin.

Skylar and Gwen sat together, rivetted by the television.

"Oh my, what amazing news" Gwen shrieked.

"Gwen," Skylar chimed in, "this is so wonderful!"

Gwen nodded her head in agreement and said, "Thank the Lord, someone's finally realizing all the prejudice that black folk have been suffering since the time of slavery!"

"Well then," Skylar said, "I say this is a cause for celebration!"

Slipping out to the kitchen, Skylar grabbed the citrus soda pop and a jar of maraschino cherries. Pouring two glasses of bubbly liquid, she grabbed with a spoon, three cherries and plopped them into each beverage.

"A special moment in history, calls for extravagance!" Skylar remarked.

They were excited to share with Gramsy, the joy of the moment seen on television. While she had recovered from her first bout of pneumonia, it had left her weakened.

* * *

In early May of 1965, Evamya became bedridden for the second time. Lying upstairs under a patchwork quilt made by Sophia, her breathing turned into laboured wheezing. Opening her eyes to see all of Gwen's prized photographs, was comforting to see.

Soon, the days saw Evamya drifting wearily in and out of sleep, as she became weak. The families pulled together and took turns comforting her.

For Gwen, it was overwhelming to see Evamya without her strength.

As Gwen placed warm compresses on her forehead, she tried to soothe her by humming hymns.

Pausing, she looked at Evamya and said, "Soon you will be entering heaven and the choir greeting you will sing greater than any on Earth."

Often, Rev. Francis came by to share with her words from his Bible. He had been witness to Evamya's discernment of things. She had a deep spiritual guidance and a keen sense of things to come.

It was not easy for Christian and Skylar, who were losing their Gramsy. They could not imagine her no longer greeting them with sweet potato pie or offering wisdom when they needed advice. Yet Evamya did not fear her end, as she would see her beloved family once again.

Earlier one morning, both Jack and Sophia, paid a visit to their dear friend, Evamya. She then asked Victoria to summon Gwen, Skylar, Christian and Frank upstairs. The drawn curtains, now opened, revealed the clouds that hung in the sky.

As droplets of rain pelted the windows, Victoria lit a single candle that flickered at Evamya's bedside, then helped propped up Evamya on her favourite pillow. The children entered, and she offered a weak smile as they gathered around her. Victoria, who had been taking care of the elder lady, had summoned Rev. Francis. As Evamya's passing was near, Victoria sat in the rocker, while Rev. Francis stood nearby, clutching his worn Bible.

"The Lord's sons and daughters have gathered for one last moment to be with their Gramsy," Evamya said. "Now, you all must listen to what I have to say, for I've not much time left. Take these words to heart, because I reckon, they are the words Our Saviour wants me to share.

"First, my little Opal; Gwendolyn-Sue. You know I gave you the name of a stone, on the day you were born, because it means hope. You embody the love of all your generations that came before you. Never let anybody say you don't have a reason to be proud of the colour of your skin.

For out of the darkness, shall come light – and that light, I reckon, comes from within your soul, no matter the colour of your flesh. Now, I want you to make me proud. Do you hear what I'm saying?"

Gwen nodded through her tears.

Evamya paused, her breath was shallow. She turned towards Frank.

"As for you, boy, the good Lord blessed you with a fine momma, who has sacrificed so much for you. You've also been a good friend to Christian. Believe me, there'll be times you're going to need each other to lean on. Know this, just as Christian's hands are a gift, so are yours. I've been blessed to know things and your hands are that of a craftsman. However, take heed of what greediness can do to a man's soul."

Next, Evamya held out her hand, its twisted fingers covered by weathered skin. She gripped Christian and Skylar's wrists. Holding on to them with her last bit of strength, she prayed over them

"May what I am about to declare, pass my wisdom along to you both."

Evamya whispered, "I want you to make me a promise. No matter how the devil tries to cover you in darkness, always remember it is simply a smokescreen. Turn to the good Lord, for he will see you through."

Christian and Skylar overcome with emotion, let the tears fall down their cheeks.

"We promise, Gramsy," they replied in unison.

"There's more," she winked. "Savour each day with one another. Do not waste your words on malice, because I reckon, you'll only be left with regrets!

"Cling to the Sitka yet be mindful of the Elder tree. As for you Christian, you've been blessed with wanting to be a good doctor. However, a time will come son when there be no remedies to help you anymore. Know when to let go and you'll be alright. As for what you pursue, choose wisely, for sometimes what we desire stems from an illusion. I pray you'll know the difference."

Christian sat quietly, pondering what she was saying to him.

Evamya focused her attention on Skylar. More tears of hers came spilling forth onto the quilt.

"My dearest Songbird. You have been through so much, my child. I recall when I first met you. Your happiness was once broken by a rotten man in you and your mom's life. It has left you with a bruised heart." Skylar looked down. Evamya clutched her hand. "Now listen here. Do not put the blame upon yourself for other people's transgressions. A child is born innocent, and God sees them without evil. So be strong girl, and rise above the sins of others. Understand me?"

The young girl nodded. Gazing into the deep recesses of Evamya's eyes, Skylar felt as if she was looking into her soul.

"One last thing, Songbird. You are not done conquering your battles.

"What you must endure is yet to come, so be not afraid when it is your time. The birds here on Earth, surround you with their beautiful songs, while the tree you find refuge in will carry you through some dark times. I have knowledge about things that comes from the wisdom of pouring over scripture. Long ago, I gave Jesus authority over the life, he created.

"In surrendering to my faith, I was blessed with discernment; a gift of knowing things that would be fulfilled.

* * *

At the stroke of 11, Evamya closed her eyes and drew her last breath. A single drop of water fell from the ceiling and landed on the candle, extinguishing the flame.

The sweet divine had called Gramsy home, and she was at peace.

A crack of light filtered through the window into the dreary room. The rays bounced off the daffodil walls, Evamya had first observed many years ago.

The next day, after Rev. Francis made the funeral arrangements. After the sermon, he announced Evamya's last wishes. The hymn "The Old Rugged Cross" was to be sung by the church choir. Her ashes would be scattered into the breeze, among the white heather.

Within the sanctuary was a gift from Evamya. On a pedestal stood an hourglass.

Inside was a mixture of sand and a handful of fine dirt, taken from around the Sitka tree. The hourglass was engraved with the following words:

Only God's Time Separates Us from Those We Love

After Evamya passed, Gwen offered to clean her bedroom. After folding the quilt, she lifted the pillow and stared at what lay beneath. Bound together with string were folded sheets of paper. Gwen gingerly picked up the bundle, bringing it closer to her. The faded outer covering was marked with greasy fingerprints. They were Evamya's, traces of her existence. As Gwen opened the pages, a tattered piece of cloth fell out. On it was the faded drawings of a star, cross and a leaf. Symbols of freedom, which connected Evamya to her roots. Overwhelmed, she understood the gift in her hands was precious. The following page had a small twig from the Sitka pressed inside waxed paper. The needles of spruce were flattened and still attached to it.

Gwen flipped through the pages of prayers, handwritten throughout the years.

The entries from Evamya, were filled with passages of blessings.

There were notes, about thanking the Creator for the piece of bark and particles of dirt, she had removed from the spruce. In the middle of the journal, one entry caught her attention.

I thank you, Heavenly Father, for the chance to be used to serve and to heal. I praise you for the little songbird that you had Ms. Skylar bring to me and for the restoration only you, Lord, can provide.

Underneath were the words:

'But I will restore you to health and heal your wounds,' declares the Lord. – Jeremiah 30:17

Skylar later shared with Gwen, how she had brought the injured songbird to Gramsy.

She told her that upon creeping back to the kitchen, Skylar watched Evamya sprinkle dirt over it and mutter some words, she thought were magic. The reality was that Evamya had been praying.

Turning to the last page, Gwen read,

Rising from the roots of this tree, you will find its purpose.

Smiling, she closed the pages and tucked them away among her things.

* * *

A month later, life resumed its busy bustle, yet the house was not the same. Skylar caught herself on several occasions walking into the entryway, expecting to hear Evamya humming in the kitchen. Gwen still found herself glancing towards the upstairs window, remembering the woman whose role in her life, was that of a mother.

As Christian prepared for graduation, his thoughts were on the difficult decisions, which lay ahead.

Although he had been accepted to one of the most reputable campus's, Norelton University. The choice to leave behind his family, friends, and sweetheart tore at him.

He applied for scholarships and bursaries, hoping they would help pay for tuition and medical textbooks. Christian's parents said they would support him financially, yet he did not expect anything. He knew how they had toiled all their lives to give him a better chance.

Even though his dreams meant a lot, family was most important.

One night, Skylar and Christian sat on the small deck of the tree house. Lavender hues cast across the twilight.

The stillness of the air, was interrupted by the whirl of a gust of wind below, which seemed to wrap itself around the Sitka spruce.

"Her spirit is with us tonight," Skylar smiled.

"It always will be," replied Christian.

Skylar slid her hand into his. The smell of musk hung around them. He had bought her a bottle of the perfume on her birthday, and she wore it only for him. Despite Christian leaving Ospero Falls, he promised to return from Norelton for visits.

To prove his devotion, Christian had taken a small strip of bark from the Sitka tree and dried it out in the sunshine. He glued a sheet of paper to the inside and wrote on it:

I, Christian James O' Connelly, lay claim to this tree uniting two lovers and declare that our roots here, will never be severed!

In his excitement, Christian forgot what his father had said long ago, about giving thanks to the Creator.

Carrying on without any thought to the custom, he surprised Skylar with the token of affection. They were just as much a part of each other, he explained, as the bark was to the Sitka tree. The narrow strip of bark, he said, symbolized the strong bond they would always have.

Chapter 11

Hikari

Ospero Falls, British Columbia was a town unlike any other. This was a multicultural society, where the effects of racism did not have any bearing on the townspeople. The Beech Lacus School was a school of mixed races, due to the diverse combination of parents working in the small town. In Ospero Falls, being a town of progression, there was no separation of people due to colour. The segregation in public schools, which swept through other Canadian communities had come to an end in 1965.

* * *

Graduation day arrived with Sophia fretting over last-minute details. She fussed to ensure her son's tuxedo pants were pressed into a straight line.

At the awards ceremony that afternoon, Christian was granted a full scholarship to study at Norelton University. When his parents stood up in the gym, applauding continually, every parent shared in their joy.

Throughout the ceremony, Frank and Christian fidgeted in their seats, excited about the prom in the evening.

After watching Christian and Frank receive their diplomas, Skylar and Gwen left, as they needed to get ready for the dance. It all felt like a dream to Skylar. She wanted the moment to come to a standstill and bind her and Christian to Ospero Falls forever.

Later, as Christian walked over to pick up Skylar, he thought how everyone else in his graduating class had a girlfriend the same age or older. He was the only one with a girlfriend younger than himself. Yet tonight was not going to be any different, as Christian knew she had already emerged spectacular in his eyes.

He remembered how she had surprised him one day by taking him up to her newly redecorated bedroom. It had been repainted in vibrant tangerine, reflecting her favourite season of autumn.

The original work of art, Gwen and Skylar had painted of the Sitka, now included a painted stick figure of Frank along with the two dots for the Saddle shoes, he had flung into the tree. Upon seeing it for the first time, the rendition made Christian smile.

He knew by looking at the Sitka tree, even though they would be separated by a great distance, the connection they shared would remain.

Christian thought about his best friend Frank asking Gwen to be his date. Even though the year before, they had decided to part ways on good terms, both remained close friends. Christian bid goodnight to his parents, with a promise to stop by with Skylar on their way to the prom. Then he walked over to his girlfriend's house.

Knocking on the Falls' door, he heard movement inside.

Opening the door, Victoria smiled. Christian's attention was drawn to the stairs where Skylar stood. Her strawberry-blonde hair was swept up in a bun and matched her pastel-peach chiffon dress. Layers of soft frills cascaded down the plunging neckline. His eyes were drawn to the front of the dress.

Walking down the stairs in a pair of ivory heels, Skylar had been transformed into a woman.

"You look nice," she whispered, sensing his jitters.

"You look stunning," he murmured, fumbling with the corsage. She blushed.

He reached for her hand and placed a spray of carnations around her delicate wrist.

She tucked a lace handkerchief in his front pocket, leaving a corner hanging out.

There was another knock on the door. Victoria opened it to find Frank awkwardly standing with a bouquet of handpicked wildflowers.

Victoria welcomed him in, and Skylar hollered for Gwen to hurry up.

Soon after, Gwen appeared on the stairs. Her naturally spiralled curls, were pulled back away from her face, in a large bun. The pale blue dress she wore was covered with sequins. Her lips shimmered with a hint of gloss. In her hands, she held her precious camera.

Skylar could not contain her excitement and squealed in delight. Gwen walked down the stairs. Christian poked Frank in his side, jarring him.

"Well, my goodness Gwen," Frank stammered, "you're all sparkly!"

Christian rolled his eyes.

Gwen knew that was the best compliment she could expect of Frank.

"Why thank you, Frank!" she said. "Your outfit matches your shoes."

The foyer filled with laughter. Victoria grabbed hold of each girl's hand and stepped back.

"Oh my, both of you are the picture of elegance," she said. "If only our sweet Evamya were here to see the four of you together now." They smiled, knowing she was in their hearts.

"Look at you handsome young men. Take good care of my girls now, you hear?"

"Of course, ma'am," Frank said. "We reckon we'll have them home in time for you to fix us breakfast."

Victoria snapped her apron at him. "That's enough out of you!"

She turned and grabbed Gwen's camera.

"Smile nicely for me now," Victoria said, clicking photos.

The foursome stopped in at Christians house, where Sophia, Jake and Olivia all eagerly waited to have additional pictures taken.

The photographs captured happy memories, a time when everything was perfect in their lives.

Arriving to the school gymnasium, the space was transformed into the theme of the prom – Electric Evolution.

Rhythm-and-blues music pulsated from the electric guitars of the band on stage. Silver and black helium balloons bobbed against the ceiling.

Neon stars illuminated a checkered blue backdrop where couples posed for pictures.

As the music filled the room, it sent vibrations through the mass of dancing bodies. Skylar charmed anyone who encountered her. Pulling out her hairpins, she let loose and shook her hair out.

The shy girl now wore confidence, as if it was a new hat. For Skylar, the night was electrifying.

When the band announced the last dance, Skylar grabbed Christian's hand firmly.

Spinning him onto the dance floor, she giggled. Throwing her head towards the ceiling filled with balloons, Skylar looked back at him and declared,

"This one's for us!"

Everything about the evening set the stage, for what was yet to come.

Skylar liked how she was much shorter, and her head pressed firmly in the crevices of his arms. Christian glanced over at Frank, who also held onto Gwen securely.

After the prom, there was a surprise that Christian had previously arranged. He told Gwen, Skylar, and Frank to join him at the dock. A week before, he spoke to Mr. Stevenson and asked for a favour. Christian had offered him money to take the four of them over to Averston.

Even though it was late, Mr. Stevenson passed on any money as he knew how significant the Sitka was in their lives. He piloted the ferry into the still waters, lit up by the ferry lights and the full moon.

Shortly after midnight, they landed in Averston. Christian promised Mr. Stevenson they would be back at the dock in a few hours. This would allow enough time for him to rest and be ready for the early morning sailing. Before getting off the vessel, Christian and Frank, indicated their gratitude with a fistful of dollars that they refused no for an answer. Mr. Stevenson smiled, nodded and bid them a good night.

* * *

Despite Jack's reassurance that the kids would be all right, Sophia and Victoria struggled to go to sleep until all four of the friends were safely back home. Jack told his wife that he was retiring early, as his day began at 4 a.m.

His current job along the water's edge, saw extra work available, as a newly cut forest saw him form the logs into booms. They would be towed to the sawmill, along the shoreline.

While some men disliked the morning shift, he savoured the quietude of early dawn. He would often leave the house, to see the sun rising over the glacial mountaintops, to welcome a new day.

The water's edge, where Jack worked, teemed with life. Sometimes he would arrive early to sit upon a rock and inhale the brisk air of the cove. For him, this is where life began. He had grown accustomed to observing the seals playing in the harbour. Farther out in the bay, a school of dolphins swam together, coming up out of the water, then dropping into the vast ocean. In comparison to the sea, there were fond memories of the upper lake around him. It was here, men embraced their love of the outdoors, while christening their fishing gear in the pristine waters. In the meantime, the white-spotted backs of sandpipers, probed the shores for their meal.

Within the peace felt by Jack, he did have one regret; his son did not know where the enthusiasm for literature originated.

Christian assumed Jack's parents had taught him about the written word. Yet, Christian never knew them, since they had died before he was born. At times, Jack had taken solace in that, yet still, he held onto the guilt of who his father really was.

Jack grew up three hours north of Ospero Falls, in a small fishing village on Hattner Island, with his parents, Harold, and Ida. He was their only child. One summer, when Jack was twelve, he met an elderly Japanese man who was a 2nd generation Canadian. His name was Eishi Hara. Jack helped him dock his fishing boat, and Mr. Hara took a liking to the boy straightaway. Mr. Hara's calm demeanour drew Jack to seek refuge with him, whenever he came into harbour.

Mr. Hara's Canadian-born wife Asuna and ten-year-old son, Sota, lived with relatives on a strawberry farm, while he worked fishing on the ocean. For that reason though, he mostly kept to himself, Eishi enjoyed Jack's company immeasurably.

They would drink Sencha – a traditional Japanese tea from Mr. Hara's intricately designed teapot, in a layered design of green, crimson, and indigo hues. The spout was the dragons head, while his tail wrapped around, to form the handle. The top of the lid had another dragon head in shimmers of gold.

The teapot, Mr. Hara told Jack, was all he had connecting him to his Japanese roots.

Therefore, he kept it protected in a crate, away from prying eyes.

Mr. Hara took notice of how easily Jack retained the knowledge of everything he was taught. Whether it was how to haul in a net full of fish or how to scrub the deck clean, Jack always showed a willingness to learn.

One day, Jack's father Harold asked why he wasted his days away down at the inlet. He proudly told his father about Mr. Hara and everything he had learned from him. The young boy was not prepared for what happened next. He recoiled as his father raised his clenched fist. Though he didn't hit him, he flew into a rage, spouting off about traitors. Jack found out firsthand how intolerant his father was of other cultures. He hollered the Japanese were better off with the black people and both deserved to be separated from white society. He made Jack swear he would never go near any "coloured" folk of any kind – or else he would get the whipping of his life.

As he sat on the rock near the water, recalling the horrible incident, tears welled up in Jack's eyes.

He remembered the times he snuck away to be with Mr. Hara, who sensed something was wrong. When Jack finally told him, in between sobs, Mr. Hara patted the boy's trembling shoulders.

He told Jack to take pity on his father, for his ignorance only stemmed from mistrust. When Jack confided that he was made to swear to never speak to him, Mr. Hara's face softened.

"Seek what's deep in your soul and listen. You will find guidance when you read the scripture."

With that, Mr. Hara handed Jack a Bible and said, "You may borrow this as long as you wish."

On the inside cover was a word written in Japanese.

"What does that say?" Jack asked.

"Hikari – it means Light," Eishi replied.

The young boy, began carrying the Bible with him, whenever he went to meet Mr. Hara. Much to Jack's delight, the elder man would recite verse after verse, explaining that everyone interpreted the holy words differently. Whatever dwelt in the heart of those who read the good book, Eishi said, would emerge from the scripture.

"If like you, a person has a pure soul," he said, "then blessings will follow. However, if hatred dwells within your soul, then the enemy will find a gateway into your life.

Remember this, the Lord will be your best teacher if you listen to Him. If you want a heart-to-heart connection, then seek Him in order to understand the spoken words, written upon the sacred pages."

Jack wanted to spend his days visiting Mr. Hara, so he diverted his father's attention away from himself. It was not hard, considering Harold's interests included producing moonshine.

The last day of summer, Jack waited to read the final passage of the Bible in front of Mr. Hara. Afterwards, Jack thanked his mentor. Heading home, he was unaware of the menace that awaited him.

Arriving at the gate that led to the grey shack they lived in, Jack was terrified to see his father, waiting. As he drew nearer, Jack smelled the stench of whisky. It disgusted him.

Harold did not say a word, as he placed a knife in his son's trembling hands.

Jack winced, knowing what he had to do.

Walking over to the willow tree, he saw his mother, Ida, peer through the paper-thin curtains of the shack. As their eyes met, she turned and walked away.

Ida was a weak, bitter woman who had never stood up for her only child. Time and time again, he felt betrayed by the one person who should protect him. His stomach knotted up, as he realized she might as well be the one, doling out the beating.

Reaching for a branch, Jack knew it would have to be just the right size to please his father – or there would be even more hell to pay. He picked a thick one. In a daze, he sawed at it, until it snapped off in his hand.

Slowly, he walked back to his drunken father. Harold could barely stand up, and the young boy knew this punishment would be worse than any before. Jack removed his shirt, and under the hot setting sun, the whipping began.

A strange thing occurred that day. As hateful, racial words spewed forth from Harold's lips, Jack began reciting the Lord's prayer. Suddenly, he could no longer feel the unbearable pain of the switch stinging his skin. A sense of peace overcame him, and he felt free inside; God was with him, easing his torment.

When Harold finished, he clutched his chest and collapsed. The front door flew open as Ida came running out to her husband's side. As they watched, Harold gasped for air. Ida spat at Jack, who was in shock. Clawing at the dirt, he muttered, "The devil is taking me home!"

With one final gasp, he drew his last breath.

Ida turned to Jack. "Look at what you've done!" she hissed. "You're going to pay for this, you worthless boy."

Jack struggled to stand up, blood oozing from wounds all over his body – he looked into his mother's dark, beady eyes.

"May God forgive both of you," he said.

Ida flung dirt at Jack as she cradled her dead husband.

"Get the hell out of my sight!" She lunged and spat at Jack. "Go see if your scummy friend will take care of you now!"

Jack turned and walked away, blood trickling down his back.

Seeing the whipped boy, Mr. Hara wept and fell to his knees, asking God to wash away the transgressions from Jack's open wounds. He left for a few moments and came back with an oval-shaped emerald container. On the lid was a lotus. Mr. Hara lifted the lid and spread the salve on Jack's wounds. It was after, when they had a plate of salmon between them that Eishi invited Jack to live on his boat, as he had no where else to go. He also insisted that Jack no longer call him Mr. Hara, but by his first name Eishi. When it grew dark, Jack was given a warm blanket and a cup of Sencha. Upon waking the next day, Jack was stunned to find his cuts healed. Miraculously he was relieved of the pain, and never questioned what had taken place. Soon after, he was introduced to Eishi's wife, Asuna and their son, Sota.

Eishi had spoken to them about Jack many times and they understood, the boy had no home.

As the years passed, and under the care and guidance of Eishi, Jack flourished and grew into a proud young man. He learned the art of fishing from Eishi. The techniques would see Jack be able to catch a fish in a quick manner. They read the Bible together and one day when Jack was twenty, Eishi asked Jack if he would like to be baptized? The profound gesture saw Jack say yes. There in the calm waters, the elder Eishi placed his hand on Jack's forehead and asked,

"Do you accept Jesus Christ as your personal Lord and Saviour?"

Jack answered, "Yes, I do."

Carefully dunking Jack into the salt water, Eishi stated:

"I baptise you in the name of the Father, Son and Holy Spirit."

Two years later, when the Second World War broke out, Jack enlisted. Upon his departure, he did not know it would be the last time he would see Eishi Hara, the man who had been more father than friend.

As he huddled in the trenches, Jack received letters from Eishi Hara. In one, Mr. Hara described how Asuna and Sota were enroute to Ospero Falls, when they were seized in Averston. Away on a fishing trip, he was powerless to stop the authorities from taking his family away, to the internment camps. He carried the burden of guilt for being far away from home when his family were rounded up and placed in captivity, along with over 20,000 other people of Japanese descent.

Despite his hardship, Mr. Hara was not a bitter man, but embraced life with heiwa – harmony.

When Jack received a letter from another old fisherman in his former village, it was to say Mr. Hara had passed away in his sleep. Jack removed from his pocket the tattered Bible and kissed it.

Opening it carefully, he found the wooden cross tucked between the pages.

Years before, he gifted Eishi the simple cross – carved from a willow switch – during a conversation about forgiveness. It was shortly after Harold had died. The cross was hewn, from a branch of the same tree, his father used to whip him as a youngster.

Before Jack shipped off to war, Eishi gave the wooden cross back. He told Jack that severing the root of bitterness, helps to make peace with the past. Jack was given the gift for himself, as a reminder of what he had endured. Carrying the cross like an olive branch, represented the extinguishing of generational sin.

Years later, when Christian asked about his grandparents, Jack said they had died many years ago. The truth was, when he came back from war, Jack found his mother long gone, and their home left in shambles for the mountains to come and claim. The dwelling was unrecognizable, enveloped by vines, moss, and thick shrubs. Christian sensed Jack's reluctance to talk about his parents, assuming it was too painful, because he missed them.

Even Sophia did not know of Eishi Hara's existence, and was unaware of the crate in the shed that held the Japanese Moriage teapot, Eishi had left to her husband.

Standing up from the rock, Jack decided it was time he told Sophia, of the man who had taught him what it was to be loved. He was eager to share with his son Christian, where his enthusiasm for the written word, stemmed from.

Walking out onto the saturated logs, Jack gazed upwards to see a sparrow, looking down as it flew over. He smiled, as thoughts wandered to the surprise graduation gift awaiting his son.

* * *

The four friends sat in their retreat, silent and reflecting on their imminent separation. Both Frank and Christian, had secured jobs in Norelton, to earn money while they attended school. Pursuing a career in architectural design was Frank's goal while Christian wanted to be a doctor.

As the auburn sunrise began to overpower the light of the half moon, Skylar's thoughts shifted, as she had a lot on her mind.

For the time had come for Christian's departure from Ospero Falls, his family, and her. Yet, all she could do, was try to hide the worries she had.

Christian knew it would be difficult to leave Skylar behind. He had offered reassurance by reminding her he would be home for the last long weekend before the fall semester, and on holidays.

As the sun began to rise over the horizon, the two of them gazed at each other.

The silence was broken by Frank, whose words seemed to dangle in the cool air.

"We don't have much time left, before Mr. Stevenson is expecting us back."

Christian slid closer to Skylar. Leaning into his chest, she looked at his hands and smiled. She found comfort, knowing one day he would use them, to save lives.

Frank glanced over at Gwen.

"Why don't we take a walk, Opal, for old time's sake," he said.

She still fancied how he called her by her childhood nickname. As Gwen descended the ladder, Frank gave Christian a wink.

Skylar nestled close in Christian's arms, the only place she felt secure. He held her tight and whispered in her ear.

"Know you the land where the lemon-trees bloom? In the dark foliage the gold oranges glow, a soft wind hovers from the sky, the myrtle is still, and the laurel stands tall. Do you know it well? There, there, I would go, O my beloved, with thee!"

"Johann Wolfgang von Goethe," she said.

"You've been studying, Piper."

"I have the best teacher," she smiled.

Her attention was drawn to the daybreak that was upon them.

"Look at me Skylar," Christian whispered.

She stared deep into his eyes. He cupped her delicate rosy cheeks, and as his lips touched hers, he felt her tremble. When they parted, he was amused to see she had kissed him with her eyes open.

"I love you, Piper. Long as the roots of our Sitka are bound to this forest, my love for you will continue to grow.

She breathed in every word and let them settle within her.

"Oh Christian, I love you too. If you want, we can do something special to remember this night forever."

He was not surprised by how easily she aroused him. Skylar, filled with passion, enticed Christian with her sensuality. He swallowed the lump in his throat.

"No, Skylar. As much as I love you and want to be with you, I don't think you are ready to give yourself to me… then have me leave for university."

Relief overcame her and she let out a sigh.

"When the time comes," he said, "and we feel it is right, I know it will happen here. You are the one. Just as this tree is alive, so is our love for one another."

"You promise?" she asked.

He looked into her eyes and saw himself reflected.

"A promise is a promise, Piper," he said, placing his left hand over his heart.

"By hook or by crook?"

"Absolutely. By hook or by crook," he chuckled as they clasped their hands together.

"I can accept that for now," she giggled.

The shrill of the ferry horn heralded dawn's arrival. It was time to go. Then the horn sounded again, and Christian knew something was wrong. Skylar reached for his hand, and they hurried down the ladder. Gwen and Frank were waiting below. Again, the horn sounded. He counted every blast as they bolted through the woods.

When the horn finally stopped after seven, short horn blasts and followed with one long blast, Christian felt the hairs on the back of his neck rise and immediately, he wanted to get sick.

At the dock, they found Mr. Stevenson pale and distraught. They thought maybe he had taken a fall and was using the horn to call out for help. When he turned and looked at Christian, the nausea swept over him again.

"I am so sorry, boy," Mr. Stevenson said. "I don't know how to tell you, but I just received a call from the coast guard. Seems your father took a slip on the logs and fell back, knocking him unconscious."

Christian's eyes widened in horror, while Skylar clutched his jacket. Frank and Gwen shook their heads in disbelief.

"They reckon he slipped into the frigid waters this morning. When ol' man Aldrich found Jack an hour ago, there was no saving him." Mr. Stevenson made his way to Christian. Putting his trembling hand on the young man's shoulder, he sputtered, "Your father is dead."

Chapter 12

Affirmation

FOR CHRISTIAN, THE FOLLOWING DAYS PASSED IN A BLUR OF GRIEF AND denial that his father was gone. He held back his tears, though, trying to be strong for his mother.

Friends of the O'Connelly's supported them as much as they could.

Frank assisted Christian who, along with Jack's workmates, carried his father's casket from the mill, through town to the cemetery. With every step they took closer to the final resting place, the ground underneath grew sodden with the downpour of rain interspersed with mourning.

The cemetery overflowed with people who came to pay their respects to one of the hardest-working men they had known. Although Jack kept to himself, he had never hesitated to help anyone in need. All the businesses in town, closed their doors for the day. The lumber mill stopped running for the first time in 20 years, to honour the man who had died, doing the job he loved.

The 10am service for Jack was a haze of condolences, speeches, and a promenade of tears.

Afterwards, Mr. Aldrich approached Christian. His eyes were rimmed with red circles, and his mouth was downturned in grief.

"I have something for you," he said.

He extended and opened his hand to reveal the pocket watch that Jack had worn every day. It had a crack on the glass surface, yet to Christian, it was a treasured connection to his father. He accepted the broken item with tears welling up in his eyes.

"Thank you kindly, Mr. Aldrich," he said.

As the two parted, Christian examined the face of the timepiece. He imagined how his father had used the numerals to structure every moment of his life.

Christian closed it and was about to put it into a pocket when he noticed something.

On the back was an inscription. Peering closer, he read, *"I am the vine, and you are the branches" – John 15:5.*

The inscription was a reminder of the importance of abiding in Christ, just as the branch abides in the vine, to bear fruit.

Slipping the pocket watch into his jacket, he did not think of it any further. A week remained before he was to leave for Norelton, and amidst all the turmoil, all he wanted was a moment of peace.

Wanting to be alone, he made his way to the pier.

The ride was rough with swirls of choppy ocean slamming the sides of the ferry. Hank Stevenson called Christian inside the bridge and let him steer the old vessel. The two of them stood quietly for a while until finally, the silence was broken.

"I think there's something you should know," Mr. Stevenson said, his voice shaking. "Many times while you were in school, after your father worked long morning hours; he would board Carnelian here to travel into Averston. I often wondered why Jack spent so much time there, but as a man's business is his own, I dared not ask for fear of offending him. Besides, your father was a man who was well-respected, and it was not my place to question his actions.

"However, a few weeks ago – the day before your graduation – Jack went out as always to Averston. Upon returning, he told me how proud you made him, especially your dreams of becoming a doctor. Jack never doubted your success for one minute. I'll be darned if your father didn't confide in me where he went all those times in Averston.

You see, your father would walk the same worn path you had travelled many times, out to your beloved tree house. He wanted to go to the place that connected you both.

Jack told me, how he fondly recalled you scaling the Sitka, as a young boy with big ambitions.

"He shared with me, how he cried the night before your graduation. It tore him up to let you go, but knew it was time. Jack said, "I placed something under the old rug, that was lugged up there years ago. It was with reassurance; you would know what to do with it."

Christian stood, quietly as Mr. Stevenson slid into the captain's chair to take over the controls. He turned on the spotlight to make it easier to see, as the sky poured down around the ferry. Mr. Stevenson was a seasoned captain and docked the ferry safely. Placing his hand on Christian's shoulder, he gave it a firm squeeze.

"We all need something to believe in," Mr. Stevenson said. "Whatever enchantment that tree holds within its towering limbs has brought a lot of people closer together. If I were you, I would never let go of that. I knew your father well enough Christian, to say that he would want you to become the best doctor you can be. You are the reason he laboured all those years. Just remember, these are the times in our lives when our faith is tested. What you need to do now is whatever it takes to get through this… Your old man deserves that much!"

Christian managed a faint smile and shook Mr. Stevenson's hand, thanking him for the advice.

"I'll see you in a while," Christian said. "I have some thinking to do."

The rain softened. Christian sought out the pathway, as a brisk wind blew through the dense forest. Evamya and Jack were gone, he knew, but memories of them remained.

At the Sitka, the strapping 19-year-old reached for the rope ladder. Looking upwards, he whispered, "This one's for you, Dad!" Dropping the dangling, weathered piece of twine, he looked at the buttressed base of the spruce and touched the large, scales of the tree.

It would be difficult to climb but not impossible, as his father would say. Christian visualized his ascent and started to scale the trunk. As wet bark packed under his fingernails from several failed attempts, he gained hold of the grooves and climbed the tree. Stopping to catch his breathe, Christian leaned back against the sturdy branches to peer out at Rogue's Bluff.

Inside the treehouse, lay the rug Sophia had given them years ago. Christian climbed in through the window and bent down. Lifting a corner, it revealed a piece of masking tape. Peeling it off, there was a key, along with a folded piece of paper. Picking up the items, Christian turned over the key to notice the word *Doc*, was inscribed upon it.

With trembling hands, he opened the paper. He was filled with sorrow as he began to read.

My Dear Son, Christian

If you are reading this, then every step you have taken has led to this moment. Being your father has brought me great joy, while watching you grow into a young man has given me strength. At times, you made me see through your eyes, the beauty this world has to offer. I can recall a moment when you came to Skylar's defence and how proud I am of you back then having concern. You are blessed with your mother's kindness and my passion for the written word. I only pray that in the future, I can share with you, the roots of where I came from.

This key I have given you, is to something I know you'll cherish. Thank you for allowing me the privilege to be your father. I am honoured to say you are my son.

I look forward to seeing you become a brilliant Doctor. Remember to see your patients as people and not as their diseases, for this will be your redeeming quality. I Love you, son.

With my Profound Respect, Dad.

Christian's tears mixed with the ink of his father's letter. He wondered what the key was for and guessed his mother would know.

It was early evening when he got home, to find Sophia sobbing, at the kitchen table. They had not shared in their sadness over Jack's death, both trying to be strong for one another.

He pulled up a chair beside his mother and placed his arms around her.

"I am here for you to lean on," Christian whispered.

She looked up; her face wet with grief.

"You made him so proud with everything you've accomplished," she said, dabbing her eyes. "Did you go out to the tree house?"

He nodded. "What's the key for?"

She shrugged. "All I know is, he hoped it would lead you to another adventure."

"You mean he never said a word to you about what it was for?" replied Christian.

Sophia shook her head and answered, "I haven't a clue. But as you know, my aunt left us a great deal of money when she died. Since Gloria and her husband Frederick had no children, and they were both so fond of me, I inherited their fortune. It caused a lot of tension between your father and me. Because of his pride, he never wanted to take handouts. He swore that he would never touch a dime of that money. Nevertheless, when you decided to become a doctor, Jack understood that we would need to use some of the money. We agreed to set aside a portion for your education. Unknown to us was that you would receive a full scholarship. Therefore, this money can be used for your personal expenses. After all those years of being staunchly opposed to the idea, your father asked to withdraw some of the inheritance. He also started to work extra hours, which I think had to do with the key. I never questioned the matter any further, as I knew it must be important to him. Your father told me if something were to ever happen to him, that I should make sure you went to the tree house.

Upon your return you would need to go see Divino Canetti, whose son Francis worked at the mill with your father."

"But what about you?" he asked. "I can't leave you to go to Norelton, when you are in so much pain."

Sophia shook her head in defiance.

"Now you listen to me, son. Just as your father did not want you to give up on your dreams, I don't either! You need not worry, as I have Victoria and Olivia to check in on me. Besides, the church needed a new secretary, and Rev. Francis offered me the job. You know, Christian, deep down in your heart, leaving's the right thing to do. Now take this key to Divino Canetti. Your father made certain he'll know what it's for."

Christian leaned forward and kissed her on the forehead, inhaling the smell of her rose perfume.

Under the evening moonlight, he strolled the few blocks to the Canetti's house. Knocking several times, he was about to leave when the door opened.

Divino Canetti had emigrated years ago with his large extended family to Ospero Falls, hoping to find a place to call home. He was a man who cared about his community. His family's homemade Italian food was well-known throughout town at their restaurant, Canetti's Diner. Often, Divino would walk down to the docks to bring Francis a hot meal and always offered Jack some of his wife's cooking.

While the men ate, they would converse about the latest automobiles released on the market. All three were fans of Chevrolet cars and debated which model was better. In the end they would laugh, knowing nothing compared to the latest model, the General Motors Company produced in their busy factories.

In 1959, Divino's older brother Jon lived in Flint, Michigan and was employed by General Motors as a quality-control manager. Since he worked in a factory, Jon had firsthand knowledge of the cars rolling off the assembly line.

Bursting with excitement, he called Divino to tell him about the latest Cadillac unveiled at the Detroit Motor car show. Divino shared his brother's enthusiasm yet knew that he would never be able to afford, such a luxury. However, when Jack heard of the impressive automobile, a smile came across his face.

Only a few months ago, Jon made special arrangements for a delivery to Divino's residence. It would arrive in Ospero Falls, via the ferry, from the nearest car dealership in Averston.

Divino made preparations with Hank Stevenson, to have the car transported late in the evening, so no one would see it. Its arrival was to be kept secret, and the car stored in Divino's garage, until the time was right.

With Christian standing in the doorway, Divino Canetti slipped on his worn leather boots and motioned for him to follow.

At the door to the garage, Mr. Canetti turned on the light. Something lay concealed under a brown tarp. He gestured to Christian to help him remove the cover and as they did, both let out a deep sigh.

There, in front of Christian, was a candy-apple red 1959 Cadillac convertible with high tail fins and a white leather interior. As if in a daze, Christian let his fingers glide over the smooth surface. Mr. Canetti smiled and patted him on the shoulder.

"I believe you have the key to this beauty?"

Christian could only nod, reeling in disbelief at the gift his father left him. Reaching into his pocket he pulled out the key. His fingers traced the grooves of the word *Doc*, as the realization sank in that he was the proud owner of a car, many in town could only dream of driving.

Christian remembered the times Jack held him on his lap, so he could steer the old Chevy pickup.

Then later sitting in the driver's seat, Jack beside him, coaching him on how to manipulate the pedals.

Opening the driver's door felt surreal. Not until he slid behind the wheel and inserted the key into the ignition did reality sink in.

Mr. Canetti opened the double door garage. Christian waved him over to get into the passenger seat. When he turned the key, they smiled, as the engine purred to life.

Soon they were driving the quiet, gravel roads of Ospero Falls. Under the streetlights the glossy paint glistened. As the young man drove, Divino enthusiastically listed the Cadillac's features.

Christian's head swirled as Mr. Canetti detailed the four-speed automatic transmission equipped with a 325 horsepower, V8 engine. The whitewall tires, power seats and windows only enhanced the car's appeal.

After a short while, Mr. Canetti asked Christian to drop him off. Stopping in front of Mr. Canetti's home, they shook hands. Leaning in he said to Christian, "While I am deeply sorry Jack's not here with us, I'm sure his presence will be felt as you drive your new car."

Christian adjusted the mirror, then drove off to his home.

Pulling into his driveway, he tooted the horn. Sophia came running out of the house, holding her hands up to her cheeks.

"Oh, my Lord!" she exclaimed.

Christian laughed as he swung open the passenger door.

"Get in, Mom, we're going for a ride."

The commotion brought Victoria, Skylar, and Gwen out to their front porch. When they saw Christian behind the wheel, they whooped.

Christian pulled along the curb, put the car into park, and walked over to his girlfriend. Extending a hand towards Skylar, he brought her to the Cadillac.

Opening the door, he led his sweetheart into the back seat.

"My dear lady," he said.

Skylar blushed; Gwen's mouth dropped open.

"Well, I'll be darned," Christian said, "Gwen is speechless for a change!"

Skylar slid onto the seat's interior, in awe of the extravagant vehicle.

"I'll be back later for you two ladies," he winked at Victoria and Gwen.

The swift car hugged the rugged road alongside the ocean, while the moonlight blanketed the seaside community. After a few miles, Christian turned off the road to where his father had laboured, for years.

Slowing down, he drove out to the entrance of the gate to the mill and stopped on the other side of the ocean. Putting the car in park, Christian gazed up at the sky, layered with diffused starlight. Leaning back, he sunk into the seat. The leather seemed to mould to his body. Placing his hands behind his head, he inhaled the scent of the ocean that hung in the air.

The three sat in silence. The car, Christian knew, was more than a symbol of luxury – it represented the freedom to travel and get the most out of life, which Jack wanted for his son.

"This is where your father's life really was," Sophia said. "It was where his day began and, sadly, where his life ended. However, the truth is, he never left us in spirit.

Christian nodded before speaking, "I remember when I was nine years old. He took me here one morning to his favourite place to think near the dock. There was a large boulder that he would sit me beside him."

Sophia was filled with sadness. She patted Christians hand and said, "Your father spoke of the importance of giving to others the best of who you are and never forgetting where you came from."

The grief Sophia felt was brimming at the surface, yet she remarked in a soft whisper, "He reminded you the value of your roots, placed here by the hands of the Creator."

"He always saw the beautiful simplicity in everything," Christian said.

"I always felt your father was a protector," Skylar said.

"Since I didn't have someone to watch over me, he made sure to do that."

Sophia turned to face Skylar; tears began rolling down her cheeks.

"Thank you, sweetie, for saying so," she said, patting her hand.

They sat quietly for another few minutes.

Sophia spoke softly, "We best be going now."

They drove around for another 10 minutes, before returning home.

Christian stopped and parked in order to go inside and grab a sweater. Coming back downstairs, he found Sophia and Skylar sipping hot cocoa.

"I am off to pick up Gwen, Victoria, and Frank."

After a kiss on the cheek for each of them, Christian bolted out the door.

He offered Victoria and Gwen a ride, but first wanted to surprise his best friend Frank, about his father's gift. It was around 10 o'clock when he drove over to Frank's house and Christian was not sure if he would be awake.

Yet news travelled quickly in the small town. Pulling into the Whitman's driveway, Christian saw Frank waiting outside.

"Whoo-wee!" Frank said. "Thomas was right. It sure is a masterpiece! He saw you earlier, driving it around town with Mr. Canetti and came right over to tell me."

"Hop in buddy, let's go for a ride!" smiled Christian.

Frank got in the back with Gwen. Listening to the story about the car, he was torn between envy and happiness for his best friend. Once

Christian had gone back to drop off Gwen and Victoria at the house, Christian turned towards Frank.

"Would you like to take her for a spin?" Christian asked.

Frank felt a lump in his throat and nodded. Christian got out to let his best friend in the driver's seat, then walked around to the passenger side to get back in. With both hands firmly gripped on the steering wheel, Frank drove cautiously. Nearing the docks, he dropped his best friend off. Pulling away, Frank reached over and turned on the radio. Rock and roll beat through the speakers. As he got comfortable in the driver's seat, Frank began to whistle to the music.

Christian sat perched on the same boulder, his father had so many times before. As the moon's rays sparkled on the glistening sea water, Christian pulled out of his pocket something he had found in the car's glovebox. It was the Bible that had belonged to Jack. Tucked between the frail pages, was a yellowed envelope marked with his father's scrawl.

19th Day, 11:00 hrs.

"The measure of a man's life is through the honourable deeds he stands up for, and how he values forgiveness." To those who have taught me about triumphing over darkness: Eishi Hara, Evamya, Sophia, and Christian James O'Connelly.
Thank you for filling my world with so much love."
Signed,
Jack O'Connelly

Christian felt tears welling up and closed his eyes. Taking a deep breath, he decided to open the envelope. Carefully, he slid out the contents and unfolded the pieces of tattered paper. It was a letter. Christian began to read the remarkable story of Eishi Hara.

After he finished and wiped away his tears, Christian found at the back of the Bible the cross that Jack had carved from the willow tree. Attached to it was a piece of paper with a verse:

'Come now, let us reason together,' says the Lord. 'Though your sins are like scarlet, they shall be as white as snow; though they are red as crimson, they shall be like wool.' – Isaiah 1:18

Clutching the cross, Christian could see Frank pulling into park. Hopping off the boulder, he tucked the cross back into the Bible and made his way back over to the car.

* * *

The week passed quickly as Christian, and Frank prepared to leave Ospero Falls. Their travels to Norelton, would be a time of adjustment, in a new city.

As Sophia and Olivia fussed over their boys, Skylar and Gwen were not prepared just yet to send them off. Unbeknown to the two young women, Frank and Christian had planned one more night with them.

The evening before the boys' departure, they took the girls to Blackfine Theatre.

They sat in the middle row munching candy buttons and sipping fizzy sodas, laughing at the on-screen antics, and revelling in each other's company. After the movie ended, they headed home in the Cadillac. Neither Skylar nor Gwen, spoke of the approaching goodbye.

Frank helped the girls out of the vehicle. He looked over at Gwen and smiled.

"You'll do well in life, Opal. Remember the wisdom of our Evamya when life gets you down."

"You're alright, Whitman," she said, giving Frank a hug.

"Don't forget," Christian said to Gwen, "that you can't get rid of me that easily. I'll be back before you know it."

"That's good to know, because I will be waiting to pester you!" Gwen snickered, then stuck out her tongue.

Laughter filled the air.

"Don't worry about this old boy," Frank said to Gwen, winking at Christian.

"He's in the best of hands with me."

Skylar groaned and rolled her eyes. "Oh, please! We all know Christian's gonna be lost without his sweet Songbird."

Although she was joking, everyone knew deep down, she was hoping for it to be true.

Frank walked over and gave Skylar a hug.

"Everything will be alright," he said.

As they parted, Skylar nodded.

As Frank walked Gwen over to the house, he glanced at Christian.

"See you in a few hours buddy. We have a long day ahead of us."

Skylar fought back tears. For the first time, an awkwardness divided them. As much as he did not want to let her go, Christian knew they were only delaying the inevitable. Skylar sensed his reluctance. Gathering her into his arms, he kissed her soft lips.

"See you under the Sitka," he said, brushing her cheek.

"We will always have our tree," she smiled, then added, "I love you."

He placed his hand, over his heart, then touched her lips.

"Till we meet again, my Songbird. I love you with all my heart." Christian assured her.

Skylar turned, overcome with emotion, she burst into a sprint towards her house.

In the middle of town, the glare of the mill clock shone down.

Chapter 13

Routes

CHRISTIAN AND FRANK WAITED AT THE DOCK TO DEPART ON THE larger Seabliss Ferry to Norelton. As they stood beside the Cadillac, Sophia and Olivia said their farewells. In saying his goodbye's Christian scanned the crowd, looking for Skylar. Although he had discouraged her from showing up, Christian hoped she would anyway.

The ferry berthed and began to unload. Frank turned to his mother.

"Mom," he said, hugging her, "I will never forget all the sacrifices you made for me since Dad died. I promise to make you proud and build you the most beautiful house one day."

"Smiling, Olivia replied, "I have been blessed as your mother to watch you grow into a fine young man, now go on and make your dreams come true."

Christian leaned into the car and pulled out from the glovebox, the Bible that Eishi Hara had given Jack years ago. He placed it into Sophia's trembling hands.

"Father wanted us to have this," he said, "It is something he hoped to share with you and me one day when the time was right. I think now is that time. Please take it home. It will help you to understand and maybe discover a side to him that neither of us knew."

Sophia clutched the Bible, near to her.

Opening his hand, he showed her the wooden cross, Jack had carved as a young boy.

Christian explained, "Mom, I wanted you to see this before I take it. The letter inside the Bible will tell you all about Dad's faith and courage. I want to hang this cross from my rear-view mirror, so I never forget my roots and all that was sacrificed for me.

Sophia nodded her head in agreement, tears streaming down her cheeks.

"I love you, son. Never forget the path God has chosen for you."

He bent down and kissed Sophia' s cheek.

"I best be getting on Mom," he said. "I have a schedule to stick to. It will be a long three-hour ride for us."

She nodded and walked up beside Olivia.

Christian climbed into the driver's side of the car, with Frank in the passenger seat.

"Take good care of my Piper," Christian said to Sophia. "Tell her I…" He stopped mid-sentence. Sophia smiled and waved.

Watching the ferry sail off into the distance, the mothers stood arm in arm, until the ship became a speck on the ocean. Finally, they began the walk back to their homes.

It was afternoon, before Victoria decided to wake Skylar. All through the night she had heard her daughter sobbing.

Gwen returned from errands to find Skylar slouched over a cold bowl of porridge. She looked dreadful, with circles under her red, swollen eyes. Gwen pulled up a chair and placed an arm around her.

"Want to talk about it?" she asked. Skylar shrugged her arm and scowled. Gwen took the hint and got up. Walking away she sighed, then remarked, "Suit yourself, Bird Girl!"

As the weeks of June came and went, Victoria made sure Skylar kept busy, with Rev. Francis's sanctuary project.

The exterior completed and the roof placed, volunteers began to decorate the interior with modest furnishings. Enhancing the pristine setting of the sanctuary, was the lake full of brook trout. Skylar found herself drawn to the fresh, calm water many times, to cool off from the heat.

As the construction neared completion, Rev. Francis asked Skylar to suggest a name for the sanctuary. She was thrilled.

One night, she had a vivid dream where Evamya was pushing her on a swing. She smiled tenderly at Skylar, pointing towards the forest was a door, wrapped in Sweetbrier. A breeze came upon the girl, and in the wind, she heard the whisper of a name.

The next day, after service, Skylar shared with Rev. Francis the name – the Whispering Rose Fellowship. He liked how the name rolled off his tongue. Following a meeting with the church elders, Rev. Francis announced their approval. After a visit to Pebbleside Art store, Skylar brought the supplies to the sanctuary, to paint the name above the front door.

The doors to the sanctuary were to open in September. Skylar spoke to Christian on the telephone, telling him of her participation. He told her how proud he was. When the moment came to say goodbye, each said, "See you under the Sitka."

* * *

For Gwen, the summer had been a reawakening to her roots. She found as she grew older, more questions were arising from her African lineage.

In her spare time, Gwen studied people integral to the civil rights movement. Her attention focused on Rosa Parks, who had stood up in the 50's against prejudice and Martin Luther King Jr., who was now confronting the discrimination still rampant in the south.

Gwen was motivated by reading about previous generations of African-Americans who had sacrificed so much for their freedom. She was elated to hear of two missionaries from Swahili coast who had moved to Ospero Falls. One Sunday, after service ended, she introduced herself to Amos and Jawana Hurston.

Before long, the Hurston's encouraged Gwen to investigate her history and to be proud of her ancestry.

The young girl would sit for hours, listening to Amos and Jawana's recollections of a church mission they participated in, while tending to the needs of African people.

Even though they often suffered from illness, malnutrition and a lack of adequate shelter, the African people showed immeasurable kindness to the Hurston's. No one blamed God, Amos said, but instead praised the Lord for offering salvation.

An unbreakable faith bound the people steadfast to one another.

What began as a simple mission to provide the necessities of life, led the Hurston's to donate time and money to build a schoolhouse. When the Hurston's showed Gwen pictures of the school, she told them about her prized possession, the Brownie camera.

The gift from Evamya, had opened a world of photography, which Gwen cherished.

She often found herself travelling on the ferry to Averston to capture images of the Sitka tree. Passionate as she was about photography, word began to travel fast. Before long, Gwen was hired to take pictures of children's birthday parties. She was delighted to be paid for doing something she loved.

* * *

Mayor Georgio Ditton and Rev. Francis decided a celebration was in order, on the last long weekend, in September. A gathering was to be held, as a tribute to the opening of the Whispering Rose Fellowship. This was to acknowledge the hard work of the volunteers. A community barbeque was to take place in the Ospero Falls' town square.

Women baked strawberry-rhubarb crumble pies, while the men built a fire-pit for Melvin the butcher, to roast his pig. A group of youths began arranging various picnic tables, to be later adorned with red, gingham tablecloths.

The day before the September long weekend celebration, Christian and Frank arrived back home to the delight of their mother's, who eagerly awaited their arrival.

Skylar and Gwen knew it would be nice for the mothers to have some quality time with their sons. Therefore, they agreed to meet up after supper at the tree house.

It was a warm evening, with hues of scarlet the dusk. Skylar, dangled her feet over the side of the tree house. She became more excited as she saw from her view the Cadillac.

Christian and Frank got out of the car. Their appearances had changed over the past few months.

Frank sported a blond moustache, while Christian had let his hair grow. They looked more mature, which caught Skylar and Gwen off-guard. A gentle breeze ruffled the hemlines of their dresses, which were both white, with pink polka dots. Skylar had thought it would be fun to buy the matching outfits. Her sleek curves made the dress even more alluring.

The young men climbed the rope ladder and seated themselves on either side of the young women.

Frank whistled, while Christian scanned Skylar up and down.

"Oh my!" Christian said. "I would have to say you two are the finest looking ladies in town."

Skylar's cheeks reddened as she averted her eyes.

"Now you hush, boy," Gwen said. "You are talking like a fool."

"Nice to see you are still full of spunk," Christian said.

They laughed and began talking at ease. Christian told Skylar about his pre-med studies and dissecting a heart. Frank impressed Gwen with everything he'd learned about architecture.

As night deepened, they realized it was time to go home. The next day was to be full of activities.

Upon reaching home, Frank and Gwen exchanged quick goodbyes at her doorstep, while Christian and Skylar lingered in the front seat of his parked car.

The glint of the curved moon behind a cloud radiated across Skylar's delicate cheekbones. Christian moved close, tracing the outline of her mouth with his fingers, sending shivers down her neck. She yearned with every breath for his lips to touch hers. Leaning in, he cupped her face and parted her sun-kissed mouth with his. She tingled with warmth.

He wanted her more than ever. As they cradled each other, they listened to the strident melody of the crickets rubbing their wings together.

In the distance, the sea collided with the granite cliffs, echoing the forceful passion that Christian and Skylar felt, between them.

It was not until Victoria flicked on the light outside, that the mood was broken.

Christian opened Skylar's car door. Holding his hand out, he looked at how the dress hugged her curvaceous body. Marvelling at how she had blossomed over the summer, Christian drew her close for one last kiss. A minute later they finally parted. Winking at her, Skylar smiled and waved.

"Good night, Christian," she whispered.

"Good night, Piper."

Closing the door behind her, Skylar lingered, thinking of the time they had spent together. Slowly, she began to climb the steps to her room.

Christian awoke in the morning to the inviting aroma of breakfast. He stretched out, relishing in how good it felt to be home again. Gazing out the window, he smiled, thinking how easy it was to slip back into the simple life of Ospero Falls.

His thoughts drifted back to seeing Skylar's striking appearance.

She had always been beautiful, but she was maturing – and every curve of her body lured him. He found it difficult to be a gentleman when his hormones told him to seduce her. Christian knew how easy it would be for her to succumb to him and realized how selfish that would be. He pushed the thoughts from his mind – for the moment, at least.

Downstairs, Sophia greeted Christian with a peck on the cheek. She set before him a feast of potato pancakes, buttermilk waffles, and peppered bacon rashers. As he ate, they chit-chatted, Sophia telling him how busy she was volunteering at the sanctuary and working at the church.

Christian spoke highly of the summer pre-medical program intended to prepare him for his major, and of his part-time job at Norelton's aquatic centre.

Years of swimming in rivers and the ocean, under the watchful eye of his father, gave Christian a strong set of lungs. If someone was drowning, then he would be ready in action. He soon got to know by name, the people who frequented the pool for lessons and leisure. There was Eleanor, a bright, vibrant young lady who excelled at swimming and dreamt of going to the Olympics. Another person who stood out, was a lively red-headed girl whose blue eyes drew in the attention of many men. Christian had conversed with her on a few occasions. She liked to be called by her initials J.C. She was a girl who was unsure of her pursuits in a specific career, enrolling only to please her wealthy family. This bothered Christian; however, they were nothing more than acquaintances.

Once home, Christian had chosen to tell Skylar about his new friends. However, he decided it was best not to mention the girl with soft, auburn curls. He knew his girlfriend would interpret things the wrong way. Besides, he did not want to start an argument over anything.

After Christian had eaten breakfast, he finished helping Sophia with dishes. His thoughts were on the planned activities for the day.

Skylar had told him how blessed she was to be the one to pick a name for the sanctuary. It was her candor that Christian loved about her. He decided to do something for Skylar.

Waving goodbye to his mother, he sauntered out the door. Sunshine – a pleasant, unusual sight in rain-soaked Ospero Falls – greeted him. He savoured any chance to have the Cadillac top down.

Skylar had spent most of the night tossing and turning. Christian would soon be going back to university, only returning for holidays and breaks. It bothered her how much time he needed to dedicate to his career. He would spend at least seven years at university, plus a one-year internship, before he would earn his license. The duration was unimaginably long.

It was mid-morning when she realized she still had not heard from him. Hurriedly, she dressed in a red blouse and white skirt, and pinned her hair up for the sanctuary's opening ceremony at noon.

Racing down the stairs, she heard her boyfriend driving up. She hollered out to her mother that she was leaving. Outside the front door was a surprise she did not expect. Standing there was Christian holding a necklace made of intertwined poppies and daises. Skylar blushed.

As the two exchanged glances, she was noticeably touched by his simple gift, pleasing Christian with her reaction.

"I thought these would look nice on you today," he said modestly.

They are lovely, thank-you," she replied.

He leaned forward and gently placed the string bouquet around her neck, kissing her before stepping back. The sweetness of her lips made him smile.

She coyly added, "Juicy strawberry lip gloss. I bought it because I thought you would like it and it goes with my red outfit."

They laughed and walked hand in hand to the car.

Driving the few miles out of town, they were greeted by a large, bright sign stating:

Welcome To The Whispering Rose Fellowship.

Christian winked at Skylar, and she beamed with pride. He pulled into the dirt parking lot, looking at the sanctuary with awe. It was the first time he had seen the completed project.

He was impressed. Handcrafted logs interlocked to form the frame. His father had spent many hours stripping and sanding the wood, that now fit together like pieces of a jigsaw puzzle. He knew his father would be proud of the hard work everyone had put in, especially Skylar.

Stepping out of the car, they were greeted by Frank, Olivia, and Gwen. Victoria and Sophia arrived a few minutes later in the old pickup of Jacks. Rev. Francis stood at the entrance, welcoming everybody to the grand opening.

As all of them toured the sanctuary, Christian peered into each room, and inhaled the scent of pine that wafted throughout. It was bright yet cozy, offering comfort to those needing respite. Within Ospero Falls were various individuals, who needed a place to live out their days surrounded in beauty and peace. It was a place to say goodbye.

Outside again, Frank breathed in the crisp, mountain air.

"Now this here, my friends," he said, "truly is where God's hands have sculpted the land."

They nodded in agreement and mingled with the endless stream of townspeople who had started to arrive outside.

At 11 o'clock, Rev. Francis rang a chime that was hung by the door.

Leading his congregation to the front of the building, he placed a birdcage with two doves upon a structure draped in ivory cloth and waited for everyone to be quiet.

"Good morning to all," he said. "I want to thank each one of you, for attending today's special ceremony, to celebrate the opening of Whispering Rose Sanctuary.

Ms. Skylar Falls suggested the name, and after conversing with the elders, I was pleased to embrace such a spirited appellation. It brought me great joy, to see this young woman among the many volunteers, who devoted themselves to turn this project into a reality.

"Among them was one remarkable man who is no longer with us, who worked countless hours and dedicated his life to God. In his honour, I offer this dedication."

Rev. Francis lifted the birdcage and gently placed it on the ground. He pulled off the cloth to reveal a five-foot cobblestone monument with an engraved plaque. Clearing his throat, he read the inscription:

With this stone, we honour a man of wisdom, faith, and humility, who touched the lives of all those who were blessed to have known him. This marker is placed in memory of Jack James O'Connelly (1918-1965), who was committed to family, friends, and those in need. You are not forgotten.

Rev. Francis paused for a moment, before proceeding on:

"I never was able to tell Mr. O'Connelly about something that united us in our shared faith, and I will always sorely regret it. You see, before I became a minister, I struggled along the way to redemption. I was not convinced I would make a good preacher and even contemplated a career in the lumber industry. It was good work with decent pay. When I was a younger lad, I thought it might be my way out of seeking a spiritual path. Well, my mind was soon changed when at the ripe old age of 16, I showed up to work the woods. Back then, I thought I knew it all, and no one could convince me otherwise. All that changed when I met my new boss, Mr. Jack O'Connelly."

A murmur rippled through the crowd. Rev. Francis waited
for silence.

"Mr. O'Connelly took one look at me. He asked what a scrawny
stripling like me was doing working in the forest? Before I had a chance
to answer, he posed another question:

'What are you running away from?' His candidness caught me
off-guard. I mumbled, 'I'm not worthy of becoming a minister.' I will
never forget his reply to me. Looking me square in the eye, he said: 'The
world needs people of the cloth more than it needs men of the woods. My
advice to you is simple – turn around and march right back out of here
so that you can make something out of your life, son. Someday you will
thank me for it.'

"I never got the chance to thank the man who changed my path in
life, yet this is one of the reasons I wanted to see this sanctuary built. It
was an opportunity to serve the Lord and give back to Mr. O'Connelly
and the whole community. This was my way to redemption and now this
place is for those who are at a crossroads in their lives."

Reaching down, he opened the latch on the birdcage. The doves took
to the air.

Christian and Skylar cried freely, holding Sophia's trembling hands.
Even Frank couldn't hold back the tears. Olivia put her arm around him
when Gwen began to sing,

"Blessed Be the Tie That Binds."
From sorrow, toil, and pain,
and sin, we shall be free;
and perfect love and friendship reign
through all eternity.

Voices joined hers to sing the chorus, filling the woods with
harmony. Afterwards, Rev. Francis led them in prayer, asking God to

bless the sanctuary and give hope to those in need. He called on Sophia and Christian to join him in cutting the ribbon. Cheers arose as the scissor blades severed the red ribbon, signifying the official opening of the Whispering Rose Fellowship.

The congregation gathered inside to eat lemon pound loaf and sip blueberry tea. While Rev. Francis poured himself a cup, the O'Connelly's approached.

Christian shook his hand, while Sophia struggled to find the appropriate words to say thank you.

"Today, I am sure my father is smiling down upon us, giving you his blessing," Christian said. "Your dedication deeply touches Mom and me, and we know he would be proud of you."

"Thank you for your kind words," the Reverend said, bowing his head.

Struggled to contain her emotions, Sophia realized that Christian, with his kindness and love, was becoming his father. At times, Jack's loss was unbearable – yet today, she felt his presence.

As the congregation dispersed to head to town for the evening's festivities, Rev. Francis reminded them that he would see them at church in the morning.

Driving back, Christian and Skylar exchanged few words, revelling in the glory of the day.

He parked near the town centre and, as they got out of the car, the community of Ospero Falls welcomed them. An array of hanging baskets suspended from posts lined the area with bursts of colour. The bustling of people, intermingled with aromas of the bakery and deli.

Melvin the butcher stood steadfast at the fire pit, basting the slow-roasted pig, with his renowned tangy sauce.

Skylar and Gwen placed the gingham tablecloths onto each picnic table.

A few hours later, suspended across the twilight sky, were puffs of cumulus clouds.

Melvin remained near the spit-roasted pig until its skin cracked and browned. He took great pride in his work and was a perfectionist when it came to the finished product. Melvin guarded the browned pig that was nearly fully cooked.

Years ago, a group of young lads tricked Melvin into leaving his prized pork sizzling on the open, red coals; by telling Melvin his butcher shop was on fire! The Forrester boys had diverted his attention away for a few moments. Meanwhile, Gareth Percy Willy darted from the bushes to steal what Melvin called the crowning jewel of the pig; a bright, large apple, perched inside the mouth of the roasting beast.

As Gareth pulled the soft, cooked fruit from the mouth, he had not accounted for one thing – it was full of steaming heat! Gareth's bloodcurdling screams could be heard throughout town, as his hand was branded with a circular shape. He dropped the fiery apple and hobbled away.

Discovering his shop wasn't on fire, Melvin came running to see what all the commotion was about and at first seethed with anger that someone touched his masterpiece. However, his temper soon subsided when he spotted the wailing boy, hopping up and down, immersing his arm into a bucket of water. With a grin, Melvin wandered over to offer his assistance.

Years later, Gareth Percy Wilson bore the scar from that day and was teased for the nickname he had acquired, *Apple Willy.*

When night fell, fire illuminated the darkness, casting tall shadows onto the buildings. The festivities picked up with more merriment. Soon Divino Canetti brought out his violin, and everyone paraded around the crackling orange flames. Christian and Skylar danced along with Gwen and Frank, until others joined in. Casting off the brick structure of the Postal Office, were a spectacle of shadows cavorting, underneath the moonlight.

When the festivities ended, Christian drove Skylar home and walked her to the door. He leaned against the yellow paint of the entryway.

"I am glad I was a part of such a memorable day, Piper," he said.

Skylar was not tired and wished they could watch the sunrise together. Instead, she drew close to him and they stood kissing until they needed air. Letting out a deep sigh, she reached behind her for the door handle. Her attention elsewhere, Skylar leaned back to find the door flung open.

Victoria had arrived home a few hours earlier, exhausted from all the work she had done. She'd fallen asleep on the couch.

At this moment, Victoria was not amused to be woken to see her daughter traipsing in at daybreak.

Skylar lost her balance and fell onto the porch, her ruffled skirt coming up high above her knees. Christian laughed, but the look on Victoria's face showed she was not amused.

"Pick yourself up off the floor, Skylar Reigh Falls!" her mother demanded.

"Listen, Ms. Falls," Christian said, chastened. "I am very sorry for bringing Skylar home so late. It's my fault. We were having so much fun!"

Victoria softened, before replying, "Christian, I know today was a big day for you, but as a young man you have to understand that this is my daughter you are keeping out till the early hours! For goodness' sake, we all have to be in church this morning."

Skylar straightened out her dress, embarrassed.

"Sorry, Momma," she said, turning to walk upstairs to her bedroom. "Goodnight, Christian."

"Go on now, boy!" Victoria said. "I expect to see you bright-eyed in church today."

As the rooster crowed from the fence, Rev. Francis looked out at the sad sight of his congregation. Dark circles were predominant throughout the crowd; some people yawned. The night's festivities had gone on far too long, he thought.

A smirk came across his face as he understood that his audience needed to be woken up. He turned and nodded to the choir.

They then began to play, "He's Got the Whole World in His Hands." Soon the high-pitched sounds of the choir, saw everyone sit up in the pews, alert and listening to Rev. Francis's sermon.

"Where is your mom?" Christian whispered to Skylar.

"Can you believe it?" Skylar said, shaking her head.

"After all the lecturing she gave us to be at church, she told me this morning that she was not feeling well."

Christian was surprised, as he never knew Victoria to miss a service. Not wanting to probe, he decided to mention his concerns to Sophia later.

Back at the Falls' house, Victoria stood in front of the full-length mirror. Her brow was furrowed, and her hands were shaking.

Reaching under her nightgown, she fumbled for the same spot she had discovered several nights earlier. Probing the lump under her breast, she flinched in pain. Victoria was overcome with fear, as her body was revealing something she didn't want to believe.

Chapter 14

Deception

AFTER CHURCH, MUCH TO THE DELIGHT OF SKYLAR, CHRISTIAN TOLD her that he had planned an afternoon for them. Since he and Frank were due to catch the 6 o'clock ferry, they had to make the most of every moment together.

Although Christian was excited to be back home, the pressure of dividing his time between his mother and girlfriend, was building inside. When he was with Skylar, he worried about Sophia, and vice versa. Being unable to return to Ospero Falls, until Christmas, weighed heavily on him. Skylar sensed his restlessness.

"Is everything alright?" she asked.

"Just thinking about how much I miss this place," he said, "and the curves of your sexy body."

Blushing, Skylar ran her fingers through his thick, black hair.

Christian pulled over in the Cadillac when they came to Picea Point. It was a quaint, secluded area overlooking a turbulent run of the river. Skylar smelled autumn clinging to the mist. The leaves had begun to change colour.

Reaching into the back of the car, Christian retrieved a picnic basket Sophia had packed for the couple. It was filled with a selection of Skylar's favourite foods. They walked through the woods, away from the road as they wanted privacy. Bursts of lilac, yellow, and orange speckled the meadows.

Christian pulled a blanket from the basket and placed it on the grass. When they sat, Skylar leaned over and kissed Christian's neck. He was overwhelmed with the temptation to make love to her. For Skylar, the feeling was mutual. Every time her hands touched his skin, she shuddered. Abruptly, he pulled away.

Skylar frowned and twirled a piece of grass between her fingers.

"Why do you always stop?" she asked. "You take me out here all alone. What do you expect me to think?"

He could tell her feelings were hurt.

"Piper, I honestly brought you out here to have a picnic and share the day with the most beautiful girl in the world. I want you so much that it drives me crazy. But you know my parents raised me to be a gentleman. We are just not going to do it right here, with me leaving in a few hours. I know how that would hurt you even more."

Grabbing a clump of grass, she flung it at him, playfully. As much as she wanted to deny it, she knew he was right.

"Well then, let us see what goodies my mom packed for us," he said, opening the basket. He pulled out a jar of mint lemonade and poured them each a glass. They snacked on cucumber sandwiches and cubes of smoked cheese. Skylar's eyes lit up when she saw Christian had included something special for two of them. The lovers, fed one another a peach, drizzled in maple syrup.

When it was time to go, she helped pack up the leftovers.

Driving back, he could tell she was sad. The unspoken concern, arose every time he had to return to Norelton, making each goodbye harder than the last.

Christian put his arm around Skylar and squeezed her shoulder. She leaned in closer, savouring the moment.

They decided it was easier not to bid farewell at the docks. When they reached her house, Skylar tried not to linger. Looking into his eyes, she concentrated on the imminent separation. Pressing her body against his, she kissed him with the same desire they both felt earlier.

She got out of the car before her emotions took over.

"Hey Piper," he said.

Turning, she avoided eye contact, afraid she would run back and beg him not to leave.

"See you under the Sitka," he said.

"See you under the Sitka," she murmured.

"I love you, Piper!" said Christian.

"I love you, too," she mumbled.

Her strawberry locks, bounced up and down off her shoulders, as she ran to door and opened it.

Dashing into the house, she closed and leaned against the inside of the doorway. Wanting the pain to go away, she headed to her room. However, Skylar stopped when she heard the muffled sobs of her mother coming from the kitchen.

She quietly crept around the corner to see Victoria down on her hands and knees, scrubbing the floors; her tears mixing with the scent of Mr. Clean.

All Skylar wanted to do was wallow in her self-pity, so she hesitated to make her presence known.

However, Victoria's red hands were furiously scrubbing the same area over and over. Skylar knew something was wrong.

Walking up to her, Skylar bent down to gently touch Victoria's shoulder, startling her.

Her mother screamed, then demanded, "Why are you sneaking up on me like that?"

"Sorry, Momma, I did not mean to frighten you. I was wondering if you are okay," a stunned Skylar replied.

Avoiding her gaze, Victoria stood up and walked towards the sink full of dishes.

"I didn't hear you walk in. Sorry for snapping at you, but I am not feeling well.

Must be the flu I caught… Anyway, I just need some rest and I will be fine."

It did not make sense, Skylar thought. If she needed rest, then why was she scrubbing the floor and washing dishes? Something was upsetting her. Not wanting to provoke an argument, she decided to leave it alone.

"Okay, Momma," Skylar paused then asked, "How about I do the dishes and then fix you some tea?"

Victoria managed a faint smile.

The clinking of dishes, echoed from the kitchen, as Victoria slumped into the living room chair. Although terrified of the lump she had found, she was even more scared of a doctor diagnosis. Expecting the worst, Victoria felt betrayed by her body. She had never smoked; she ate well and walked every day. Why her?

Bitterness gripped her, much like the mass that clung to her breast.

Soon, the smell of chamomile tea wafted throughout the house. Skylar entered the living room with two, steaming mugs on a tray.

They looked at the clock after a long conversation and were surprised to see that it was past 8 o'clock. Despite the circumstances, it had been an enjoyable evening for mother and daughter. Heading off to bed, Victoria, and Skylar both had a lot on their mind.

Walking past Gwen's room, Skylar realized how much she missed her best friend. She was spending the night at Amos and Jawana's, which had become her second home.

Skylar slipped between the sheets, concerned about her mother.

* * *

September brought brisk weather, along with the change of the season.

For Christian and Frank, the adjustment from small town boys to university men required effort. In contrast, Gwen and Skylar eased back into the routine as senior high school students. Engaging herself into various studies, Skylar spent her down time reading books, which piqued her interest.

Gwen surrounded herself with people who were fighting for equality. Her bedroom walls were a shrine to those with whom she felt a connection. She was mesmerized by a handsome boxer named Muhammad Ali, who had made a name for himself in the United States.

Surrounding those who were seeking tolerance and clamouring for unity, was a nation full of discord.

With Christmas soon approaching, Skylar felt overwhelmed. Between her studies and volunteering at The Whispering Rose

Fellowship, the young girl was spreading herself thin. She was also part of the planning committee, for a Christmas Eve meal to be served to those less fortunate, at the sanctuary. As a result, she sometimes caught herself falling asleep during class.

Gwen occupied herself with an equally busy schedule, but still found time to follow the political unrest unfolding across North America. She was incensed by reports of black people in the southern U.S., being terrorized by white supremacists, calling themselves the Ku Klux Klan.

The information she gleaned came filtered through the Hurston's. Upon hearing of black people being mistreated continually, they decided to take action.

* * *

A few days before Christmas, when Christian and Frank were expected home for the holidays, a terrible storm hit the town. With it came gale-force winds and heavy flurries, which transformed the streets into mounds of blanketed snow. A weather advisory on the radio cautioned people to stay inside. Two days passed, before workers restored power.

Sophia, Victoria, Skylar, and Gwen were gathered at the Falls', huddled around the old, wood stove, when Hank Stevenson came to deliver the bad news. Being a ferry operator, he had heard on the radio about the poor visibility on the ocean. The phone lines were jammed; therefore Hank had come to be the bearer of bad news. Christian and Frank were stranded in Norelton and would not be coming home for Christmas.

Upon hearing the information, Skylar, disappointed, reached for Gwen's hand.

The realization that Christian would not be sharing a Christmas meal or opening the presents made her unhappy. She knew that it would be difficult if they came for Skylar's birthday and found themselves stranded in Ospero Falls. They had their important studies and lives in Norelton.

For the first time, the lovers would be apart for the Christmas holidays.

On Christmas Eve, realizing they were stuck in Norelton, Christian and Frank decided to make the best out of a bad situation. They agreed to meet at the HavenFayre Cookhouse for dinner at 6 o'clock. As they parted ways at Christian's dorm, Frank noticed a striking red-headed girl walk towards his friend. He reminded himself to ask at dinner who she was.

Returning to his tiny and cramped basement, where Frank lived under his relatives, he had gotten use to the small, lumpy cot. With his Aunt Ettie and Uncle Thomas away, until their annual New Year's Eve party, Frank thought it would be nice to invite Christian over to hang out after dinner. The space was not much, but it had a separate entrance and a key of his own. With the bad weather, he hadn't bought any food to stock up on yet. All his small fridge had in it was a jar of olives and old cheddar cheese. Frank assumed his uncle had left a separate key to the main level of the house in case he needed it. However, he was dismayed when getting home he found nothing and the upstairs locked. In a rush, they had forgot to leave a key behind.

Frank opened the fridge, delighted to find a bottle of cream soda chilled to his liking. About to open it, he changed his mind. After all, Christian had offered to splurge for supper and a few drinks. Looking at the clock, Frank sighed. It was only 5 o'clock, and his stomach was rumbling.

* * *

Meanwhile in Ospero Falls, Rev. Francis said grace over the abundant feast the women prepared, at the sanctuary for those in need.

The meal was special for it helped to bring cheer to those dealing with hardship. Three white candles were lit at the head table in memory of Oliver, Evamya, and Jack, while two smaller ones were lit by Sophia and Olivia for the safety of their sons far away.

When the time came to set the table, Skylar and Gwen placed an additional setting. His curiosity piqued, he asked who it was for? The Reverend smiled when they explained how it was a tradition in their family to set a spare plate, in memory of those who had passed away. Also, if anyone should show up unexpected, they would already have a setting ready for them. It brought the girls comfort, in knowing those they loved were still in everyone's hearts.

Meanwhile, Skylar was still struggling to come to terms with Christian's absence. Even though they spoke several times on the telephone, she expressed her frustration over the distance that separated them. The knowledge that he would not be coming home until a break in March, almost three months away, only bothered her more.

Yet, preparing Christmas Eve dinner for those in need, gave Skylar a sense of appreciation for things she had been taking for granted.

After dinner, they savoured a deep dish of spiced Christmas pudding with rum sauce. Stomachs and hearts full, they gathered around the hearth to sing hymns.

* * *

Frank waited, shivering under a telephone pole outside of the HavenFayre Cookhouse.

At 7 o'clock, he walked the two miles back to his uncle's house. Frustration replaced his worry, as he wondered why Christian had stood him up. What was worse, he had left his wallet in Christian's car and had no money for food or beverages. Clenching his teeth and rubbing his numb fingers, Frank trudged through the bitter cold and, with every step, cursed Christian under his icy breath.

Unbeknown to his best friend, when the red-headed girl had walked up to Christian, it was to ask for a ride home. Her car had run out of gas. Instead of worrying her parents, who were busy with Christmas plans, she spotted Christian and thought he would not have any objections.

He was courteous when she made an excuse that someone later would come for her car.

Driving through the outskirts of Norelton, they were enveloped in the soft glow of Christmas lights that swathed the city. The noise of the snow crunching under the winter tires reminded Christian to take it slow.

They were talking about school, careers, and family when Christian became sullen. He realized his mother would be spending her first Christmas, without her husband and son. The girl noticed his quietness and asked if everything was all right. For the next hour, Christian poured out his heart to her. She reached over and touched his hand. He took the gesture as a show of sympathy and thought nothing more of it.

Finally, they reached a mansion that stood prominently above Norelton's city skyline. It was a remarkable sight. Endless lights shone their lustre around the house festooned in swags of greenery and gold garland.

For a moment, Christian was speechless.

The girl asked him to come inside for a cup of cocoa, before he left. Not wanting to be rude, he accepted, thinking he would only be a few minutes.

The butler greeted him, and her parents introduced themselves. Upon finding out how kind he had been to give their daughter a ride, they thanked him and led him into the dining room. The large oak dining table was groaning with a buffet of assorted dishes, some of which he had never seen before.

The temptation was overwhelming, and he found himself heaping a plate tall with delicacies that seduced his palate. When he finished eating, the girl motioned for the butler to remove his plate. He was charmed by the way she commanded attention.

She leaned close towards him, and he noticed the dancing flames of the fireplace reflected in her steely, blue eyes.

For a moment, he was gripped by her red hair and ruby lips as if enchanted, until the crackling popping from the fire, snapped him back to reality. Shame overcame him as he understood she was trying to entice him. He abruptly stood up.

Looking at his watch, he saw that it was already 7 o'clock. He had forgotten his dinner plans with Frank! Panicked, he rushed towards the door, startling the girl.

"Sorry," he mumbled, "Thanks for the food!"

The snow had been falling steadily. As he swept off his car, he cursed himself for being caught up in the moment and not thinking of those who truly meant something to him. He hopped in, hoping he could make things right with Frank.

* * *

Skylar finished washing the last few dessert dishes in the kitchen of the sanctuary. Glancing up, she saw the guests mingling in the living room, enjoying each other's company.

One of the recent arrivals to the sanctuary was a woman with tangled strands of silver hair and white, glazed eyes that frightened Skylar. The elderly lady was blind and needed to use a wheelchair. She had been left on porch, with only a note tucked into her wrinkled blouse, stating they could no longer afford to care for her. She was taken in at the sanctuary, with the Reverend making inquiries. Ospero Falls was a tight knit community, and yet no one knew who she was. It did not help; the woman never spoke about where she came from. Though she was blind, she could detect the presence of anyone in the room, without them uttering a word. On occasion, she upset the others by pointing a bony finger and – in a whiny voice – murmured something about them.

One night, leafing through his Bible, Rev. Francis read again the passage about discernment; a spiritual gift allowing some individuals to be aware of things that had happened or were to come.

He thought of Evamya who was similar in foresight. Since the woman did not speak of her name, the word *espy* came into his thoughts, as it meant "to catch sight of."

Shortly after providing her with a namesake, there was an incident at the sanctuary. One day, Espy levelled her finger at Sophia. Speaking in a raspy voice, she said, "Do not despair, your husband Jack died a quick death. He did not suffer in the waters."

Sophia grew pale as silence penetrated the room. Rushing over to her side, Rev. Francis sputtered out an apology.

"I am so sorry Mrs. O'Connelly," the Reverend said. "Espy must have overheard one of us speaking about the tragedy that claimed Jack."

Espy snorted and wheeled her chair around.

The episode upset Sophia. From then on, she refused to have anything to do with Espy. Whenever Sophia came to visit, Espy was wheeled onto the back porch or into her room.

* * *

As Christian pulled up to Frank's bachelor suite, he was dismayed to see no lights on. He exited the warmth of his vehicle and walked to the door of the basement. Knocking loudly, he knew if his best friend were asleep, it would wake him up.

Frank sat inside bundled up in layers of clothes, miserably cold and hungry. His uncle had forgotten to turn the heat up, before leaving for his holiday. Upon arriving back at the house, he had devoured the olives and cheese, then guzzled the cream soda. By now his mouth was dry, and his stomach rumbled. Still, if he allowed himself to answer the door, it would only be to deliver a swift punch to Christian.

After nearly 10 minutes of standing in the biting wind and snow, Christian left, feeling like a coward for betraying his friend on Christmas Eve.

Driving off, he felt all alone in the world. The truth of Evamya's dying words weighed heavily upon him.

As for what you pursue, choose wisely, for sometimes what we desire stems from an illusion. I pray you'll know the difference.

In that moment, he wished he were back in Ospero Falls.

* * *

Driving home from the Bay Hospital, Victoria fought back tears, desperate to confide in Skylar about the lump. On more than one occasion, she tried to reveal her shameful secret to Sophia. However, the excuses kept piling up. Over wracked with guilt, she thought it best to keep the misery to herself.

Meanwhile, the lump grew. With every passing day, it consumed her thoughts and seemed to overtake her flesh.

She saw it as a solid mass covering her entire body, threatening to suffocate her in an instant.

Skylar's pending birthday weighed heavily on her mind. Victoria grew more depressed.

To ease the responsibility, Victoria asked Gwen to plan Skylar's 17th birthday, suggesting the party take place at Canetti's Diner.

As Christmas Eve turned to Christmas Day, nestled deep in the forest, covered in mounds of snowfall, stood the Sitka tree. An extended tip lay bare at the top, while the branches drooped beneath. In the isolation of winter, the treehouse waited to be enjoyed again in the spring.

Across the way, from the window of her room in the sanctuary, Espy gazed towards Averston. With her gnarled left hand clasped onto the arm of the wheelchair, she bent three fingers of her misshapen right hand inward.

Pointing with her twisted, index finger towards the mansion on Rogue's Bluffs, her lips curled at the corners.

Chapter 15

Complexity

On Christmas morning 1965, the Fall house filled with laughter and the aroma of honey cloves, basting a roasted ham. Olivia, Sophia, and Victoria were in the kitchen, hovering around numerous pots and pans on the stove. Each filled with traditional dishes; recipes passed down through the generations.

At eight o'clock, before the serving of breakfast, the woman grabbed their cups of tea and sat down in the living room.

To their delight, the snowstorm had passed, and streams of light filtered in through the icy windows, brightening the parlour.

Skylar and Gwen, drowsily came down the stairs and into the room. Within a few minutes, the young women ripped and tossed wrapping paper, towards every corner of the room. Victoria revelled in the joy on Skylar's face when she opened her gift: a cross-stitch of the beloved Sitka tree.

For Gwen, she adored the collection of frames that all three mothers bought for her, from the local photography store.

When it was her turn, Victoria removed the decorative paper from Skylar's gift. Opening the folds of tissue, she saw the crimson blouse she had been admiring for months. Its billowy sleeves were offset by hemlines of lace; a bright, red bow lay in the centre. She wondered how her daughter could afford such an extravagant gift.

"It's not the original blouse from the dress shop," Skylar said, "but I bought the material from Miss Jeans fabric store and Gwen helped me sew it!"

Victoria was overwhelmed. "It's beautiful, Songbird!"

Skylar stood up and hugged her mother, who pulled away rather quickly due to the pain.

This concerned Skylar, who made a point to remember to ask her mother later, about it.

Turning her attention to Gwen, Victoria said, "Thank you for helping, sweetie."

Skylar noticed, coming from the top of the Christmas tree, a shimmering sparkle. Moving closer, she drew in a deep breath. Reaching forward, Skylar saw it was a stunning bracelet.

Gwen stretched out to see. "Well, what is it?"

Skylar spun around. Tears welled up and she let out a soft "oh," as she clutched the silver jewellery.

"Christian bought the bracelet a few months ago," Sophia said, "and gave it to me so I could take it to Mr. Atwood for engraving. He spent months saving his money to buy it. While Christian could not be here with you today, your gift waited among the branches."

Gwen wandered over to see the bracelet. It consisted of interlocking sections of tree branches and, on the silver-plated band, it was engraved with the word *Piper*.

The timer on the oven buzzed; breakfast was ready. Everyone except for Skylar retreated into the kitchen. Gazing outward through the opaque window, she placed her warm hands on the glass, melting the frost on the other side. Blowing a kiss across the ocean, she wished Christian were with her.

* * *

In Norelton, Frank awoke Christmas morning to the pounding of fists on the basement door. Slowly, he stretched his aching body that had been curled up all night, shivering. The heat had also been forgotten about and was left only on low. Shielding his eyes, he reached for the doorknob, fumbling to open it.

Standing there in the brisk wind was Christian, holding a box of food.

In Norelton, a small convenience store was the only thing open. This resulted in Christian having to pay twice as much, yet he had a lot of apologizing to do. Frank saw pepperoni, bags of potato chips, and a package of buns. Jutting out of the box were two six-packs of chilled creamed soda, and a container of whipped shortbread. On top, was his wallet that he had forgotten.

Frank's mouth watered, but he was not about to let Christian off the hook that easy.

Looking at his shivering friend, he frowned.

"Leave the box here… you can go." he wryly said.

Christian stood there, shocked.

Frank slapped him on the shoulder. "Come on in, you fool! Man, you are lucky you brought a peace offering, after the crap you pulled last night."

Christian huddled in the dark basement, feeling even more terrible, when he realized how much Frank could have used his company.

"Listen, let me explain," Christian said.

"Forget it, man. I do not need to hear any of your pitiful excuses. Let's eat!" Frank smiled and rubbed his hands together.

After the hearty meal warmed their bellies, Frank and Christian decided to do something special to honour their fathers and their loved ones in Ospero Falls.

They were welcomed into the Cove Shelter by a youthful minister named Leon. He handed them aprons and put them to work, helping serve a holiday meal to those in need.

After dishing out countless plates of food, Christian and Frank finished up and returned to the university dorm. Attached to Christian's door, they found a note.

"I wished you could have stayed longer at my house, for dessert. Maybe another time… Merry Christmas, Chris. Luv Jaycee."

He had never been called Chris before, and it did not sit well with him. Looking sheepishly over at Frank, who had one eyebrow raised, he crumpled up the piece of paper.

Inside the warm room, he felt the urge to talk to Sophia and Skylar.

"I need to call home. The phone is down the hallway; I will be right back."

Frank nodded his head, picking up a car magazine of Christian's.

Wandering down the corridor, he stopped in his tracks, when he saw Jaycee approaching. "Listen," he snapped, "I got your note. I just want you to know that last night was a big misunderstanding. I have a girlfriend back home, and I am not interested, so back off."

"Sure," Jaycee said, unfazed, "whatever you say. I was only going to grab a jacket I forgot in my friend's room. Regarding last night, I was thankful to see a familiar face, in a time when I needed a friend. Sorry if you read more into the situation."

She went through the door of her friend's open room, grabbed her coat and sauntered back out, past Christian, without saying another word. His face reddened. Not wanting to draw attention, he retreated to his room.

"Are you alright?" Frank asked.

Christian struggled to regain his composure. After sitting down on his bed, he managed a weak smile.

"Yeah man, I'm okay. Just a little tired from all the work we did today!"

Frank began to set up the table for a game of cards. "So, how are things back home?"

Christian winced. "Oh, the line was busy," he lied. "I will try again later. Besides, I need to use the bathroom and there is usually a line -up."

When Frank felt it was clear to go, he snuck down the hallway to make a call.

* * *

Skylar sat waiting by the telephone for Christian, who she thought for sure would have contacted her by now. Everyone else was chatting and enjoying their presents. She wanted to thank him for the delicate bracelet that fit her wrist perfectly.

The conversations were interrupted by the ringing of the phone. Skylar picked up the handset.

"Hello?"

"Hey there, Skylar," Frank said. "Merry Christmas!"

"Hello Frank," she sighed. "Merry Christmas to you, too."

Frank looked down the hallway to make sure no one could hear him.

"Say… Has anyone been tying up the phone tonight?"

"No, I have been waiting by this darn thing half the evening! Why do you ask?"

"Oh… maybe the lines were jammed because of all the calls."

"Yeah, I guess so. Anyway, is Christian with you?"

Frank was about to reply when he turned to see the glare of Christian. He handed over the telephone. Christian turned his back on Frank.

"Hey, Piper! How are you?"

"Oh Christian, the bracelet is so beautiful! I was surprised to get it and only wished you were here so I could thank you properly."

Christian's guilt over the stupid decisions made by him in the past 24 hours. Turning around, he saw that Frank had grabbed his jacket and was leaving. Christian panicked.

"Listen, Skylar, I have to go. I will call you right back."

He hung up and dashed down the hallway after his friend. Catching up with Frank on the stairwell, Christian grabbed his arm.

"Just where do you think you're going?" he questioned.

Frank shook his head, "Listen, I have no clue what kind of crap you are trying to pull, but I do not want any part of it!"

Christian knew with Frank upset, that he only had one chance to explain. He motioned for Frank to follow him back to his room. Inside, Christian shared what happened with Jaycee and how he had screwed up by being at her home.

"I dunno, even though this Jaycee says you are reading too deep into things," Frank said, "I see it another way. From what you tell me, her body language is saying something different. If I were you, I'd stay clear of her. She sounds like nothing but trouble."

Christian nodded, relieved he had not misread her intentions.

"Thanks for the talk, buddy. I really needed it."

Christian remembered he had hung up on Skylar. As Christian bolted towards the door, Frank burst into laughter.

"Man, oh man! You better hope that bracelet will keep her from tearing a strip off you," Frank yelled, then added, "I will be waiting for you here in your room to whip you at game of crib."

Christian nodded and nervously dialed the telephone.

The phone rang once before Skylar answered.

"Why the heck did you hang up on me like that?" she demanded.

"I am so sorry, Piper. Frank and I had a slight disagreement about something, and we had to settle it."

Although it was only part of the truth, he felt better sharing it with her.

"Well, just as long as everything's okay now, I forgive you! Besides," she laughed, "how many times did you have to wait patiently, while Gwen and I squabbled over the years?"

"I love you so much," he said, relieved, "and I wish you were here with me right now."

"I love you too, Christian. I cannot wait until we are together again."

They spoke for over a half-hour about school, the sanctuary and loved ones no longer with them. Christian wanted to speak to his mother, but Sophia had fallen asleep by the warmth of the wood stove, Skylar said. Christian assured her he would call again on New Year's Eve to speak to her and Skylar then.

Back in his room, Christian and Frank spent the rest of the evening, playing crib.

* * *

The next few days passed quickly. Preparations were underway, for Skylar's surprise 17th birthday party, planned for New Year's Eve.

During the day, Skylar was kept busy by Rev. Francis, needing assistance to put away the Christmas decorations at the sanctuary.

Victoria, Sophia, and Olivia decorated Canetti's Diner, which was closed to the public. Gwen adorned the booths with colourful streamers and balloons. Sophia put the finishing touches on Skylar's favourite dessert, a three-layer carrot cake with buttercream icing.

Back at the Whispering Rose Fellowship, Espy's health was failing. Rev. Francis discussed with staff it would not be long before she passed away.

All this time, he was perplexed by the mystery resident. Every night, before retiring to his room, Rev. Francis would lift her into bed; and yet each morning, somehow, he found her sitting straight up in her wheelchair, facing the window. It spooked him to the point where he would ask the night nurse to check on her periodically through the night. Try as he might, to find who was responsible, the Reverend never received any answers.

After Skylar finished tidying up, Sophia drove Victoria to pick up Skylar. Olivia followed behind in her car, with Gwen in the passenger seat.

As a gesture of thanks, Rev. Francis invited them into the sanctuary for a cup of tea.

Skylar had finished helping for the day and wanted to change into the clothes, she brought.

Going into the bathroom, she pulled on a sweater and a pair of jeans. Twirling in front of the mirror, the light glinted off her bracelet.

Her thoughts were interrupted by the shrill ring of the telephone.

Coming into the kitchen, Reverend Francis motioned for Skylar to pick up the receiver.

"Hello, The Whispering Rose Sanctuary, how may I help you?"

"Hey Piper, it's me Christian, I wanted to wish you a happy birthday early!"

"Well, thank you. I just wish you were here," she sighed.

It felt good to hear her sweet voice again. Sophia had told him about her surprise birthday party, and he knew Skylar would be thrilled to celebrate with family and friends.

"I guess since I am speaking with a lady, should I be jealous of whose company you might be keeping tonight?"

"Stop that, you silly boy! You know my heart belongs to you."

Skylar looked at the wall clock and added "Oh my, it is already half past 5. I need to go, Christian. Please call me tomorrow."

"Okay Piper, have a goodnight. Until then, see you under our Sitka."

"A promise is a promise," she said, then hung up.

Christian sighed, wishing he could be there to share her special evening.

After the fiasco on Christmas Day, he had accepted Frank's invitation, to ring in the new year. The party would be hosted by his Uncle Thomas and Aunt Ettie, who had returned from their travels.

When the doorbell rang, Uncle Thomas, who was in the midst of a conversation, told Christian to answer it. Opening the front door, he was startled to see Jaycee and her parents.

* * *

As Rev. Francis escorted Sophia, Victoria, and Skylar towards the door of the sanctuary, he was about to close it when they all heard a piercing wail echo throughout the corridor.

Rev. Francis dashed down the hallway to Espy's room. Instinctively, Victoria, Olivia, Gwen, and Skylar followed. Only Sophia hesitated. When she entered, Sophia was not prepared for the sight before her. Lying in bed, Espy clawed her chest and gasped, while her pearl eyes bulged from their sockets.

They called for the nurse. While Sophia stood aghast, Victoria tried to help Rev. Francis clear the woman's airway. Espy's arms shot upwards, and she grabbed Victoria by the blouse Skylar had made for her. At first, everyone thought she was overcome by convulsions. However, the room went eerily silent when her flailing ceased, eyes focused on Victoria, she spoke.

"An affliction of the flesh curses you," she said in a raspy, broken voice.

Victoria paled as she struggled to free herself, from the old woman's grip.

As she broke free, the ruby ribbon on her blouse tore off in Espy's hand.

Pushing herself away, Victoria watched, stunned, as Espy's last breath rattled out. Attention turned to Victoria, who was trembling. Her limbs hung heavily, and the room began to spin. Closing her eyes, she slumped backwards. Skylar shrieked.

Chapter 16

Burdens

Sirens of an ambulance, rushed Victoria to Bay View Hospital in a blur of bright lights. In shock, Skylar sat beside her mother in the back. The Staff called ahead to the hospital, for when Victoria came to from collapsing, she needed assistance. Olivia drove Sophia, and Gwen in her car, into town. As the ambulance arrived at Bay View, an attendant put Victoria into a gurney and wheeled her mother away. An upset Skylar, followed inside, and slumped into a cold, metal chair. Olivia arrived with Sophia and Gwen. They took turns pacing the corridors.

Finally, someone escorted Skylar into Victoria's room.

While frost heaves created needle ice outside, the bitter cold clung outside as the beginning of 1966 was to be rung in within hours. Skylar sat rigid in a chair at Victoria's bedside. Her mother's paleness matched the nurses' starched uniforms.

Clinging to the hard railing of the hospital bed, Skylar could see through the half-open door, an ambulance attendant speaking to Dr. Gregson. She was numb, overcome by the fear lodged in the pit of her stomach.

Victoria looked upward at Skylar whispered, "It's okay Songbird."

Dr. Gregson entered, and placed his hand on Skylar's shoulder. He asked her to join him so he could speak with both of them.

"Victoria, upon examining you tonight, I found a lump in your breast of a considerable size. We will have to do a biopsy on the mass. There may be more surgery required if it is found to be cancerous. I will keep you informed at every stage along the way, and if you have any questions, please feel free to ask."

The word *cancerous* scared Skylar. She felt as if a blanket of stinging nettles, had been draped over her. Pressing her fingernails hard into her palms, she then released. In a daze, Skylar rose from the chair to tell Sophia and the others.

Afterwards the Doctor asked Nurse Ethel to administer a low dose of sedative. With a drip in her arm and another hooked up to a monitor, an exhausted Victoria fell asleep.

* * *

The clock neared midnight. Frank had sensed Christian's discomfort when Jaycee showed up. They watched with suspicion as the cheerful red head worked the room, commanding attention.

Christian excused himself and went into the office. He wanted to call Skylar again. Something didn't feel right. About to dial the numbers, he sensed someone behind him in. Turning around, he saw that Jaycee had followed him. She moved closer to where he stood. The smell of spicey amber sweetness infiltrated his nostrils. With heart racing, Christian looked for a way out. He panicked when she smiled, pressing her body against his.

"You like my perfume?" She cooed; "It's called Tabu."

Christian squirmed and dropped the telephone receiver.

"I just came to get my New Year's kiss," she said. "It's a tradition around here, you know, to find the prettiest girl and offer her your best wishes."

He inched past Jaycee and made his way towards the door.

"Well, I guess you will have to find some other guy, because it's not going to be me."

Frank was relieved when he saw his best friend leave the room and make his way over.

"Why the hell didn't you help me out?" Christian asked.

Frank slapped him on the back. "You did a great job of escaping without me interfering," he chuckled.

Christian rolled his eyes and shook his head.

"Will you let it go already? I mean I have paid enough for screwing up Christmas Eve because of her," he implored.

"It's all good my friend, I have your back!" Frank winked and grinned.

Years later, he would carry the regret of not intervening sooner.

Grabbing two glasses of champagne, Frank passed one to Christian. Soon they joined the partygoers, who began counting down to the arrival of 1966.

* * *

When the clock struck midnight, no one in Victoria's room cheered. Happiness had been sucked out, leaving only uncertainty.

Skylar wiped her cheeks with a scarf, Gwen had given her.

Taking a deep breathe, she resumed her bedside vigil, praying to God.

* * *

Frank and Christian retreated downstairs with a bottle of whisky they had swiped. As Frank set up two glasses, his best friend poured a vast amount into each one. Clicking their glasses together, both men said at the same time, "To our fathers!"

The next pour was for Evamya. Christian made another toast,

"To Evamya who left this world, a better place through her knowledge."

By the time the next drink was dealt, the young man, decided it was better to telephone Skylar the next day. It was late, and Christian was drunk.

* * *

Skylar awoke on New Year's Day with stiffness in her neck, having fallen asleep beside her mother. She rubbed the sleep from her red-rimmed eyes and saw that Victoria was awake.

Victoria wanted to speak, to reassure Skylar everything was going to be okay, but she was weak. Skylar took Victoria's hand in hers and tenderly rubbed it.

"Hey, Momma," she said, trying to sound chipper. Victoria smiled.

Nurse Ethel appeared, took her temperature, and wrote on a chart. Pouring a glass of water, the Nurse placed a straw inside, and handed Victoria the glass. Her parched lips drank the liquid. Sitting in silence, she mulled over the situation.

The sight of her mother's weakness made Skylar uncomfortable.

Not having the chance to speak with Christian, as she was at the hospital, only made her feel worse.

Skylar had told Gwen, Olivia, and Sophia to go back home and get rest.

It was now New Year's Day as she exited the door and into the corridor. Leaning against the hallway, Skylar was anxious with worry. Sophia who had been waiting for more news, greeted her in anticipation. Skylar began to heave with muffled cries. Knowing the young girl was physically and emotionally exhausted, Sophia wrapped her arms around her.

Olivia and Gwen, who had went to the hospital, left after midnight, and returned in the morning, with freshly muffins and hot cocoa.

Sophia brought Skylar over to them in the waiting area and sat her down.

The hospital doors opened as Reverend Francis walked through and came over to sit and speak with them.

"I apologize with not getting here sooner," he said and added, "Espy passed away and it's a complicated muddle trying to figure out what to do. With no family coming forward, she will be buried at the old cemetery by the church. There won't be a service, but I will of course say a few words. I am here now to see Mrs. Falls and let her know I am praying for her and you too young lady."

As he stood, the Reverend looked over at Skylar and said, "You're in good hands with those who care for you. Just remember God is near whenever you need him."

She remarked, "Thank you very much Reverend Francis. Momma and I appreciate it."

Nodding, the Reverend went on his way to Victoria's room 37 J.

Olivia brought out the thermos and poured a cup of hot cocoa, while Gwen handed out a warm muffin to Skylar.

"It's Evamya's recipe," she said, then added, "We had a birthday surprise for you planned at Canetti's Diner, with your favourite treat… carrot cake.

Skylar shrugged, "I won't be celebrating this year, tell them they can have it."

Gwen felt badly for her best friend and didn't respond.

As Skylar took small bites of her muffin, her stomach twisted with worry seeing Dr. Gregson approach.

"I would like a few moments alone to speak with Ms. Falls, please," he said.

Skylar shook her head, "If you have more news to tell me about my mother, then you share it with all of my family."

Dr. Gregson sat down.

"Upon examining Victoria, I discovered a mass in her left breast that is consistent with the diagnosis of breast cancer. Your mother has invasive ductal carcinoma, which is the most common type of invasive breast cancer. As far as treatment is concerned, I will be honest with you. This kind of breast cancer calls for radical mastectomy, in which we remove the affected breast and auxiliary lymph nodes.

"Like all of you, Victoria was explained in full detail the procedure, as well as the risks involved. She has given her full consent to proceed with the removal of her left breast.

If any of you have further questions, I will be available after my rounds. Right now, Victoria has asked to only see her daughter."

"I think it's best if one of us stays," Sophia said to Olivia.

Gwen clutched Skylar's trembling hand. "Do you want me to wait with you?"

Skylar shook her head. At that moment, all she wanted was Christian's hand in hers.

Standing up, Skylar walked in a daze, towards her mother's room. As she entered, Reverend Francis was praying over her mother.

* * *

Christian and Frank slept most of New Year's Day. They had passed out the previous night in a drunken stupor. When they awoke, only the lingering sour smell of the liquor remained.

Frank awoke and tussled with the tangled blankets, as he stumbled towards the bathroom. Christian tried to get up from the sofa chair he had passed out in. As he attempted to be first to the toilet, he tripped over the rug. Frank ultimately won and hung his head over the bowl with one hand against the cold cement wall for support. Yesterday's celebratory food was making a reappearance.

Christian glanced over at the clock and realized Skylar was probably wondering why he had not called.

"Something's not right," he muttered.

Frank turned around. "What did you say?"

"It's something Evamya used to tell me about the hairs on my neck."

Uncle Thomas hollered downstairs for Christian to come up, for a telephone call.

* * *

As Skylar sat quietly by her mothers hospital bed, Victoria stroked her cheek. She felt it was important to promise her daughter that everything was going to be okay, even if she feared the unknown. With the blinds closed, Victoria took Skylar's hand and placed it on her chest.

"Now you listen to me, Songbird. I know you may find it hard to understand why I'd be so eager for them to lop off a body part, but it's only just a piece of me and not what makes me complete. I'd rather them cut it out if it is cancerous, because I want to be able to grow old with you. Do you understand what I'm saying?"

Her daughter turned away, silent. Victoria understood her remining quiet, had pushed Skylar away.

"How could you not have told me – your daughter! – what you were going through?"

Before Victoria had a chance to reply, Skylar marched out of the room, leaving the hospital.

Walking back home through the bitter cold, she pushed away any misgivings.

Arriving home, the stillness of the warm space was cold with the void of life. Gwen had decided to stay over at Sophia's. Trudging upstairs with her boots still on, Skylar entered into the bedroom. Reaching for her quilt off her bed, she towed it over to the wall and nestled underneath the painting of the Sitka spruce. She imagined the branches of the tree all around her. As she welcomed the invitation to escape from reality, this was her safe haven. Within minutes, Skylar was fast asleep on the hardwood floor.

* * *

Christian reached for the telephone, knowing by the look on Uncle Thomas's face that something was wrong.

"Hello?"

"Thank goodness I have finally reached you!" Sophia said.

"What's the matter, Mom? Is it Skylar?"

"Well, yes and no, honey. It's Victoria. She is in the hospital, and they are planning to do surgery on her. She collapsed at Skylar's party."

"What is the matter?"

"Oh, I am afraid it's not good." The words hung in the air then dropped like a load of bricks. "Victoria has breast cancer."

"Oh no! What about Skylar? How come she didn't call me? Mom, where is she?"

"Calm down, dear. That is why I am speaking to you. Nurse Ethel saw Skylar leave upset. I returned to Bay View Hospital to speak with Victoria. She shared Skylar was upset with her for not telling her about the lump. She is not handling things too well. Gwen saw Skylar walk by our house in a huff and go into their place. Has she tried to reach you?"

"No, Mom, I have not heard from her. I can't believe it. Poor Piper, she must be devastated! What's the prognosis?"

Sophia managed a faint smile. The doctor in him was appearing.

"Well, they have to remove her left breast. She paused and whispered into the receiver, as if cancer was a dirty, unladylike word. "If the cancer has spread, only time will tell."

Christian's thoughts raced. He knew he should be with Skylar; she needed him.

"Damn it!"

"Watch your tongue! It is no use getting all worked up. Anger will not help the matter any."

"Sorry, Mom. You know that I should be in Ospero Falls," he lamented, "but I'm stuck here! What good is that?"

"The best thing you could do for Skylar is to write her a nice letter," Sophia offered advice.

"Tell her what is in your heart, son. Let Skylar know you are there for her."

"You're right, Mom," agreed Christian. "Please, just let me know what is going on, and keep watch over Skylar. Tell Piper that I love her."

"I will do," Sophia assured her son. "I am going to check on her later. I imagine she will be found sleeping under the painting of the Sitka tree."

Christian sighed, knowing Skylar felt safe there. Over the years, he had come to understand how important the tree was to her. He recalled the time when at their tree house, Skylar revealed her heart was connected to the spruce, in such a way, she felt it was her spirit tree.

"Thank you for calling, Mom," said Christian, then added, "I'll talk to you in a few days. I love you!"

"I love you too, dear. I will let you know if anything changes. Bye for now," replied Sophia.

Christian stood clutching the handset tightly after his mother hung up. Uncle Thomas's hand on his shoulder snapped him back to reality.

"Are you okay, boy?"

"Yeah, I'm alright. I just need some time to myself."

Down in the basement, Frank could tell he was unsettled.

"Want to talk about it?"

"No thanks, Frank. If it's alright with you, I am going to head back to campus. I just want to be left alone for a while. Your uncle wants you to call your mom. She will fill you in on everything."

"I understand, just remember, pal – I'm here for you."

As much as he was grateful for both his mother and Frank, Christian yearned to talk to his father, who he missed more than ever. He decided to leave Skylar rest and call her later from campus.

* * *

It was evening when Skylar awoke to the aroma of soup. She heard the crackling of the fire in the wood stove. Sophia and Gwen talked in hushed tones around the kitchen table. Pangs of hunger cramped her stomach as she stretched on the floor. Making her way to the stairs, she realized her boots were still on. They made the steps creak even more on the aged hardwood. The conversation between Sophia and Gwen ceased when Skylar entered the kitchen. They had set the table with some of her favourites; fresh, homemade buns and borscht. A brewed teapot of steaming English Breakfast was beside a plate of whipped shortbread cookies. Skylar could not help but smile at the thoughtfulness. Sitting down, she sighed.

"Thank you both," she smiled. "Everything looks delicious."

A look of relief swept over Sophia and Gwen. Sitting down, neither spoke of Victoria, wanting Skylar to be able to eat her meal in peace.

* * *

Christian went to the campus library and in waiting to speak with Skylar, he wrote a letter expressing his love and support. The ink flowed as he opened up, letting her know of his concern. He was relieved that mail service had resumed, and he still had a few stamps left. If everything were on schedule, his letter would arrive in a day or two via a floatplane. Licking the envelope, Christian imagined her delicate hands unfolding the paper, to reveal the letter of reassurance.

Stopping in to drop off his treasured mail, Christian was in line, when he smelled a familiar perfume. Turning around, it was Jaycee.

"Fancy meeting you here," she smiled. Her lips were covered in a shiny burgundy gloss.

Christian tried to avoid eye contact.

"Um, yeah Hi Jaycee."

Abruptly, the package she was holding, slipped from her hands. As Christian went to help her, Jaycee bent down, revealing a low-cut blouse.

The Postal worker interrupted the moment.

"Excuse me Sir, your next… in line."

Christian handed over his letter, to be mailed to Skylar, and bolted as fast as he could.

* * *

After dinner, near the warmth of the wood stove, Skylar sat sipping her tea. When the phone rang, it startled her and nearly spilled her cup.

She set it down before picking up the receiver. Skylar was relieved to hear her boyfriends voice.

"Oh Piper, finally my love!" Christian remarked.

"Christian it is so good to hear your voice!" Skylar exclaimed.

"I am so sorry to hear about your mom!" he replied.

"Thank you so much! This has been awful for her and difficult for me to deal with. Your mom has been amazing, along with Gwen and Olivia, I have been blessed to be surrounded by so many caring people!" said Skylar.

Christian did miss, how everyone in Ospero Falls looked after one another.

"That is so great Piper, as I have been worried about you," he shared. "I love you so much that it hurts to know that I am way over here and cannot hold onto you."

Skylar was relieved and wished he could be with her during her heartache.

"Christian, I love you beyond measure! I am so grateful you called. Just keep momma and I in your prayers," she said.

"Of course, I will call you in another day, I just don't want to tie the phone line up. If you need me call Frank's Aunt and Uncles home, as you have the number," Christian offered with assurance.

"Okay, I appreciate it! Skylar added, "See you under our Sitka."

"A promise is a promise," replied Christian, before he hung up.

Afterwards, Gwen and Sophia came into the parlour room and sat upon the settee.

"I am glad you were able to speak with Christian," Sophia smiled.

Gwen spoke, "I can't imagine how hard this is on you."

Skylar looked down before replying she said, "You both know she should have told me; at least then I could've helped her deal with it. Tell me one thing, did either of you know?"

They shook their heads.

"Sweetie," Sophia said, "I know you are upset with your mother. However, her surgery is within the next few days. We all understand how much Victoria loves you. Although I am not making any excuses for her, I do believe she needs you now, more than ever."

"Go talk to her, Skylar," Gwen said, "because if you don't and something worse were to happen, it would be awful. Dear Lord, if Gramsy were here, you would be getting a talking-to!"

Skylar frowned. She knew they were right but was consumed by resentment.

"You know, I just wish God had not cursed us."

Gwen's eyes widened.

"Hush now!" Sophia said. "The good Lord did not afflict this on your momma or you, child. If anything, it is the devil trying to turn you against your faith.

"No matter what, you should be driven to your knees in prayer!"

Shame swept over Skylar as she realized blaming the Lord was not the answer.

Bursting into tears, she cried, "I'm sorry!"

Gwen and Sophia stood up and came over to Skylar. Wrapping their arms around her, they held on tight.

After some time had passed, she excused herself and went to her bedroom.

When she awoke, her eyes struggled to focus. Looking over at her watch, she saw it was after 11 o'clock. She decided to get up to go to the kitchen for a late snack.

Sneaking downstairs, she made her way to the refrigerator and opened it to grab the glass milk pitcher. Turning toward the counter, something out of the corner of her eye, caught her attention. Skylar dropped the pitcher, which smashed all over the linoleum. Sitting a few feet away at the breakfast table, with a stern look on her face, was Evamya.

Gwen heard the commotion and scrambled down the stairs, leaping two at a time. When she flicked on the kitchen light, she saw Skylar hunched in the corner, whose face was pale. Shards of glass, twinkled in a pool of milk, spread across the floor.

Gwen backed away and pulled on her gumboots. Stepping around the glass, she made her way to Skylar, who had a blank stare on her face.

"Hey Skylar, it's okay. It's me, Gwen."

Skylar kept looking off into the distance.

"Alright, that's enough now. You're scaring me. Say something, will you?"

Skylar pointed at the empty chair where she had seen Evamya.

"S-S-She was right there," Skylar stammered. "I swear to God!"

Gwen turned slowly, an eerie feeling creeping over her.

"Who was there, Skylar? I didn't see anybody."

Skylar looked into Gwen's eyes.

"It was… I mean, I could have sworn that I saw Evamya staring at me."

Gwen stood up quickly and leaned back against the wall.

"Okay, this isn't funny anymore, Bird Girl. If you are trying to get back at me, then you're gonna be really sorry for it."

Skylar shook her head and rubbed her eyes.

"No, Gwen. I promise you I'm not playing any games. I came down here to get some milk. When I turned around, Evamya was sitting there… And boy, did she look furious!"

Gwen knew by the look on Skylar's face that she was not pulling a prank.

"Okay, well guess what. I have some news for you – Evamya's dead!"

Skylar rolled her eyes. "Yeah, no kidding."

The telephone rang, startling them. Gwen picked up the phone.

"Hello?"

"Hi sweetie, it's me, Sophia. I was having trouble sleeping when I saw your lights come on. Are you girls alright?"

"Yes, Mrs. O'Connelly, we are okay. We wanted a glass of milk, that is all. Thanks for your concern, though."

"I will speak with you tomorrow then, dear, goodnight!" replied Sophia.

As Gwen hung up the phone, she saw the colour return to Skylar's face.

"Oh, we're alright, Mrs. O'Connelly. Skylar here is only seeing dead people!"

Skylar stood up and reached for the mop, sulking as she began to clean up the mess.

"Quit your joking and go on to bed, Gwennie, I've got this," she retorted.

Gwen shook her head, "Oh, I certainly will not be getting any more sleep tonight. How about I make some tea, and we never talk about this again, okay?"

Skylar nodded in agreement, "Fine by me."

In the morning, Skylar had turned to her room and drifted in and out of sleep, exhausted from the night before. She woke to see Gwen sitting on the edge of her quilt, holding an envelope.

"This came for you today," she said. "I thought you would like to read it."

Skylar took the envelope and recognized the handwriting.

"I will leave you be for now," Gwen said. She wanted to talk about the incident in the kitchen but doubted there was an explanation.

Christian had never written her before, Skylar thought. Opening the letter, she imagined the tenderness of his lips brushing against the paper and his tongue licking the envelope. She pulled out the letter with trembling hands.

Carefully unfolding the pieces of paper, she sighed and began to read his gentle scrawl.

Dearest Piper,

I write to you offering my deepest sympathies concerning your mother's cancer. My mother informed me about her hospitalization. You have assurance that Dr. Gregson will do whatever he can to help her. I am concerned, as I have heard how upset your mother has made you by keeping her disease a secret. I cannot imagine how helpless you must feel right now. However, I am sure she did not mean to hide her illness from you but was scared. You have to place yourself in her positions and just imagine how she must feel, betrayed by her own body. Your mother has only you in her life and needs you now.

As for the miles that separate us, you know I would give anything to be there by your side. Still, the distance between you and I is connected heart to heart. I want you to close your eyes. Now go to our special place where you and I connect; feel the love we have for one another. Now open your eyes and look around. I am right there beside you.

We are under the Sitka tree's green boughs, gazing at the flickering stars, scattered across the night canvas. As you turn to look at me, I can see tears cascading down your cheeks. Leaning over, I gently kiss them away. In the morning, when you awake, I will still be by your side, listening to the lull of the ocean, with you in my arms. For me, this is as real as the passion we have between us and the beautiful truth that Our Creator, is the master of our fate. With much love to you, this is not goodbye… It is only 'See you under the Sitka tree!' May the good Lord continue to watch over you and your mother.

Missing you beautiful Piper…

Much love,

Christian xx

The words lingered; evoking a range of sentiments. She was overjoyed Christian had written her, yet Skylar felt the burden of shame, at how she had been dealing with her mother.

Looking at the clock, it was almost noon, and a sense of panic overcame her. She placed the letter from Christian on her dresser.

Minutes later, she was out the door, running to the hospital.

A few blocks away, she arrived at Bay View Hospital. Catching a reflection of herself in the entrance, Skylar saw a dishevelled girl looking back, dark circles under dull eyes, hair wisped in a tangled mess. She regretted leaving the house, without a hat.

Inside, she hurried along the corridor to Victoria's room.

Opening the door, she saw the bed empty and stripped of its sheets. Panicking, she turned and collided with Nurse Ethel, who held Victoria's folded clothes.

"I am so sorry, dear."

Chapter 17

Renewal

In shock, Skylar couldn't respond.

Nurse Ethel shot her a puzzled look. "Are you alright, honey?"

Skylar remained speechless.

"I realize that you would have liked to see your mother before the surgery," Ethel said, "but she knows how much you love her."

Skylar grabbed onto a chair as confusion set in. Patting her shoulder, the nurse smiled.

"Now then, I have brought back your mother's freshly cleaned clothes, and her sheets will be ready before she returns. You know your mother is in good hands, with a surgeon as fine as Dr. Gregson."

Realizing she had misunderstood, Skylar let out a deep breath. Everything, she knew, would be alright.

* * *

At Norelton University, Christian paced the floor of the dormitory hallway. He had very little sleep, consumed with worry about Skylar and her mother.

Christian awaited an update from Sophia who was at Bay View Hospital. She had promised to let him know when Victoria was out of surgery. He prayed Skylar would not have to endure the agony of losing a parent, at an early age as he had.

Walking down the hallway, he stood in front of the urinal, deep in thought. At the sink, he looked up and caught a glimpse of himself in the mirror. Rubbing his chin, there in front of him in his reflection was the likeness of his father.

The stubble on his chin reminded him of Jack's long days of work down along the water's edge. He smiled, realizing the core of the man he was becoming, lay in the conviction of his faith. Christian thought how the Lord would see him strong, even in the weakest moments.

* * *

Skylar fidgeted with a piece of satin ruby ribbon, in her hand, as she sat in the waiting room. It was from her mother's blouse and had been ripped off by Espy. Skylar had bent down and put it in her jacket pocket. This morning as she paced, then finally sat down, she discovered the ribbon. Waiting with Skylar were Sophia, Olivia, and Gwen. As each stared off into the distance; they reflected on their personal loss of a loved one.

Dr. Gregson emerged from the operating room. The strain of all the surgeries performed over the years, was etched in his face. Taking the chair beside Skylar, he placed his hand upon her shoulder.

Dr. Gregson spoke, "The surgery went well, and your mother is now resting in her room. As for the cancer, it had spread throughout her left breast. I believe we removed it in time before it could spread to the lymph node. Of course, at this early stage, we will need to wait and see. However, I have performed this type of surgery many times before, and the success rate is high.

It is crucial that your mother return for check-ups to see if further treatment is required. I also recommend she join a support group. When someone loses a body part, it can be devastating. How she deals with it, is key to her recovery. I am sure though, with all of you beside her, it will not be long before she is back to normal. However, I advise that Skylar be the only one to see her this evening. The rest of you can come back tomorrow."

They breathed a sigh of relief. As the doctor turned to leave, Skylar called out to him.

"Dr. Gregson, I just wanted to thank you for all you have done."

"Well," he said, smiling, "it is my job."

As the young girl walked towards her mother's room, it was with different emotions this time. She had given all of her fears to the Lord and knew her prayers were heard.

Sitting down in the chair beside her sleeping mother, Skylar whispered her gratitude to God, for Dr. Gregson.

* * *

Christian was happy to hear from Sophia that Victoria was going to be okay. After hanging up the telephone, he hurried over to Frank's house to give him the update. Frank suggested they go to the HavenFayre Cookhouse for a drink to celebrate. Soon the two men were on there way.

Arriving inside, Christian grabbed a table, while Frank went to order a couple of cold beers.

Glancing around it was then that Christian saw her. In the corner, wearing a tight revealing black dress and sheer stockings, with red stiletto heels – was Jaycee. Taking a cherry stem from her drink, she seductively wound it around her tongue. Christian found it hard to take his eyes off of her, until Frank smacked the table with his hand. This made Christian jump and Frank sat down, looking over at Jaycee, he shook his head, and stated, "Don't even give her another look!"

Christian raised his beer to his buddy and reassuringly said, "Not to worry my friend."

* * *

When Victoria awoke there was Skylar, leaning over the railing of her hospital bed. Feeling sluggish, she opened her parched lips to speak.

"Take it easy, Momma," Skylar said. "Let me get you something to drink." Reaching over to the bedside, she poured a glass of water and placed a straw in it. "It's about time you let me take care of you."

"My Songbird," Victoria whispered.

"I am just glad you're okay. If anything ever happened to you…"

Victoria put her fingertips up to Skylar's lips.

"Hush now, you hear. I'm going to be just fine."

Victoria's gown slipped as she tried to shift in bed. Skylar saw her misshapen breast area wrapped in thick gauze and looked away.

"You know, honey," Victoria said, "you are going to have to get used to the fact that I am missing a part of me. Once I am released, I'll need you to help me wash and change the dressing."

Skylar had not thought about that. Avoiding Victoria's gaze, she nodded.

After Nurse Ethel told them what to expect during the recuperation, Victoria was discharged. She resigned herself to the knowledge that she and Skylar would have to be patient and take each day as it came.

As they arrived home, Victoria saw Sophia and Gwen standing on the stoop waiting for her. Skylar helped her mother, out of Olivia's car.

Inside, she was surrounded by friends and enveloped in the aroma of a roast dinner. Regardless of how tired she was, Victoria knew it would be impolite, to not appear gracious for the effort everyone had put in.

After the meal was complete and good-byes were said, Victoria hugged each person. However, this time even though no one said anything, they all sensed it. As she pressed against them in a distant embrace, there remained the empty spot, which had changed their friend forever.

In the morning, Skylar awoke to the telephone ringing. She stumbled out of bed and sleepily reached the phone.

"Hello?"

"Finally!" Christian said. "It is so good to hear your voice, Piper."

"I am so glad to hear from you, Christian," said Skylar. "It seems like forever since we spoke. Thank you for your prayers and writing me my first love letter."

"No need to thank me, as it all came from my heart. If you want to know something, you are the faithful one in our relationship; handling whatever life throws your way."

"I do not know what I would do without you Christian," Skylar interjected.

"I want you to reach for the courage within that fierce young girl, and continue to battle whatever comes your way," he remarked.

"I will, Christian," she said. "I honestly believe we are challenged in ways that show our real character. This disease has brought my mother and me closer together. Before all of this I assumed you and I would spend the holidays together – no matter what. I understand why you want to become a doctor, and I can see just how important it is for you to follow your dreams. I think of Evamya and your father, who knew about bravery because of what they endured."

"I agree, Piper." Christian replied.

"I have to tell you something Christian and I hope you believe me." Skylar paused, then added,

"I saw a vision of Evamya, sitting in our kitchen the other night, with a cross look on her face. At first it frightened me, but as the days passed, I searched for an answer. Finally, as I watched my mother's laboured breathing one night, it occurred to me just how selfish I had been. She was the one stricken, and all I could think of was how it made me feel. I was not considering her fears, only mine. The reality is we often believe we are in control of our lives, yet only the good Lord knows the ending. All I can do is offer my love and support. It is up to my mother how she will respond over what has taken place."

Christian pondered every word of Skylar's, for a moment, before he answered.

"Well, Piper, I believe every word you're saying. Gramsy taught me to pay attention to the hairs on my neck…who knows how I'd feel about her visiting me!"

Skylar laughed; relieved that he did not think she was crazy to speak of such things.

"By the way, I am working on plans to come home to see you in March," Christian said.

"Oh, that's wonderful to hear! I cannot wait to see you."
Skylar replied.

He thought of her beautiful face and smiled.

"You know I am here for you, no matter what. You will always own my heart," he said.

"That is why I love you so much. You are a romantic through and through," she gushed.

"Hang in there, Piper. Till we talk again. I love you," he replied.

"See you under our Sitka!" responded Skylar.

Hanging up ushered in the silence. She regretted not saying more.

The following weeks blurred together for Skylar. Between volunteering, school, and taking care of Victoria, she was exhausted. The vision of scar tissue where her mother's breast had been a shock at first. Some days, as she sat daydreaming in class, her mind would wander to the indentation that was now a part of their lives.

Moreover, she worried about her mother's behaviour, as Victoria neglected to go to her support group and made excuses to avoid seeing friends.

Then one day, Rev. Francis reappeared in town, fully recovered from his own health issues. Showing up on the front porch of the Fall's residence, with a stranger, he had come with a purpose.

After they were welcomed into the home, they say down on the settee. Skylar served tea and joined them. The stranger stood up and walked towards Victoria. Taking her hand, the woman bent down.

"My dear," she said, "we do not know each other. But 10 years ago, I was diagnosed with breast cancer. Both of my breasts were removed, cut away, as if they did not belong to me.

The depression that I went through was unbearable. At times, the cancer seemed to overpower me. Often, I wished I had died instead of being forced to live as half a woman. However, my attitude changed upon was a precocious nine-year-old girl in the hospital. Her name was Cassidy, and she was battling cancer most of her life. One day, when I went for a check-up, I saw the nurses crying and consoling one another.

Wondering what happened, I listened to them talking. 'Do you know what her last words were before she passed away? Cassidy said, "Save your tears, and remember me as the girl who loves Jesus and singing."

"Can you believe the strength Cassidy had inside her? For me, Ms. Falls, it was a turning point. I stopped pitying myself and vowed to educate others, about surviving breast cancer. The people that surround you here today are embracing life and want to see you do the same. Whatever you do, don't let cancer beat you down. Be with your family and friends, go to your support group, but most of all let go of being victimized by this frightful disease. You are, after all, a survivor!"

The words impacted Victoria, who sat silent.

The woman rose, smiling at Victoria. Turning, she walked to Rev. Francis and kissed him on the cheek. Standing, he embraced her.

"Thank you for coming, Mother," he said. "I love you."

"I love you, son," she said, patting his back.

Taking the tissue offered by the Reverend, Victoria cleared her throat.

"I owe you an apology, Skylar," she said, "for being stubborn. Over the years, I have watched Sophia, Olivia, and Gwen face their losses with dignity and faith. Songbird, I am sorry for the terrible strain I have put on you, by isolating myself. I am so blessed to have such a wonderful daughter."

"I would like to lead us in prayer," Rev. Francis said. "Dear Jesus, we thank you for the love that gives us strength and for your hand in guiding us, through this challenging journey. We ask that you continue to offer Ms. Falls guidance for her well-being. Please continue to bless those lending their support. Lastly, we pray for those facing their own battles every day. Amen."

Skylar, Rev. Francis, and his mother took turns embracing Victoria. She felt her burden lift.

* * *

At the end of February, things had changed significantly in the Falls residence. Victoria had recovered and returned to work at Miss Tasmin Jeans Boutique. She was now participating in a support group and making plans for planting a spring garden.

As the short days and long nights dragged on, Skylar adjusted to independence. One night, lying on her bed, she counted the days on the calendar, until Christian would come home again.

* * *

Christian and Frank arrived back home for March spring break in 1966. Skylar had barely slept the night before, eager to be in Christian's arms again. Seven months had passed since they last saw each other. So much had happened, and though she felt renewed, her love for Christian remained.

After showering, Skylar changed into a cream blouse with red poppies and a matching short ivory skirt. Even though the weather was brisk, spring was in the air.

Bouncing down the stairs, Skylar met Gwen, who was dressed for the weather in a mauve sweater and grey slacks.

"Don't you reckon you are a bit underdressed, Bird Girl?"

Skylar smiled sweetly and sauntered off into the kitchen.

Victoria raised an eyebrow when she saw her daughter's outfit.

"Take a sweater, Songbird. You do not want to catch a chill."

"Sure thing, Momma," she said, giving her a peck on the cheek. "I will grab one on my way out."

"I have a nice heavy one here for you," Gwen said, holding a thick wool sweater.

"That is so kind of you, thanks," Skylar said, snatching it.

Victoria smiled at Gwen, holding back laughter.

"Listen you girls, behave, and remember you have a curfew. I would like it if the boys brought you in a little earlier, so we can catch up. I will make us all some cocoa."

Skylar and Gwen sat in the front entrance to wait for Christian and Frank. Minutes later, there was a knock on the door.

As they opened it, the young girls could only stare in disbelief. There in front of them stood a pair of sophisticated, University gentleman. Where once two, young lads had nervously come to pick up their dates, Christian and Frank emerged now with poise. Having outgrown their adolescence in Ospero Falls, they returned equipped with confidence and transition into young men.

Chapter 18

Clarity

AS CHRISTIAN STEPPED FORWARD, THE GRIN ON HIS FACE REVEALED the jocular, young man Skylar adored. She was pleasantly surprised by his rugged appearance and thick stubble on his chin.

Sweeping her into his arms, he lifted her with ease, making her squeal.

"Christian James O'Connelly – put me down this instant!"

Frank and Gwen burst into laughter.

Gently, Christian placed Skylar back on the ground.

"Well, Hello my sweet Piper," he whispered in her ear.

Skylar blushed, replying with coyness, "It has been awhile, stranger."

Abruptly, Christian took her small hand in his and twirling her around, he whistled. "Now then, will you look at this pretty little lady!" he teased.

Skylar revelled in all the attention.

* * *

Sitting in a booth at Canetti's Diner, they reconnected by reminiscing over the good times.

While Christian and Skylar rekindled their love, Frank found contentment in his friendship with Gwen. They discovered both of them had in common, a great enthusiasm for a sport that Frank thought did not appeal to most girls. Years earlier, she became smitten with Cassius Clay and followed his career closely. At first, Frank was surprised by her interest in boxing, but knowing her feisty character, he understood.

"What did you think about Cassius Clay changing his name to Muhammad Ali after his fight with Sonny Liston?" Gwen asked.

"Yeah, that was some fight!" Frank replied. "What do you think about his, 'Float like a butterfly, sting like a bee'?"

She giggled and blushed. "I think anything Muhammad Ali says is sweet talk to me!"

"I think it's stupid if you ask me," Christian said. "I mean, a boxer changing his name is one thing, but trying to sound like a poet is another!"

Gwen glared at him over her chocolate malt.

"Oh and I reckon, Doc, that all that silly poetry you spout off to Bird Girl is something special?"

"Hey now, keep me out of your little dispute here," Skylar said. "I have not said a thing about your black lover boy."

Before Skylar could say another word, Gwen stood up. Seething with anger, she grabbed her malt and impulsively dumped it all over, her best friend. The shock on Skylar's face was visible to all the patrons in the diner.

"Why don't you keep your intolerant remarks to yourself!" Gwen shouted.

Leaving, she slammed down her change on the counter and strutted out the front door, with Frank chasing after. Christian knew he should be helping Skylar, but the urge to laugh was too strong. His reaction did not amuse Skylar.

"I am going home," she said, "by myself!"

As she walked towards the bathroom to clean-up, Christian stayed at the table. Realizing he had hurt her feelings, he wished he could erase the past few minutes. He did not want the night to end on a sour note.

Frank caught up to Gwen.

"Do you have any idea," she asked, "what I have to put up with that dim-wit sometimes? How do you think she would feel, if I put down her stupid tree?"

"Listen, I don't think she meant any harm by it, Gwennie-Sue."

"You know something Frank, I ought to smack you right now, for calling me that," she said, stopping in her tracks. "You're sticking up for Bird Girl, but you don't get how it makes me feel, when she talks down about my people and me."

"I think this whole thing has been all blown up out of sorts," Frank said, choosing his words carefully. "Do you know how much you mean to the rest of us?"

Gwen looked down and kicked at a puddle with her boots.
She shrugged.

"Just take me home, please."

Christian sat waiting. Skylar emerged from the washroom. What he saw was a pitiful sight. Skylar's strawberry-blonde tresses were matted against her flustered cheeks, while the once-beautiful outfit she wore was marked with drab, muddy stains. He stood and opened his arms.

"Piper, I'm sorry I acted like such a jerk," he pleaded.

"No, Christian, it's me that's sorry. I should not have been taunting Gwennie like that," confessed Skylar.

"Come on now, don't be so hard on yourself. We were all kidding around. I'm sure things will work themselves out." Christian said reassuringly.

Putting his arm around her, they paid and walked out.

Back home, Gwen headed straight to her room. Victoria tried calling out to her from the living room, but she kept quiet. Sensing something was wrong, Victoria paced the floor.

Skylar soon entered. She had bid goodnight to Christian. Their reunion was not what she had hoped it would be. The evening started wonderfully and ended terribly. Sneaking past the living room, Skylar thought she had slipped by her mother, when she heard her voice.

"Songbird, I do not know what happened between you and Gwen, but you two better work it out right now. I won't have any nonsense going on under my roof."

"Yes, Momma," Skylar sighed.

Walking upstairs, she could see the light was still on in Gwen's room, prompting her to knock on the door.

"You still awake?"

At first there was silence, and she was relieved. About to turn around and leave, Skylar heard Gwen mutter, "Come in."

Skylar opened the door. Gwen was propped up in bed, cradling a picture of Evamya with Gwen, in her hands. Skylar could see she had been crying and approached with caution.

"I just came to say I am sorry for hurting your feelings and wrecking our night together with Frank and Christian."

Gwen looked up at Skylar and then down again at the worn photograph.

"Truth be known, Bird Girl, I reckon I am partly to blame."

Skylar reacted with surprise.

"You don't have to stand there looking like the floor's gone and disappeared on you," Gwen mumbled. "I do not claim to be right all the time, you know."

Skylar inched her way onto the bed and went to give Gwen a hug.

However Gwen could not stop from giggling at the pitiful site of her friend.

Skylar broke off the embrace and nudged Gwen's shoulder.

"How about tomorrow we all go to Blackfine's and catch a movie?"

"Sounds good to me," Gwen nodded. "We can thank the good Lord we get another chance to be with the boys."

"You mean those two gorgeous men who saw us act like two-year-old's tonight?" Inquired Skylar, "We will be lucky if they don't jump the first ferry back to Norelton in the morning!"

They both burst into laughter. As Victoria walked past the closed door, the sound reassured her.

* * *

As the sun rose on a Saturday morning, after a week that seemed too short, Christian and Frank prepared to go back to their lives in Norelton.

Saying farewell, Christian sensed something different about Skylar. Usually, she choked back her tears, making him regret leaving her behind. This time however, after sharing a hug and a long, intense kiss, she didn't make a fuss. He tried to shrug it off.

"Until next time, my sweet Piper. I love you. See you under our Sitka tree," professed Christian.

"I love you too, Mr. O'Connelly," Skylar smiled.

Christian and Frank opened the Cadillac doors and got in, to board the ferry. Before leaving, they stuck out a hand and waved.

With a surge of politics transforming the lives of blacks and whites, the landscape of revolution came with knowing things had changed.

* * *

In April, Skylar rebounded with jubilation. She found the previous long, dark winter had dampened her normally happy spirit. Yearning to see the buds of colourful flowers gracing the mountainside, she was overjoyed to welcome the full splendour of spring. Her work at Whispering Rose Fellowship continued, as the young girl delighted in serving.

Victoria was in remission. She embraced the role she had in her group, supporting others stricken with cancer. Christian and Frank successfully passed another academic term at university. While Gwen achieved straight A's, Skylar struggled with mediocre grades.

Come June, returning to the majestic Sitka tree, saw her visiting often.

When she climbed the rungs of the ladder leading up to the spruce, she entered into nature's breathing space. She loved to sit silently within the branches and listen to the melodies of the songbirds. Her favourites were red-crossbill finches, violet swallows, and the boreal chickadee. Occasionally, Skylar would witness the hammering of the Red-breasted Sapsucker woodpecker, drilling the trunk of a nearby tree.

Skylar felt blessed, in being witness to a Great Blue Heron take off in flight from the riverbed in the distance.

One Sunday, as twilight neared, a breeze moved through the tree house. Skylar lay upon the rug on the floor. She was delighted when a ladybug landed on her cheek. Scrunching up her nose, its six minuscule legs tickled their way upon her freckles causing her to giggle. A minute later, as the insect flew away, Skylar was reminded of the meaning in even the smallest things.

Christian and Frank arrived back in Ospero Falls, for the July long weekend. Just in time for the grand fireworks, put on by the council of Averston. The town had the financial means and a larger budget for putting on the display. This drew in larger crowds and for the one night, people gathered together in celebration.

The evening was a magical reunion for Christian and Skylar. They held tight to one another and shared stories of their parts of the world – separated by the ocean.

After conversing among themselves, they decided to get away from the crowd and go to the tree house. Boarding the ferry in Christian's car, Hank Stevenson greeted them with a smile and nod. He was balding and age spots had appeared on his face and wrinkled hands.

Once they were on the open gravel road, under the hazy interspersion of the Milky Way, Skylar asked Christian to put down the Cadillac's soft-top. He pulled over to oblige her. After the top was down, she climbed into the back seat and kicked off her sandals.

As she stood up, Skylar felt the coolness of the leather on her bare feet. The coastal air engulfed her, sending shivers upon her arms. Her sheer blouse pressed up against her, and Christian had a hard time concentrating on the road. The drive out to the tree was less than

10 minutes, therefore he slowed the car down. She shook her sun-kissed strawberry curls in the breeze and gestured to Christian to turn up the radio. Raising her arms above her head, she stretched as if trying to hug the stars. He slowly coasted the Cadillac and parked under the Sitka tree. As they stood before the ladder, their laughter echoed into the night.

"I have something to show you," Skylar said, motioning for Christian to climb the ladder first.

Once she reached the trapdoor and entered, she took his hand and said, "Let's go stand on the platform deck to enjoy the view."

"I thought you had something you wanted to show me?" he asked.

"Of course I do, you silly boy. That's why I brought you to the tree house. Just look at the fireworks from way up here, they're spectacular!"

Prismatic rainbow hues lit up the darkened skyline. As he neared, Christian saw through her eyes, the magnificence she envisioned. Leaning in close and, before she could say another word, he put his lips to hers in a tender kiss. The rupture of fireworks exploding in the background could not hold a candle to the lovers' passion that was ignited. They playfully teased one another, with a lot of kissing and hands on one another. Christian was having a difficult time at respecting their decision to wait. Unbeknown to him, Skylar too struggled with delaying being intimate, before marriage. However, neither wanted an unexpected pregnancy to cause discord. Besides, both of them had talked and only when they were married, the decision would be to bring a child into the world. Coming up for air, Skylar gasped, "Maybe we should take a breather."

Christian nodded and replied, "Probably so Piper."

Even though he reluctantly agreed, his love for her ran deeper than a quick tryst, which could have a lasting impact.

The next day, Frank and Gwen joined them for a day of fishing. Sitting on the pier under the sweltering sun, they dangled their feet, dipping their toes into the coolness of the water.

"So, Bird Girl," Gwen asked, "what happened to you two last night?"

Skylar shrugged and baited her hook. Frank raised an eyebrow at Christian, who ignored it. Gwen decided to change the conversation.

"I bet all of you that I'm gonna catch the biggest fish here today."

"You're on," Frank said, casting off.

The rest of the hot day was spent fishing, talking, and enjoying each other's company. For Christian, time was passing far too quickly again. He would be returning to Norelton at the end of the month, to continue his studies.

Meanwhile, Frank was anxious to return to the city. He intended to come back someday – not to Ospero Falls, but to Averston. Frank was lured by promises of wealth and a career as a city planner.

Frank's bobber sank below the surface. He jumped to his feet and reeled in the line.

"Whoopee! I bet you it's gonna be a beauty of a fish," he exclaimed, heaving on his pole.

Christian, Skylar, and Gwen leaned close to get a look at the end of Frank's hook. Gwen was the first to see it.

"Well, I reckon that there is some new kind of fish," she giggled.

Frank peered down at the old boot dangling from the end of his line. Sophia and Gwen laughed, until they noticed Christian, who was staring in silence. He had turned pale.

Whispering the words that raised the hair upon the back of their necks, Christian said,

"My dad was missing one of his logger boots when they found him."

To Frank, the whole idea that he had caught ol' Jack's boot spooked him. Before anyone could take a closer look, he abruptly dropped it back, into the murky depths of the ocean below.

Without another word, everyone quietly gathered their fishing gear and headed in for the day.

Chapter 19

Rusted

BEFORE DEPARTING MID JULY CHRISTIAN FOUND HIMSELF AGAIN sitting on the pier, waiting for the ferry to arrive. Reflecting on the day before they had spent fishing, he stared into the depths of the darkened waters and caught a glimpse of himself. Slipping on his Norelton baseball cap, Christian walked over to the ferry dock, plucking a daisy along the way, as he met up with Skylar.

She met him with a kiss. Taking the daisy, Christian tucked the flower behind her ear.

"Peace be with you, Piper. See you under our Sitka tree," he said

"Hold me close to your heart," she said softly.

* * *

As the weeks passed, the lush greenery that stretched over the meadows, witnessed a blossoming. Skylar Reigh Falls was experiencing her own changes. Leaving behind the vestiges of her adolescent years behind, she was transforming into a young woman.

A few days before Skylar and Gwen were to return to school, an unexpected visitor returned. On an impulse, Christian decided to spend one last weekend in Ospero Falls. He was drawn by the memory of Skylar standing on the pier blowing him kisses. He only told his plans to Frank, who wasn't surprised, as he understood his best friend's quick departure from Norelton. Christian had shared how things had been heating up between Skylar and him. Slapping his best friend on the back, Frank just smiled, as Christian winked.

It would be a long three hours to Ospero Falls, but well worth surprising the love of his life.

He arrived back home, only to find out from Hank Stevenson that Skylar took the ferry an hour ago to the tree house.

Christian parked and left his Cadillac back in Ospero Falls, as he wanted to walk to their cherished Sitka tree and surprise the woman he loved.

Trudging through the woods, Christian heard Skylar's soft voice. Drawing nearer, he heard the words clearly, as she recited a poem, he had not heard before.

Beyond the Concrete imbedded with litter, exists a realm of purity
Where the sweetness of mother earth remains untouched
A place in which the heartbeats of the trees, pounds ceaselessly
The foliage, is dipped in shimmers, from the suspended yellow globe
As I fix my dreamy eyes upon the glistening torrents of glacial streams…

Christian moved, snapping a twig.

"Is someone there?" Skylar said.

"Hey Piper, it's just me, Christian!"

She jumped to her feet and looked down over the edge of the tree house.

"Christian James O'Connelly, you scared the living daylights out of me!"

"Well now," he grinned, "that's some way to greet your boyfriend, who travelled all this way just to see you."

Scurrying up the ladder, he was soon in her arms. Their lips met in a flurry of passion spurred on by absence, and it was a few minutes before they parted. Smoothing down her hair, she straightened out her skirt, as they settled down upon the rug.

"I wanted to surprise you, Piper. I only have two days to spend with you, so let's make the most of them."

"Oh Christian, I am so glad you came home to me."

He stroked her cheek. "What were you reciting earlier?"

"It is a poem that I wrote in last year's English class, called 'The Concrete Jungle.'

"Of course I would hear you reciting poetry to the trees," he laughed, then asked "What's it about?"

Skylar explained, "It's like a conflict of two things. How sometimes they can seem to fit nicely with one another, when really they are polar opposites.

He thought about it then remarked, "Well not exactly happy thought, eh?"

Skylar shrugged and leaned forward, stretching towards the sunlight.

Inhaling the evening air into her lungs, She asked,

"Can you smell that?"

"No, what is it?"

"The winds of change."

"The what?"

She sighed. "The winds of change blow when the end of a season is near and announces the arrival of another one. Our summer is ending, while autumn's reappearance is on the verge. It brings a smell of departure. Everything is preparing to either die or return to a deep slumber, awaiting the arrival of winter."

Christian mulled over her words.

"If you ask me, it sounds dismal," he finally remarked.

Skylar glanced at him, mystified.

"Since my momma's illness, I now look at death differently. Like when an animal dies in the woods, its body feeds others, giving them strength – while whatever remains dissipates into the ground – supplying it with nutrients. Even in the Bible, it says we should not fear death, but go into the light. Therefore, I believe in peace for the soul."

"One of the reasons I love you so much," he said, "is the way you look at things. Where I see a plant, you discover the splendour of Calypso orchids, gathering on the ground."

She wrapped her arms around him and planted a kiss on his lips.

"No one knows me like you do, my love," she said.

Over the next two days, they picnicked in the park, walked hand in hand along the seaside, and had a crab bake near the bluffs.

As always, time passed too quickly for them.

Skylar continued to sit at the pier, after watching the ferry take Christian away. She longed for Christmas when he would come home again.

* * *

The beginning of the final school year, did not appeal to Skylar. However, as winter break neared, an assignment piqued her interest.

"I understand the holidays are soon upon us," said Mr. Hill, her Grade 12 history teacher. "However, it won't be a vacation. I want you all to compose an essay on a heroic historical figure."

A throng of student's groans, filled the room with noise.

Mr. Hill motioned for everyone to settle down.

Gwen smiled, as she knew writing about Martin Luther King Jr. was sure to get her an A.

Then the teacher added a twist.

Mr. Hill announced, the essay needs to be about a Canadian in the last 100 years, since its our centennial.

"How boring is that gonna be?" said Tawni.

Snickers sounded throughout the room.

When Mr. Hill went to respond, Tawni took her long brown hair, flipped it over and put her glasses over her silly hairdo.

This prompted bursts of laughter throughout.

Mr. Hill was amused yet he did not give into the class clown's antics.

"I think if all of you do your homework," Mr. Hill said, "you maybe be surprised, who you find among the roots of our Canadian history."

The school bell ended the discussion. The students gathered their books.

"Your work is to be handed in, when we resume class after the holidays," Mr. Hill said.

"Merry Christmas to you all!"

* * *

The families gathered at the Falls' to enjoy Christmas breakfast. Christian and Frank had returned home for the holidays. The Hurston's had been invited too and joyfully accepted to be part of the festivities. The large crowd packed everyone into the living room area. Sofa's and chairs were moved temporarily. The noise level was high, as everyone was excited about opening their gifts and also what the new year would bring.

After breakfast, the dishes were cleared and the furniture moved back into the living room area, to open gifts.

Skylar looked at her bracelet and was content with whatever his present was for her.

Victoria, Sophia, and Olivia had already opened their gifts of perfume, chocolates, and stockings.

Frank gave Gwen a set of three hand-carved maple wood photo frames to add to her collection. In return, she gave Frank a photograph of him and his mother, which she had taken in the summertime.

They thanked one another with a hug.

Skylar and Victoria split the cost of a subscription to National Geographic for Gwen. The magazine was her favourite, and the message written in the card moved her to tears:

"I think of you as my own daughter, while Skylar likens you to a sister. We thank the good Lord for bringing you into our lives and our hearts. God bless!

"Merry Christmas.

"Much love, Victoria and Skylar"

Gwen gave each of them a beautiful scarf she knitted herself.

The Hurston's had asked for no gifts, instead requesting a small donation to their African charity. Jawana surprised Gwen, with the offer of a package. Opening the wrapping paper carefully, Gwen was overcome.

"I can't believe you bought this for me," she said. "I love it!"

She proudly showed off her gift, holding it up for everyone to see, it was a book.

Gingerly, she opened the cover and read the inscription: "May peace prevail over us all." She scanned the pages, losing herself in Dr. King's words, as if they were written just for her.

Gwen stood and embraced the Hurston's.

Finally, Skylar and Christian exchanged gifts.

Placing a small, wrapped present in his hands, Skylar kissed Christian on the cheek and whispered, "Careful, it's delicate."

Opening it with care, he removed a clear glass dove and held it in the palm of his hand to show everyone.

"I love it Piper," he said. "It reflects your carefree spirit."

Christian placed it on the side table. Putting his hands on his knees, he then nervously reached down to pick up a box at his feet. Standing up he looked nervous. Everyone was looking at him. Turning around, he took a deep breath in, then exhaled. Dropping to one knee in front of Skylar, she looked surprised.

"Piper," he said, "we've been through so much together, and the happiness you've brought me is unmatched. Over the years, you have been someone who truly knows me. You're my Songbird. Now, more than ever, I cannot imagine my life without you. I know you need some time to grow, but if you will accept this token of my love, I know we can grow together – and build something that will last forever."

Opening the box, he presented his gift. It was an intricate engagement ring. The band was a circle of twisted gold, which resembled roots and intertwined two solid hearts. Each one, containing a single diamond.

Skylar was astonished, as was everyone else. She had imagined this moment since she was a little girl and now the man she was madly in love with, was about to propose.

Christian placed the ring on her finger.

"Skylar Reigh Falls, will you do me the honour of becoming my wife?"

Abruptly, Skylar leapt to her feet and shouted out with enthusiasm,

"Yes, Christian James O' Connelly, I will marry you!"

Sophia and Victoria sat quietly. His mother was taken aback that her son had not even hinted at proposing, why while Victoria was not expecting the moment to happen so soon.

Frank got up and slapped Christian on the back.

"You sure kept me in the dark about this one, my friend!"

Gwen stood and hugged Skylar.

"Congratulations, Bird Girl! You deserve all the happiness in the world. Just do not forget who your maid of honour will be, when the time comes."

Skylar giggled. The thrill of the moment started to settle in. She looked over at Victoria, who walked over to embrace her.

"Oh, my little Songbird! I don't know what to say."

Sophia embraced her son. "Well now, aren't you full of surprises," she sighed. "I hope you two are going to wait a little longer?"

"As long as Skylar needs to finish up her schooling," he said, looking at his fiancée. "Then we'll move to Norelton and start our lives together."

Suddenly, it dawned on Skylar that he was assuming his fiancée wanted to leave Ospero Falls, all together. Although she understood his schooling was in Norelton, she had assumed after he was done, they would settle in Ospero Falls.

Skylar was confident that they would speak about the matter further when the time was right.

* * *

As the festivities enveloped the small coastal town, the red-haired girl in Norelton known as Jaycee, cut a picture out of the university paper. Under the caption,

"Aspiring Doctor in a League of His Own," she drew a heart around the name – Christian James O'Connelly. Smiling, she placed her lips on the accompanying photograph, leaving behind the distinct mark of her Courtesan lipstick.

Chapter 20

Commencement

As New Year's 1967 approached, Skylar looked forward to all of the new beginnings planning for her wedding.

Lying on a mountain of pillows on her bedroom floor, she busily sketched the outline of an elegant dress of her own creation. Her dress would be adorned with layers of chiffon and a satin red ribbon in the back. She imagined a lace neckline of red poppies. Gwen would be her maid of honour and carry Skylar's bouquet of yellow Gerberas, with a spray of Sitka. She envisioned Frank driving her in Christian's Cadillac to the spruce tree, where her future husband stood. All of their friends and loved ones would be present. As Frank assisted her out of the convertible, she would walk barefoot to join Christian in marriage. Abruptly, her thoughts were interrupted by Gwen bursting into the room, setting various books onto the bed.

"Hey Skylar, guess what? Reggie gave us these books to borrow from his store, since the library is on holiday hours. That means we can get started on our project." Skylar rolled her eyes.

"Listen Bird Girl," Gwen remarked, "Mr. Hill isn't going to care one bit that you got engaged. You still have to write that essay."

Skylar soon relented. Setting her sketch pad aside, she grabbed one of the books for research.

Still, an hour of going over information on Canadians who had made a difference and Skylar was growing frustrated. Then she saw the name Isabella Valancy Crawford. As she read on, the woman's story appealed to her. Ms. Crawford was a Canadian poet. Born in Dublin in 1850, she emigrated with her family to Canada, where they settled in Ontario.

She endured the loss of her father and siblings and was left to take care of her ailing mother. All the while, she submitted her writing to literary journals. Rejected time after time, Isabella's words finally made it into newspapers. Later, using her own money she published a collection of narrative poems, which garnered high praise – but sold only 50 copies. She was only 37 years old when she died and was not recognized for her many achievements, until long after her passing.

Skylar could relate to the poet who gave everything she had to follow her passion.

"Gwen, I found someone interesting."

Gwen sighed as she was still leafing through the books. While she was happy Skylar had found someone, she was about to close the last book, when the name Mary Ann Shadd caught her attention. She was an educator, newspaper editor, and civil rights advocate. Born free in Delaware in 1823, Ms. Shadd moved with her brother to Ontario in 1851, fearing a new law that threatened their freedom. There, she created a school to educate slaves fleeing the United States. Meanwhile, she was the first woman publisher in Canada offering a weekly paper that was among the first written for black people. Uncommon during the era, she often spoke in the U.S. to those oppressed by enslavement. The Shadd residence offered protection for freedom-seeking slaves, who journeyed north on the Underground Railroad. When her husband passed away, she took her children and moved back to America. She obtained a law degree at the age of 60, the second black woman in the U.S. to ever do so. Shadd acquired the law degree, to further assist in the plight of black people and the rights of women.

Gwen smiled and remarked, "I found a woman that has her roots in both Canada and America, just like my family."

Skylar looked up from the pages of the book in her hand, "Well, I think we each have found a piece of history, connecting us to inspiring Canadians."

Finally, on New Year's Eve, everyone gathered at the Falls' house to celebrate Skylar's 18th birthday.

Sitting in the living room, her mind drifted.

She thought of how her recent engagement was the talk of Ospero Falls, with people assuming she would move to Norelton with Christian.

Troubled as she was, Skylar remained quiet, waiting for the right time to talk with her future husband. He had at least six more years of schooling, before he could be licensed as a physician, which concerned her enough. Nevertheless, she hoped he would want to leave city life and come back to Ospero Falls, to start a family practice.

Surrounded by Christian and her loved ones, Skylar pushed away the worries that gnawed at her.

"Happy Birthday, Piper," Christian whispered, handing her a small package.

Unfolding the wrapping paper, Skylar tried to guess what it was. She opened the box to reveal a skeleton key decorated with a heart encircling a cross. She picked it up and turned it over. It was engraved with the words *PIPER* on one side and *FAITH* on the other.

He reached for something behind his back. He placed another box on Skylar's lap. Opening it, she found a cast-iron, Victorian door plate.

"The key," he said, "fits into this lock, which we will use for our first home – the one we will build together."

Her worries disappeared, as she assumed he meant in Ospero Falls. "That's so sweet, Christian."

"I want you to know, Piper, that you have made me a better man – a son my father would have been proud of. It is because of your good heart that I am blessed."

"I cherish this present," she said, "as I cherish you. Thank you so much."

Skylar gave Christian a kiss.

Victoria approached her daughter.

"This is for you, songbird," Victoria said, placing a package in her daughter's hands.

"Happy birthday!"

Opening the present, Skylar drew a breath when she saw what it contained. A gold heart-shaped locket engraved with a cross, hung from a delicate chain.

Unhooking the dainty latch, she gazed at the small picture of Victoria cradling her, as a baby.

Skylar's tears formed as she was overcome by the sentimental present.

"You will always be my Songbird," Victoria said.

"Oh, Momma," Skylar said.

"Can I put it on you?" Christian asked.

Skylar stood up and offered him the necklace. He took it and tenderly placed it around her neck, kissing his fiancée on the cheek afterwards.

After all of the gifts were open and the sitting area tidied, Frank turned on the radio. They spent the rest of the night chatting, listening to music, and dancing.

Since Christian and Frank would be leaving in two days, plans were made to take Skylar and Gwen tobogganing, the next day. The fresh-fallen snow made for perfect sledding conditions. Carefree, they threw snowballs at each other, wrestled in powdery mounds, and built snowmen. When they grew tired of playing around, the friends sipped from the thermos of hot chocolate and nibbled from a tin of shortbread.

Upon returning, their feet felt like ice-covered blocks. Quickly, they gathered around Sophia's wood stove. As they stripped off their wet outer clothes, Gwen glanced at Skylar's neck.

"Hey, I thought you were wearing the locket your momma gave you?"

Skylar's hand reached up to feel her neck. Panic overwhelmed her as she turned to Christian.

"Oh no, the necklace is gone!"

That evening as she sat in the living room, tears streamed down her face.

Sitting across from her mother, she confessed that she had lost the necklace.

At first her mother sat silently, mulling over the loss of the priceless gift.

"Maybe the clasp was not connected properly?" Victoria asked.

Caught by surprise, Skylar never thought Christian could be responsible for losing the necklace.

Victoria was quick to add, "You might have lost it somewhere in the house, even before you left."

"I am sorry, Momma," she said, shaking her head. "I know you worked so hard to save up for it, and now it's gone."

Victoria stood and walked over to her daughter. Placing her arms around her, Victoria kissed Skylar's wet cheeks.

"Listen to me, Songbird. If it is meant to be found, the necklace will make its way back to you."

The next day, Skylar met Christian at Canetti's for lunch.

"Christian," she asked, sulking over a plate of lasagna, "did you make sure the clasp on my chain was attached properly?"

The bitter words grasped the young man's attention. Abruptly he stopped stirring teh cream into his black coffee.

"What are you implying?" he asked. "Do you think I intentionally left it unfastened, so that you would lose the damn thing?"

"Looking up at him, she sputtered, "You don't have to get so upset at me simply asking! I should have just let my mom put it on me."

Christian stiffened, as his face reddened with anger he slammed down his fist, startling her.

"Now, you listen to me, Skylar. I did not mess with your necklace, and I certainly do not like you blaming me either!" he yelled.

Before she could say anything, Christian stood up and threw down some change. "I'm out of here!"

Sitting in the booth all alone, she watched as her future husband drove away, his pride hurt by her biting accusations.

She arrived home to find Victoria cross-stitching in the living room. Her mother could tell that her daughter was upset.

"Want to talk about it?" Victoria asked.

"No thanks, Momma. I will deal with it."

Skylar went to her room. Grabbing her quilt, she sat under the painting of the Sitka tree. Comforted, her thoughts drifted away from the pain of the argument.

Meanwhile, Christian packed his clothes in a fury. He was in shock at Skylar's insinuation.

Although he was not due to leave town until tomorrow, Christian decided to take the next ferry out. Deeply offended, all he cared about was putting distance between himself and Ospero Falls.

An hour had passed when Skylar decided to make amends with Christian, at any cost. She felt terrible for what she had said and wanted to tell her fiancé how sorry she was. Grabbing her winter jacket, Skylar walked over to the O'Connelly house. As she approached, Skylar knew that something was amiss, when she spotted Christian's vehicle gone. Knocking on the door, Sophia answered and was surprised to see Skylar.

"Is Christian home?"

"No sweetie, he said goodbye to me and left a short time ago. I assumed he was going to see you."

Skylar's heart sank. He had left without saying goodbye for the first time – and lied to his mother. Not wanting to concern Sophia, she covered her despair with a smile.

"I'm sorry. I was hoping he might have missed the ferry and come back."

"Did you not see him off?"

"There was a slight misunderstanding, that is all," she said, not wanting to lie. "I will talk to him later."

"I hope things are okay between you two."

"Everything will be alright Mrs. O'Connelly. I will be going now."

"If you need someone to talk to, I am always here for you."

"Thank you," she said, "I appreciate it."

Turning, she walked towards the pier. Huddling against the bitter cold, she trudged through the snow. The last ferry had left long ago, and she did not expect to see Christian. Therefore, she was surprised to see his car parked nearby, its windows foggy. As she reached for the handle, the door swung open, alarming the girl.

"Sorry," Christian said, "I didn't mean to startle you."

Skylar drew a deep breath in and got into the passenger side.

"Please hear me out," she said, "I am so sorry Christian for even thinking such a terrible thing! I only hope you can find it in your heart to forgive me?"

He had been avoiding eye contact; when he looked up, her sadness tore at him.

"You know something, Piper? I drove to the dock to catch the ferry, and I couldn't do it. If you want to know the truth, it was my father's voice telling me, 'Be a man about this, because if you leave with anger in your heart, there ain't no going back!' If anything, my pride was hurt, because I never thought you could ever believe for one moment that I would intentionally cause you pain. Skylar, I fall more in love with you as each day passes. Of course I forgive you, and I hope you promise to do the same if ever the time comes."

A feeling of reassurance swept over Skylar as she bent down and kissed him.

Smiling, she replied, "From my heart to your heart, I promise Christian."

Back at the O'Connelly house, no one discussed the incident. They also decided not to talk about the future. Frank called; thankful to hear things had been sorted out.

In the morning, Skylar came over to speak with Christian. She found him outside, tossing his bag into the back seat of the car.

"Coming down to the pier with me?" he asked.

"If it's alright with you," she said, kicking at the snow, "I've decided to see you off at the house. It is getting harder each time you have to leave."

"I understand, Piper," he said, lifting her chin in the palm of his hand. "Thank you for your honesty." They exchanged a tender kiss. "My heart is yours, my soon-to-be Mrs. O'Connelly."

She blushed, hearing him call her, by his last name.

"Remember, before you know it, you will be back for my graduation in June," she said. "Then we will decide on a wedding date."

He slid into the Cadillac, holding the door open. In his rear-view mirror, he saw Frank walking towards the car.

"Of course, Piper. We will talk more then, see you under our beloved tree."

* * *

Skylar's routine of school and volunteering at the sanctuary resumed its familiar pace.

She and Gwen eagerly handed in their essays, proud of the research they had put into their assignments.

The following week, in class, Mr. Hill held the marked papers in his hands. Handing them out, he said, "I was impressed to see how much work most of you put into your writing," waving the papers.

Mr. Hill added, "However, there is one essay that stood out. I could tell that this individual truly connected with their Canadian hero and are proud of their roots. I wanted each of you to understand the significance of being Canadian, comes from people who are immigrants. For every person who has a foundation here, came from settlers to our country. This student took on a duo role that is connected to their own family and escaping slavery.

Mr. Hill announced, "I ask Gwen Walker to come forward and read her essay."

Skylar began clapping heavily and stood up for her best friend.

As Gwen walked to the front of the class to receive their essay, Skylar gave her a high-five.

After school, they decided to celebrate their accomplishment with hand-dipped strawberry shakes at Canetti's. Skylar could not refrain from cracking a joke,

"Mmm…its much better to eat a shake than to wear it." Skylar said, then laughed, prompting Gwen to take a swipe of her whipped cream and dab her friend on the nose.

"Is that so Bird-girl!" replied Gwen.

Both of them burst into loud laughter and savoured the moment.

That evening, Skylar telephoned Christian about Gwen's winning essay, along with hers.

"I am so proud of you both Piper," he said.

"I appreciate that, Christian. I love learning about history. I think I have found my calling in life. If you look around the coastline here, we have so much history around us. Maybe I could become a summer guide or something."

She heard nothing but silence. For a moment, she thought they had disconnected.

"Christian, are you still there?"

"Yeah, I am still here."

"What's the matter? Did I say something wrong?"

"Piper, I see bigger things for you. Why would you want to be a summer guide in Ospero Falls when you will be moving to Norelton?"

She hesitated. "You know, we really have not discussed all of the options, Christian. You made the decision for the both of us, without asking me how I felt."

It caught him by surprise that she was not as eager to join him in the city. As he lingered on her words, Christian felt as if there was more, than just an ocean separating the two.

"Well, I guess we have some serious talking to do when I come back in June."

He did not want to start an argument. Changing the subject, he asked, "So, how is your mother doing?"

"Oh, I haven't told you! Mr. Canetti was having some difficulty running both his stall at the summer market and the restaurant. So he offered Momma the opportunity to manage the market for him, full-time. He is paying her well, and if I want to make some extra money, I can work with her too.

Isn't that great?"

"You do not need to make extra money, Piper. I am going to take care of you."

"I do not need to be kept under lock and key, Christian. Can you not be happy for my momma?"

He knew there was no use discussing it further.

"Yeah, of course, that's great. I wish her all the best. Anyway, it's time for me to go. I have a lot of studying to do. I will call you in a few days, Piper."

After hanging up, she felt miserable. Every time they talked lately, she thought, the conversation left a sour taste in her mouth. To shake off her bad mood, she went to return the books lent to her and Gwen from Reggies book store. She liked the way he had set out corners inside with mounds of various comfy pillows to sit and read.

Skylar had brought a tin of mincemeat tarts and a card of thanks for the elderly man. He truly was happy with his little bookstore, as he enjoyed reciting poetry and giving recommendations. After conveying her and Gwen's gratitude, for letting them borrow books for their essays, she founds herself scanning the shelves for something to preoccupy her thoughts.

She found a book on feminism. As she glanced at the back of the book, Skylar grew more interested in what it had to offer.

* * *

Days passed with no word from Christian. One week turned into two, and Skylar found herself agitated. She felt herself growing stubborn as the month of January passed.

It was February when she called Frank's house. A woman answered. Skylar thought she had dialled the wrong number, as she always recognized the voice of Ettie, Frank's aunt.

"Is Christian O'Connelly there?" Skylar asked.

"No, I'm sorry. Christian went to buy us some coffees. Who should I say is calling?"

Skylar slammed the handset down. How could he do this to her? Who was she? Skylar looked at the shining engagement ring and clenched her fist.

A few minutes later, the telephone rang. She was the only one home, so she had to answer it.

"Hello?" she said, sniffling.

"Piper, is that you?" asked Christian.

"Just who do you think you are?" she screamed into the receiver. "It has been weeks since we last spoke. Then I call you, to find out another girl is answering the phone! Do you think I am stupid?"

"First of all," he said, "that was Samantha – Frank's new girlfriend – who answered the phone, since Frank was busy talking to his uncle. I stepped out to get coffee because we were studying here. Anything else you'd like to know?"

She felt ashamed that she had thought the worst. "I have not spoken to you in so long and – "

He cut her off, "I am swamped with classes and work. I was going to call you this evening and make amends."

Skylar felt torn. "Oh, Christian. Can we possibly start over again?"

"Yeah," he sighed, "sure thing, Piper."

"Christian, I… Never mind. How about you call me back tomorrow?"

He knew she was sorry, yet he was irritated.

"That is probably for the best, Skylar. I will talk to you later."

She heard a click.

The next day, she waited by the phone. Around noon it rang. She sprang to her feet and picked it up on the first jingle.

"Hello? Christian, is that you?"

"How are you, Piper?"

"Listen," she said, "about what I said yesterday…"

"It's in the past."

She sighed, thankful for his forgiveness.

They spoke for almost half an hour, keeping the conversation light.

"I love you, Christian," she said at the end. "Don't you worry about me; everything is going well." She masked her true feelings.

"I love you too, Piper. Take good care of yourself. I will be in touch."

She hung up, trying to ignore that he had not said, "See you under the Sitka."

* * *

March saw Ospero Falls awaken from the grip of icy slumber, and Skylar yearned for the sunshine, to touch her skin again.

Gwen was happy when she secured her first photography job.

The Montgomery's, a wealthy family in Averston, hired her to take pictures of their daughter Ashley's spring wedding.

Soon, it was April and wedding bells were about to ring, for one of Averston's finest.

Upon arriving at the Montgomery manor, Gwen planned to seek out the bride-to-be. She wanted to photograph her, before the ceremony started. Knocking on the door, Gwen waited. An elderly black man, dressed in formal attire, answered.

"May I help you, miss?"

"Yes, I'm the photographer for Miss Ashley Montgomery's wedding."

He welcomed her in. As she went to open her camera case, a servant carrying a tray full of delicacies approached.

"You must be the dishwasher; we've been waiting for you?" she asked.

The butler shook his head. "No Sissy, this is the young lady who's here to take Miss Ashley's pictures."

Sissy hung her head and curtseyed. "I am so sorry, miss. My mistake."

Looking at another woman of colour dusting the stairwell, Gwen was overcome with memories, of her and Evamya.

Gwen's cheeks flushed, as she realized the Montgomery's servants were all black.

"Now you listen here, there won't be no bowing to me!"

Hearing the commotion, Mrs. Montgomery came dashing over.

"What is all the noise about?"

"You should be ashamed of yourself!" Gwen shouted.

Mrs. Montgomery's face showed displeasure.

"Excuse me, young lady! Who do you think you are marching in here and speaking to me that way"?

Gwen stood defiant. Looking straight at the mother of the bride she said, "Go find someone else, who will be subject to your slavery, because I will have none of it!"

Mrs. Montgomery was furious and slapped the young girl's face, seething with outrage, she mocked, "How dare you come into my home and insult me, after I was willing to pay you a fair amount. You should feel privileged!" she taunted. "All you black people are the same, never respecting where their freedom came from!"

Gwen grabbed the tray from the stunned maid. She dumped its contents onto Mrs. Montgomery's satin gown. "Us black people! We don't like to be told by white bigots like you, where our roots of freedom come from!"

Gwen turned and stormed off.

"I am going to make sure you are never hired as a photographer again!" Mrs. Montgomery yelled after her.

It was not long before the news spread all over Averston and Ospero Falls about the chaos that had unfolded at the Montgomery estate. Gwen expected some fallout, and when she next visited Averston, people cast glances over their shoulders when she passed on the streets.

At the beginning of the school year, Gwen had been asked to take photos at the formal dance and she had gratefully accepted.

Now a rumour circulated that none of the students wanted their picture taken by her. Even though she had been chosen to be valedictorian, she began to feel classmates were now ignoring her.

Gwen decided to back out of the special night. Before all of the drama unfolded, she had already written her valedictorian speech, on some of Evamya's old recipe cards. Feeling rejected, Gwen threw them in the garbage.

The next day, Skylar – who had tried to convince Gwen not to back out – pulled from the trash, her best friends address to the Class of 1967.

Though Gwen accepted her shunning, the reality that no one had asked her to the formal, upset J & J Hurston's. They felt Gwen should be treated with dignity and that someone should escort her to the dance. Inviting her over for dinner, she listened to their plan. Despite her reluctance, Gwen agreed to go. They only had one condition – she could not utter a word of their intentions to anybody, even Skylar. With only three weeks until the dance, the Hurston's began to put their plan in motion.

Meanwhile, Skylar and Christian spoke weekly. With the excitement of her big night looming, she wanted everything to be perfect. While he was happy to hear that his fiancée now was chosen as valedictorian, he sympathized with Gwen in her struggle.

Finally, the weekend arrived for both the graduation ceremony and the formal dance. The school had decided to split the festivities over two days, to accommodate the large graduating class.

Arriving in the morning, Christian was given strict orders not to see Skylar until after the ceremony. He guessed if they were to meet beforehand, she would be too emotional to get through her address to the graduating class. They made plans to celebrate later that evening at Canetti's.

Frank thought it was best, to stay behind in Norelton with his girlfriend Samantha, yet he felt remiss not being there for Gwen.

As Gwen helped Skylar fix her hair in the bathroom, neither realized they each had surprises planned for the other.

Walking out into the foyer, Skylar turned to Gwen and embraced her.

"I love you so much," she said. "Tonight, when I get up to say my speech, I hope you know that you should be standing where I am."

They waited in the foyer for Victoria. Meanwhile, Christian sat with the crowd in the Beech Lacus School gymnasium, in anticipation of the ceremony.

Around 6 o'clock, the students filed in.

After Principal Carter's address to the grads, each student was called up to receive their diploma. Skylar's speech was to conclude the ceremonies. When the time came, she walked on-stage and stood fidgeting in front of the podium.

"Good evening ladies and gentlemen, and the graduates of 1967," she said. "It is an honour to be chosen to speak on this occasion. As valedictorian, I hope to convey a message that reminds us of our roots here in Ospero Falls, while preparing us for the future. One word encapsulates the significance of that message, and we should never take it for granted. That word is freedom. Here among us, there is someone who knows far more about the value of freedom than me or anyone else I know. She should be standing where I am. Skylar paused, then took a deep breath in, she exhaled. "Gwen," Skylar said, holding up the recipe cards, "will you come up to the stage and share the speech you prepared?"

Murmurs filled the room. All eyes turned to Gwen; in a moment, the community of Ospero Falls would never forget. Praying for Evamya to give her courage, Gwen stood up.

She wished Evamya was there to give her some wisdom; yet she felt her voice reminding her of her roots, tethered to the past.

On stage, Skylar hugged her. "Your momma Cecilia would be so proud."

The tender words caught Gwen off-guard. She stood quiet, at the podium for a moment, before looking out at the expectant crowd.

"Good evening to all of you," she said. "First of all, I want to thank the late Evamya Walker for always believing in me and reminding me to be proud of where I came from." She glanced down at her cards , and began to read:

"Freedom, to me, is being able to stand before everyone, to speak without restraint or fear of retaliation. Freedom to me, is being able to write an essay on my Canadian hero, who was black. On October 9, 1823,

Mary Ann Shadd was born free in the United States. Then they changed the laws. Speaking of her country, she said, 'Were it not for the monster of slavery, we would have a common destiny here – in the land of our birth.'

Freedom is being able to speak those words without my voice stifled for uttering them.

"Like my hero, my family came to Canada to be free. The night my Grandmother Clara died; a small, torn rag was found in her dress pocket. On it was a drawing of a star, a cross, and the Canadian Flag – three symbols that together, represented freedom to her. It was all she had, to connect our family to its past and our faith. My Grandmother, or Bibi as I fondly refer to her as, made it so that she would never forget where we came from.

"As I stand here tonight, I am thankful to her that I live in a country where I can be free. I am free to worship, free to share my opinions, and free to pursue a career of my choice. I am free to give a voice to the voiceless, and I am free to stand up for what I believe in – without being punished. So, I ask all of you sitting here today to consider what the word freedom means to you. I hope that while you chase your dreams, you remember that someone – just as my hero, and my grand-mother, and my great-aunt, and countless others did for me – someone sacrificed their liberty… so you could be free!"

When Gwen finished, whispers passed through the audience. Then thunderous applause resounded from within the gym walls as the audience stood, clapping.

When the graduating class gathered in the lobby, Skylar watched as one by one, their classmates walked up and embraced Gwen. Apologies were given, while some hugged her, embarrassed for the way she had been treated. Standing off in the distance, Skylar felt a presence behind her. Turning, she envisioned Evamya, smiling among the throngs of people.

Chapter 21

Purity

AFTER THE CEREMONY, EVERYONE GATHERED AT CANETTI'S FOR free pizza and bottles of cola. The front door swung open. As Gwen walked in with the Hurston's, the place erupted in cheers.

"I reckon what you did for Gwen goes beyond the bonds of friendship," Jawana said to Skylar. "May God bless you for having the courage to speak up."

"You always amaze me, Skylar," Gwen said. "I do not know what I ever would do without you, my sister in faith. Thanks for making tonight so special. I know Evamya would be so proud of you."

"Of us!" Skylar said.

The next day, Skylar and Gwen awoke earlier than usual. They had a lot to do to prepare for prom. Gwen had kept her promise to the Hurston's, and not even Skylar knew she had a date. Everybody assumed she was going on her own.

The anticipation of the evening's dance, made the young women anxious, as they tried on their dresses in front of the full-length mirror. Gwen chose to let her tight, raven curls tumble down to her shoulders, whereas Skylar opted for an upswept hairstyle, allowing only a few wisps of strawberry-blonde locks to frame her face.

Victoria and Sophia had spent months sewing the dresses and finished in time for the formal. While Gwen would wear a striking red smock with billowy sleeves, Victoria was not sure about the short length. Skylar politely reminded her mother that it was now the style. Gwen had saved all of her money, to purchase a pair of white, mid-calf, flat-heeled boots that complemented both her outfit and long, slender legs.

Skylar wore a sleeveless armada mini-dress with sparkles in the front. A detailed golden-arched design of sequins, embroidered on individually by Victoria, emphasized her curves. The tailored lines glittered under the lights. Skylar knew that with her dazzling outfit, Christian would find her hard to resist.

The young women rushed around, applying last minute touches of make-up and bursts of hairspray. They finally emerged into the sitting room to the delight of Victoria, Sophia, and Olivia. As the women checked them over for any zippers undone or straps sticking out, Victoria fought back tears.

"My two baby girls are grown young ladies," she said.

"Do not embarrass me, Momma," Skylar blushed.

"Oh Bird Girl," Gwen said, "let her have her moment."

A knock on the door interrupted them.

Gwen went to answer. Opening the door, she saw standing before her a tall man dressed in a dark mahogany suit complemented by a silver-and-amber striped tie. He had a commanding presence, with chiselled features, his brilliant white smile captivated Gwen. Above his left pocket, a boutonniere of a single tiger lily was pinned to his lapel.

"Good evening my lady," he said with a thick accent. "You must be the beautiful Gwendolyn Walker the Hurston's told me so much about." Putting her hand out, he took it in his and kissed it. "It is truly a pleasure to meet you, miss. My name is Abimbola."

"It's nice to meet you, Abimbola," she said.

Victoria welcomed him and chimed in, "Do you have a last name?"

"No, miss, just Abimbola," he smiled. "Where I come from in Africa, last names have no significance. It is your first name that commands attention and symbolizes something."

Victoria couldn't resist asking, "If you do not mind me asking, what does your name mean?"

"It means born wealthy."

"Who is your friend?" Skylar asked from the sitting room.

"Will you come in for a moment?" Gwen asked. Abimbola nodded and followed her in.

"This is Abimbola," she said. "His parents are friends with the Hurston's and are in Ospero Falls for a visit. Abimbola graciously offered to escort me to the formal."

Shaking hands, he impressed the women with his manners. Skylar was stunned by how handsome he was.

Tucked under his arm was a small, clear box. He presented it to Gwen. Inside, she saw a beautiful corsage of sherbet tiger lilies. They matched his attire. She was speechless.

"Pretty flowers for a pretty lady!" he said.

"Thank you so much, Abimbola."

He pinned on the corsage. She was swept up in the moment.

"Do you want some photographs taken, Gwen?" Skylar asked.

She blushed, realizing how smitten she must be to forget to take pictures.

"Oh, of course," she said. "Let's not forget to get some of us too."

Taking Gwen's camera out of the bag, Skylar snapped a few photos. Victoria took the camera and captured several more of the two friends.

"I think we should go now," Gwen said. "I promised Amos and Jawana that we would stop in before the dance. I will see you there, Skylar."

"It was nice to meet each of you," Abimbola said.

As the door closed, Skylar smiled, happy for Gwen.

"Well, my good heavens," Sophia said, "did you see that young man? Any girl would be happy to have a well-dressed fellow like that on her arm."

They smiled and nodded in agreement.

Victoria saw Skylar fidget. "Songbird, there is no need to worry. Christian will be along soon."

"He said he had a few last-minute things to do," Sophia said, "and then he will be around for you soon, sweetie."

Before they were off to the prom, Victoria looked over at her daughter, with tears forming.

"I have been waiting for the right moment to give you something songbird and I feel this is it."

Walking over to Skylar, she opened her hand. In her palm was a striking, green, sparrow brooch. The eye was a simple pearl and the outline of it was surrounded by silver.

It's so beautiful momma," said Skylar.

Holding her hand to her lips, Victoria was trembling as she spoke,

"This brooch is made out of aventurine and is a treasured gift from someone, who loved both you and me."

Skylar became overwhelmed, at the notion, of who it once belonged to.

Victoria placed it in her daughter's hand, which was now shaking.

"Your father Eli, gave me this on our wedding day."

The other women in the parlour room were overcome with their emotions and passed a box of tissues, to dab away their tears.

Victoria pinned the brooch carefully on then added, "I thought I would have waited to give it to you, but tonight is a new chapter with Christian. You have always taken care of me, now it's time you spread your wings. You will always be my baby-girl, yet I know there are things on the horizon, which will see you have your own new beginnings."

"Oh, momma I love you and this so much!"

Skylar's tears covered her cheeks.

Victoria shook her head.

"Oh my sweet songbird! I have gone and messed up your make-up!"

Olivia and Sophia went to the kitchen for more tea and tissues, but Skylar could hear them whispering. Hugging her mother, Victoria then joined the ladies. Looking down at her ring, the glint of the sparkling stones made her sigh. She touched the bracelet Christian had given her. Reaching for her neckline, she felt disheartened. The necklace and locket her mother had given her, would have completed the outfit. Olivia came back out with a fresh, steeping pot of Earl Grey.

"He will be here soon, no need to fuss." She said reassuringly.

Looking at the clock, Skylar smiled, hoping she was right.

Olivia stood and wandered back into the kitchen. As she sat alone, Skylar peered out the window. A ribbon of lavender separated the evening skyline, as the light of day faded into night.

On the verge of tears, she stood to go fix herself up in the bathroom when Victoria stopped her.

"Go upstairs and fix up your make-up. Be sure to grab your shawl, so you do not catch a chill. Besides, then you will be ready to walk out the door."

Skylar nodded. Her disappointment turned to frustration, and she marched up the stairs two at a time. Once in the bathroom, Skylar began to twirl the engagement ring on her finger, when the noise of a pebble hit the outside casement. Wandering over to the window, she opened it.

In the backyard, were burning candles placed in the shape of a heart. In the middle, was the word that bound Skylar and Christian together: *Sitka*.

"What's the earth, with all its art, verse, music, worth, compared with love, found, gained and kept?" Christian recited.

"Ah," she swooned, "Robert Browning."

He held his hand out to her. "Skylar Reigh Falls, come sail away into a night we shall never forget."

"I will be right down, my captain," she giggled.

Running down the stairs, Skylar stopped when she saw Sophia, Victoria, and Olivia waiting for her at the door. She realized they knew Christian's plan all along and had kept it secret.

He walked in and presented an aromatic corsage of violet and yellow freesia.

"It is the flower that represents innocence and trust," he said, putting it around her wrist.

Sophia held up the camera to photograph the couple, but Christian interrupted her.

"Please wait for just a moment," he said, reaching into his pocket. "Something is missing."

Skylar looked puzzled as he pulled out the necklace and locket she had given up as lost.

"Oh my goodness!" she said. "Where did you find it?"

"I spent all day searching for it, in the area where we were sledding in the winter," he said, motioning for her to sit on the Davenport beside him. "I thought it was lost forever, but then the strangest thing happened. I was walking back along some rugged, steep terrain when I thought I heard a bird chirping. It grabbed my attention enough to make me look. I saw something shimmering on the tree branch, where I thought the bird was perched. As I drew nearer, I instantly recognized the locket. It was a bit weathered, so I took it to Mr. Hadly. He polished it up, remarking on its beauty, and how lucky I was to find it. I telephoned your mother, and we shared in the joy that the necklace had made its way back to you – with a little help! The strange thing was, I never did see any bird."

Placing the necklace around her neck again, he tenderly kissed her shoulder.

"From what I see in front of me, I would say you bathed in beauty today," he said.

Skylar blushed.

"Speaking of birds," she remarked, "Momma gifted me this beautiful brooch that my Daddy gifted her on their wedding day."

Christian bent down to take a closer look, then replied, "How perfect is that? I can only imagine what it means to you Piper."

Tipping her over, he smirked, "Looks like I am one of the luckiest men on earth, to be attending tonight's festivities, with a sparkling gem like you!"

Skylar appreciated how handsome he was, sporting a mod haircut that fit with the sleek, merchant navy suit he was wearing. His buttoned-down, pale blue shirt revealed dark chest hair that enticed her touch. Skylar's body tingled when his hand brushed up against her sleek frame.

"Well, thank you," she said. "I must say that this beauty has a charming date tonight."

Urging them to stand up, Victoria snapped several photographs.

"You two best be going if you are going to make it to the dance," she said.

Christian took Skylar's hand and escorted her to the Cadillac. She smiled when he opened the car door, revealing a string of rock roses and daisies linked together around her passenger seat.

"Your carriage awaits," he said.

Soon after arriving they joined Gwen, who introduced Christian to her date, Abimbola.

"Oh my goodness," Gwen said, seeing Skylar's locket, "where did you find it?"

Skylar slipped her hand into Christian's, marvelling at how they fit together perfectly.

"Christian found it on the branch of a tree. There's more to it, but I will share later."

As the night unfolded, Skylar and Gwen revelled in their new-found freedom. When the last dance of the evening was announced, Skylar found herself wrapped up in Christian's embrace.

After the dance ended, Gwen went up to Skylar and pulled her aside.

"Well, what are you two up to now?" she asked.

"I don't know," Skylar shrugged. "Christian says it is a surprise."

Gwen smiled her mischievous grin and said,

"I bet he has a big surprise for you."

Skylar gasped and began to blush.

"Oh my goodness, Gwendolyn-Sue, you bite your tongue now, girl!"

"I am going to Canetti's with Abimbola," Gwen announced, walking away.

"He is such a dream!"

"The Hurston's sure made your prom night special!"

Gwen turned around and ran back to Skylar. As they hugged, she said, "You're the sister of my heart, forever and always."

Moments later, their dates escorted them off the dance floor. Indicating they should leave; Christian offered his arm to Skylar.

"The night awaits, Piper."

Wrapping her arm around his, they strolled towards the door. Skylar turned around just in time to give her best friend a wink.

* * *

Abimbola and Gwen sat across from each other in a booth at Canetti's.

"I had a wonderful time this evening," she said. "Thank you."

"The pleasure has been well worth my time," he smiled, looking intently into her eyes.

Over the next few hours, they talked about many things, including the Civil Rights movement and the quest for equality, which they both had strong connections to.

Gwen sat mesmerized, listening with sadness, as Abimbola spoke of the conflict their people struggled with. Such as South Africa being barred from the Olympics because of their policies on apartheid.

There were the three civil-rights workers in Mississippi, who went missing and were later found dead. Both of them shared the same concerns.

They shared a reverence for Martin Luther King Jr. and toasted his accomplishment in winning the Nobel Peace Prize, years earlier, by raising and clinking their glasses of cream soda. She felt connected to the man who, only hours earlier, was a complete stranger.

* * *

Skylar unbuckled her seatbelt and shifted next to Christian, as he drove the Cadillac towards the dock. Upon arriving, they waited for Hank Stevenson to motion them aboard.

Christian grinned, "Our Sitka awaits."

Hank was silent as he navigated the ferry across.

He spoke once the ferry docked, "Will you need me to wait on you?"

"Thanks, but we will not be returning till morning," Christian said, passing him a few dollars. "I appreciate your time tonight."

"I will be back to get you two around 8 o'clock," Hank winked.

"Good Lord, Christian," Skylar whispered, "my poor Momma's gonna flip out!"

"Your mother gave me permission, Piper," he said, grabbing her hand. "I told her after all these years, you and I have shared so much at the Sitka, we never had the chance to spend the night – just the two of us."

Her cheeks reddened.

Driving the Cadillac off the ferry, they soon arrived and parked under the tree. As he turned off the engine, she grabbed his hand.

"Please leave the music on for a bit longer," she said, "as it is only us out here."

He turned the radio back on to hear the night fill with song.

"Let me go up first, Piper," he said, "I have to make sure everything is just right."

Closing her eyes, she wished the moment would last forever.

When she opened them, she saw a soft glow in the darkness of the tree house. After a few minutes, Christian returned.

He opened the passenger door. Reaching into the car, Christian slid his arms underneath her, and lifted her up out of the Cadillac.

"Alright Piper," he whispered, "your evening of pleasure begins."

* * *

The crowd dwindled at Canetti's, but Abimbola and Gwen did not want the memorable night to end. They spoke of their futures, as if they had known one another, for some time.

He listened to her thoughts on Vietnam and how Americans had become divided over their involvement. She added her voice to those of the protestors across the nation, who echoed Dr. King's call for an end to the war.

After the episode with the Montgomery's in Averston, Gwen was standing up once again, for what she believed in.

She proudly spoke of Evamya and her own family's journey to freedom long ago, and of their harrowing escape from the chains of slavery that bound their bodies, but not their spirits. Abimbola listened intently, as she shared her personal ancestry, which was a common thread between them.

As if reading the words stamped on her soul, he wanted to impart to Gwen, the wisdom passed along through the generations of his own family. Peering deep into her eyes, he said,

"We are bound by our roots, not by our feet."

Gwen reached across the table and took his hand in hers.

Looking at their similar skin tone, they both felt the equality between them.

* * *

At the treehouse, Skylar kicked off her heels to climb the ladder. Christian waited at the top. He placed his hand over her eyes when she arrived at the entryway.

"Tonight is a special night for us, Piper," he whispered. "I want you to imagine what is before you."

Inhaling the night air, she was delighted to smell the aroma of sandalwood. The warmth of candlelight danced on her skin, and the yearning to make love to Christian overwhelmed her.

He dropped his hand, and her eyes adjusted to the brightness of the candles placed all around the tree house. On the floor, was a white feather quilt with vermillion sheets overtop. In the corner, a bottle of homemade strawberry wine was chilled, beside two, stemmed glasses. Next to the makeshift bed was a decanter of patchouli oil. The musk earthy aroma permeated the wooden walls. In a mason jar, a bouquet of hand-picked daisies nodded at her.

As she stood in wonder, he took her hand and led his future bride to sit with him on the crisp sheets. He poured her a glass of wine. The liquid tingled as it slipped past her lips. Reaching behind her, he kissed her neck, sending shivers all over. Warmth enveloped her as he undid the zipper on her gown. Both knew nothing was stopping them as they finally gave in to desire. Gone were any remnants of their childhood, as their skins yielded to one another's touch. Making love was as natural as the tree that held them.

As he stripped off her clothes, Christian's eyes roamed Skylar's nakedness. Quickly, he took off his own clothes, and she found herself staring at his exposed physique. Christian slipped off his underwear, and she drew a deep breath when she saw him bare, for the first time. Basking in the flickers of candlelight, he tenderly lifted her face and gazed intently into her eyes.

"You look more heavenly than I ever could have imagined all these years," he whispered.

His words put her at ease, and she gave in to the sensations.

"Make love to me, Christian."

Without hesitation, he took his hands and lightly stroked her backside. Reaching down for the massage oil, he poured some of the liquid Patchouli between the palms of his hands and on her shoulders. His sexual play was hypnotic, as he caressed every inch of her sensual curves. Skylar's breathing deepened, as she arched forward absorbing into her, the pleasure he was giving. Lying back down on to the fresh sheets, Christian extended his hand outwards to Skylar, seducing her with his hungry mouth as she drew closer to him, her heart beating faster. His eyes turned to Skylar's exposed soft honey breasts; he gravitated toward their beauty, and he ran his lips over her rose-pink nipples. Back and forth, his tongue flickered, savouring the taste of her sweet scent. She could feel every inch of manhood pressing against her inner thighs, moist with pleasure. Her body inflamed with a yearning desire, she in no way had experienced before. Skylar's moans intertwined with his deep breathing, and as she parted her legs unto him, she thrust forward, inviting in the passion that had been building for years.

There, in the solace of the Sitka tree, they exchanged without words something that could never be taken back. They made love, connecting in a way she never imagined possible.

* * *

Abimbola and Gwen walked arm in arm. Leaning towards her, he brushed his lips against hers. The distinct taste of cinnamon lip-gloss lingered.

"I want to see you again, Miss. Gwendolyn," he said softly.

"I don't want you to go," she added hastily, "When are you leaving?"

"Tomorrow. I must return to the city to attend to my business.

After all we talked about, I can't believe I never asked what your plans are now that you have graduated."

"I want to pursue photography," she shrugged, "but the courses are far too expensive."

"Gwendolyn, if you want your dreams to come true, then you will find a way. May I call you in a few days?"

"I would like that," she smiled.

Arriving on the front porch of the Falls' house, they said goodbye.

"Thank you for such an amazing evening," she said.

"It is I who am grateful," he said, "for the privilege of spending time with such a fine young woman."

* * *

In the morning, Gwen stumbled into the kitchen for a late breakfast, still half-asleep. She saw Victoria stooped over her black coffee, dark circles around her eyes. Victoria had spent most of the night tossing and turning. She second-guessed the decision, to let her future son-in-law take her daughter away, to the tree house for the night.

Gwen grabbed a blueberry muffin before settling into a chair beside her.

"Morning, Ms. Falls," she said.

"Hello, dear. How was the formal?"

"It was a wonderful evening. Abimbola is such a charming person."

Victoria smiled. "So, when do you see him again?"

"He had to leave this morning but promised to call me in a few days."

"That is great to hear, Gwen! I hope it works out for you, sweetie. You certainly deserve it."

"Thanks, Ms. Falls. So where is Skylar this morning?

Let me guess, she is probably still under a heap of covers upstairs, right?"

Victoria fell silent for a moment, not sure of what to say.

"No dear." she paused, then added, "Christian and Skylar spent the night out at the Sitka tree."

The words fell like bricks from her mouth, tumbling out into the open. Gwen was stunned. She had no idea of their plans and found herself at a loss for words. Victoria reached over and patted the girl's hand.

"It's okay, honey," Victoria said, patting her hand. "I knew about it and could not do anything to stop them. After all, they will be married before we know it."

Gwen shook her head. "I am sorry Ms. Falls, but gee-whiz, I cannot believe you are okay with this."

"Listen to me, Gwen. I am just happy she is with the likes of Christian O'Connelly and not some fellow who only wants one thing, then is gone forever from her life."

Gwen nodded in agreement.

"Skylar sure is lucky to have you as her momma."

"I am like a momma to you as well young lady," Victoria smiled. "Please never forget that."

The front door opened. Victoria and Gwen watched as Skylar tried to sneak by and up the stairs. "Good morning, Songbird," Victoria said.

"Hey Momma," Skylar said, freezing in her tracks, she mumbled, "Just please let me sleep for a while and we will talk later. I am tired, as I didn't get much sleep."

Skylar bit the bottom of her lip, as the words made her wince.

Gwen wanted to burst into laughter, however, knew the timing was not appropriate.

Okay sweetie, we will have a chat after," said Victoria. "Get some rest songbird."

She knew it was no use pursuing the matter any further.

Gwen quietly stood up and began to wash the dishes, secretly envious of her friend's life.

Skylar fell fast asleep into a terrible nightmare. She was running frantically on black sand surrounded by molten lava. The ground split in two, engulfing her.

She woke up screaming. Gwen bolted into her room. Beads of sweat had gathered on Skylar's forehead, and she struggled to catch her breath. Gwen smoothed her dampened hair.

"Are you okay, Skylar?"

"I am alright. It was just a bad dream."

Gwen left and came back with a glass of cold water. "Do you want to talk about it?"

Skylar was reluctant at first yet wanted to confide in someone.

"You know what," she sighed, "I thought it was going to be like fireworks going off, this fantastic thing, which some of it was. But to be truthful, I kind of enjoyed the whole making-out part better than the actual… Well, you know."

"No, Bird Girl," Gwen said, raising her eyebrows, "I don't know."

They burst into laughter, and Skylar shared the details with Gwen.

"Did it hurt?"

"It did at first, but then after a short time this warm, glowing feeling came over me. I know Christian really enjoyed it."

Gwen giggled, until her sides ached.

Standing up, she slapped her friend on the shoulder and casually remarked, "Well, thanks for the information, but when I asked if you wanted to talk…I was referring to your nightmare!"

Skylar's mouth fell open. She threw her pillow at the bedroom door Gwen was exiting out of and hollered, "Gwendolyn-Sue, you get back here right now and spill the beans on your date!"

"Unlike you," Gwen said, peeking around the corner and sticking out her tongue, "I don't kiss and tell!"

Skylar laughed at her best friend's antics. Slowly, she got up to go into the shower.

Christian had made plans to meet up later that afternoon before he went back to Norelton.

As she was about to leave, Victoria caught up with her.

"Listen, honey, I think we should talk. Don't you?"

Skylar was dreading the moment. She sulked back into the sitting room. Sitting down beside Victoria, she let out a sigh.

"Momma, I know how hard all of this must be for you, but it was bound to happen, and I am glad it was with Christian!"

"I hope you took some precautions. I do not want to see you get pregnant at this stage."

"Yes, Momma," she blushed. "Christian was very careful."

"Is there anything else you want to talk about?" inquired Victoria.

"Not right now, but when and if I do, I will make sure to come and see you first."

Victoria hugged Skylar, who had slipped out of adolescence and further away now as a young woman.

Skylar met Christian at Canetti's. He looked refreshed and as handsome as ever. Upon sitting down, the two lovers looked at each other quietly for a moment, unsure of what to say.

"What can I get you two?" the waitress asked.

"I think two pieces of your lemon meringue pie please," said Christian.

Skylar bit her bottom lip, as her favourite pie was saskatoon berry.

After the waitress left with their orders, Christian spoke.

"Hear me out before you say anything, Piper. Last night was so incredible for me. I have spent half the day wondering if it was for you too. I got to thinking… I can come back on July long weekend, and you can return to Norelton with me."

Skylar's heart began to pound as she struggled to tell him how she truly felt. Even after making love, her views had not changed, about wanting to stay in Ospero Falls. She averted his eyes.

"I don't think I can go to Norelton with you," she mumbled.

Chapter 22

Strife

CHRISTIAN SAT MOTIONLESS, TRYING TO UNDERSTAND WHAT SKYLAR was saying. He was confused by her decision.

"I do not understand, Skylar. We are planning to get married and are supposed to be preparing our future together."

She could see his anger build and tried to defuse the situation.

"I just need some more time to think things out, Christian. I want to go with you, but I am scared. If you will be a bit more patient, I am sure everything will be fine."

He slammed his fist down on the table, startling her. His eyes narrowed as he clenched his teeth.

"Then what the hell was last night about? Damn it, woman! You cannot toy with my emotions like this, Skylar. You are tearing us apart!"

The tears welled up in her olive eyes. She twisted a napkin in her hands and looked away. Christian was lost; he did not know what more he could do. Her avoidance was driving a wedge between them. Why did she not realize it?

"You do not want me to push you away," he said, "yet you are not giving me any other choice."

She looked intensely into his eyes. Staring back at him, was uncertainty.

"Give me more time, Christian. I will be able to plan our wedding soon, and both our mothers can help the way they always wanted to. We will set a date right here, and as God as my witness, I swear to you that will be it."

As much as he did not like leaving her behind once again, he knew that if he pressured her anymore, she would run the other way. Further, it would make both Sophia and Victoria happy if they waited. His face softened, as he took her trembling hand in his.

"Okay, Piper. Just say something that I want to hear."

"All that is promised to be will happen under our beloved Sitka tree."

He stroked her hand and smiled.

"Well then, when shall we take the plunge?"

"How about an autumn wedding? You know how I have always loved that season. September would be nice, maybe around the end of the month?"

He felt relieved. The waitress came back to the table.

"Pick a number between one and 30," he said to her.

"Twenty-five," she answered, caught off-guard.

He clapped his hands once.

"Then it's settled, on September 25th, 1969, you shall become Mrs. O'Connelly."

The waitress congratulated them.

Skylar was relieved. She had bought more time to convince Christian, why they should settle in Ospero Falls and not Norelton.

Back at the Falls' house, they shared their exciting news with everyone. Both Sophia and Victoria tried to hide their relief in their decision to wait.

Christian needed to go back to the city, therefore he made his round of goodbyes.

Standing on the front porch, he held on to the girl he adored. Once so delicate, she now felt solid in his arms.

"I think it is a good thing that you stay," he said. "Maybe with your mind on the wedding preparations, time will fly by. Besides, I know that if you give Norelton a chance, you will love it."

"Thank you, Christian, for everything. I know in my heart there is no amount of distance that can ever separate us."

They shared one last passionate kiss before parting. As he walked off, Christian felt a piece of him stay with her.

* * *

As summer of '67 began in Ospero Falls, Skylar found herself busy with her volunteer duties at the sanctuary.

Further up the inlet, in a residential school, stood a man dressed all in black – with the exception of a white collar. He fingered the wooden beads of a rosary, mumbling prayers under his breath. His words were stained with the blood of their spirit – defiled by the deeds he'd committed against those he was supposed to save – yet considered them as savages.

Hidden amongst the tree line, was the emaciated frame of a fourteen-year-old boy, named Makwa. The thick lines underneath his dark eyes, showcased the anxiety he had already suffered throughout his adolescent life.

The young boy's skin bore the marks of beatings, in the residential school he attended. Removed from a loving family when he was six, his name was stripped like cedar bark, from a tree. At the new residence, he was number 72. This was a means of eliminating the true identity of the boy.

Whenever Makwa spoke his family's language, he was disciplined in ways unfit for animals. In a shed on a mattress tainted with transgression, the suffering he endured at the hands of his enemy, was inflicted daily. He learned to conceal his roots – or else it was struck from his weary carcass. Despite his isolation, he had heard and seen at his own school, the severity of similar abuse, spread across the Canadian landscape.

There was only one priest who treated Makwa kindly.

He snuck him dry biscuits that were treats, compared to the mash of bug-infested gruel, the children were normally forced to eat.

As months went by, the pangs of hunger and starvation, took the lives of the children that could not endure the prison-like conditions. Yet even death was preferable, to the acts perpetuated by the deviants who sinned, while acting in the name of God.

The priest who befriended Makwa, appalled by the violence occurring every day, reported the abuse. One night, Makwa overheard the priest speaking with another. They talked of how the sickening actions of some priests, in the name of education and the Lord, were leading to genocide and the wrath of God. Shortly after, Makwa never saw the two priests again. Unbeknown to him, they had found themselves removed from their positions and sent away.

Staring out of the large room he shared with others, Makwa had heard noise out in the backyard area of the Residential school. Being curious, he quietly snuck to see a gathering of priests. At first Makwa could not make out what they were doing with shovels and mounds of dirt. Knowing the morning call was early, he went back to his stained mattress shared repeatedly amongst his brothers. They had slept in the same bed before him, then were removed and never seen again.

In the early morning as others were stirring, Makwa went back to the window. He discovered numerous mounds of dirt had been dug and all that was left were small, oval mounds of earth. As he began to add up the mounds, a sickening feeling was settling upon him. He lost count after 200, yet there were far more. It was then that Makwa planned his escape.

With no one to speak up for him, the young boy knew it could be any day, when he became a pile of dirt.

In between class one day, he slipped out of the residential school and ran off into the bushes.

He searched through the forest, near the water's edge, for a log worthy of his expedition. Makwa found a thick Sitka spruce he could dig his nails into. The bark would allow him to float on the log, like an unfinished canoe. Before pushing off into the frigid waters, he closed his eyes and thanked the Creator for guidance and the means of escape, using a tree. Once the ocean touched his skin, he let the salt waters of Mother Nature cleanse his wounds. Without a destination, he knew that putting as much space between him and the island of evil spirits would be his only salvation.

* * *

When Skylar met Makwa for the first time in person, it was
by chance.

One day, taking a shortcut to the sanctuary, Skylar stumbled across a
boy picking berries among the bushes. Even though she was startled, she
did not make a sound.

He took one look at her and continued picking the berries. Her eyes
studied the thick, chalk-like scars upon his back. She knew every bit
of his delicate frame held a story, as his skin bore one thing – survival.
Slowly, Skylar walked up to him, and she began to quickly pick
the berries.

At first Makwa stood rigid and unsure of what to do. Then he saw
the mushed berries in her hand. Instinctively, he shook his head and
pointed to the mush of fruit in her hand, staining her palm a bluish-
purple. Makwa looked at Skylar and then to the bushes. Even though he
was hungry, he plucked the ripened berries carefully, as they were full of
juice. She smiled, watching him take such care. He thought her method
was wasteful. As if her fumbling, was the result of it being her the first
time she had ever picked fruit from such laden thickets. Skylar did not
know where he was from or if he spoke English. She did not want to
frighten him away, so she quietly picked the berries, in silence. Later as
they parted, she had a sense that they would see each other again.

A few days later, farther up shore, she saw him write something in
the sand with a stick. She read it.

"Makwa, Is that your name?", she asked.

He nodded.

Over the next few weeks, Skylar spent a lot of time in the woods
seeking him out. Although he never spoke to her, they shared a
connection in their reverence of nature. Sometimes she would lead

him down to the river, where she would read to him from her nature magazines. The words seemed to calm him.

He was curious, yet not willing to speak a word.

One day, she observed him whittling something, and as she approached, Makwa hid it from her. The next day, she was delighted to see him back at the same spot, carving intensely.

Meanwhile, when she spoke with Christian numerous times, she never mentioned Makwa. Skylar felt he would stop her from seeing the young boy, based out of fear. She was disheartened when Christian told her on the phone that he would not be able to come back home, even for a short visit. His third year of schooling had begun, and he was working to save up for the wedding.

As for Gwen, she had shared with Skylar her feelings for Abimbola. They spent two weeks together in the summer. Before his departure, he asked Gwen to come with him.

After discussing the matter with the Hurston's, they shocked Gwen by giving her an envelope full of money. Jawana explained since they had no children of their own, they wanted to see Gwen pursue a career in photography. Through donations made by other church members and using some of their own savings, the Hurston's had saved enough for her to complete the first year of a three-year arts program.

After they first met, Abimbola returned to the city to tell his family about the beautiful girl who exuded wisdom and dreamt of being a photographer. His family supported him and offered to help them out financially. Gwen cried when he told her, overjoyed by their contribution.

All her life, she had wanted to see the world through a camera lens. Now she was being afforded the opportunity. She accepted graciously and broke the news to Victoria and Skylar.

They were thrilled to hear the exciting details. Within a few hours, Gwen had packed her precious belongings, kissed the picture of Evamya in the hallway, and bid farewell to her best friend and adoptive mother. She promised to write and be back next autumn, for her best friend's wedding.

Everything had happened so fast that for Skylar, it all seemed like a dream. Life was full of many changes that brought new challenges along the way.

As summer dwindled, she mulled over the idea of taking Makwa to the tree house. However, she saw the tattered clothes he wore and knew people would talk. One evening, Skylar waited near the blackberry bushes where they had first met. She brought him some new clothes purchased out of her wedding money. Makwa went behind the nearest tree to change, yet Skylar could again see his scars, as he slipped into the shirt. Were they the reason he did not speak?

At the ferry, Hank Stevenson raised an eyebrow.

"Miss Falls, is everything okay?"

"Certainly, Mr. Stevenson. Skylar assured him and continued, "Thank you for your concern, I have someone from the Sanctuary with me. I plan on taking my new friend here, to see our beloved Sitka tree."

Soon after, the ferry docked, Mr. Stevenson said, "I will just wait for you both to return safely."

Hank Stevenson was like family and Skylar understood his apprehension.

Arriving at the tree house, Makwa could hardly contain his excitement. He felt instantly at home with the giant, sprawling Sitka, and he scaled the tree with ease. Stopping at an opening in the branches, the young boy caressed the trunk.

Placing his ear to it, he listened for something Skylar could not hear. Smiling, Makwa placed his fist over his chest and mimicked the thumping sound of his heart. She was happy to have brought him to her cherished place. After climbing the ladder, she made her way to the platform. Motioning for him to sit beside her, they peered out in silence.

After several minutes passed, he put out his hand. For the first time in years, he felt at peace.

"My hand says we belong to this space, and we respect this land."

This surprised Skylar and she asked him,

"Where did you learn to speak so well?"

Abruptly, Makwa grew silent and shook his head.

Skylar felt it was better to remain quiet beside him.

As the days turned into weeks, Makwa prepared to leave Ospero Falls to find his own family. Skylar accepted his decision, as she always felt he was simply passing through.

When the time came for him to return to his village, he sat with her and told her how he was taken from his family with the promise of a good education. He trembled as he revealed his terrible secrets. When he finished speaking, they were both in tears.

At the dock, she asked Mr. Stevenson to assist Makwa with where it was, he needed to go.

He agreed, as she explained it was time for the young boy, to reunite with his family.

While sad to see Makwa leave, she cherished the experiences they had shared.

Before leaving on the ferry, he turned towards her and placed something in her hands. She opened them to find a songbird carved from wood, each feather flawlessly detailed. She smiled, realizing he had spent the summer carving it – and had hidden it from her, until he was finished.

"It's beautiful, Makwa."

He nodded, pleased with her reaction. When Hank indicated it was time to depart, Makwa turned and pointed to her with one hand. Clenching the other into a fist, he placed it over his chest.

"Good heart!" he said.

With tears welling up in her eyes, she watched him sail off. It occurred to her that Makwa had honoured the spruce tree with the very same words of good heart, when he first encountered the beloved Sitka.

* * *

Autumn passed by too quickly for Skylar, and soon another bleak winter fell upon Ospero Falls.

Two weeks before Christmas, she was instructed to open the present Christian had sent early. She was excited and nervous when she opened the card and read the handwritten invitation. Skylar was to join him in Norelton, for the annual party, at the home of Frank's Uncle Thomas and Aunt Ettie.

The party was planned for three days before Christmas, since Frank's aunt and uncle were going away for the holidays. Christian had made prior arrangements with them, to have Skylar stay at their house, during her visit.

He thought it would be the perfect opportunity for her to meet his friends. As well, Christian hoped it would quell any fears she clung to, about moving to the city.

He made plans after the Christmas party, to surprise her with a romantic sleigh ride around Norelton. They would return to Ospero Falls the day after to spend the holidays with Sophia, Victoria, and Olivia.

Gwen was spending her first Christmas away from Ospero Falls with Abimbola in Oakerson, a coastal city farther north. Meanwhile, Frank split his Christmas vacation between his relatives and his girlfriend Samantha's parents.

Skylar bid farewell to a tearful Victoria and boarded the ferry to Norelton. As the ship rounded the mountains, leaving Ospero Falls behind, a sense of emptiness overwhelmed her.

Anxious to see Christian, Skylar wondered about fitting in with the city folk of Norelton. Regardless, she hoped her presence would be welcome. With a sense of naivety, she could not foresee a songbird had left its nest too soon.

* * *

Christian met her upon arrival and offered assurances of a wonderful time. Once settled in with Frank's relatives, they left to join Frank and Samantha at HavenFayre Cookhouse for some holiday cheer. Since Skylar was still 18 (for another 2 weeks), she drank Shirley Temples, which made her feel a bit out of place. However, she was in the company of good people and liked Frank's girlfriend.

Samantha had a fair complexion, big blue eyes, and golden hair. She worked for Uncle Thomas as his secretary. Frank met her through him. It was evident to everyone, by how they clung to each other, they were deeply in love.

Afterwards, Christian and Skylar went for a walk. As the snow fell upon the hustle and bustle of the city, she noticed how bleak everything looked. With tall, grey buildings blotting out the mountains, it reminded her of a concrete jungle. She had to bite her lip, not wanting to offend her fiancée.

As they walked hand in hand, Christian engaged her in conversation.

"How are the wedding plans coming along?" he asked.

Skylar winced. She had not even tried on her finished wedding dress. She had made excuses to Sophia and Victoria, about how she was busy with the sanctuary.

"Oh, they are coming along nicely."

Christian, sensing her tension, changed the subject.

"So, what do you think of Samantha?"

"I think she is a lovely girl. They seem so happy."

"Just like us," he smirked, "they're mad for each other."

They returned to the house to join Frank and his relatives for an extravagant pre-Christmas dinner. Everyone enjoyed themselves – except Skylar. Though she tried to include herself in the laughter and discussion, her mind kept wandering back to the events taking place without her, at the sanctuary.

As her thoughts drifted back to Ospero Falls, which seemed a million miles away, she did not hear Christian speaking to her. He nudged her. Realizing all eyes were upon her, her cheeks reddened. Excusing herself, she apologized for being tired, and slipped away from the table to the guestroom.

Moments later, he knocked at her door. Part of him was ruffled by her conduct, but he sensed how uncomfortable she was.

She opened the door a crack.

"Sorry Christian, but I am exhausted," she whispered. "I will see you in the morning."

The door closed in his face. He had no choice but to return to the others, who kept their thoughts to themselves.

In the morning, she rose slowly. She was glad, she had her own bathroom to get ready in.

She wanted as much time to herself, as possible. After the awkwardness of leaving the dinner table abruptly, she wondered how she would be able to face everyone again?

At last, she left her room and walked past the kitchen, where maids cleaned and cooks busily prepared congealed salad, oysters on the half shell, and platters of cheese from around the world. A butler stood near the front door. She now realized why Frank's father, Oliver, was the outcast in the family.

He had chosen a hard-working life, over the riches of the wealthier existence of his brother. A large part of Thomas taking Frank into his home and offering to pay for his education arose from guilt in shunning Oliver. He had never accepted his younger brother's rudimentary lifestyle, at times ashamed to admit they were related. Frank's mother Olivia had only accepted Thomas's generous offer, to end the feud of the Whitman family. She understood it was the only way Frank would ever be able to, pursue his dreams of becoming an architect.

Aunt Ettie greeted Skylar.

"I trust that you slept well, dear?" she asked.

"Yes," Skylar said, "I most certainly did, thank you."

"Do not worry about last night, honey," Ettie winked. "It always takes some time to absorb all the crap that goes on around this house." The blunt words startled Skylar. "Oh come dear, do not act so surprised.

Believe it or not, I once was just like you. I, too, came from the wrong side of the tracks. Then one day when I looked in the mirror, I had to ask myself: 'Do you want to be a poor man's wife, popping out babies and slaving over a hot stove all day, or would you rather be a rich man's trophy, clinging to his side for everyone else to envy?'"

Pinching Skylar's cheeks, she puckered her smoky mocha tinted lips and winked.

Turning, she strutted away on her red high-heels. Each step clicked on the polished, marble tile.

Skylar wanted to fly as far as she could from Norelton.

She knew this was not the life she wanted to live. Headed back to the guest room, she bumped into Christian. Clean-shaven, he smelled of Old Spice. She was torn by the conflict between heart and mind.

The couple decided to go out for lunch together. On the way back, she dove into a pile of snow, as she used to when they were young, and made a snow angel.

When she looked up at Christian, she was saddened to see a look of disapproval upon his face. Try as he might to hide it, what once used to bring a smile to him, now evoked a sense of embarrassment. Skylar stood and brushed the snow from her. Walking slowly in silence, neither of them knowing what to say.

Back at the house, she excused herself to her room, where she stifled her sobs in to the satin pillows. Around 5 o'clock, she opened her suitcase and pulled out the simple black cocktail dress that Victoria had made her. As if going through the motions, Skylar showered, put her hair up, and took one last look in the mirror, well-aware that the woman who looked back was not the one she wanted to be.

The party had already started, with guests trickling in and mingling around the room. She looked for either Frank or Christian, but they were nowhere to be found. Standing by herself in a corner, Skylar fidgeted with her engagement ring.

A red-haired woman pranced over and shoved an empty martini glass towards her.

"Will you be a dear and go fetch me a drink?" she asked.

"I am not the hired help!" Skylar said.

"Oh my, I am so sorry," she said. "I just thought with your attire and all…"

Skylar had all she could stand and stormed upstairs.

Changing into a pair of jeans and a sweater that Gwen had knit for her, she stuffed her belongings in the suitcase.

She knew by hurrying, it would be possible to make the six o'clock ferry, to connect back to Ospero Falls.

Skylar was about to leave, when she looked down, at her engagement ring. Removing it, she placed it on the pillow. Knowing that there was no going back, she exited the room.

Her stomach churned with the harsh realization for the first time in her life, Skylar was breaking a promise.

A half-hour passed, before Christian started to worry, where she was.

Sneaking away from the party, he knocked on her door. After not getting a response, he opened it. The sweet aroma of musk perfume lingered, but Skylar and her suitcase were gone. Glancing over to the bed, he drew a deep breath when he saw the engagement ring resting on the pillow. As he sat quietly upon the bed's layers of satin and lace, Christian picked up the ring. Holding on to it, he knew deep down inside that she was gone for good. Cupping his hands over his face, he wept.

Chapter 23

Soul Catchers

BACK IN OSPERO FALLS, SKYLAR STOOD CRYING BEFORE SOPHIA AND Victoria, explaining that the wedding was off. They knew her decision was firm. Although they shed tears of sadness, the mothers were relieved their children had not made the mistake in to hastily marrying.

As they hugged the young girl, Skylar felt as if the door to a birdcage had swung open.

All she wanted to do now was climb into her bed and forget about breaking her solemn promise.

The news spread quickly, throughout the small community, of the broken engagement. The townspeople, who had watched the couple grow up together, were dismayed by the announcement. Their fairy-tale romance once unfolding within Ospero Falls, now signified the finale of something magical.

When Gwen telephoned home on Christmas Eve, Victoria broke the news to her in a hushed tone. Disheartened to hear of the break-up, but knowing Skylar had her reasons, Gwen offered her sympathy.

Sophia, offered to place the wedding dress in storage, in the attic of her house. She and Victoria covered the gown to protect it from dust. Before hanging it up, Victoria tucked the trailing edges underneath with a sigh. She had embroidered bluebirds around the long train, symbolizing hope and happiness – two emotions that her daughter no longer felt.

Skylar hid in Gwen's room to avoid the painting of the Sitka tree and would not come out except late at night. Immersed in sadness, she made a request of not celebrating the holidays. As Christmas Day passed and as Skylar's 19th birthday approached, she emerged.

Returning to her bedroom, she lamented over the painting of the Sitka.

A small piece of her wanted to cover it up, as if making it disappear would break her link to Christian.

Wandering downstairs, she found a note that Victoria was out on errands. Skylar glanced around the house, and seeing all of the unopened Christmas gifts, she felt guilty. Even under the circumstances, her mother had made the effort to decorate the house with a tree, ornaments, and a beautiful collection of candles.

Skylar decided to surprise Victoria by joining her for dinner. Lighting the candles on the stairwell, she put on her favourite Christmas album. The sounds of "Silent Night" filled the room. Bringing two candles, Skylar went upstairs to have a bath.

She immersed herself in a tub full of bubbles. The relaxing scents of cranberry and cinnamon filled the room, and the music soothed Skylar's nerves. She did not hear the knock on the front door. As she slipped deeper into the comforting warmth, the water muted the sound of footsteps on the stairs.

When she opened her eyes, wiping away the foam, she screamed. Standing in front of her was Christian.

"What are you doing here?"

"You know," he said, pacing, "I thought at least I deserved to be told to my face, why you did not want to marry me."

Still inside the tub, she reached for a towel.

"I cannot believe," she said, covering herself, "that you honestly expected me to leave everything behind, to follow you around like some lovesick puppy dog – just so you can show me off!"

He pounded his fist against the wall. "I would have done anything for you, Skylar. I was faithful and, trust me, I had opportunities.

"You made me wait too damn long to have sex and I still didn't stray. I was willing to build a future for us, and you wanted to throw everything away for this shitty little town! You expect me to waste my dreams on Ospero Falls?"

The words tore at her heart. The implication that he had turned down other women for her was belittling. Adding to the pain, was how he referred to what they had shared as sex, and not making love. She cringed at his negative comments about their hometown. Stepping out of the tub while holding the towel around her, she looked him straight in the eye.

"You should be appalled at who you have become, Christian James O'Connelly! Your father worked himself to the bone every day, so you would be raised in such a wonderful community. This town has been there for you through every wretched turn in your life. And look at how you are so quick to turn your back on it. I gave you everything I had, including my virginity, and you compare it to just having sex? Right now, I am ashamed to know you." She pointed to the door. "Get out of my home, and may God forgive you for the scathing words you have uttered here today."

But in his anger, he would not let her have the last word.

"I want you to know that I mean every damn word I have said," he sneered, turning his back on Skylar, Christian added, "When you wake up tomorrow, I hope you remember that."

He knew that coming was a waste of time. Fortunately, Frank's Uncle Thomas had let him have use of his float-plane. He was grateful he had told the pilot to wait.

All he wanted to do was leave behind the reminders of his meagre existence in Ospero Falls and return to Norelton, where he was worth something. Slamming the front door behind him, he did not notice a candle fall to the floor.

Skylar returned to her bath. As the taste of salt on her lips dropped into the lukewarm water, she slapped at it in anger.

Upset at what had happened, she turned on the hot water, to stifle the sobs coming from her shivering body.

As the float-plane took off and curved around the mountainside, Christian thought only of Norelton. He was unaware of the fire that was about to engulf the Fall's residence.

Victoria was on her way home when she saw the flames. Screaming, she dropped her packages into the snow and ran frantically, while sirens pierced the winter calm with their urgency.

Firefighters doused the flames, ensuring the fire was extinguished.

She was distraught as Skylar was nowhere in sight. Sophia spotted her friend collapsed onto the ground, screaming Skylar's name. Rushing to Victoria's side, she placed her arms around the hysterical woman. Suddenly, Olivia appeared in the distance, waving her arms to get their attention.

Abruptly she shouted, "Ladies, it is okay. Rev. Francis rescued Skylar; she is going to be alright!"

Victoria stopped her sobs midway, and thanked God as he had answered her tearful prayers. Sophia helped unite mother and daughter. Skylar, despite being wrapped in a blanket, stood in the dark night shivering.

Rev. Francis had come by to visit Skylar, Olivia said. When he saw flames leaping from the roof, and heard Skylar's screams, he didn't hesitate to charge into the house. He bound up the stairs two at a time and kicked in the bathroom door. The firefighters said that Skylar was lucky to have been in the bathtub – soaked and wrapped in a wet towel, she had avoided being severely burned.

Rev. Francis was not so lucky. He had burned his hands and inhaled smoke. Paramedics were treating him in the ambulance. Victoria and Skylar went over to say thanks.

In the midst of the chaos, prayers of gratitude mingled with the smoke rising, to the heavens.

Before long, word of the fire reached Norelton. Olivia telephoned Frank, who went to the dorm to wake up Christian and tell him what happened. Christian was shocked to hear about the fire but was relieved that Skylar and Victoria were okay. He did not know that he had caused it. Ashamed by the horrible things Christian had said to Skylar, his remorse prevented him from reaching out.

Much to Frank's disappointment, Christian refused to return to Ospero Falls. Instead, he telephoned Fancy-Mae's Florist Shoppe and paid for a bouquet of flowers to be delivered to his home. He heard that Victoria and Skylar had temporarily taken up Sophia's offer, to stay with her.

On Skylar's birthday, firefighters allowed the Falls to visit the house to see what they could salvage. The settees they had spent hours sitting on were burnt to the coils, and a melted pile of plastic was all that remained of the radio. The Christmas tree was reduced to a bluish-grey ash. Gone were cherished ornaments – mementos of previous holidays spent together.

Fortunately, the stairs and upper bedrooms suffered slightly less severe fire damages, with the walls scorched from the extreme heat.

The fire chief wanted to show Skylar and Victoria something, which had caught his attention.

Due to the extensive damage, the unsafe stairwell could not be trusted. The Fire Chief did not want to put the young women at risk, should the stairs give away.

With the assistance of two ladders, they peered into the main bedroom, through a window.

Victoria cried, when she saw Skylar's bed, scorched all over.

The chief drew their attention to the wall. Skylar gasped. The wall was burned, but the painting of the Sitka and the stick figures remained untouched.

"In all my years," the chief said, shaking his head, "I have never seen anything like it."

Word of Victoria and Skylar's plight travelled as far as Oakerson. All along the coast, people offered food and clothing. An elder from the small village that Makwa lived in, arrived by canoe with an offering of sage braided into three strands. The sage, he explained, represented the life-giving strength of a woman. Makwa had proudly told his family it was Skylar who helped him return to them.

In the Falls' biggest time of need, Rev. Francis, who had recovered from his injuries, came forth with a generous offer from the church. When the sanctuary first opened, it was intended to house only a few temporary guests in crisis. However, Rev. Francis found the need within the community was greater than anticipated. A larger building, closer to the church in Ospero Falls, was necessary to fill the demand. In addition to the help from Olivia and Sophia, the Reverend wanted someone to plan events and fundraise for the church and sanctuary. He put forward a proposal that was approved by the church elders. A new sanctuary would be built nearby. The church would then donate the former sanctuary, to Victoria and Skylar, to serve as their new home. Rev. Francis then offered Skylar the position of church planner. It was a paid position with all the benefits of working in an environment that she thrived in. Skylar was delighted at the thought of serving those in need. Victoria agreed. For Skylar, she knew it was where she belonged.

* * *

Soon after, the fire was ruled accidental, as Skylar admitted to leaving candles burning, when she went to have a bath.

She never spoke of Christian coming to the house in a rage and confronting her. She could not imagine him, even in his anger, doing anything to cause her harm.

Meanwhile, staying at Sophia's home grew uncomfortable for Skylar. Even though Christian was not around, his presence was everywhere. She avoided his room and slept on the couch instead. Knowing the Falls were staying with his mother, he called to speak to Skylar on the telephone, but to no avail. She just shook her head, indicating to Sophia that she did not yet want to have a conversation with him.

When Gwen found out about the near-tragedy, she returned to Skylar's side, knowing her friend needed someone to talk to. After reuniting at the O'Connelly's, Skylar told Gwen about the incident. She mentioned how the fire spared the painting of the Sitka tree.

"I reckon Evamya was watching over you," Gwen winked.

Gwen told Skylar how thrilled she was with Abimbola in her life. Between classes, they took part in protests for equality and against the Vietnam War. They dedicated their time to the environmental movement, which was beginning to garner attention. In a society besieged with inequality and conflict, they fought for freedom, in every way possible.

The day came for Gwen to return to Oakerson, and Skylar found herself saddened to see her best friend leave. Much like the Sitka, their lives burgeoned, unceasing, from their roots in Ospero Falls. Before Gwen left, Skylar handed her a photograph salvaged from the fire. It was a portrait of their dear Evamya.

The burnt edges could not take away the sentimentality it held for both of them. The tears welled up in Gwen's hazel eyes, as she touched the smudged photograph.

"Thank you!" she said smiling.

As Gwen boarded the ferry, she waved at Skylar – the only person who loved her like a sister.

* * *

Springtime was a welcome sight in Ospero Falls.

Construction on the new sanctuary started. An endless stream of volunteers came out to build a place of solace, for those in need. The community reinforced in Skylar why she had chosen to stay.

The morning of April 5th, the ringing of the telephone pierced the quiet of the house. Picking up the handset and saying hello, she could barely make out Gwen's words, through the sobs.

"Did you hear what happened?"

"What, Gwen?"

"Yesterday, Abimbola surprised me by taking me to hear Martin Luther King Jr. speak in Memphis. We travelled a long distance to hear him deliver a very moving spiritual address. He spoke at The Mason Temple of strife and unity, weaving them into an inspiring sermon he called 'I've Been to The Mountaintop.' There I was with Abimbola, taking photographs and living in the moment, watching a piece of history unfold before my own eyes. Later, the unthinkable happened! Martin Luther King Jr. was shot at his motel. He's dead, Skylar!"

Skylar could not believe what she was hearing.

"I am so sorry, Gwen! The Lord knows how much he meant to you and to the world."

Gwen began to sob into the phone,

"It truly is a day of mourning. How can a man deliver a speech about peace, love, and putting an end to prejudice, then be gunned down? It's just like Medgar Evers all over again. I cannot imagine anyone being so ruthless!"

Abruptly, there was silence between them, until Gwen murmured,

"I have decided to come back to be with the Hurston's. They are also in shock.

I am flying into Norelton and taking the first ferry out. I need to see you."

"Oh Gwen, you know that I am always here for you."

"You are, without exception, the best friend a girl could ever have. I will see you in a day or two."

As Skylar held onto the silent handset, she reeled from the news that Dr. King was dead. Newspapers, radio programs, and television shows pieced together the horrible details of the tragedy in Memphis. Dr. King's death threw a nation into a tailspin, as people struggled to come to terms with it.

Skylar coped in her own way. She decided to help ease her friend's pain by doing something special. She grabbed her easel and sketching pencils, walked down to the ferry, and travelled to the Sitka tree.

Days later, in the late afternoon, Gwen appeared on the Falls' doorstep. Before she could knock on the door, Skylar opened it, threw her arms around her best friend and the two girls broke into sobs together. Rocking back and forth, on a porch where the colour of their skin did not matter, was the essence of what Martin Luther King Jr had fought for – equality.

After some time, Skylar offered to grab some Kleenex. Retreating into her home, she soon returned holding a large, wrapped parcel.

Thrusting it forward, she said, "This is for you – just a little something to remember him by."

Gwen opened the brown parcel wrap to reveal a charcoal sketch done in the likeness of Dr. King. Throwing her arms again around Skylar, she sputtered, "God bless you, Skylar! I will cherish it forever."

Afterwards, while they sat on the porch, Skylar listened to Gwen's recollection of Dr. King's address. Hours later, glints of stardust pierced the darkness of the evening sky.

Skylar took Gwen's hand in hers.

"Our loved ones are keeping company with some of the greatest," she said.

Gwen returned to Oakerson, and Abimbola convinced her to put together a collection of her photographs for an art show. Without hesitation, she set out to show the world what she saw through her eyes.

Christian's long journey to becoming a doctor would finally see him obtain his degree. After a year-long internship, he could finally apply for his licence. But consumed by self-indulgence, he did not realize how misguided his dreams were.

Another blow landed when on June 6, 1968, U.S. Sen. Robert Kennedy was assassinated. People still affected by Dr. King's death, now had to swallow the bitter truth that no one was invincible.

In Norelton, Christian dealt with the loss alone. He buried himself in his studies and work. Yet he still could not shake the coldness of Jaycee's remarks about the mayhem afflicting the country.

"What a pity!" Jaycee said. "Guess all the money in the world cannot buy you security these days."

Christian, filled with anger over her callous remarks, had to refrain from lashing out.

Forcing himself to keep busy, so he would not dwell on what might have been, he tried his best to avoid the girl.

Sophia chastised her son for not coming back and lending his support to Skylar and Victoria. Claiming it was the decent thing to do, she still held onto hope of their broken hearts mending.

It was no use. Unknown to Sophia, he was coping with the shame by drinking. Unable to face Skylar after flinging bitter words at her in anger, he chose to write her a letter expressing his regrets. Although addressing it to her, he never put any postage.

His intentions were not to send it.

The letter sat on his desk for several days. It was forgotten, until his roommate casually remarked that he did Christian a favour, by sending off his mail for him. Panic gripped Christian; he was mortified to think his private thoughts were on their way to Skylar. He had no idea how she would react. He shook his head, at how fate had chosen, to intervene.

As the days passed, Christian slumped into a deep depression, as he tried to cope with losing the only woman he had ever loved.

Struggling to come to terms with his immeasurable loss, he began to frequent the local pub, The Norelton Underdog. There, long-haired hippies drowned out the American dream by dropping acid and chasing it with bottles of Molson Canadian. However, the young medical student was more interested in ousting his personal demons plaguing him, than striking up a conversation with anyone.

The guilt he harboured, along with the emptiness he felt inside, exposed his vulnerability.

With the summer of '68 upon him, Christian found himself at the pub in the company of the red-haired girl he had spent the past years avoiding.

At first, he thought it was strange that she would frequent such an establishment. However, after several drinks, he realized they had something in common – they were both drinking to avoid reality. Jaycee was tired of her parents' constant meddling in her love life. Several failed attempts, to match her up with a respectable suitor from their country club, had left her bitter. She was bent on rebelling in any way possible.

Unbeknown to him, she had heard through her inner circle about Christian and Skylar's engagement breaking off and rejoiced in the news.

As she sat next to him in the cigarette haze, she ran her fingernails along his groin, making clear her intentions.

It was not hard to seduce him. Checking into a nearby motel, she did not hesitate any longer to show him the pleasures her body had lusting after. Soon, they lay with their bodies pressed together, beads of sweat dripping off their naked flesh.

They engaged in intercourse twice that night, under the lights of a cheap room, while outside a storm brewed. As gusts of wind rattled the windows, the menacing clamour reminded him of his letter to Skylar.

After he felt numb, void of any feelings towards Jaycee. As he lay beneath the sordid sheets, an overwhelming sense of betrayal engulfed him. Remorseful of deceiving Skylar, who he still loved, he sprinted to the bathroom. Lunging over the toilet, he threw up.

If the young woman was turned off by his outward projection of guilt that spewed from him, she did not show it.

She did not care that he had been drinking heavily or that his thoughts were not of her while they had sex. What was important, was the silent claim to victory that she now had ownership of him – an unclaimed prize she had won.

For over two years now, he had been the ultimate challenge that at last, she had conquered triumphantly. Jaycee convinced herself that Christian now belonged to her. He had given in to her desires. The thrill of control she now had over him, gave the young woman an immense feeling of satisfaction.

* * *

In Ospero Falls, the townspeople celebrated the completion of the new sanctuary. Its foundation was placed a block away from the old church, between the pine, cedar, and spruce trees. Interspersed was foxtail grass and salmonberries. Adding more colour around the new building, Skylar and Victoria sprinkled around it, a mixture of wildflower seeds.

The morning of the sanctuary's consecration, Skylar spent time at the inlet, where she collected three shades of green stones polished by the sea. While Rev. Francis watched, she placed them in front of the sanctuary, one on top of another, forming a silent tribute to the past. She took out her Bible and shared her inspiration. Referencing Joshua 4, she spoke of stones being placed to commemorate those who came before, and the power of the Lord in their lives. Closing her Bible, she smiled.

"Jade is a stone that means benevolence," she said, "and these stones I laid for Oliver Whitman, Evamya Walker, and Jack O'Connelly."

Intrigued by her actions, the Reverend asked if she had thought of a name. Skylar smiled and said,

"The Heart of Jade Sanctuary."

Within days, Victoria and Skylar moved into the old sanctuary. They were overwhelmed by the generosity of the people who helped them.

Charlie Swenson made country furnishings out of salvaged wood. Divino and Maria Canetti brought a small freezer filled with homemade delicacies, including Skylar's favourite – sweet pepper and feta lasagna. Melvin the butcher brought wrapped packages of various meats, and Mr. Jacob showed up with boxes of bread and sweets from his bakery. Miss Tamsin Jean delivered new outfits from her boutique, and Ms. Wigensworth warmed Skylar's heart, when she brought a collection of bound books, full of her favourite poetry.

The Falls settled comfortably into their new home, and life returned to normal.

Before long, Skylar came across a box containing unopened mail forgotten about in the chaos of the move. She held in her trembling hands a letter from Christian.

Tearing open the envelope, the lingering scent of Old Spice escaped from the paper.

Sitting underneath the painted sign of The Heart of Jade Sanctuary, she drew a deep breath.

Dearest Piper,

Words alone cannot express the sorrow I feel deep inside knowing how much I've hurt you. I brought all of this grief upon myself and have only myself to blame for how I treated you that night at your house. The rage I let out on you repulsed me. It was as if I had my own Dr. Jekyll and Mr. Hyde within me! I am a man torn in two, who does not deserve the immeasurable love you have given me.

Throughout the years, I have watched you grow, physically and spiritually. Your golden heart touches so many through your generosity. When you finally gave yourself to me under the Sitka tree, I knew that I could not live my life without you!

Wisdom and kindness are just two of the gifts that you possess. I now realize why your heart may belong to me, you will forever be connected to Ospero Falls and our beloved spruce.

It seems clear what your purpose is in life. I am so sorry, as it is selfish of me to expect you to sacrifice your roots. Please forgive me… I only pray that it is not too late for us! As always, I will say, "See you under our Sitka" and hope that, for the first time ever, this is not goodbye.

I also want you to know how sorry I am to hear about the fire. I can only thank the good Lord that you are okay. Keep the faith, Piper.

Much love,

Christian xx

Tears fell on the piece of paper in her hands. She wept quietly and wondered if maybe things could be worked out somehow, between them? Sitting at the oak table in the kitchen, she grabbed a sheet of paper, knowing that if she did not write back now, she never would.

Dearest Christian,

I just found today among the mail, your letter to me. First, I want you to know that I forgive you from the bottom of my heart! I could never stay angry with you, my love. I understand it must have been difficult for you, when I left my engagement ring behind in Norelton.

You must understand, I don't ever want to be so self-centred that I would want you to give up everything, you've worked so hard to be with me! I support you in your own dreams and want to pursue mine. I wish I knew of an easier way to make our lives uncomplicated. I have prayed endlessly to the Lord, asking him for guidance, and only hope that we will find our way back to each other.

Please, do not lose faith that we will be together again someday. Know in your heart that nothing is impossible – it is only an obstacle! In saying this, I sometimes feel as if we are two ships, caught in a storm. The harder we try to unite, the more we find ourselves capsized.

I know you have demons that you battle, Christian, and it terrified me to see you with such anger! Yet, my faith has shown me the power of prayer, and I will not give up on you… as long as you stand by me.

I have to share with you the other day, I found myself thinking of our impending wedding, when we were supposed to be married. I don't believe either of us were ready just yet, to truly decide, where we should settle down and raise a family. But if you will be patient with me, I promise it will all be worth the wait!

I also have some happy news! Since the fire, Momma and I have settled into the old sanctuary. It feels like it was always home to me!

Often, I will go and rest by the stone plaque, placed in memory of your father. I just sit in silence, knowing that I am close to both you and your family. No matter what may happen, Christian, you and I will always be bound to one another and our Sitka tree. I Love you!

Eternally yours, Piper xx

Sealing the envelope, she walked outside and placed it in the mailbox before she had any second thoughts.

* * *

Christian returned to his studies, trying to avoid the red-head that had become his shadow. Jaycee showed up every day after classes, fondling him and leaving traces of her scarlet lipstick on his cheeks and neck.

She called him Chris in front of others, which annoyed him enormously. Adding to his displeasure, Jaycee's constant displays of affection, were making his life unbearable. Sober and with a clear conscious, he deeply regretted having sex with her.

He pushed her away, hoping Frank would never find out about them.

One day after class, as he headed towards the dormitory, Christian felt a smack on his shoulder. Turning around, he saw Frank bristling with anger.

"You know, man," he yelled, "I expected better of you! Just what the hell were you thinking bedding that rich bitch, Jaycee?"

Christian felt sheepish and gestured for Frank to keep it down.

"Oh, now you want me to shut my mouth! Did you think I was not going to be upset by how you continue to hurt Skylar? She is my friend too, you know. Any way you look at it Christian, you are a real coward. You never even went back to Ospero Falls, after the fire, to help out!

"All you sent were some cheap flowers."

Frank turned to walk away. Christian put his hand on his shoulder, but he shrugged it off.

"To hell with your shit, man," he said, walking away. "You and Jaycee deserve each other!"

Christian slumped against the stone wall of the building. He remained in a daze as the minutes passed. Slowly, he stood and went to his dorm room. Upon arriving, he flung off his jacket.

On his desk, he saw Skylar's handwriting on an envelope addressed to him. His heart was beating faster. Reaching for the mail, he sat down on his bed and opened the envelope.

Pouring over her loving words, his emotions ranged from remorse to anger to deep loss. Crumpling up the letter, he knew that after what he had done with Jaycee, she was lost to him forever. Skylar could forgive his anger, yet he knew that sleeping with another woman was the ultimate betrayal.

Grabbing his jacket, he headed to The Norelton Underdog.

After several drinks, he saw Jaycee strutting towards him. Her curves fit just right into the snug, velvet green dress she wore.

A smug look on her face, Jaycee straddled the seat next to his at the bar and whispered into his ear.

"How about you and I find some place?"

Something in him snapped. He grabbed her hand and led her out to his Cadillac. Inside, he pulled up her dress and, dropping his pants, started to thrust himself on her. He was rough and she liked it. The steam from their bodies gathered on the windows, and she squealed in ecstasy.

With a burst of intensity, he pushed himself deep into the crevice, between her robust legs. She bucked forward to meet him in an intense rhythm, erupting into an outburst of moans. No sooner had they started, than the deed was done. Jaycee, cupping his face with her long fingernails, sloppily kissed his lips, leaving a stain of berry-red lipstick. Exiting the car, she blew a kiss and sauntered off into the night, like a stalking cat who had just devoured its prey.

* * *

Talking on the telephone, Skylar delighted in Gwen's stories. They also shared their fears. The conflict had escalated in the Vietnam War, with the U.S. suffering significant losses.

There was reason for concern, but Gwen reassured Skylar that she was in good hands with Abimbola by her side. Skylar thought she was holding back on something, and after much prompting, Gwen divulged what it was.

She and Abimbola had eloped a few weeks before. They spent their honeymoon in a small village in Africa, among the people he had helped, on a missionary trip. She had been reluctant to tell Skylar. After all her best friend had gone through, she did not want to seem boastful. Gwen also was sad that Skylar was not able be her maid of honour. She prayed her sister in faith would find just as much joy and love in her life, as Abimbola had brought her.

Skylar took the news with the same grace she handled everything, wishing Gwen and her husband, all the happiness in the world. Her best friend promised to send some wedding pictures, commemorating the event. After a few more exchanges of pleasant conversation, they both bid each other good-bye.

* * *

After a gloomy winter, which had seen fierce storms pounding surf along the coastline, the vivid colours of spring were a welcome sight to the landscape.

The sun brought forth life with its radiance. Emerging from the crags and crevices of the mountainsides were glacier lilies, spring beauties, and globe flowers. Two of Skylar's favourites were Trillium and Ladies Slippers that she would merrily graze tenderly with her fingertips, as if to say hello.

While Skylar was a lover of nature, Victoria would spend her spare time watching Peyton Place on Sophia's small, black, and white television. The friends were fans of the show and gathered around the tube when it came on, losing themselves for an hour, in another world.

Skylar waited for Christian's reply. Yet as the days turned into weeks, and the weeks into months, there was no word from him. She grew disheartened. Try as she might to push him out of her thoughts, her mind raced. Why had he not written back?

At the end of June, Christian came home to Ospero Falls – and all hell broke loose.

* * *

Skylar was in Dufrayn's General Store, enjoying a strawberry swirl cone, when the front door swung open.

Silhouetted by the shining sun was Christian. Her heart pounding, Skylar rushed towards him and leapt into his arms.

The rigidness of his body told her something was wrong.

"Hey, Skylar," he said, unwrapping her arms from around his shoulders.

Still holding her cone, she stepped back.

Taking a closer look, she was surprised by his gruff appearance. His dark beard and moustache made him look several years older.

She smelled the pungency of whisky on his breath and realized he had been drinking. He opened the door, and she watched a woman with long, auburn hair enter.

In a tight, sleeveless dress with a lined bodice that pushed up her breasts, the woman slid her arm around Christian's waist.

"Hands off, sugar," she slurred. "This man's all mine!"

Staring in disbelief, Skylar felt a hand of stone reach in and crush her heart.

She recognized the woman as the guest at the Christmas party in Norelton who had mistaken her for a maid.

Mouth wide open, Skylar tried to say something, but the words stuck. Then remembering the melting ice cream in her hand, she shoved the cone right into Christian's face.

Bursting into tears, she ran away to escape the humiliation.

Chapter 24

Rebellion

WHEN SKYLAR BURST INTO THE HOUSE WITH HER TEARS TRAILING behind her, Victoria wondered what had happened? After following the overwrought girl up to her bedroom, Skylar's mother patiently waited for her daughter to share. Between sobs and sniffles, Skylar went on to explain everything. With each word, Victoria grew more infuriated by Christian's behaviour.

Brewing a pot of red rose tea, Skyler's mother helped to settle the girl's emotions, with a long embrace, kiss on her forehead and reassurance that God had a plan for everything.

She drew a warm bath for Skylar and waited until her daughter was surrounded by warmth and bubbles, before stepping out to go to the market.

Walking past the O'Connelly house, Victoria saw Sophia chase Christian off the front porch with a broom. The woman Skylar described to her earlier was pulling on his arm, eager to flee the wrath of her new boyfriend's mother. Defiant, he turned and stood to face his mother. Victoria could not hear what he said but watched in shock as Sophia lifted her hand and smacked his face with such force that his head jerked to the right. Victoria gasped and hurried on.

Christian placed his hand up to his stinging cheek. Turning, he walked away. He ushered Jaycee into the Cadillac. When he spun out, the screeching of his tires could be heard.

As he sped away, the dust settled on the broken hearts scattered throughout the tiny coastal town.

Word spread quickly about his unexpected return. That morning, Hank Stevenson shook his head in disappointment when Christian drove onto the ferry. Demanding to be taken to Ospero Falls, Hank wanted to knock the rudeness out of him. He did not know Christian was concealing a mickey of rye whisky. That afternoon, Divino and Maria asked him to leave their restaurant when he and Jaycee carried on in a booth.

Rev. Francis had waved Christian and Jaycee inside, when they stumbled past his church. While the young woman had burst into laughter at the invitation, Christian waved him off, muttering about sowing one's seeds.

After the episode in Ospero Falls, the couple spent their nights drinking, smoking pot, and having careless sex back in Norelton. Frank stopped speaking to his best friend. Christian's boss called to tell him he was fired. Everything was out of control in the young man's life as he was spiraling downward.

After a month of recklessness, Christian received a letter in the mail from his mother. It stated if he did not clean himself up before school began, he would be cut off from the trust fund money set aside for his education. At first, he brushed it off. But when Jaycee read the note, she panicked. Without his money, she would have no choice but to beg her parents for support.

She quickly set about sobering him up, desperately trying to get him back on track, for school in September. After enduring several miserable weeks of his wretched behaviour, she succeeded. Christian was rehabilitated – not into who he had been, but close enough so that he could focus on his studies. Jaycee made him write an apology and send a dozen yellow roses to his mother, to reassure her that he was a changed man. Out of concern for her son, Sophia accepted his request for forgiveness, while Jaycee set about her next move.

Meanwhile, Skylar sought peace through her prayers, in dealing with the loss of the only man she ever loved. She endured a time of confusion, sorrow, and regret. The letters they had exchanged had renewed her hope, and a belief they would be together again one day.

She had never seen his betrayal coming, and found solace speaking with Rev. Francis. When he asked what the source of her hurt was, she did not hesitate to share. As tears fell, she said how Christian had not stood up for her, when she needed him most.

Rev. Francis reminded her that everything was a test of faith.

* * *

As summer ended, the glory of autumn brought a returning contentment to Ospero Falls.

Skylar started teaching Sunday school at church and continued to work at the sanctuary. She also enrolled in art classes. Taking the ferry out to the Sitka tree, she spent countless hours sketching. Not once had the thought occurred to her of never returning to the place that she cherished. There, she reflected on the good times she had shared with Christian, along with Jack, Gwen, Evamya, and Frank. Nor did she forget Makwa's words about the tree having a good heart.

After the fire, Skylar had spent time salvaging what she could from their house. In a small box, she found the carved necklace Evamya had gifted her and Christian. Back then, she saw it as a symbol of harmony between Christian and her – a love that would endure. Despite the darkness that had eclipsed her life, Skylar would never forsake the Sitka. She knew the tree held within it, nature's energy, placed there by the Creator.

The autumn months crept towards winter. Christmas came and went without incident. Skylar spent her birthday celebrating with only her mother and a few close friends. They knew Christian's name was not to be spoken in her presence.

Even when Sophia and Victoria had tea together, neither mentioned him. It was as if Christian O'Connelly's existence was removed from the community, to allow Skylar to heal.

When Frank announced his engagement to Samantha, Olivia wavered over whether to spread the news. However, life went on she knew, even though it was now changed. Upon hearing the announcement, Skylar smiled, holding back her tears. Such a cruel twist of fate, she thought, that she and Christian – once destined for happily ever after – had their ending rewritten.

In Norelton, Christian moved with a new crowd.

To please Jaycee, he began to associate with the city's wealthiest residents. Fortunately, her father liked Christian enough to give him a job at the manufacturing plant he owned, allowing him to earn enough money to sustain him through the winter.

Though busy with work, his studies, and Jaycee's demands, he made a point of telephoning Sophia every week. The conversation was friendly, but he knew the grief he had caused still resounded. She made it clear that Jaycee was not welcome in her home. They never spoke of Skylar, understanding that too much pain lingered.

The distance allowed Sophia to remain hopeful. She prayed Christian would return to Ospero Falls, to open a practice of his own one day. To care for those who cared for him, when he lost his father, only seemed right she thought.

Christian was still plagued by remorse. He had betrayed the only woman who had loved him completely. Christian always felt treasured by Skylar. Try as he might, he could not erase the image of brokenness he had created by his actions. His caustic words had caused misery, to someone who already had experienced such heartache, in her life.

He gave up reading poetry, which Jaycee likened to nonsense. Once, he made the terrible mistake of mentioning to her the Sitka tree. She knew the meaning it held for him and Skylar. As punishment, Jaycee cut him off from sex for a month.

Still, Christian was attracted to the control Jaycee had over him. She revelled in knowing her domineering nature appealed to him; he approved of her erotic appetite. While Christian and Skylar shared passion and love, he and Jaycee merely indulged in fulfilling her insatiable sexual desires.

As time passed by, the young man found it easier to be consumed by the world she had created for him.

It became apparent that Evamya's foretelling of things which stem from greed, were bearing truth in all areas of his life.

* * *

The onset of 1970 saw a continual upheaval in the economy and people as individuals full of peace and love, reached out to the clashes of indifference. Trying to mend the conflict between them, while the drums of war beat on, was Skylar – who continued to touch the hearts of others.

In the spring, her routine was interrupted by a surprise visit from Gwen and Abimbola. They laughed at the memories they shared of their youth and reflected on everything that had changed.

Gwen showed Skylar a photograph she had won an award for. It was of the four friends. Unable to refrain from showing her emotions, she burst into tears. While her best friend consoled her, Abimbola knelt beside Skylar.

"You know something, Ms. Falls," he said, offering her a tissue, "in the small village my mother came from, they had a belief that if you treasure something by nurturing it with love and respect, you must also guard it against the outside world. It is important to always be mindful of where it is. For once it was released, it would surely die, because it would not know how to live without you.

"However, we know that because of our faith, we must let it go to be free. Only our Creator knows its outcome. You also must believe the union you and Christian shared will never be broken. The promises you two made to each other will be honoured, even if in death."

* * *

As summer approached, Frank and Samantha came back to Ospero Falls, to visit Olivia and prepare for their August wedding. Frank had obtained his bachelor's degree in engineering and architectural design. He secured a high-paying job in Averston as a planner and urban designer.

Even though Frank and Samantha planned to live in Averston, they made Olivia happy by announcing that their ceremony would take place in Ospero Falls. The reception, on the other hand, would be held in the city.

For the young man, he was happy upon returning to Ospero Falls. Filled with pride at his accomplishments and the love of his devoted fiancée, saw the townspeople gather together, to commemorate the achievements of Oliver Whitman's son.

Samantha was a pleasant girl, who everyone got along with, including Skylar.

The two became friends quickly. Skylar missed having someone around who was close to her age. On a hot July day, she took Samantha to see the Sitka tree. Her reaction pleased Skylar, as she was in awe of the impressive spruce. Later, the two sat under the shade of the tree and talked. Skylar shared how the Sitka was a big part of her relationship with Christian. Samantha empathized with her, as she could easily see how the tree was the place for them, where love began.

Meanwhile, Frank hung out at the pier, thinking about who to ask to be his best man. As much as he hated to admit it, he knew the only person who should be standing next to him was Christian.

Frank would occasionally see him in Norelton. He always seemed to have Jaycee clinging to him. In order to avoid a confrontation with her, Frank dodged both of them.

As he stared into the depths of the ocean, he wondered if he was about to make a serious mistake. He remembered a conversation with Samantha. She had urged him to make amends with Christian, reminding him that life was too short to live with regrets.

The next morning, without telling anyone except for Samantha, Frank boarded the ferry back to Norelton to see Christian.

With only a few weeks to go before the wedding, he knew he was taking a risk.

After spending a long-time deliberating, while leaning on the railing of the ferry, Frank figured out how he would handle the situation.

Arriving at the dorm, he found Christian buried under a mountain of medical books. Seeing each other again after so long, they acted as if they had never been apart. Extending his hand outward, Christian grasped Frank's palm with a firm grip and smiled.

"Good to see you, man." he said.

"Same here. It's been awhile…"

"Not to worry, buddy."

Christian motioned for Frank to sit down among the papers that covered the bed.

"What can I do for you?"

"Well, it's like this. Samantha and I are getting married in several weeks and it just wouldn't seem right if you're not there as my best man."

Christian began to rub his chin like Jack had so many times before. As he sat quietly mulling over the words, Frank's anxiousness caused him to exclaim, "Aw hell, I knew this was a mistake!"

Christian looked straight at him and knew their reunion would be bittersweet if he was not honest with Frank. He sputtered, "Listen man, you and I have to think this seriously over. It is not only us we have to consider here. First of all, is the wedding in Ospero Falls?"

Frank began to fidget in his seat, uncomfortable at how the situation was turning out. Nodding his head, he muttered, "Of course it is man, that is where it should be!"

Christian could sense the tension between them and hesitated for a moment before blurting out, "I couldn't deal with it, if Skylar found out on your wedding day, about Jaycee being pregnant!"

The shock spread across Frank's face, "What did you just say?"

"You heard me right," Christian sighed. "Jaycee told me over two weeks ago, and I have been a wreck ever since.

I mean, one day my life seemed like it had a bright future with a woman I loved like no other, and then bam! Here I am, having to do the right thing. We're planning on getting married ourselves, soon."

"Does your mother know?"

"No, I cannot bear to cause her any more pain, Frank. I am unable to go back and see all those people who I have hurt so much. What the hell am I going to do?"

"Do you know if it's yours?"

"Yeah. As far as I know, I am the only one."

"Did you go to the doctor's office with her?"

"No, I did not… but damn it, Frank, I am a doctor myself! Don't you think I would know if she was lying?"

"Hey, I'm sorry, man. I don't know what to say."

"It's not your problem. But I need you to know, for everyone involved, it is best if I do not attend your wedding. Don't get me wrong. I am happy for you and Samantha. She is a great girl."

"It's just not fair, Christian," Frank said, chewing his lower lip. "You and I both know that you two do not belong together! What is it going to take for you to damn well realize that?"

"It's no use giving me hell over what I already know. What is done is done. I have to do right by Jaycee. I know you might not understand it, Frank, but it is the proper thing to do." He walked Frank to the door and slapped him on the back. "Thanks for dropping by my friend. It meant a lot to me. I wish you well, and please… let me be the one to tell my mom."

Frank nodded, numb. He walked down the hallway and turned back. "If ever you need me for anything, buddy, I will be there."

Christian nodded.

Back in Ospero Falls, Frank told Samantha what happened. She thought it was awful, and he agreed. Yet knew he had to adjust to the reality that Jaycee had gotten what she wanted, after all.

Frank focussed on finding someone else to be his best man. He was about to give up, when he received a telephone call from Divino Canetti.

"Word among the folks in town is you're looking for the best man at your wedding," he said. "I reckon I am probably not the best guy for the job, but I did know your pop, and he was a fine man. I've watched all of you growing up as you hung out at our restaurant. If you are willing to let me help you out, I would be honoured."

"That means a lot to me Mr. Canetti. Thank you!"

"No need to thank me. That's what community is all about."

On an overcast August day in 1970, family and friends witnessed the union of Frank and Samantha. Though Mr. Canetti and Skylar stood up for the happy couple, all of the townspeople witnessed the nuptials and rejoiced in them. One of their own had come back home and made them proud.

While the citizens of Ospero Falls celebrated, Christian drowned his sorrows in Norelton. As he picked another cold beer out of the fridge, he heard the whining voice of his future bride nagging at him, to rub her feet.

If Skylar hoped Christian would make an appearance at the wedding, she never told a soul. Even though she was uncomfortable being in Averston, Skylar moved through the crowd at the reception looking beautiful and full of grace.

She visited every table, personally making sure every guest was looked after. When it came time for speeches, Skylar had everyone laughing then in tears, as she recalled as a little girl, meeting Frank for the first time.

Even after Frank and Samantha slipped away for their honeymoon, she stayed behind to clean up. Carrying all the gifts into Olivia's car, Skylar then drove the exhausted woman home.

As always, she saw life through rose-coloured glasses.

* * *

In Averston, Frank and Samantha enjoyed their married life. Soon after being wed, both of them were overjoyed to discover Samantha was pregnant with twins. While Frank was given congratulations from all over Norelton, Ospero Falls and Averston, it was the one call he received that bothered him the most.

In late September, Frank received a telephone call from Christian, who told him that Jaycee had miscarried. Frank offered his condolences, while feeling ashamed at the relief he felt. Maybe the turn of events would encourage his best friend to dump Jaycee, so as to leech off someone else. However, Frank was shocked when Christian said he still had plans to wed her. There was no way he could back out now, knowing Jaycee had just endured an unbearable loss. Their conversation ended, when Frank heard Jaycee demanding to know who the hell Christian was talking to for so long.

As time moved on, the pressure mounted for Christian to wed Jaycee. He kept on stalling, speaking of the importance of his studies. However, when cornered by her family during Thanksgiving dinner, he relented.

"Next year around this time would be fine," he said.

Later, Christian seethed over how they browbeat him into marrying her.

He had no backbone, even though there were times he could stand up for himself and those he truly loved, he always chose poorly. Not wanting to dwell on his fate, he focused on becoming one of Norelton's finest doctors.

Meanwhile, the winter of 1970 went onto the record books, for the most recorded snowfall. The people of Ospero Falls hibernated under the cold spell, waiting for spring to come.

For Skylar, the winter overcast put her in a sullen mood. All she wanted to do was visit the Sitka tree, imagining it yearned for her company. After the fire, she had asked one of the firefighters to remove the original painting of the beloved spruce, treehouse, and friends. With scorched edges, she placed it on an easel, in her new room at the former sanctuary. The childish artwork brought comfort still, whenever she needed it.

A few nights later, Skylar had a nightmare. She was walking barefoot in the forest and saw a light up ahead. As she got closer, flames were consuming the Sitka and the tree house. When Skylar awoke, her nightgown clung to her sweat-covered skin. She thought of Christian and what they had become – a page ripped from a book, with an unfinished ending.

Chapter 25

Alliances

THE STIRRINGS OF A NEW YEAR, SAW THE CITIZENS OF OSPERO FALLS, go about their days in usual fashion. As the lumber mill sustained a population, the fellowship they shared, saw the resident's lives be well known to another. Within the coastal community, everyone looked after each other. When something happened that ruptured the sense of honour felt, they gathered together in support.

Soon they would discover the trappings of a line had been set, in order to corner one of the town's former finest.

Frank and Samantha, prepared to relocate to the well-to-do suburbs of Averston. He had built an addition – a guest house for his mother to move into. At the end of March, Olivia bid farewell to her friends.

Meanwhile, Christian resolved to call Sophia and tell her about his wedding. Since he put off telling her for so long, Jaycee gave him an ultimatum: If he did not tell Sophia, she would.

He called Sophia and told her that he and Jaycee were to be married in the fall. Sophia responded with silence. She could not fathom how he could ever marry such a woman and could not lie to him about her feelings. After an hour of trying to convince him to reconsider, she gave in, realizing he would marry Jaycee with or without her blessing. The conversation ended with Sophia promising not to tell Victoria and Skylar.

Jaycee decided the ceremony would be held in Averston. Unaware of her intentions, Christian was pleased. He saw no reason to upset the people of Ospero Falls, who still clung to the hope that Christian James O'Connelly would return to set things right.

He thought she was in control, but he learned it was her father Luther Campbell, who really pulled the strings.

Mr. Campbell, a wealthy businessman, knew that Averston was where Christian wanted to set up his practice. Therefore, he made him a proposal. Knowing Christian, was set out to be an ambitious doctor, Mr. Campbell offered to establish a medical practice. He would cover all start up costs needed.

Christian was leery at first, not wanting to feel indebted to the Campbells. But Mr. Campbell was a cunning businessman. He was convinced Christian's loyalty could be bought, if only he knew the price.

After talking to Jaycee, another meeting was arranged. Mr. Campbell offered not only to set up Christian's practice in Averston, but to buy him the house he had desired, since he was a boy.

Mr. Campbell held in his hands the deed to the mansion on Rogue's Bluffs. The stately home Christian had gazed at so many times, from the tree house in the Sitka. Mr. Campbell was offering Christian the title to the dwelling that he had sworn would be his; the residence he had told Skylar and Gwen he would live in one day. However, it was the very same place that Evamya had warned him about, so long ago.

"Sign here, son," Mr. Campbell said, presenting a pen, "and it will be yours."

Christian took the pen, dipped in the thick, black inkwell of his adversary, and wrote his name.

Finally, he felt like he was a somebody. Seeing his name on the title to his new home brought him affirmation. He believed his life was about to change for the better, not knowing he had just sealed his fate; despite all that had been done previously to avoid it.

* * *

In June, as the wildflowers flourished, word of Christian's impending wedding to Jaycee spread through Ospero Falls.

Try as they might to keep the details from Skylar, Sophia and Victoria could not protect her from the wrath of the bride-to-be.

One summer day, weeks before the wedding was to take place, Jaycee decided on a whim to take the ferry to Ospero Falls.

Skylar spent her days at The Heart of Jade Sanctuary. She still struggled to accept the ocean dividing the two former lovers, would always keep them separated. As much as her love for him remained strong, she knew in her heart, he had chosen another woman over her.

On her way to the sanctuary, she was surprised to run into Jaycee. As they came face to face, neither showed signs of being intimidated.

Skylar was the first to trigger a conversation, by pointing in the direction of Norelton, she remarked dryly,

"You must be lost. The rich live that way!"

"Actually," Jaycee said defiantly, "I was in Averston checking out our new home. Did you hear? My daddy purchased the mansion on Rogue's bluff, you know…the one where Chris has yearned for all these years! How perfect will that be – us overlooking you – the peasants!" she laughed. Then she delivered the final blow by adding "Christian and I will be married there and everything my little heart has desired, will have come true!"

Skylar did not flinch. Placing her hands on her hips, she looked Jaycee squarely in the face.

"You know something? You may have a man to call your husband, but every waking moment he will be thinking about his Piper. Remember this on your wedding day: You may control him, but you will never own his heart. It will always belong to the only woman he has ever loved – me!"

Jaycee spun on her high heels and stormed off, seething.

Afterwards, Skylar travelled on the ferry, with plans to spend time at the Sitka tree.

Walking along the path, embedded with her footprints, Skylar's world of solitude was now being disturbed. Nearby, was the noisy construction, on the parcel of land known as Rogue's bluffs.

Following renovations to the mansion and landscaping of the overgrown area, the bluffs were swarming with people working, to ensure Jaycee's wedding day went smoothly. Only a few weeks to go before the nuptials, she was in a state of panic, bellowing out orders to anyone who dared get in her way.

Numerous times throughout September, Skylar had thought it best to avoid the area, but then would change her mind. Her devotion to the Sitka was a reflection of her faith.

"As God created this tree," she reminded herself in moments of uncertainty, "for me it shall always be!"

Without realizing it, her, and Christian narrowly avoided meeting each other, numerous times.

Since he wanted his mother to attend the ceremony and reception, the young man found himself, back at his childhood home.

There, he reminisced with Sophia as if nothing had changed. Except, promises had been broken and lives permanently altered. A union that was once the envy of all lay scattered among the rubble that Christian left in his wake.

He made a point of avoiding the Fall's residence, choosing instead to slip quietly back and forth. Ospero Falls was where Christian James O'Connelly's roots began. Even though he knew he had caused painful rifts, a part of him, wanted to make amends with the townspeople. Although he wished he could somehow transform the community back to its former self, with the old Christian in it, this was not possible.

However, two weeks before the wedding was to take place, Christian – channelling his father – found himself making the rounds.

For those in Ospero Falls, a part of Jack O'Connelly, remained forever in his son. Christian offered sincere apologies to Divino Canetti and his family, and to Hank Stevenson, who he had disrespected when visiting with Jaycee. They were pleased to see Christian humble himself. It felt good to be able to at least set some things right.

Christian's repentance meant the most to Rev. Francis, who welcomed him back into his church. Hesitant at first, the burden Christian shouldered proved to be too heavy, and he found himself divulging his sorrows. As they sat in the pews, Rev. Francis listened, knowing he needed the relief confession would bring.

As consoled as he was, Christian made sure Jaycee never knew what he did, to undo the harm he had caused. Mr. Campbell had made a point of reminding his soon-to-be son-in-law just how powerful his connections were in Averston. Should Christian ever betray the family, he warned, it would guarantee the end of his career as a doctor there and he would be removed from the mansion. From then on, the young man made a point of steering clear of anything that might jeopardize his chances.

Fortunately for him, Jaycee did not want anyone from Ospero Falls, except for Sophia, to attend the wedding.

When Frank heard about Christian's new practice in Averston, he tracked him down to wish him well. Even though his best friend was not invited to the wedding, it did not bother him. He loathed the woman, who had come between all of them.

The night before the wedding, he found Christian down at the Averston Country Club nursing a martini.

"Well, well," he said, slapping Christian on the back, "if it ain't the cream of the crop sitting here among the swankiest people in Averston!"

"How the hell are you, Frank?" Christian smiled as Frank sat down. "You know, I don't know if I am allowed to be seen with you." Christian shrugged and knocked back his martini.

"That bloody bad, eh?"

"The old man owns my balls now, too."

They burst into laughter, and for a moment, it felt like the way things used to be. They exchanged small talk and a few jokes, before Frank stood to go on his way.

"You have always been like a brother to me," he said, placing his hand on Christian's shoulder.

The words, though simple, had a profound effect on Christian.

"Right back at you, buddy," he said, grabbing Frank's hand and clenching it tightly.

Later that evening, Christian drove around aimlessly. Unable to return to the house on the hill, as Jaycee had kicked him out, due to the superstitions of seeing her before the wedding. He found himself travelling down the gravel road to the place he needed to see, he thought, for the last time.

Arriving at the Sitka tree, he quietly coasted his Cadillac under the dark stillness where the half curves of the moon hugged the night sky. Stepping out of his vehicle, Christian grabbed the lantern at the base of the spruce. Before making his way to the ladder, he lit the lantern and climbed up as he had done so many times before.

Standing at the entry of the tree house, he was caught by surprise. Nestled in a hammock was Skylar, fast asleep under the warmth of one of her mother's quilts. She did not stir as he stood there, oblivious to the fact the former lover was in her presence. The rounded features of her face were still as beautiful as ever, prompting Christian to smile, faintly. She seemed at peace.

Under the canopy of the Sitka, a flicker of light from the lantern played off the tree and illuminated Skylar's sun-bleached curls. He longed to run his fingers through them.

He looked at her wrist and saw the bracelet he had bought her, several Christmases ago.

As his eyes adjusted to the darkness inside the tree house, he noticed the additions she had made. White-frilled curtains with the pattern of bluebirds covered all the windows except the one facing the sea. She had shut out the view of Rogue's Bluffs completely, he realized. Beside a stack of books, one lay open. It was a collection of P.K. Page's poems. On a cushion sat a carved wooden bird. She had laid claim to the tree house, he knew, making it her own.

It was then, the light of the lantern, captured the words he saw scrawled in chalk across the ceiling. *See You Under the Sitka,* he read, wincing. Staring back at him, he felt were his broken promises.

He wondered when she had written the words. Could it be that she had clung to the hope that they would reunite someday? Maybe it was just a painful reminder that their timing had never been right. Whatever it was, tears formed in his eyes. He wanted to sweep her into his arms and erase the grief that plagued them. However, he could not change how he had traded their love for his dreams, which suddenly felt hollow.

A cold shiver ran through him, as he now fully realized Evamya's eerie predictions had come true. Turning to leave, he heard the sweet, familiar voice.

"Christian, is that really you?"

He hesitated then wiped the tears from his red cheeks.

"Yes, Piper, it's me."

"What are you doing here?"

He stepped closer, so that she could see him, in the light of the lantern.

"I don't know why, but I felt drawn to our Sitka. I had no idea you were here."

"I usually try to make it out to the spruce as often as I can before winter comes. I don't know who gets lonelier, me or the tree."

They smiled, easing the tension of their reunion.

"I like what you have done with the place," he said, putting the lantern down beside her.

"I thought I would decorate it with my collection of bird stuff," she shrugged. "It only seems appropriate."

"It sure reflects your personality." He stopped, knowing he was treading into deep water.

Abruptly, Skylar spoke the words she had carried with her, "I have not stopped loving you, Christian."

The truth felt like a load of bricks were upon him.

"You do not have to say anything in return. I have accepted your decision to move on and found peace within myself."

"Piper," he whispered, "I have never stopped loving you either, not for one second. Yet I am so wrapped up in everything that I cannot find my way back to you." He fell to his knees, wanting to beg for forgiveness. "Tell me, what am I supposed to do?"

He did not grasp that she had already granted him absolution. She slipped out of the hammock. Bending down, she threw her arms around him.

"Shhhh… It's okay Christian, I am here."

He looked deep into her eyes. They offered refuge. Giving in, he cupped her flushed cheeks with his palms. Kissing her full lips, their tongues danced together.

Suddenly, the time they had spent apart, erupted into a bout of heated lovemaking. Christian thrust his weight upon her body with a hunger Skylar could not recall. His lips touched every crevice of her nakedness. With every breath she took, her body quivered. He guided her hands to parts of him that she never had felt with such intensity. The young woman arched her back, as he made love to her repeatedly, under their Sitka tree.

After, as Skylar lay trembling in his arms, Christian looked up to see the words that she had scrawled on the ceiling staring back at him, taunting. Closing his eyes, he wished that when they awoke, the nightmare he had plunged them into would be over.

In the morning, she rose from her slumber to find him gone. If not for the way his scent lingered on her skin, she might have thought his visit was just a dream. Stretching, she pulled back the curtains and leaned out the window. Across the river and up the hill, a gazebo was being erected on Rogue's Bluffs. Biting her lip to hold back tears, she understood that he had been hers again for one night only. He had made his choice.

* * *

When Christian awoke with Skylar in his arms, he knew he had done wrong. Wanting to cleanse his guilt, he sought out Rev. Francis and told him what had occurred. Not wanting to persuade Christian either way, the Reverend said, "Do what you think is the right thing."

Afterwards, Christian vowed never to tell anybody else what had happened with Skylar.

The wedding of Christian and Jaycee took place on a brisk autumn day. As Jaycee walked down the aisle towards her future husband, a ladybug landed on her bridal bouquet. Try as she might, she could not shake the bug off. Using a single finger, she flicked at the insect marring her beautiful flowers, but it would not budge.

In the days following the wedding, Christian doted on his new wife. He clung to the belief that he could make his remorse disappear, by creating the illusion of a perfect marriage.

Several months later, he discovered that Jaycee was harbouring her own dark secret.

Chapter 26

Turnabout

LATE IN THE MORNING ON CHRISTMAS EVE, JAYCEE'S FATHER LUTHER paid Christian a visit. After pouring them each a tumble of bourbon, they sat in the study.

"I just wanted you to know, young man," he said smugly, "that you have done right by my daughter."

Christian nodded, averting his father-in-law's eyes. Guilt plagued him every day, making him paranoid.

Luther continued, "I know as a doctor, it must frustrate you about Jaycee's unfortunate inability to produce the growing family, I am sure you both had hoped on having. However, I have the finances to provide you with whatever resources, you need for more tests. There is also the option of adopting that I am sure my daughter is open to. Nevertheless, it is now between you two, to decide what to do about her infertility. You will have our support, either way," he added with reassurance.

Christian felt the room spin. His hand released its grip on the glass, dropping it to the floor where it shattered into tiny pieces of crystal. Luther's words raced through his mind as the truth settled in. She had tricked him into believing she was pregnant, then faked a miscarriage! How could he – a doctor – have been so naive?

"Are you okay?" Luther asked.

"No, I am just overwhelmed by your genuine concern." Suddenly, the maid showed up to have the mess cleaned up. "If you don't mind Mr. Campbell, I need some fresh air by myself to think things over." Luther nodded his head. Christian paused then said, "Thanks for the talk… It is nice to know what kind of a family I married into."

"Well, young man," Luther said, standing to shake Christian's hand, "you will soon realize that we stick together. Everyone knows that we go out on a limb for people. But wrong us and you will be sure to suffer the fury," he winked.

Christian waited for Jaycee to return from shopping. He sat in a leather chair in the bedroom with the curtains drawn, thinking about what he would say. There was relief, he had persuaded his wife against hosting an elaborate New Year's Eve party. Using the excuse that the renovations needed to be completed, he hid that he was using it as an excuse to cover Skylar's birthday. He also panned the idea of a Christmas gathering, as the mansion was still in disarray. Mulling over his thoughts, the young man reflected on how the only thing Jaycee and Christian were good at, was exchanging lies.

Entering the room, Jaycee did not notice him sitting in the shadows. She had begun to undress when Christian flicked on the lamp beside him. She shrieked. He put his finger up to his lips.

"Hush now," he whispered. "I am sure you don't want anyone to hear what a conniving, lying bitch you are."

Her face turned red. "How dare you talk to me like that!" she hissed. "Just who the hell do you think you are? I can call my father right now and end your career with a snap of my fingers!"

He put his hands together and smiled, knowing he had gained the upper hand.

"Just go right ahead and call him. Then when he shows up, I will let him know how you deceived me with a fake pregnancy and then lied to me about a miscarriage. I will finish off this corrupt marriage, by letting them know how you forgot to mention, you're unable to have children!"

Sitting down on the bed, she burst into tears.

"I did not think you would find out, at least not this soon.

"I figured if you gave us a chance, you would fall in love with me and we could work through anything. I never meant to hurt you."

He looked at her with scorn.

"You took me away from the only woman who ever has meant anything to me!" he yelled. "You sabotaged my love for her with your deception and inflicted upon her a pain, like no other. You ruined the friendships I had with people who respected me. You brought grief to my own mother. You are in my mind, without a doubt, the worst trash of Norelton! You hoped I would fall in love with you? I despise you! You are ugly to me, inside and out. I loathe the day I ever met you!"

She crumpled on the bed, sobbing. He strode past, throwing his ring down beside her.

"You explain to your family, what a sham our marriage is. I no longer have to answer to you!"

For the first time in years, his confidence returned. As he sauntered out of the mansion into the briskness of winter, he thrust his closed fist upward and extended two fingers in a V.

He believed everything would change for the better, but Evamya's unheeded advice had more misery to bring forth.

* * *

Time passed for Skylar with no word from Christian. She resolved herself yet again, to accept the painful reality that his greed was stronger, than his love for her.

Meanwhile, she was coping with a crisis of her own. Shortly after their rendezvous at the tree house, she had taken ill. At first, she was nauseated and tired, but then the dizzy spells began. Added to the symptoms was a tenderness in her breast, which she noticed while bathing. Not wanting to make a fuss over nothing, Skylar tried shrugging it off. However, when she realized her period was late since the night with Christian, she began to worry.

All the same, she did not want to upset her mother and decided to keep her concerns to herself.

With the new year upon them, she looked forward to Frank, Samantha, Olivia, Gwen, and Abimbola coming back to spend the holidays in Ospero Falls. Everyone would be together, including Sophia, except for Christian, who would be missing.

They enjoyed a traditional Christmas dinner, expressing contentment with their lives – except for Skylar. The pain in her breast had worsened, and she noticed a worrying discharge. In spite of the pain, she suffered in silence, planning to visit the doctor after her birthday.

On the morning of New Year's Eve, Gwen showed Skylar a portrait of Evamya that she won a prestigious award for. Skylar noticed that Gwen was hiding another photograph under the award-winner. She playfully grabbed the photo out of her hands. It was a stunning black-and-white portrait of Christian and Gwen standing underneath the majestic beauty of the Sitka tree. Skylar recalled the day vividly. They had spent the hot, July day picnicking and frolicking along the riverbed. Skylar had offered to take the picture.

The photo was hard for her to look at, but she knew how much it meant to Gwen.

"I couldn't have seized such a beautiful moment, if it hadn't been for your camera," Skylar said.

"You're truly the best, Bird Girl."

They hugged, and Gwen noticed Skylar flinch.

"What is the matter?"

She turned, trying to avoid Gwen's look of concern.

"It's nothing, I have just been feeling a little tender lately in my right breast."

Gwen knew something was amiss. When she and Abimbola had arrived at the Falls' home, they noticed how pale and weak Skylar looked. Gwen shared her concerns with Victoria.

She remarked that Skylar was probably exhausted, from all the volunteering she was doing for Rev. Francis. Victoria made it clear that after all they had been through, Skylar would never hide anything from her. Gwen shifted the conversation, but made a mental note, to keep a close eye on her best friend over the holidays.

As Skylar prepared to have a quiet birthday, a chance encounter would again bring her and Christian together.

The afternoon of her birthday, before the celebration was to begin, Skylar excused herself. She went to take a walk along the frozen sands, leading to the pier. Although it was bitterly cold in the middle of a fierce winter, she needed to see the ocean.

Walking along the wooden pier that creaked mournfully underneath her steps, she found herself standing at the edge, inhaling the seaside into her lungs.

As the wind howled, a sharp cramp made her double over in pain. She collapsed on the wooden pier, clutching her sides in agony, and went limp. While her unconscious body lay exposed, a nearby lone figure could be seen running towards her.

* * *

When Skylar awoke, it took all her effort to grasp her surroundings. Whispers in the distance became audible.

"Poor thing, such a shame what is happening to her."

"If you ask me, I think the whole family's cursed."

Skylar raised her hand towards them.

"Oh my goodness, she's awake! Go get Dr. Gregson."

It was then she realized she was in Bay Hospital.

Almost immediately, she was surrounded by Dr. Gregson and the two nurses she had heard chattering.

He proceeded to check her heart rate and blood pressure. She could tell by his expression that he was worried by whatever ailed her. She could not stand the silence any longer.

"What's wrong with me?"

The doctor raised an eyebrow and asked the nurses to get Victoria. She entered the room clutching a crumpled handkerchief in her trembling hands. Upon seeing her daughter, Victoria ran to her side.

"Oh Songbird," she said, grasping Skylar's pasty hand. "If only you had come to tell me, maybe then…"

"Would someone please tell me what is going on?" Skylar blurted.

Victoria's face paled. "You mean," she asked Dr. Gregson, "she doesn't even know?"

"No," he said, shaking his head. "I thought it would be better if you were here, when I told her."

Victoria nodded, tears cascading down her face.

"I love you," she said, clutching Skylar's hand tighter.

Dr. Gregson brought a chair over and sat.

"You have been diagnosed with the most serious breast cancer there is, inflammatory carcinoma. The skin over the breast becomes swollen because the lymph vessels are blocked by cancer. Although you are in the first stages of it, the prognosis for this type of cancer is the least favourable. I'm sorry to say I cannot offer you any hope, Ms. Falls. The likelihood is that you are not going to survive."

Skylar tried to grasp his words, but they floated like fragments in the air. Before she could even begin to fathom all he was saying, the doctor continued.

"There's something else you should be aware of," he said, his voice hesitant. "When we ran some tests on you, we found out that you are in your first trimester of pregnancy."

"No!" Skylar screamed.

Her anguished cries echoed through the corridors of the hospital. As Sophia clutched Christian, sitting in the waiting room with the others, they knew something dreadful had happened.

Victoria held her overwrought daughter in her arms. Dr. Gregson waited for the sobs to subside before he proceeded.

"In my experience, it is uncommon that someone can become pregnant when they have this type of cancer, but it is not impossible. The problems that arise from this situation are, obviously, on a grand scale. What is worse, the surge of estrogen from pregnancy can rapidly speed the growth of the cancer. Usually, being able to proceed to full term is not an option. However, I will do all that I physically can as a doctor, to ensure your life is not jeopardized any further by the pregnancy. There is, of course, another option."

Skylar's olive eyes widened. "If there is any hope that this child can survive, I refuse to senselessly get rid of it."

Dr. Gregson nodded. "You'll need to take some time to think everything over. If you carry on with the pregnancy, then you must understand that you would be living your days here in the hospital under strict supervision. There will be no drugs or radiation administered to you, out of concern of damaging the fetus. Also, you would require a Caesarean, as there is no way you could physically give birth. However, with the type of cancer you have, I see the chances of you surviving to full term are not favourable. I'm very sorry, Miss Falls. My sympathy goes out to you and your family. I will leave you to think over everything and later we will talk through your options. Before I leave though, I would recommend you tell the father of your baby.

"He has a right to know."

As soon as they were alone, Skylar looked at her mother with the same fright she felt, when Trey Wickett was a part of their lives. Victoria continued to hold onto her daughter, knowing a part of what she was enduring. On the other hand, she could not imagine being given a death sentence and being told about the new life growing inside, all at the same time.

The hands of the clock ticked deafeningly.

"You know Christian's the father, Momma. What am I gonna tell him?"

"I know, honey. Would you like me to talk to Sophia?"

"No, Momma. We are all adults. I think it is best if I tell him myself. I just do not know how to reach him."

"Good Lord," Victoria said. "Nobody told you it was Christian who found you on the pier. He came by looking for you, telling us he had some wonderful news to share. I told him that you had gone for a walk along the wharf. Thank goodness he came by or else you surely would have frozen to death, you and the…"

"Just look at what has happened," Skylar sputtered. "It's all my fault!"

"Now you listen to me, Skylar Reigh, none of this is your fault. The cancer has not taken you away from us yet, and I am not going to watch you give up so easily. We all have to gather our strength and faith – and pray for a miracle! Please have the courage to believe that both you and your baby will survive this."

Skylar nodded, then asked Victoria to get Christian. As her mother left the room, Skylar began to pray.

When Christian walked in and sat down, his hands were trembling. Stripped of his stethoscope and white coat, he sat exposed.

They looked into one another's eyes, and he did not like what he was seeing.

"Christian," Skylar said, uttering the words that would torment him forever, "I'm dying."

His world crumbled as he listened to her grim prognosis and that she was pregnant with his child. They cried for a long time, and he vowed to do whatever he could, to ensure she would live long enough to see their baby. Yet he knew the probability of beating the cancer was slim, and that it would take a miracle for their unborn child to survive. In the back of his mind, it occurred to him that if Jaycee found out, she would try to regain control again. At the very least, try to even the score, in the twisted game they played.

Over the course of one day, many lives had been changed forever.

Unbeknown to them, the fallout would seep into the next generation, yet to come.

* * *

Before long, one by one, those closest to Skylar had heard what was happening to her. From Gwen's pleas of mercy to Frank's outburst of tears in the waiting room, everyone reeled with shock over Skylar's battle – not only for her life, but for that of her unborn baby. Sophia clenched her fists when Christian told her. Her only hope, since Jack's death, was to hold her future grandchildren. She was overcome with anger, that someone else she loved so dearly, could be taken away.

Back home, Christian told his mother why he had showed up at the Falls' residence. Something Evamya had told him long ago stuck with him, he said. His intentions were to leave Jaycee.Finally, Christian was giving into the belief, their misery loved one another's company. Although Sophia empathized with her son, she urged him not to tell Jaycee about Skylar, just yet. His mother reminded him that Jaycee was full of malice towards Skylar, and she feared retaliation. He agreed to hold off and decided to return at some point to Averston, to see if Jaycee had told her family what she had done.

More important to Christian, though, was that Skylar was not alone on her birthday. He told the others to go home and offered to shoulder her tremendous sorrow. He told Skylar about Jaycee's deception. In her typical forgiving manner, Skylar expressed only empathy, for the desperate lengths Jaycee had gone to.

Later, Nurse Ethel shed tears when she looked in on her patient. There she saw Christian cramped into a chair with Skylar curled asleep in his arms. They were wrapped in a quilt of songbirds around them.

While they clung to each other in a hospital room, anxious for a miracle, cheers from the throng of people spilled out onto the streets of Ospero Falls, as the new year began.

In the days that followed, Rev. Francis and Victoria kept vigil by Skylar's side. More tests were conducted, yet they came back with the same grim conclusion – there was no hope. Abimbola had to go back to the city. He came to bid farewell to Skylar, who he found awake.

"In my family," he said, leaning over her, "we do not fear death, but see it as an extension of one's life that goes on through the generations." He placed his hands upon her belly and whispered with reassurance, "It's a healthy baby. As we say, 'mtoto wa kike.'"

When Abimbola kissed her forehead, Skylar felt a surge of warmth flow through her.

After saying goodbye to her husband, Gwen returned to the room. She brought photographs of the four friends taken throughout the years. Meanwhile, Frank and Samantha helped Victoria gather a variety of Skylar's favourite bird collectibles from their house, to bring some cheer to the dismal room.

Grief brought everyone together, and yet life was never the same. Skylar had spent her days in prayer and was at peace with the heavenly father. She began to think about who would help Christian, raise their child, when she was gone.

* * *

Sitting across from his wife Jaycee at the dining room table, Christian carefully chose his words. The ticking of the grandfather clock echoed through the empty hallways of the half-renovated mansion. They sat in silence, not looking at each other, ashamed of the guilt that consumed them.

"Damn it," he said, slamming his fist on the table. "Just once in your life, will you admit to what you have done? Maybe if I could see a glimmer of remorse from you, we could try to settle this mess we call a marriage."

Jaycee sat defiant, refusing to take any accountability for the pain she had caused.

"I want a divorce," he said, fury clouding his judgement. "I do not give a shit anymore what you or your family does. Right now, as I speak, the only woman I really love, is sitting in a hospital room dying. Skylar is pregnant with my child, and all you can do is think about your own greedy self!"

Suddenly, Jaycee leaned forward. Looking straight into his eyes, she demanded to know, "What do you mean she is dying and pregnant with your baby?"

"You heard me. Not that it's of any concern to you, but Skylar has cancer and is expecting at the same time. She will be lucky to live long enough to have the baby."

Jaycee burst into sobs and covered her face with her hands.

"I am so sorry to hear that, Chris. I truly am."

Taken aback by her display of grief, Christian sat quietly, unsure of what to say. He was prepared for a battle; she had caught him off-guard.

"Please hear me out," she said. "I never told anyone in my family what I did because I am ashamed of myself. It really does not surprise me that you had a rendezvous with Skylar. In fact, she once told me, your heart would always belong to her.

"If only I had been honest with you, maybe we would have stood a chance, but now I know that is impossible. If you want me to sign divorce papers, I understand. But in spite of all that has happened, I want you to know that I truly do love you."

He remembered what Skylar had said about taking pity on the poor soul and found himself standing up to console Jaycee. She wept in his arms.

"Be with her, Christian. She needs you more right now, than I do."

Walking out the door of the mansion, his feet couldn't carry him fast enough. From the window, Jaycee watched him get into the Cadillac and drive away. A crooked smile stretched across her face.

"You will reap what you sow," she whispered into the darkness of the night.

Chapter 27

Compromise

BACK AT THE HOSPITAL, CHRISTIAN WAS STILL PERPLEXED BY Jaycee's reaction to the news about Skylar. He waited until late in the afternoon the next day to tell Skylar.

"I never have been able to understand her at all, Piper. She is so different from you. At times she is heartless and then, like flicking a switch, she is caring."

While he shared his thoughts, he tried to imagine life without Skylar. Reaching over, he stroked her hand and breathed in her scent of sweet musk.

Skylar seized the moment to share her intentions with him.

"I would like you to listen carefully to what I have to say," she said. "I have discussed my options with both my mother and Rev. Francis. At the same time, I have been praying to the Lord for an answer. Since you are the father, and our child needs a home with the love of a mother, I want you and Jaycee to raise our baby."

The magnitude of the words weighed heavily upon Christian. He could not argue the truth and knowing it would be of no use anyway, the young man simply replied,

"I cannot imagine how hard it was for you to come to this decision," he said. "Thank you for giving me a second chance. Maybe I can set things right, with our child at least."

"I will have the papers drawn up when the time comes," she said. "I only ask for two things from the both of you: I want to name the baby, and I want our child to know who I am, when the time is right."

He nodded as tears flowed down his face. He held her hand tightly and began to sob, knowing that she was making the ultimate sacrifice.

"I will always be a part of you, Christian," she whispered. "A promise is a promise."

Upon returning to Rogue's Bluffs a few days later, Christian told Jaycee of Skylar's offer. Jaycee threw her arms around him.

"Oh Christian!" she said. "It really is the best thing to do. I promise to take such wonderful care of the baby and of course abide by her special requests. You will not regret this."

He was not convinced, but giving her the benefit of the doubt, he resigned himself to accepting Skylar's offer.

A week later, Jacqueline's family were told about the circumstances. Both Christian and Jaycee could see the shock on Luther and Savannah's faces. However, in the best interest of their daughter, they accepted the news knowing how much she wanted to be a mother.

In the hospital, focus shifted to caring for the expectant mother to ensure the survival of the child. When she was first diagnosed, Skylar was allowed to move about the hospital. Sometimes the nurses would find her reading poetry to the elderly and smile. However, as the months passed, she was restricted to her bed for rest. Her body had started to show the physical signs of the disease. Regardless of her situation, she managed to give thanks. Lying in bed, she would marvel at how her belly grew, while the rest of her diminished. She considered each day a blessing for her unborn child. Closer to her due date, Dr. Gregson, who had kept his promise to make her a priority, reminded Skylar she could have a caesarean, at any time.

The days seemed to go by quickly and Skylar read her bible daily, as the scripture offered comfort, when she needed it.

One day, as she arrived for a visit, Victoria saw through the room window that Skylar was crying, while writing something on a piece of paper. Not wanting to intrude, she lingered in the waiting room. When she finally went in, whatever Skylar had been writing was nowhere to be seen.

She sat and patted her daughter's hand.

"Is everything okay, Songbird?"

"Last night," she sighed, "I dreamt of finding a sparrow. It was hurt and I was overwhelmed with such sadness."

She fell quiet.

Clearing her throat, Skylar made a request.

"No matter what Jaycee says, you are to be part of this child's life."

Victoria grabbed hold of her daughter's hand and giving it a gentle squeeze, she nodded her head in reassurance.

Over the following weeks, meetings took place between Luther and Savannah, along with Victoria and Sophia. Though awkward at first, everyone was polite in front of Skylar. Arrangements were made for the adoption papers to be drafted.

Time passed and the due date approached. Victoria found it harder to watch as her beautiful daughter slipped further away. She struggled over how to contend with Jaycee in raising her grandchild. Many times Victoria sought the guidance of Rev. Francis.

Jaycee, too, was having a hard time coping with the situation. She had watched as her husband took care of his soulmate, with a tenderness, she yearned for herself.

One day, she came by the hospital to visit Christian and Skylar with paint swatches for the nursery. Her eyes fell on the bird decor that adorned the hospital room.

"Would it be alright," Jaycee asked Skylar, "if I took a few items for the baby's room?"

"Of course," Skylar said, her face lighting up. "I'd love that."

While everybody warmed to Jaycee's portrayal of a compassionate mother-to-be, two of them remained unconvinced. Gwen and Frank discussed her intentions with unease.

They prayed for a miracle, that Skylar would somehow pull through to raise the child herself.

Returning to Bay View Hospital at every opportunity, Christian began to loathe the smell of death that haunted every crevice of the building. As a doctor, it had not bothered him before. Yet now as Skylar neared her end, he began to understand the deeper connection to his former patients, whose lives had ended too soon.

In March, Christian sat with Victoria at her home.

"I want to tell you personally, Ms. Falls," he said, sipping his tea, "how sorry I am for all the pain I have caused both you and Skylar. I never meant for things to happen the way they did. I regret so much…" his voice trailed off.

Victoria looked tired, yet her eyes held the same sparkle as Skylar's.

"I do not hold anything against you, Christian," she said. "My daughter and you have always shared a special bond. Even though she does not recall how you came to protect her from Trey Wickett,

I have never forgotten. You always have been and will continue to be welcome here."

Christian cleared his throat as he fought back his emotions.

"Thank you," he said, reaching over to hug her.

He saw the reflection of where Skylar's kindness came from.

"That means a lot to me. I do have one question though," he hesitated then continued, "why didn't you offer to raise the baby?"

She fidgeted with the lace on her handkerchief.

"With the history of cancer in our family, and the possibility of a recurrence happening to me, I just could not take the chance. I would not want to raise the baby and then have to burden the child if I were to pass away suddenly."

"I do not understand why you both have suffered so much," he said, touching her hand. "However, I do know how blessed I am to know you, Miss Falls. You truly are a wonderful mother."

Her face softened and she murmured, "Thank-you for your kind words."

Christian spoke again, "I wanted to ask you about something very important to Skylar. She has requested, if she lives past the birth of the baby, that I bring her home… here." He cleared his throat. "She wants to die in peace among the trees…"

Victoria looked away, then nodded.

Christian continued, "I have asked Frank if he could come to see you about adding a loft to the house, a place where Skylar would feel comforted by her surroundings. I, of course, would cover all the costs, and Frank offered to give his services for free. It is our way of giving back to Skylar, a little of what she has given us through the years."

She smiled, knowing how important it was for him to come to terms with Skylar's illness.

Victoria's hands wrapped around the handkerchief and twisted it. She wanted to scream, "No! Not my babygirl." Yet instead she replied, "I think it is a wonderful idea, Christian. I do not want to see my Songbird, pass away, in a dreadful hospital room."

"You have my word that it will be completed on time," he said, rising to hug Victoria again.

True to his words, the addition of the loft was completed in a few months.

With only two weeks before the due date, everyone put their lives on hold for Skylar. Gwen and Victoria spent their days adorning the new room with birds. Hand-sewn by Victoria, Calais curtains with a sparrow pattern, were hung from the window. Gwen placed photographs taken during their early years atop the dresser. Her favourite was a close-up of Skylar, her soft freckles emphasizing her natural beauty. Christian brought from downstairs the painting of the Sitka; she had cut it from the wall after the fire. He placed it upon her easel.

A quilt embroidered in songbirds covered the bed. Surrounding the mattress was a wrought-iron frame. Each porcelain post, adorned by brushstrokes of red hearts. Frank wrestled upstairs two rocking chairs that he had carved from cherry. On the back of one, etched into the wood, was a solitary sandpiper.

As they worked side by side, no one dared mention that Skylar might never see the room.

Her body had become so weak that Christian gave her liquids using a straw. He would dip the straw into the glass and put his finger over one end, to drop the liquid into her parched mouth, slowly. He applied cool cloths to her brow and balm to her cracked lips. Christian's constant vigil over Skylar was a testament to their love and he faithfully stayed by her side, as much as possible.

When Christian was busy with his new practice in Averston, Gwen stayed with her best friend.

Soothing Skylar's dry, taut skin with lotion made of almond oil, Gwen tried to help take her mind off the pain. She held the albums of photographs snapped over the years and flipped through each one. Whenever Skylar spotted a picture of the Sitka tree, she would point to it and smile faintly.

One day, as she peered upon the photograph of Christian and Gwen standing underneath the tree, Skylar said, "That is where I want my ashes to be released."

"Of course," Gwen said.

"One more thing. I want my baby to know about our beloved spruce only from you, Frank, and Christian. No one else is to enter the tree house, especially Jaycee. It is a sacred place, Gwen, one that holds special meaning to me, and I do not want anyone dishonouring it."

Nodding her head in assurance, Gwen replied, "I promise to take care of it for you."

On June 2nd, 1971, Skylar's baby came into the world by Caesarean delivery.

It was a healthy, baby girl weighing in at 5 lbs, 2 oz. Abimbola had been right when he had bent down and said in his language: mooi meisie, meaning "beautiful girl." The joyous moment was marred only by the knowledge that Dr. Gregson was not expecting Skylar to survive the night.

After the baby was whisked away to the maternity ward, everyone gathered in the hospital chapel, to pray for a miracle. Christian hoped that Skylar would live long enough to look into the eyes of their child.

Rev. Francis prepared his visit to Skylar to read her last rites. No one wanted to let go. Around 3 am, Nurse Ethel ran out of Skylar's room looking for the doctor.

When Christian, Sophia and Victoria were awakened from their sleep in the chapel pews by Nurse Ethel, they feared the worst. However, once in Skylar's room, they were surprised to see her conscious and holding the baby. Skylar cooed softly, a placid smile on her face. Sophia, Christian and Victoria were amazed, until Dr. Gregson took them aside.

"It is not unusual," he explained, "to see cancer patients nearing the end have a burst of life, as if everything is normal. I believe Skylar has made it this far through sheer perseverance and faith. I have let her know that I am abiding by her wishes to be released into your care. Nurse Ethel will come along to ensure Skylar has proper medical attention. Since you are a doctor yourself, Christian, I know she will be in good hands."

"Of course, Dr. Gregson," Christian said. "Thank you for taking such wonderful care of Skylar over the past few months. Each of us is grateful!"

Victoria and Sophia shook his hand and offered their thanks through tears.

"Yes, we appreciated the quality of care you have given her."

The Doctor nodded, then turned to Christian.

"I only wish," Dr. Gregson said, patting him on the back, "that I could have done more."

Christian finally understood, looking inward, why becoming a doctor had been so important to him. He had the gift to save lives. When all possibilities of hope had been exhausted, it was still up to him to see a family through their grief, right up to the end.

"You did your job as well as you could, Dr. Gregson," he said.

After the doctor left, they turned their attention to Skylar. Despite the tubes jutting over her gown covering her emaciated body, Skylar emitted joy. Her colour though, was like the yellow buttercups, poking out of a nearby vase.

"Come here, Christian," she beamed, "and say hello to your baby girl, Aurelia. It is pronounced a-RAY-lee-a, and it means the golden one. My favourite season is autumn, and I wanted her to have a connection to her momma."

"What a fitting name for such a beautiful girl," Sophia said.

"She will always be blessed to carry such a wonderful name," Victoria added.

The mothers watched, shedding tears, as Christian and Skylar saw the life they had created.

Skylar gestured for her mother to come hold her granddaughter.

"You do look just like your momma," Victoria said, carefully holding Aurelia's head, which was covered in wisps of strawberry curls. She cooed at the baby, "I will call you 'little golden sparrow.'"

Skylar smiled at the sound of it. "Promise me that she'll know how much I love her," she said.

Christian leaned down and kissed her tenderly, said, "A promise is a promise, Piper."

Looking deep into his eyes, she could only hope this time, he would keep his vow.

"Thank you for seeing me through these moments," she said.

"You do not have to thank me, Piper. Ever."

The special moment for the family was shattered, by the abrupt interruption of Jaycee, bursting into the room.

"Oh," she squealed, "is that my precious little bundle you have there?"

Victoria and Sophia tried not to show their displeasure, while Christian and Skylar braced themselves for the moment they never wanted to arrive. Victoria slowly handed Aurelia to Jaycee.

"Oh my goodness, she is so perfectly beautiful. I cannot wait to bring you home."

"Her name is Aurelia," Skylar said.

Jacqueline stopped gurgling to the baby and was quiet for a moment. Finally, she replied,

"Of course it is! What a … unique name."

"Like it or not," Victoria said, "my granddaughter is to be called by that name."

Jaycee's eyes narrowed, and Christian felt the room fill with tension. He gestured for Jaycee to hand the baby back.

"Do not start anything," he whispered in her ear. "I mean it."

She bit her tongue and handed the baby to Skylar.

"Our lawyer will be by in a few hours to go over the final papers," she said, heading towards the door. "I will return then."

Skylar was filled with overwhelming sadness.

"Please leave me be with Aurelia for a while," she said, tears flowing down her pale, freckled cheeks. "I really need to be alone with her."

Christian, Sophia, and Victoria left quietly.

As Skylar clung to her baby, swaddled in a blanket embroidered with bluebirds, she stared into her bright green eyes and murmured, "Listen to me Aurelia, this isn't good-bye…whenever you want to find your momma, come visit me under the Sitka tree.

"While I only wish I had more time with you, I know I will see you once again, when we reunite in heaven. I pray the light of the Lord will be the love of your life as you seek him. With the Holy Spirit as your guide, I speak the words from my Bible over you, *Do not ever forget kindness and truth, wear them like a necklace. Write them on your heart, as if on a tablet. Then you will be respected and will please both God and people.*

"I will always be with you… when you close your eyes I will be the gentle breath upon you as you sleep. When you take your first steps, I will be there like a mound of autumn leaves, ready to catch your fall. If ever you doubt how beautiful you truly are, look at the raindrops upon the windowpanes – for the droplets will be tapping out the words, 'I love you, my little golden sparrow.'"

Skylar's tears fell upon Aurelia's head, anointing her with her mother's lament. Rocking back and forth, Skylar clung to her bundled miracle. In the daylight of the room, mother and daughter bonded. Meanwhile in the shadows lurked Jaycee, ready to take from Skylar, her purpose for living.

When the lawyer arrived, an exhausted Skylar – not wanting to prolong her suffering – signed with trembling hands, the papers that made the adoption of Aurelia Dawn O'Connelly official. Afterwards, she asked to be left alone again. Dr. Gregson came in and gave Skylar a sedative, to help her sleep. The pain she experienced physically and emotionally, proved to be overwhelming.

She drifted off to sleep, knowing she would be returning home to the former sanctuary, to live out her final days.

Arriving at the hospital in the morning, Christian was stunned to see how Skylar's skin tone had dulled to gray again. Life was seeping out of her, he thought, as the cancer spread.

While Victoria and Gwen packed up Skylar's room, Christian made a special request of Dr. Gregson. After much persuasion, the doctor agreed, as long as Nurse Ethel went along.

In mid-morning, Skylar – to her amazement – was wheeled out to Christian's Cadillac. Nurse Ethel sat in the back seat. Skylar would take a final ride with the soft-top down next to the man she loved. Christian made sure she was comfortable before Dr. Gregson gave her another shot of pain medication.

Driving slowly to allow Skylar to savour the moment, Christian looked over as she tilted her face upwards, to the shining sun.

Closing her eyes, she inhaled the scent of the ocean, as they travelled along the winding road. When she opened them again, she smiled, seeing a flutter of sparrows chase the car.

Victoria and the others were waiting to welcome her home. Christian parked, opened the passenger door, and carefully lifted Skylar into his arms.

He carried her into the house.

"Just look at our beautiful sanctuary," she said to Victoria.

He carried her upstairs to the loft. Upon reaching the top step, Christian gently set her upon a chair. Pulling a skeleton key out of his pocket, he inserted it into the keyhole of the unique door plate. Skylar's tears began to fall, as she recognized the Piper/Faith key and the doorplate he once gifted her; which was supposed to be for their future home.

Lifting her delicate frame, he entered through the door, assisting her into the room. When Skylar saw what had been accomplished in her honour, she sighed.

"This is so breathtaking," she said.

Nurse Ethel helped Skylar settle into the bed designed just for her.

Glancing around the loft, Skylar saw the photographs taken by Gwen lining the dresser top. She gazed at the windows, sunlight filtering through the Calais lace curtains, trimmed into the outline of songbirds. Skylar spotted, among the decorations, the wooden bird Makwa had whittled for her, along with the woven basket. Things that held memories of her beloved Sitka tree's good heart.

Christian, she realized, had driven out to their tree to retrieve the bird. Unbeknown to her, in the same place their child had been conceived, he had fallen to his knees at the base of the Sitka. Finally submitting to the Creator and releasing his claim over the tree. Looking up, he imagined the silhouette of his true love, with light radiating from the tree. The broken man now understood, he never had ownership over the spruce, as this Sitka – was Skylar's spirit tree.

As she peered around the room, the beautiful wooden rocking chairs drew her attention. She knew from the craftsmanship that they were Frank's handiwork. Reaching out to him, he drew close. She kissed him softly on the cheek.

"You are a marvellous man, Frank," she said. "I love you with all my heart, not only as the dear friend you have been to me, but to Christian as well."

"I love you too," he said, choking back tears. "You are family to me. We are the lucky ones to have you a part of our lives!"

Behind him stood Olivia, whose lips quivered as she recalled him as a young boy, saying goodbye to his father. When he stepped aside, his mother leaned in towards Skylar and conveyed what everyone in the room had been feeling, "If ever I have seen a person both so gentle and full of grace on the inside and out, it is you. My Franklin has always spoken highly of your strength and admiration, for standing up for your convictions. I think all of us have had our lives changed for the better because of the way you see life, Skylar."

"I cherish your kind words, Mrs. Whitman," Skylar smiled. With that, Olivia and Frank left.

Gwen moved closer to the bed.

"I want you to know I am not ready to say goodbye just yet," she said, "so I will keep this short and sweet. I am coming back tomorrow after you have rested. Be prepared to have your ears talked off."

Skylar grinned. Gwen turned to leave, but Skylar reached for her hand. They held on to each other tightly, just as they did when they were little girls skipping alongside the river, singing songs.

"Gwennie-Sue," she said, "you are going to have to let me go."

"Yeah, but today is not gonna be the day, Bird Girl."

Skylar let go of her hand. Gwen walked out, as the tears spilled down her cheeks.

Sophia and Christian drew close, struggling to accept what was happening to the woman they both loved dearly. Their time together was dwindling. Sophia bent down and gave Skylar a peck on the cheek. Careful not to move Skylar, Sophia gently propped herself on the side of the bed and said, "When Jack passed away so suddenly, I wished that I had been given a second chance to tell him again how much I loved him, as a caring husband and a devoted father. As you know, life is full of unpredictability.

"I am both sad and grateful at the same time, that I have this precious moment with you my dear. Therefore, it is important you know how much my life has been enriched, because of your gentle spirit and selfless nature. I have watched you grow throughout the years from a shy, little girl into a woman full of love for others. I believe you were blessed with a gift from the good Lord. For you Skylar were meant to shine.

"People are drawn to you for this reason, and you are fortunate enough to have realized your gift. Evamya use to say that the grace in you was from the heavens. I can honestly say that I now know what she meant by that!" Sophia dabbed her eyes with a tissue. "I do not know how we will carry on without you. I take comfort in knowing your spirit will always remain here in Ospero Falls." She could not bear the heartache any longer. "As you shined here on Earth, you will brighten the heavens, too." She stood and tried to smile. Walking away, she glanced back. "Tell Jack I miss him dearly."

"I will," Skylar said.

Sophia walked out the door. Victoria sat in another rocking chair in the corner. Her eyes were swollen from the bouts of sorrow. She was overwhelmed by the gravity of the moment, watching her daughter say her good-byes at such a tender age, was unfathomable.

Christian was slumped over in a chair next to the bed, his face buried in his hands. Unable to speak, he listened to the kind words spoken to the love of his life and the mother of his child. He tried to summon the courage to bid her farewell but couldn't.

Skylar touched his hand. Taking hold of his palm and, she placed it to her heart and said, "It is okay Christian, I am at peace. Soon, I am going home to be with Jesus."

Her declaration proved too much for the young man.

Suddenly, he bolted upwards and exclaimed, "I just cannot do this Piper! I am sorry, I have to meet Jaycee at the hospital to go pick-up Aurelia."

Abruptly he fled the room. Unable to face his own fear; the death of a loved one, was proving to be unbearable.

Victoria came over and cradled Skylar's head.

"I'll be okay, Momma."

"I'm sorry, Songbird. I cannot help my motherly instincts."

"It's okay. I guess you never stop being a parent, do you?"

"No, Songbird. No matter what, you always worry about your babies. It is God's way of making sure all his children are taken care of."

Realizing with anguish that her daughter would never see her own child grow up, Victoria struggled to maintain her composure.

Skylar smiled. Knowing Aurelia would be loved, brought her peace. She trusted Christian would keep his promise to tell their daughter about her someday. It was the best she could hope for.

Victoria tucked her in, praying it would not be for the last time. Skylar saw the painting of the Sitka tree, on the easel, in the corner.

"Momma," she asked, "can you do me a favour and bring the picture over here beside me?"

Victoria nodded, knowing how much it meant to Skylar. She placed it beside the bed. Skylar felt comforted, recalling the countless times the Sitka's lofty branches protected her through the years.

* * *

At the hospital, Christian met Jaycee to bring their baby girl home. As he drove back towards the mansion, he felt he was in a dream.

Glancing over at his wife, he imagined Skylar's sunny face smiling back at him, blowing tender kisses into the soft, cool breeze.

The cries of the baby brought him back to reality.

"I certainly hope it's not going to do that all the time," Jaycee scoffed.

He tensed up and made a mental note to hire help for her, to deal with the newborn.

Once home, they settled their daughter into the nursery. After, Christian flopped onto the couch, exhausted.

"Well," Jaycee asked, "did you say goodbye to her today?"

His muscles tightened into a thousand knots.

"No. There was so much going on. With everyone else wanting to be with her, I did not get a chance. You know, she tires easily. I thought I would go back tomorrow."

"Well, the sooner you deal with it the better, Chris. You have a family of your own to think about now. I think I've been very understanding, considering the uncomfortable situation I was put in."

He wanted to shake her. "Yeah, you are the best, honey," he muttered. "I will make sure to tell Skylar how lucky I am, to have married a woman like you."

He retreated to bed, before Jaycee could dig her claws in, any further.

Around 2 am, Christian was awakened by the baby wailing. He tried several times to get Jaycee to tend to the child.

"You get up and deal with her," she said, rolling over.

While Christian sat in the nursery, feeding Aurelia a warm bottle, he looked into his daughter's eyes. For the first time, he saw the same look of innocence that Skylar projected. Rocking back and forth, he recalled the words he'd whispered so long ago under the Sitka tree.

"Know you the land where the lemon-trees bloom? In the dark foliage the gold oranges glow, a soft wind hovers from the sky, the myrtle is still, and the laurel stands tall. Do you know it well? There, there, I would go, O my beloved, with thee!"

Aurelia was lulled back to sleep by the tender voice of her father. A lump formed in his throat. Once again, he realized he had deserted Skylar, when she needed him most.

Chapter 28

Awakenings

IN THE MORNING AT THE FALLS RESIDENCE, SKYLAR AWOKE TO THE chirping of sparrows outside the window. As she shifted, trying to get comfortable, Victoria came in with her pain medication.

"Good morning, Songbird. How was your sleep?"

"Just fine, Momma."

As she wiped the sleep from her eyes, Skylar could not shake her dream and the peace felt afterwards. She was at the Sitka, kneeled around the base of the tree. The young woman wore a flowing dress, with a pattern of poppies. Suddenly, the thin layers of purplish, grey bark began to peel back, exposing a wooden cross. Under the heavens, a banding of darkened lavender and coppery clouds gathered, as a Goldfinch soared above the spruce. As the bird flapped its wings, she was covered in feathers. Upon waking, Skylar felt light weight.

Interrupting her thoughts, Victoria came over to her bedside.

"Rev. Francis telephoned me this morning, to find out if you could handle, a few more visitors today."

Skylar's curiosity was piqued. "Of course I would love some company momma, but who else wants to see me?" she asked.

"Oh, there are a lot more people you have impacted in your life. Just wait, my Songbird. You will see."

Waiting was not easy for Skylar. Though she had accepted her illness, every moment alone without her Aurelia, brought sorrow. Her daughter was going to grow up without knowing her birth mother. Gwen had placed around the room several photographs of Aurelia that she had taken and framed. Yet the heartache of looking at them was too much for Skylar to handle. Reluctantly, Victoria tucked them away in a drawer.

Laying her head back on the pillow, Skylar heard a knock on her door.

"Come in."

The door opened. Standing before her, was someone she had never expected to see again.

Makwa's coal-black hair was braided in two. The young man's eyes were the same darts of obsidian as she remembered.

Without a word, he sat down on the bed and touched her face with his hand.

"I come with a grateful heart and a broken soul," he whispered.

Reaching into a deerskin bag, he took out a woven basket.

"This is part of your Sitka tree," he said. "Intertwined into it, is the love story of you and Christian. Long ago when you met, you were united together. Just as the tree is bound by its roots, so are you to the Creator. That no matter what, not even death can claim you.

It is known among my people that we do not choose trees – they choose us to protect, shelter, and preserve. The Sitka is a symbol of female protection; a guardian in the woodlands known as the "mother tree." This is why you are connected with the spruce Skylar, for it is your spirit tree."

Makwa placed his hands upon hers. Looking into her eyes, he said, "You and your guardian tree share the same good liveliness."

Skylar's soft cries could be heard echoing throughout the old sanctuary. Makwa's wisdom allowed her to fully understand her dream and the true purpose of the Sitka.

Victoria quietly entered the room. As Makwa stood he clenched his fist and placing it upon his chest, he said, "Good Heart."

This prompted Victoria to choke back her tears. Walking him out of the room, she mumbled, "Thank you."

Soon after, Rev. Francis stopped in to see Skylar. He could see how tired she was.

"Your time here with us," he smiled, "may have been limited."

Then the Reverend continued, "Yet to those whose lives you have touched with your love of the Lord, it is precious."

You have overcome so much as a child and risen above the pain, seeing to it that others benefited from your kindness. You have never wavered in your faith. Even when burdened with so much grief, you have shown that your devotion to our Saviour is unyielding. One day, I will see you again in Eternity."

He took her hand and placed a Bible in it.

"Hold true to the word till the end, for you have nothing to fear in death, when it comes."

I will be staying in your home downstairs, until the time comes that you require me," he said with reassurance, before parting.

"Thank you," Skylar replied.

Walking out the door of the loft, Rev. Francis said, "Peace be with you, my child."

Once again, it was silent in the room.

Skylar clutched the good book, holding it tightly to her chest she declared, "Jesus, I love you."

* * *

Christian awoke in the rocking chair. He had slumped back into the chair and dozed off, after putting Aurelia back into the crib. His body ached from sitting upright half the night.

Although he wanted to see Skylar, he was left that day alone with Aurelia. Jaycee had gone shopping for more baby things. She also had a salon appointment. The new father pricked his finger when he changed Aurelia's diaper and fumbled with the endless snaps when he dressed her. Christian cursed underneath his breath, when at 4 o'clock Jaycee sauntered through the door, with a variety of packages mostly for herself.

"Hello, Chris!" she chimed.

"Where have you been all day?" he grumbled.

"Don't you use that tone with me," she said, glaring. "I tried to get back earlier, but I ran into the Thurlingtons and had to have lunch with them, to share about little pumpkin here."

"Her name is Aurelia."

"Yes, of course it is. Anyway, I figured you could always visit Skylar tomorrow. My mother's coming over in the morning, to help out with the baby."

"Damn it, woman! I don't even know if Skylar has another day to live, and you're out shopping with no regard for the woman who blessed us with a child. What the hell is wrong with you?"

Aurelia started to cry.

"Now look at what you have done," Jaycee said, picking her up. "You are upsetting her! I think it is best if you sleep down here tonight." She turned her back on him and cooed to Aurelia. "Don't you worry now; Mommy is here to take care of her snookums."

"I'm out of here," Christian said, grabbing his jacket.

"You had better come back here tonight," she yelled after him, "if you know what is good for you!"

Screeching his tires, he sped away, wanting to put as much distance as possible between him and the wretched woman he had married.

He soon found himself sitting under the Sitka tree. Pressing his body against the trunk, he balled his fists. Standing up, he turned and fell to his knees in despair, grinding his teeth. He threw punch after punch, unleashing his grief and anger, onto the bark of the tree that had sheltered him and Skylar. Knuckles bloody, he collapsed against the lower trunk and wept. As his tears subsided, he noticed a tiny root sticking up.

Before examining it any closer, Christian stood and looked to the heavens. Extending his arms upwards, the young man made a declaration.

"Oh great Creator, I come before you a broken man. With no one to blame but myself, I have been torn from the loving arms of my soul mate, Skylar Reigh Falls. I am humbled in knowing, this Sitka was never mine to claim. I do not deserve your mercy, yet I have one last request of this tree. You know what's inside my ruined heart and I plead with you to bless what it is I am asking for. In return, I surrender all my wealth and the greed that stems from it."

Christian continued to stand under the massive spruce in silence. Unexpectedly, a pine cone made its way down, cascading unto the branches and finally coming to rest at his feet. The young man took this as a signal to indicate his request had been heard and granted.

Grabbing the Piper/Faith key he secretly kept hidden in his wallet from Jaycee, Christian used it to take a piece of their beloved tree with him.

Driving back home, he prayed she would hold on for one more day.

Skylar awoke the next morning weaker than before. She needed her mother's help to sit up. Victoria opened a container of lip balm and gently swathed her daughter's chapped lips to prevent more cracking. Next, she covered her with a soft sheet to ward off the cold and sponge-bathed her, trying to avoid more bedsores from afflicting the young woman.

Afterwards, Victoria sat in the rocking chair. She tensed up, every time Skylar clenched her fists, and grimaced in pain. Tears seeped from her closed eyes. Even though she was in agony, Skylar never complained. Everyday, Victoria wished she could take her daughters place.

For a mother to have to watch helplessly while her child suffered, was heartbreaking.

There was a knock at the door, and as Gwen walked into the room, she was glad to see her best friend. Victoria stood and kissed Skylar on the cheek.

"I will let you girls talk. If you need anything, Songbird, I am going to be right downstairs."

"Thanks, Momma."

Gwen clasped Skylar's hand.

The contrast of their skin colours made Skylar look even more sickly.

"I have something to tell you…" pausing for a moment, she continued, "I see Evamya in my room every night since I have been up in the loft. At first, I thought I was dreaming.

"However, late yesterday evening, I was lying here in the darkness when I saw Evamya rocking back and forth – in the same chair you are sitting in now."

Gwen's arms tingled. "Evamya passed on a long time ago."

"Of course she did, silly! I am just telling you that Evamya was here, humming to herself 'Old Rugged Cross.' She was smiling from ear to ear, and her teeth were pearly white. She was at peace and there was a glow all around her."

Evamya's apparition, Gwen knew, surely meant that death was near.

"Did she say anything?"

"No, but I feel she is telling me to not fight any longer."

Gwen began to cry, wiping the tears falling from her eyes she said,

"Listen, I am not good at this stuff. There are no right words to say how I feel, and my prayers for a miracle to cure you failed." She sighed.

"Tell me, how is someone supposed to say goodbye to their soul sister?"

Skylar squeezed her hand. "Even though I am not going to be here for you to pester anymore, my spirit will live on – just like Evamya's. You captured the magical moments in our lives. Every time you look at your photographs, you will remember me."

"I always could depend on you being there for me, Skylar. Truth be told, it was you who carried our friendship, all these years. You always comforted me and made me laugh. You are one of the truest friends I ever had. What am I going to do without you?"

"You have Abimbola."

"That's a different kind of love. You are the sister I never had, my safe haven where I felt loved and sheltered. I never felt I was different when we were together, because you accepted me for who I am."

"Gwen, I have trusted you with my deepest secrets and admired you for your courage. Your roots run deep. You have a family I was envious of. Even though we are not true sisters, we share a special bond that cannot be broken. If I had not known you, a part of me would be missing."

Gwen reached into her pocket. She opened her fingers, and Skylar saw a polished, heart-shaped stone, glinting rose with fragments of white.

"Oh Gwennie… Where did you find something so beautiful?"

"It is called rose quartz and is a stone of unconditional love," Gwen said, choking back tears. "I bought it from a little girl in Africa. In her hands, it emanated light. It made me think of you and how your golden heart has always lighted the way for others." She put the stone into Skylar's clammy palm. "It is meant for healing. She paused, then added, "My timing has never been good..." her voice trailed off.

Skylar held onto the soft, polished heart for a moment and then gave it back.

"I believe you will need this more when I am gone. But for now, please put it on my nightstand."

Gwen knelt by the bedside. "I guess this is where we say goodbye… for now."

Skylar touched Gwen's cheek; wet from the tears she had shed.

"Always be proud of who you are, Gwendolyn-Sue. Remember that the good Lord has blessed you with a gift. Continue to seek knowledge and understanding from Him.

"Take comfort in knowing God granted us years of friendship, which throughout our lives have brought a great deal of joy. Even though I will be gone, I remain in your life through what we shared as sisters in faith. You will always find memories of me, lingering at the Sitka."

Knowing every word was true, her best friend nodded.

As she let go of Skylar and stood, she saw a sparrow perched on the window ledge.

"Gwen whispered, "Reminders of you will never be far away."

Closing the door behind her, she realized how much Skylar sounded like Evamya. Walking down the stairs, Gwen knew it was the last time she would see her friend alive.

In the early evening, Skylar awoke to see Christian, who had been watching her as she slept.

"You looked so peaceful," he mumbled. "I didn't want to wake you."

Her illness had taken its toll on Christian. Black circles hung under his eyes, and dark whiskers covered his face. Glancing down at his hands, Skylar saw white dressings stained with blood on his knuckles. She did not ask, only assumed the need to release his fury, stemming from her looming death.

Reaching out, he tenderly clasped her delicate hands with gentleness. He struggled as to what to say.

"I prayed that you would come," she spoke softly.

Christian held onto her, the mother of their child. Knowing, if possible, he would give up all he had attained. For the torn soulmate, Skylar was the closest to heaven, Christian feared he would never be.

Taking a deep breath, he replied, "I never imagined myself sitting here conveying to you what I should have so long ago." Pausing for a moment, unsure if he could carry on. Taking a deep breath in, Christian continued.

"From the first time I laid eyes on you, there was something that drew me in. You have a warrior's spirit – and have since you were a young girl. Your grateful heart has given me and all of Ospero Falls, so many blessings! When you speak, you speak a rare truth. Your words… they dance off your tongue and come alive in the hearts of others.

"That is only one of the reasons I fell in love with you, Piper. No matter what, you will always be the keeper of my heart. I will treasure forever the love that we shared. Know that when I look into our daughter's eyes, I will see you."

He struggled to finish, as the tears came swiftly, his lips began to tremble. Skylar wept, knowing their love for one another through all of its imperfections, was being declared.

"I will never forget your passion for the written word, Piper, nor your love for the Sitka tree that you have cherished so deeply. It is something that always belonged to you, not me. I never deserved to claim the Sitka as my own, since I did not appreciate the value of its existence. I only used the tree to see past it, to Rogue's Bluffs and the riches I so desperately sought." He lamented. "Ol' Evamya knew what she was talking about, when she warned me to stay away."

"Listen now," Skylar interrupted, not wanting to talk about what could have been, during their precious time remaining. "I know that you have more things to say, but please let me speak for a moment."

He nodded, fearing they could be her last words to him.

"It's time you understood just how much you changed my life. I have always drawn strength from the power of your words that you shared with me. It connected me to your father, who I truly respected. He taught us about the spirit of the Lord, found among the mountains and forests. Yet it was through your trek in the woods, the spruce was discovered. By sharing the tree with me, I was able to be rescued away from the frightened, young girl trapped in disgrace.

"Throughout the years, you and I combined our love for poetry in nature. Under the boughs of our Sitka, we immersed in the power and beauty of words. This helped me overcome the trauma I experienced, as a child, that one tragic night.

"At such a young age, you were willing to protect me at any cost, by never speaking of what you saw. Over the years, you continued to shield me from my painful past. For that, I am indebted in a way you can never fully comprehend."

He mulled over what she was saying.

"You mean to tell me, after all these years, that you knew I was there?"

She nodded. "I do not remember everything Christian. However, there were many times beforehand, my momma and I suffered over the years at the hands of Trey Wickett. That terrible night, even in a daze, I sensed you. It is a deep bond we share, where I believed somehow our lives were united together long ago. You see, you have been my Captain, during the storms of my life."

Christian grasped onto her words and asked,

"Why didn't you tell me before?"

"I never wanted my past to come between us, so I chose to deal with it in my own way. I could not bear to have you fall in love with me, only because you felt pity. I wanted our relationship to be based on devotion, not on the terrifying moments in my life. You showed me through your devotion, how I was not to be ashamed. When you looked at me, I felt loved.

"This allowed me to embrace my strength, to deal with whatever caused me pain. Honestly, I think had we allowed the wickedness into our lives, it would have overshadowed the pureness of our love. You helped me overcome my fears and see the world through the eyes of you – the grand adventurer."

Christian sighed deeply, "Piper," he replied, "I do not deserve all the credit you are giving me."

Skylar carried on, "You do, Christian. You saw something in me, worth risking your own safety for that night. You jeopardized never seeing your own family again.

"You left the comfort of your home, for the chaos of mine. Momma told me that when we were taken to Bay View, you stayed at the hospital, until you knew I was alright. Don't you see? Your selfless act that night, helped transform me from a victim, into a survivor. As for our sacred Sitka, it was a healing place for my wounds. It brought my scarred heart together with yours."

Christian began to weep, realizing the difference he had made in her life, by disobeying his father and following him into the Falls' home. Up until then as an adult, it never occurred to him what the consequences may have been, if the outcomes were changed.

What if he did not find the frightened girl that day on the ferry? What if Trey Wickett's belt broke in his jail cell and he lived? Christian grasped the magnitude of the choices made.

He knew the stories of their lives, were a series of books on a shelf, with some of the pages frayed. While some books were written in joy, others were penned in sorrow. One had been missing – until now. The book, containing the answers to the questions raised that fateful night, was finally slipped onto the shelf. No longer did any mystery divide their lives. Instead, the truth tied them together. The shelf was now full.

Skylar sensed that Christian finally understood what she had known all along: A seed that grew into a tree of life, had brought them together. And in the end, her existence – much like the solid trunk of the Sitka – would remain rooted forever.

As she lay still under the quilt, Skylar needed to finish what she had started.

"There is something that you have to promise me, Christian," Skylar hesitated then spoke,

"I want you to make sure that Jaycee raises our daughter with love and allows her to become whoever she is. Please, when the time is right, take her to our beloved tree and let Aurelia know how much her momma loved her."

Christian began to sob.

He was reluctant to make a solemn promise on something he was not even sure of. However, seeing the desperation in her eyes made him vow to do so.

"Of course Piper. Our daughter will be properly looked after. I will tell her the truth about everything when the time is right."

Standing up, Christian pulled something from his pocket. It was a wooden box, with a songbird painted on it. Sitting back down beside her, he showed it to Skylar.

"How pretty," she sighed.

Christian opened it, to reveal a unique ring.

It was the small root he saw at the Sitka. He had woven it together, in the shape of the infinity symbol and looped it through.

The tiny figure eight was delicate.

Skylar looked at it, then at Christian.

"Is it from…" she asked, her voice tapering off.

Nodding his head, they both shed tears together.

Taking her fragile left hand in his, Christian placed it upon her pinky finger.

Looking deep into her eyes, he announced: "A promise is a promise."

Skylar drew a shallow breath, startling him. Over the last few hours, it had become slower with long pauses in between. He knew it was only a matter of time before she ceased to exist.

Christian once again concentrated on her chest, watching it rise and fall to the familiar rhythm as a doctor, he had been trained to look for.

Skylar looked at him and made one last request.

"Please go now, Christian. I do not want you to see me die. I want to watch you walk out that door one last time. Remember me differently, than you have seen me here today.

"Picture the good times we shared and hold them in your memory forever. In the same way you love me now, love our Aurelia. Through her, you will always have something to remember me by."

Christian knew then that although he was losing her, the love they shared would remain with him eternally.

"How is it that you can even turn a sorrowful goodbye into something so beautiful?" he asked.

"You should know better by now, Christian James O'Connelly, that this is not goodbye.

"I will see you again under our beloved Sitka tree."

He stood, then bending down, gave one, last, tender kiss on her forehead.

"A promise is a promise," he murmured.

Not another word was spoken, as Christian walked out of the loft for the last time.

Glancing over at the rocking chair in the corner, Skylar saw the vision of Evamya.

She smiled at the young woman in bed and softly whispered,

"It's time songbird, for you to come home."

Chapter 29

Resolutions

Lily sat quietly listening to her grandfather's story retold over the span of the afternoon. Once he had shared about the passing of Skylar, he fell quiet, tears running along the lines of his face.

"What happened to Aurelia, Grandpa C.C.?"

She waited patiently for him to speak again. Yet Christian haunted by retelling his life story, reopened old wounds. Looking into his eyes, she could see the remorse that lingered. Her grandfather never was able to let go or forgive himself, for what had taken place. His hands trembled, holding the strip of bark, he once claimed ownership of the Sitka.

"It's okay, Grandpa," she said. "I'm right here. Just breathe."

Exhaling, he took out his handkerchief and dabbed the sweat from his wrinkled brow.

"Before I can answer your question," he said, "I must finish my story. You need to know what happened after, so you can understand. Upon Skylar's death, when her pillow and linens were removed, Victoria found a white lace pouch. Inside the satchel was dirt – not just any kind of soil, but the earth from beneath our cherished Sitka tree. It also contained the bark necklace carved by Evamya, and a poem that Skylar had scrawled onto paper. I believe as darkness overcame her in the hospital, she battled with every last spark of light she had."

Reaching under the pillow on the wrought-iron bed, Christian removed the white pouch.

Emptying its contents into his hand, he then poured the dirt onto the nightstand. Unfurling the tattered paper, Christian cleared his throat.

People come into our lives and go like fallen cones off a Sitka spruce...

Within the winter season, the tree is left with exposed shadows

As the barren tree grows strong, the trunk – the Soul of the tree – never leaves it...

The roots, taking from its true mother, the pure nutrients

Thanking her – it grows tall and sturdy – enclosed in bark

Some will try and trample the tender tree, while others will find comfort and refuge

In the end, it will continue to grow, with parts of its trunk and branches left with scars

Yet, this will not change its wondrous beauty...

The years will pass like the ocean breeze, while the extent of energy contained within the tree,

is never fully revealed...

Eventually, all those who sought shelter under its commanding grace;

find the tree's immortality, is embedded within each of them...

What remains – is the tapestry of memories – weaved amongst its lofty branches

The ones that tried to bring the tree down, will realize how much it meant to others...

As they age and try to resolve the heartache caused by them,

They will weep at the cracks and holes created, to see how their destruction; echoes the void space, where love once sprang from...

"I thought this was solely meant for me," Christian said, "then as the years passed, I realized that Skylar saw through Jaycee's cruel intentions all along. With no future before her, she could only mourn what was to become."

He paused and took a deep breath in. Exhaling, he continued on, "Oh, my dear Lily, I'm getting ahead of myself. I need to share about Skylar's celebration of life! It was something else.

"It was as if every flower in God's garden was brought to Victoria's house, to honour the memory of her daughter. People came from all over to pay their respects one last time. Even though everyone – including myself – thought I should say a few words, Jaycee would not hear of it. She went on about, how much suffering, she had already gone through. Shouting at me about all the shame and grief my tryst with Skylar, caused her and her family. I should have known then; things were only going to get worse.

"Nevertheless, I was grateful to witness the spreading of Skylar's ashes. They were brought to the Sitka and scattered underneath the tree that meant so much to her. A plaque was placed on top of a granite stone, with her name etched above two simple words: 'Good Heart.' Later, I discovered from the local First Nations people that granite is the stone of protection. It only seemed appropriate that she was laid to rest there. After all, it was underneath the Sitka that Skylar and I fell in love, shared our first kiss, became lovers, and conceived our child. So much happened there that was inexplicable yet felt so natural.

"It was many years later, before I was able to return to the spot where both her spirit and our memories dwelled. Jaycee forbade me from ever visiting the old Sitka, while we were married, knowing how much Skylar meant to me.

"My practice in Averston never brought me the satisfaction I sought. Despite all those years imagining the good fortune that awaited, it never occurred to me the price I would pay for it. I was plagued with guilt and never forgot the heartache I brought to Skylar's life, through my betrayals.

"Try as I might to stay in touch with Victoria, Frank, and Gwen, my hectic schedule and the constant demands from Jaycee, kept us apart. I heard Gwen won a prestigious award for a portrait of Skylar, earning her the recognition she rightfully deserved.

"When her daughter Ophelia Rose was born, Gwen knew Evamya was shining upon her. Frank and Samantha's twin boys kept them busy, and his dreams of success came true. As you know, Lily, we did patch things up, but only after a long period of time apart.

"As for Aurelia, I loved her to the core of my being. I spent every minute I could with her. When she was little, she loved to lie on my chest, where she would fall fast asleep. When her mother was not around, I read her Skylar's favourite poems by Wordsworth, Frost, and Hemingway.

"When autumn arrived, she and I would fall into the mounds of leaves and laugh so hard our sides hurt. There were days I could not imagine my life without her, and I couldn't foresee the event that would tear us apart forever.

"It was the autumn of '79 and I was driving with Aurelia in the front seat. I stopped and bought us identical Pralines 'n cream cones, at Johnnie's Parlour in Averston. Cruising along the winding back roads with the top down on the Cadillac, we were enjoying the gentle breeze in our hair. In between licks of our melting treats, we sang along with the songs on the radio, not a care in the world. I still remember the disc jockey saying, 'Now, here is a popular song called "Songbird," by Fleetwood Mac.'

"Listening to the words, I felt like I was driving down a road I had not been on in years. I can recall the look of surprise on Aurelia's face when she asked,

"Daddy, where are you taking me?"

"To see a special tree," I said.

"I then drove out a few miles and finally came to rest upon the sprawling mass of the ol' Sitka.

"Parking under the spruce, I took a deep breath in. It was still magnificent to me, but after years of neglect, an eerie presence surrounded it. I did not feel welcome. Something was telling me to turn back, prompting me to reconsider my intentions. However, I felt I had a promise to keep.

"Gently taking Aurelia's hand, I led my daughter out of the car.

"When we reached the marker, we stopped. Encircling the lichen-covered stone was a burst of red poppies, Piper's favourite flower. Sitting down with Aurelia, I began telling her about Skylar.

"Looking back now, I honestly do not know what I was thinking. She was just a child. There I was, expecting her to understand things that even still haunted me. I shattered Aurelia's world that day. In doing so, crushing the illusion she had, of who her family really was. I will never forget the look in her eyes when she gazed upwards and said,

"Does my real mommy watch me from heaven?"

"I had not taken into consideration the retaliation that awaited, when Jaycee found out what I had done.

"After Skylar died, I signed papers stating that I was never to tell Aurelia who her real mother was. It would be grounds for an immediate divorce, and I would have to give up my parental rights. With so much to lose, I was never tempted to take the chance, until I heard that melody. The significance of the day seemed to leave me with no other choice.

"You see, it was seven years to the day that Skylar had died. I had broken my promise to her, not once but twice, and the guilt I felt threatened to swallow me whole."

Touching his hand tenderly, Lily asked, "What did Jaycee do?"

"True to her word, she immediately kicked me out of the house. She would not even let me say goodbye to my own daughter. In a single day, Aurelia's life was torn to pieces. Even though she had nothing to do with it, she would suffer for the sins of others.

"Jaycee's father Luther saw to it that my practice was closed. I became homeless and alone, with nowhere to go, except the one place I had turned my back on years earlier: Ospero Falls. I was ashamed to see my own mother, remorseful of who I had become.

"Yet she welcomed me back into our old house and said something that I will never forget.

"She lifted my chin and looked into my eyes."

"You made Skylar proud, son, seeing to it her promise was kept. Aurelia and you were living a lie, spun by Jaycee, who wanted to control both of you. Now finally even after her death, you stood up for Skylar, and it is honestly all that she ever wanted. Remember, what your father used to say, about a man who does not keep his word. He is not worthy of respect.

"Have no shame. Evamya, your father, and Skylar are smiling down upon you."

Christian's hands were trembling, as he continued on, "For the first time since Skylar died, the man everyone once loved and respected was re-emerging. I had done right by her and my father, Jack, but at an immeasurable cost. It did not take Jaycee long to get rid of anything in the mansion, which reminded her of Skylar. She threw everything that once belonged to her, in a box at the top of the driveway. Thankfully, I was able to retrieve it. You would think Aurelia had suffered enough. However, Jaycee's last calculated act of cruelty was declared, when I received papers of Aurelia's name change. I tried to fight it, but I did not stand a chance against the power and wealth of Jaycee's family.

"Eventually, I established a small clinic in Ospero Falls, but lost my passion along the way. I retired early and took to this haven in my sorrow. All the while, I tried to escape the painful memories.

"Don't worry Grandpa C.C.," Lily said, "Everything will be okay."

"That is sweet of you to say, Lilybug. Yet what I am about to say, concerns you directly."

"What is it?" Lily asked.

He clasped her hand. "Jaycee was my former wife's nickname. Her full name is Jacqueline Campbell. She changed our daughter's name from Aurelia to Katrina. Your grandmother was not Jacqueline, as you were brought up to believe, but Skylar.

You are in actual fact – Skylar Reigh Fall's granddaughter."

Lily smiled and patted her grandfather's hand.

Taking a deep breath, she exhaled and let out a soft sigh.

"I think a part of me knew it, as you shared your story," Lily said, "but I needed to hear you say it, Grandpa C.C."

For the young girl, things finally made sense. As the truth had been told, it revealed the answers to many questions Lily had been kept hidden from.

Shaking his head, her grandfather grinned, remarking, "I should have known better that out of anyone you would understand Lily. It is a quality that Skylar had."

"Am I really so much like her?"

Christian began to tremble, not out of fear, but with joy as he replied, "You have a vibrant spirit, a talent for sketching, and deep olive eyes, just like your grandmother. The way you dress, with your flared pants and crocheted vests, reminds me so much of Skylar. I know, if she were still alive, she would love you and never let go."

"Can I ask you something, Grandpa C.C.?"

Christian nodded, "Of course. Whatever you want. You have a right to know. Besides, you have been denied the truth long enough, and much pain has come because of it."

"Earlier in the story, you told me about the fight with your mother when you brought Jacqueline to Ospero Falls for the first time. Still, you never told me why she slapped you? It must have been really awful, to make Great-Grandma react that way."

Christian sighed, then responded, "I put my own mother through so much unnecessary pain, yet she always forgave me. Jacqueline not only kept Aurelia away from me, but from everybody who meant something to me.

"My poor mother was one of the innocent people, who bore the pain of my transgressions. That particular day has stayed with me forever. Although your great-grandmother Sophia has forgiven me, I have never been able to forgive myself."

He looked down.

"You see, I taunted her that day on the porch, saying I bet she wished I had died, instead of my father."

Lily was shocked.

"You didn't mean it!"

"I apologized later on, but I could never take back the hurt I inflicted on my mother. It haunts me to this day. You see, Lily, when you say something with malice, you can never undo the damage it causes."

"What about Skylar's mom? What happened to her?"

Christian blew his nose into a handkerchief. "Now there was a strong woman! What she endured and survived is a testament to her faith. Even after Skylar's death, Victoria saw to it that her daughter's work continued on. She took over working at the Heart of Jade Sanctuary and taught the children at Sunday school. At first, Jacqueline allowed her to have contact with Aurelia. However, the visits were monitored, and Victoria was not allowed to leave Rogue's Bluffs with her own granddaughter. Jacqueline told our daughter that Victoria was a distant aunt. The situation caused many arguments between Jacqueline and me. No good ever came of them, though. The incident at the Sitka with Aurelia, unleashed the wrath of Jacqueline upon those who loved the precious, little girl. Victoria was cut out of their lives. She lost not only her daughter, but her grandchild as well.

"Then one day, the cancer came back with a vengeance.

"Having nothing left to live for, Victoria did not put up a fight. She chose to die at Bay Hospital.

"But before her death, she asked Rev. Francis to retrieve me. As I sat at Victoria's bedside, she said she was happy to let go, knowing she would be reunited with Skylar. In spite of the grief I had caused, Victoria forgave me. Her last words to me were, 'Christian, I know how much the Whispering Rose Sanctuary meant to you and Skylar. Therefore, I have left it for you to inherit upon my death and ask you to please keep the loft as it is. I pray that someday Aurelia will come looking for the answers, only you can give her."

Christian paused, then continued, "I promised to keep Skylar's memory alive. Victoria died holding my hand. She and I could never have imagined that it would be you, Lily, who came instead of your mother."

"Grandpa," Lily said, "do you think that maybe I was supposed to be the one who found the key?"

Christian slowly stood up and embracing his granddaughter, said,

"I would like to think so, Lily. Now please come with me, I have more to show you."

Downstairs, Christian removed the trophy rainbow trout mounted above the door. Lily smiled as she read the inscription underneath:

The Whispering Rose Sanctuary.

"I had it covered up all these years," he said, "as it was too painful a reminder."

He placed the fish on the counter and pulled from a drawer a flashlight and a hammer.

"Follow me."

In front of the cabin, they stopped at what Lily had always been told was a dried-up, boarded-over well. Christian used the hammer to pull out the old, rusty nails one by one, until he was able to remove the wooden covering. Turning on the flashlight, he shone it inside. Lily peered in and was shocked by what she saw.

"But Grandpa C.C.," she asked, "Why?

They stared at the stone monument placed in memory of Jack when the sanctuary was first erected. Christian wiped the tears from his eyes.

"I just could not bring myself to face this reminder every day. I was ashamed to admit I was not the man he hoped I would be. I was a failure as a doctor, as a husband, and – most importantly – as a father. When I moved in here, I hid everything that reminded me of the way things were supposed to be. I never realized that all along, no matter what I did, they could never be forgotten."

Lily put her arms around her grandfather. Even though her life had changed forever in one day, she felt it was for the better. She finally understood why her mother was filled with deep resentment.

"I know if my mother knew the truth, she would give you another chance," she said.

"I do not hold out much hope for a reunion anymore. It hurts too much when your dreams are crushed. Skylar knew all about that, firsthand."

As they walked back into the house, Christian kissed Lily on the cheek.

"Time for us to get some supper, young lady. It has been quite the day for this old man. I reckon it will be an early turn-in tonight."

"I do not know how you expect me to sleep tonight, Grandpa C.C."

"I am sure you will have some pleasant dreams, my dear."

"You know, nothing you said changes how much I love you."

"That means a lot to me, Lily. I love you too. Now let's fix us some dinner."

Afterwards, Christian refilled his lantern and brought it out to the porch.

He set it on the table and soon fell asleep in his rocking chair. Lily waited until she heard him snoring, before coming to check on her grandfather.

She saw the lantern light glowing on his face, illuminating his peaceful state of rest. Bending down, Lily turned off the flame.

Going back into the kitchen, she dialled the numbers on the telephone. After three rings, she was about to hang-up when Katrina answered.

"Hello Mother…" Lily whispered into the receiver, "it's me, Lily. We have to talk."

* * *

In the morning, Lily awoke to the daylight shining through the window, into the stillness of her room. Throwing off the quilt and glancing over at the clock, she had slept in. The quiet was interrupted with a song coming from the record player.

Stretching slowly, she smiled. Lily felt as if there was a chance to finally bring her shattered family together.

Wandering through the hallway into the kitchen, Lily waited for the kettle to boil. Adding a tea bag into her cup, she poured hot water in, to let her Red Rose steep.

The young girl replayed over in her mind the conversation that had taken place earlier with her mother. Katrina listened to Lily, as she shared how Christian deserved another chance, to explain and make peace with the past.

It came as no surprise, her mother's reluctance to meet at the proposed spot by her daughter; the Sitka tree.

In spite of Katrina's doubts, Lily was persuaded to at least hear some of what Christian had shared with her. After much prompting by her daughter, a time was set to meet.

Stepping out the door onto the front porch, she found her grandfather covered with the quilt from the bed in the loft.

Bending down to give him a peck on the cheek, she realized his eyes were closed, and his lips gray-blue.

"No!" she cried out.

Dropping the Wedgwood teacup, it smashed into pieces. The young girl grabbed him by the shoulders and began to shake her grandfather. After several minutes had passed, Lily wiping her tears away, said,

"It is going to be okay, Grandpa C.C.," she sniffled, "I promise."

Looking over at the side table, Lily noticed the box with the songbird on it. She reached across and put it in her pocket.

An ambulance arrived at the old sanctuary, followed by Frank. By the time everything had been dealt with, the sun was beginning to set. Frank offered to take Lily back home as Samantha had dinner waiting. However, she told him of her oath to Christian and vowed to keep her word. Putting on her coat and mittens, she went outside. Glancing at the gilded lantern she had turned off the night before, she was surprised to see a flame now flickering, inside the glass. Taking hold of the beacon of light, Lily headed to the ferry.

Earlier in the morning, Katrina was told of Christian's death, and found herself overwrought with grief. Even though she harboured a lot of animosity towards her father, she still loved him. Throughout her life, she often wondered how things would have turned out, if she had been raised by Christian and Skylar instead of Jacqueline.

In Averston, as the sun went down, Katrina drove the gravel road to the Sitka. Consumed with sorrow; she never allowed her father the opportunity to keep a promise.

Christian died without receiving her forgiveness.

As the ferry approached its destination, Lily leaned against the railings on the deck. Inhaling the central coast air, she knew what needed to be done. Peeling back the layers of the past, Lily was now the storyteller. In sharing with her mother the truth, she was determined to spill open the secrets, which had taken its last victim.

Arriving at the dock in Averston at dusk, Lily looked up to see a quarrel of starlights fly overhead. Her grandmother Skylar was heavy in her thoughts. Relighting Christian's lantern, she walked the path both grandparents had trodden countless times before. Lily was overcome with excitement. Once in the clearing, the Sitka tree welcomed her. She turned up the flame of the lantern, to catch a better view of the treehouse. Still dangling from the outstretched branches were several pairs of old, weathered, Saddle shoes. Clumps of moss covered them, along with the former treehouse. Nature had come to reclaim the past. Near the spruce's trunk, she saw her mother wiping the overgrowth, from a stone marker.

Wind gathered from the ocean and rushed inland, shaking the branches of the tree. As Lily drew close, she could see that her mother was crying.

Reaching into her pocket, she pulled the infinity ring out of the box and placed it on her left pinky.

Gently, Lily took hold of Aurelia's hand. Shining the light on the marker, she said,

"A promise is a promise." 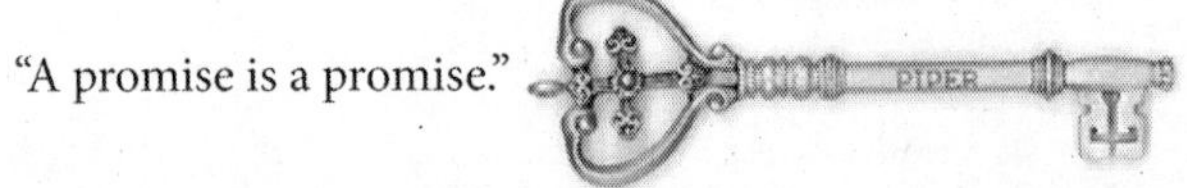